The W

Rachael Dymski

Production by eBookPro Publishing
www.ebook-pro.com

THE WOMEN OF JERSEY ISLAND
Rachael Dymski

Contact: rachael@dymski.com

ISBN 9798335610162

THE WOMEN OF JERSEY ISLAND

A WW2 Historical Fiction Novel

RACHAEL DYMSKI

ReadMore Press

DISCOVERING THE NEXT BESTSELLER

Sign up for Readmore Press' monthly newsletter and get a
FREE audiobook!

For instant access, scan the QR code

Where you will be able to register and receive
your sign-up gift, a free audiobook of

Beneath the Winds of War
by **Pola Wawer,**

which you can listen to right away

Our newsletter will let you know about
new releases of our World War II historical
fiction books, as well as discount deals and
exclusive freebies for subscribed members.

For A.J.G.,
Who has always been gold.

PART ONE

CHAPTER ONE

VIOLET

Jersey, 1911

In the morning light, Violet thinks about pearls.

She stretches on her bed, breathing in the scent of blooming wisteria outside her open window. A block away, the steady drum of the sea washes back and forth over the sand like a heartbeat.

In school last week, Violet learned about oysters making pearls, and it confirmed what she's always believed about the ocean being a treasure chest waiting to gift people with its wonders. She is obsessed with finding one.

"It's a one in a million chance to find one naturally," her classmate Louisa had said, eyes shining, the sun catching her curly blonde hair so it looked like it glowed. "You'd be the luckiest girl in the world if you found one."

Violet smiled at her and continued to sketch an oyster spitting out a perfectly round pearl on her paper. All her life, she's known the ocean as the giver of good things: sea glass and conch shells, perfect sunsets and summertime picnics. She's sure the ocean won't withhold this.

Today is the first morning of Easter half term, and she decides to spend it at the beach, collecting shells for a science project. She'll go alone: her father is busy pruning the climbing roses; her mother is meeting old Mrs. Griffith for coffee.

"I'll be home by lunchtime," her mum says in the kitchen as she spreads homemade strawberry jam on Violet's toast. "We'll have sandwiches in the garden; you can show me your treasures."

Violet's mum is tall and willowy and always smells of gardenias. Her soul is the color of turquoise, warm and serene. She looks nothing like the other mums Violet knows: mums who are sturdy and wear old house coats and smell like fresh bread.

Violet's mum sees the colors, just like Violet. She wasn't surprised at all when Violet came to her as a little girl and told her about the turquoise pooling up around her ankles. She'd only smiled and said, "This is how you'll learn yourself and other people, my girl. Find a person's color and you'll know their soul."

According to Aunt Felicity, Violet's mum came from Money, and that's why she is so different. Though she has no hired help, she hovers above daily life, just a bit too grand to get bacon grease on her clothes. This morning, her mum wears a peach dress and a string of rose gold pearls, which sway in front of Violet's face as she sets the plate on the table.

"You know your necklace came from the sea, right, Mum?"

Her mum laughs. "From oysters, you mean? Maybe you'll find an oyster with a pearl today at Greve de Lecq."

Violet slouches. "Mum, I can't go to Greve de Lecq," she complains, pushing her toast away. "There's nothing interesting there. I want to go to Plemont Bay; that's where all the good shells are."

Plemont Bay is her dad's favorite place to go on a summer's Sunday. The beach, surrounded by jagged cliffs on three sides, is only accessible at low tide by a set of steep, slippery stairs. On those days, her mum makes a bean crock, and her dad lowers it over the cliffside with a rope. They swim in the brisk water, then wrap themselves in blankets and sit on camp chairs, sipping the thermoses of tea while the wind whips their hair. As the tide inches closer, they pick up their chairs and scoot back until there is almost no beach left.

Her mum stiffens. "No," she says sharply.

Then, with a smile, she pats Violet's hair. "You're not old enough to go to Plemont Bay on your own. It's too dangerous; too many coves and cliffs."

"I'm nearly eleven, Mum," Violet protests.

"You're too young. That's the end of it."

"But—"

"Enough."

"Okay," she sighs.

"That's my girl," her mum says cheerfully. "You go on to Greve de Lecq and come home for lunch. Stay away from Plemont. The last thing you need is to spend your holiday with a broken arm."

Violet sighs again.

"However," her mum passes Violet a coin. "You are old enough to buy yourself an ice cream while you're out."

Violet brightens. She jumps up, kisses her mum on the cheek, and pulls on her shoes. Collecting her pail and shovel, she opens the door of her Tudor-style row home, blocking the exit so that Tess, their unsocial cat, cannot escape. Across the street, she can see the sand of Greve de Lecq beach stretching out forty feet in front of her until it reaches the sea.

She should stay at Greve de Lecq. She should pass the morning wandering the flat sand, hoping to find a scallop shell or a limpet. But Violet wants to explore coves and race across a field of wet, mushy sand that never quite dries until her chest is tight and her calves burn, stopping only when she reaches the edge of the ocean. She wants to find a pearl for Louisa, because Louisa is kind and lovely and didn't think Violet was silly when she said at recess one day that she saw people as colors.

"Seeing people as colors?" the other girls had snickered. "What a ridiculous idea!"

Louisa hadn't laughed, though. "What color am I?" She asked, eyes bright with innocent curiosity.

Eggplant purple, Violet had been about to answer, *the color of royalty.* But the teacher rang the bell to resume, and Violet remembered what her mum had said about the colors: you can't go around telling everyone what they are. They need time to grow into their colors, to decide for themselves.

Violet thinks about Louisa's lovely, carefree way and knows she has never wanted anything more than to be her friend, to impress her and win her over. In her first-ever display of rebellion, Violet mounts her bicycle and rides not across the street to the beach but inland along hedge-lined country roads. Pausing every hundred yards to make sure her parents aren't following her, she passes cow pastures, fields of lavender, and rows of potatoes. Legs full of adrenaline, palms sweaty, she pedals up the hill until the lane opens up at Plemont Bay.

Parking her bike at the entrance, Violet carefully descends the steep, wet stone steps to the bottom, clutching her shovel and pail. When she reaches the sand, she pumps her fist in the air, triumphant that she's proven herself right: she *is* old enough to go to Plemont Bay on her own.

Her mum calls Plemont Bay Treasure Island. The beach completely disappears at high tide and then leaves hundreds, thousands of treasures to be discovered as the water recedes. When it's empty at low tide, Mum says Plemont Bay looks exactly like the type of place Captain Flint could have landed: just barren and wild enough to contain something truly magical.

Violet makes her way toward a far cove on the other side of the bay, stopping to pick up a shell or to explore a tidal pool. She finds several limpets, a tiny crab, a handful of seaweed, and a gorgeous piece of turquoise sea glass that feels like her mum. She imagines the pearl she wants to find and the way Louisa's deep purple will shimmer when she shows her. Violet puts the treasures in her pail and continues to explore, the sun warming her face and arms.

Violet's own color is a warm blue, like the sky on a sunny day: full of possibility. She turns her face up now and wishes she could pull a piece of the sky down to give to her mum with the sea glass. Her gaze travels over the expanse of air to the cliff's top. A meadow lines the steep edge, where walkers often pause to observe the spectacular view below.

Violet cups a hand over her eyes as her gaze leaves the seagull. It lands on a couple who stand far above her, at the cliff's edge.

They have their arms wrapped around one another in what looks like a passionate embrace. Violet stops running and stares at them, feeling both uncomfortable and curious. They are standing close to the edge. Too close, Violet thinks. Dogs die every year from falling off as they run after a seagull, learning too late they can't fly. This couple is only a shoe's distance away from the same fate. Violet wonders if she should call up to warn them.

The woman wears a peach dress. It flies behind her in the wind, and she wears her hair pinned back in the same style as her mother.

Then she realizes, with a jolt, that this woman *is* her mother.

But her mother is with Mrs. Griffith and her father is pruning roses. Her parents never show affection like this toward each other. In all her eleven years, Violet has never seen one give the other more than a peck on the cheek.

Violet shouldn't be at Plemont Bay, but her parents are too close to the edge. If they take another step, they'll fall. She'll be in trouble when they see her, but she can't just let them stand there.

Violet yells out to them. "Mum! Dad!" she drops her pail and shovel, waving her arms to get their attention. "Move back!"

The man turns his head first. Violet's heart catches in her throat. This man is not her father; she can tell from a hundred feet below. His hair is too blond, his body too thick.

He has a familiar look to him. Quickly, she runs through the possibilities in her head. He is not the milkman, not the headmaster, not somebody from church, but she knows him.

Her mother turns next, and when she sees her daughter, terror falls like a curtain over her face. "No!"

The familiar man takes a step forward as her mum steps back, yanking her arm away. The air does not support the man Violet cannot place, and he tumbles over the cliff's edge.

Violet stands there, the sound of her own scream reverberating inside her head. Her mum puts her hands to her face and moves out of Violet's sight. Violet runs, her lungs burning, racing toward the end of her life as she knows it.

She gasps: *I'm sorry, sorry, sorry.*

CHAPTER TWO

MARCY

1940

"Mind you don't burn that toffee sauce," Marcy's mum, Violet, says from the table, where she folds a pile of laundry. "It needs a careful eye, and you worry me, staring out the window like that."

Marcy nods and returns her attention to the mixture of sugar, butter and cream simmering in the saucepan. She has been looking out over the potato fields, thinking about something her gran had told her when she was little.

"People are colors," Gran had said to Marcy matter-of-factly as she sauteed mushrooms in garlic and butter while Violet laid the table. "We are walking fragments of the rainbow, our colors blending and meshing together to make a complete picture."

"What color am I?" she had asked, taking a slice of a baguette and trying to dip it into the pan.

Gran swatted her hand away from the stove playfully. "Now, my girl, I can't answer that. You've got to find that out for yourself."

Violet had bumped the table then, tipping over a water glass. Marcy was sent to get the mop.

Now, Marcy turns off the heat on the stove and gives the sauce a final whisk. She's always pictured herself as a light beige. Neutral, neat. Unremarkable but also unembarrassing. This morning, she thinks it would be so nice to be gold: shimmery, wise, full of warmth and sparkle.

Marcy knows she's not supposed to label others with their colors, but she can't help herself. She studies people quietly, coaxes the pigment out until, in her mind, they start to ooze with their true color.

Her best friend Annette is a magenta pink, startling, beautiful and loud; her mum is a pale blue around a locked-up suitcase, all her feelings buttoned up and punctual.

This morning, she finally knows Eugene's color. It came to her while she was meant to be stirring, watching over the pastures where the Jersey cows graze, and it is so obvious and vivid that she wonders how she ever could have missed it. Yellow. He walks around with a puddle of goldenrod everywhere he goes and leaves his trace when he's been somewhere, a mark of yellow on a doorknob or in the middle of the grass field. Eugene is goldfinch and sunset, rows of daffodils. He is yellow like the lemons they squeezed together as children as they made lemonade in the garden with their mums, yellow like the front door of Jo's bakery in Rozel.

Fleetingly, she daydreams about telling Eugene his color. She wonders if she could walk up to him and say, "I've got it, Eugene. You're yellow," then smile and flip her hair back the way Penelope Campbell (emerald green) does.

She shakes her head and opens the drawer for a spoon. If she were a gold, she could do that: leave him breathless with a few words. But beiges aren't like that. Beiges always follow the rules. Besides, she reminds herself, you've got to let people figure out their colors for themselves.

"Is that finished then?" Marcy's mum asks as she lines up the edges of a pillowcase.

"Think so, Mum." Marcy dips the spoon in the toffee sauce and brings it to her mouth. Notes of caramel and burnt sugar swirl around her tongue. "Mmm," she says, closing her eyes in pleasure.

"Marcy," her mum scolds. Marcy opens her eyes to her mother's narrowed, disapproving ones.

Instinctively, she puts her hand to her blouse, which pulls around her tummy. Her mother had insisted on buying it a size too small. "It'll help you, really," she had said when she brought it home. "Per-

15

haps it will motivate you when you're tempted to visit the sweets cupboard after school. I want you to be happy, you know that, right?"

Now, Marcy says to her mum, "I just wanted to make sure it was okay."

Violet leans over to look in the saucepan. She nods tersely.

Marcy knows the sauce is perfect. She knows her mum knows it, too.

"Right then," her mum says. "You better get to Gran's. Those roses aren't going to prune themselves."

Violet turns back to the pile of laundry, face etched into a frown.

Marcy loves the smell of fresh laundry: the way it picks up the scent of lavender grown across the island and, on windy days, droplets of the sea. Occasionally, when she thinks no one is watching, Violet will lift a washed shirt or towel to her face and breathe in its scent with her eyes closed. It is always then that Marcy feels most safe.

"Mum," Marcy says as she digs around the shoe pile for her left wellie, "Do you ever think about colors?"

Violet picks up a single woolen sock. Behind her, light filters in through the living room window, which her mother keeps so meticulously free of smudges it poses a danger for birds. "What kind of question is that?" she asks as she searches the basket for its pair.

"I mean the way Gran does. How people are colors. Do you ever think of people that way?"

Violet's shoulders tense. Marcy remembers the spilled water glass. "It's nonsense, Marcy," Violet says. "People are people."

Marcy yanks her navy wellie over her foot. "I know I'm a beige." "Enough," Violet snaps. "You're late enough as it is, and Gran will be waiting."

Marcy should have known. Her mother lacked any of the imagination required to see people as colors. The thought itself was likely far too impractical for her even to entertain.

"I can't find my other wellie," Marcy protests. She peers under the table, then opens the door to the living room. Marcy is always losing things. Just this week, she's lost a glove, a headband, homework, and a five-pound note.

It drives her mum mad. Losing things, Violet always insists, is an entirely avoidable part of life. If one were simply responsible, one wouldn't lose things.

"Honestly, Marcy," Violet says now. "You should really just take your boots off at the same time."

Just then, Marcy's six-year-old brother, Peter, comes bounding down the stairs and into the kitchen, wearing a navy boot on his head. "Look, Mummy, I'm a duck-boy," he says, bumping into the table and knocking a pile of folded shirts to the ground.

"Aha," says Marcy, plucking the boot off his head and jamming it onto her foot. "I'll take that."

"Where is that other sock?" Violet mutters, continuing to dig through the pile.

Marcy is grabbing her bag when her cousin, Arthur, who lives on the dairy farm just up the lane, opens the kitchen door and walks in, waving a sheet of paper.

"I've enlisted!" he says, brandishing it like a flag. "I leave Friday next, Auntie Vi. Off to do my part for the war."

Violet looks up from the washing pile, resting her hands on her slender hips. She frowns at him, sticking out her delicate chin. "Gosh," she manages. "Have you told your mum?"

Auntie Ethel, her mum's sister-in-law, has been saying for weeks how important it is for the young people to do their part.

"Yes," says Arthur, plucking a scone from the counter and scarfing it down. "Hasn't stopped crying all morning, poor lass. But I know she's proud. We've all got to do our bit."

Marcy is slightly embarrassed at her cousin's lack of manners. Peter stands in awe at Arthur's ability to take a scone without asking. He inches toward the counter, as though intent on doing the same. Marcy shoots him a warning look.

"'Cept, ain't only me, of course," he says with a mouthful of food. "Loads of boys have enlisted. Ran into Eugene Westover—Louisa's boy—on my way here. He's just got his papers, he has. Hasn't even told his mum."

A sharp pain courses through Marcy. No. Not her childhood best friend. Not her secret crush. Eugene couldn't leave; he couldn't because Marcy couldn't imagine a reality without him in it.

To her surprise, her mum, always the picture of control, has turned white. She grips the edge of the table. "Not Eugene," she says.

Marcy and Peter both look at her.

Recovering quickly, she begins sorting laundry again. "Is he?"

"Yep," says Arthur, oblivious to the effect his statement had. "Well, I've got to go get my affairs in order. Basil's right livid. Couldn't pass the eye exam and so he'll miss out on all the action."

Marcy feels a twinge of relief. Basil, Arthur's twin, had always been her favorite cousin. She's glad he is staying.

Violet says nothing to Arthur as he leaves. Instead, she pours out the entire basket of laundry on the table and sorts through it violently. "Where is that damn sock?"

Peter, sensing his mother's mood, picks up a train from the floor and disappears upstairs.

Marcy walks to the door. Turning back, she sees Violet, her head in her hands, shaking over the pile of unfolded clothes.

In another life, she would walk back in and put an arm around her mum's shoulders and make her a cup of tea.

In another life, her mum would let her.

CHAPTER THREE

LOUISA

1940

Louisa Westover shivers at the edge of the sea. She tugs at the swimming costume that bunches around her thighs.

"Come on, Lou," she mutters to herself. "Just dip in so you can dip out."

She pushes her hair out of her face, annoyed that she does this to herself on the first of every month. Louisa is not a strong swimmer, nor does she particularly enjoy the water. But for nearly ten years now, on the first of every month, she drags herself out of bed to swim.

"Normal people give things up when it's not fun anymore, Lou," her husband Jon said that morning as he cut into his fried egg. "They find a new hobby. Maybe even something they actually enjoy."

"Of course I enjoy it," Louisa said, snapping up her towel and walking past him in a huff.

A wave surges forward, submerging Louisa's bare feet and legs. "Oh, alright then!" she yells over the water. "I'm coming!"

Taking a deep breath, she jumps off the rock and plunges into the water, bracing herself for the shock of cold. She kicks her legs and comes up for air. "Take that!" she calls out to the empty beach. "I do like this!"

Within minutes, Louisa is back on the rocks, drying herself off with a towel, willing the feeble April sun to warm her. She jumps in place until her lips stop chattering. Throwing a housecoat over her wet swimming costume, Louisa trudges up the footpath near Devil's

Hole, back toward her home at Sorel Point. She walks quickly, the prospect of a warm cup of tea propelling her forward.

Her dad had loved to swim. Louisa remembers the breakfast table as a child, buttering an extra slice of toast for her dad, who would come in sopping wet after a brisk morning dip and take it out of Louisa's hand on the way upstairs to change. Louisa wishes the passion would have been passed along with the nose she inherited, but it seems to have permanently eluded her.

As she reaches the lane, she closes the gate to the footpath, fiddling with the finicky latch.

"Louisa?"

Louisa stops. She knows that voice, and it belongs to the person she wants to see least in the world right now. Slowly, she turns, arching her shoulders, trying to look dignified in her old house coat and wellies, hair plastered to her cheeks.

"Hello, Violet."

Violet Foster is, as usual, perfectly put together in a navy frock and jacket, hair coiffed and pinned back, carrying a wire basket of scrubbed-clean eggs. For a fleeting moment, Louisa sees Violet as a child, sitting up straight in a classroom chair, pencil in her hand and papers stacked perfectly on her desk. Her whole life, Violet has been the epitome of poise.

Louisa pulls her old house coat tightly around her waist.

"I was just taking some of our eggs over to Mr. Brown," Violet says. She raises an eyebrow at Louisa's appearance. "Still swimming then?"

"Clearly."

Violet flinches, shoulders drooping slightly. "Yes, well, obviously, I–"

Be kind, Louisa says to herself. She fishes for something friendly to say. "It would be a hell of a lot easier if we lived in the tropics. Maybe then I'd stick with it more than once a month."

Violet smiles. "You're still only doing it on the first, then?"

Louisa shrugs.

The silence hangs between them.

Finally, Violet says, "I thought you were absolutely mad when you burst into my kitchen to ask me to swim with you. It was January, wasn't it? About ten years ago now…"

"I thought we needed some excitement to get us through the winter, shake out all the cobwebs."

Louisa remembers that Violet had been baking bread and the whole kitchen smelled of home. After their swim, they devoured the bread as they dried off by the fire. With the memory comes a stab of longing. She tries to shake it off.

"Marcy loved being in the water that first time we went," Violet says. She seems desperate for the conversation to continue.

Louisa cannot help but smile. "The cold didn't seem to touch her," she says. "We had to practically drag her out."

Violet shakes her head. "I thought she was going to get pneumonia. Her lips were so blue."

"And Eugene refused to get in," Louisa adds, enjoying the memory despite herself. "We were in the water for two minutes total, but he spent the whole time shouting warnings to us on the rock about hypothermia. Hard to believe how much he likes to swim now."

At the mention of Eugene, Violet shifts. "He's so grown up. And now look," she says. "There's a war on and so many boys off to it. My nephew Arthur came round this morning to say he'd enlisted."

Louisa pities Ethel, Arthur's mother. "There are a lot of boys headed off. But not Eugene," she says, a little too firmly. "He won't go."

Eugene, she's sure, is too soft for a place like war. Subconsciously, she pulls on her necklace: a piece of sea glass tied to a string that she's worn every day for years.

Violet opens her mouth, as if she has something more to say, then closes it.

"Well," says Louisa, "I'd best get on. A cup of tea and a change of clothes is in order."

"Yes, of course you must," says Violet. "Only—"

"What is it?"

"I just can't believe you keep swimming. Even after we stopped going together."

Violet leans forward, clutching her basket of eggs so tightly that her knuckles turn white.

Louisa pushes her wet hair out of her face. "I'd better get on, Vi."

Violet starts at the use of the old nickname, and Louisa corrects herself. "I mean, Violet."

She turns, thinking about the words she was unable to say: about the swim, about everything else.

I just can't seem to give it up.

CHAPTER FOUR

VIOLET

1911

Violet's mum used to talk about the Land of Lost Things. Every time a household object disappeared, a spoon, a pen, a knitting needle, her mum would throw up her hands and laugh. "Another item off to visit."

Violet used to imagine the Land of Lost Things as a carnival of sorts, where miscellaneous objects went to relax and get away from the drudgery of daily use.

On the beach, as she runs toward the man who fell, gasping for breath between her screams, she thinks about the Land of Lost Things. It had never occurred to her to apply that thinking to humans.

She knows this man. Violet cannot think of why. He is vaguely familiar as a background character in her life, much like the wallpaper of a room she sat in but never paid attention to.

Violet doesn't remember reaching the man. She doesn't remember the authorities arriving, the man being rolled up in a black tarp and taken away. She doesn't remember the kind elderly gentleman who helps her up the steps, nor does she remember bicycling home.

The next thing Violet remembers, after the thought about lost things, is the solid door of her Tudor-style row home, which she arrives at sticky, out of breath, and covered in sand. She opens the door. Tess bolts out with an angry hiss.

"Vi? Is that you?" Her father's voice comes from the living room along with the flapping of pages as he turns the newspaper. Every day at a quarter past twelve, her father arrives home from work for exactly thirty minutes. Mum makes him a marmite sandwich and a cup of tea, and then he cycles the fifteen minutes back.

Violet stands in the front hallway and wipes her sandy feet on the front carpet. She steps around the corner. He sits in his rocker, his glasses halfway down his nose, in front of the walls he has filled with books: history, mathematics, religion and geography. She knows her dad is a rich burgundy, but his colors look muted today, like he is floating away from her. She wants to rush forward and grab him.

"Violet," her father says softly as he lowers his paper to look at her. "What happened?" He sits with his legs crossed, a gap of skin exposed between his black sock and trouser pants.

Her mum comes around the corner, carrying a tray. Violet freezes where she is on the blue carpet of the parlor, sopping wet and shivering. Her mum's eyes get big and her mouth goes slack, but she recovers quickly.

"Goodness, girl," her mum says brightly. "You look like you've had a busy morning. Why don't you run up and change before you get sand all over my carpet?"

Violet's mum looks perfectly put together, but she also looks different. Less turquoise, more stormy. A hardness forms behind her eyes that keeps Violet from saying anything about the beach.

Then Violet realizes her mum is wearing a blue floral dress.

Fleetingly, hopefully, Violet thinks that maybe she imagined it. It was some other lady on the cliff wearing a peach dress. Her mum was here making lunch all that time.

"Mum," Violet asks. "Did you change your dress?"

Violet's mum stiffens, then laughs. "Dress? No, my girl. I've been wearing this all day."

Violet turns and runs up to her room. She flings onto her bed, knowing she'll be finding grains of sand between the sheets for days, and buries her head in her pillow.

There is a knock on the door. Her mother enters, carrying a cup of tea.

"Hello, my darling," she says, sitting on the edge of the bed.

Violet sobs, a mixture of relief and grief washing over her. She buries her face in her hands.

"What is it?" her mom asks, stroking Violet's hair.

Violet can only respond with a half-sentence: "Called out—didn't hear me—so sorry."

Finally, her mum nudges Violet back into a sitting position and looks at her with the same firm expression she had in the sitting room downstairs. "Did you see something at the beach that frightened you?"

"The man. The man fell off the cliff."

"What?"

"The cliff," says Violet. "The cliff at Plemont Bay."

"What were you doing at Plemont Bay?" her mum asks.

"I know I shouldn't have gone, but I wanted to find an oyster shell with pearls inside."

"I told you not to go to Plemont."

"Yes, I know, I'm sorry. And now the man's fallen off the cliff and it's my fault."

Violet's mum laughs, but it is without warmth. "My darling, I don't know what game you were playing, but you couldn't possibly have seen a man fall off a cliff. If someone had fallen off the cliff at Plemont Bay, we'd have heard about it. You must have imagined it."

"I didn't imagine it. Mummy, I saw him fall. I know that man, but I'm not sure why. And there was someone there who looked just like you."

Her mum says firmly, "I wasn't there, Violet. I was with Mrs. Griffith. I was nowhere near Plemont Bay. And you shouldn't have been either, but I'm sure whatever you saw was imagined."

"Do you really think so?" Violet looks at her mum, begging it to be true.

"Of course, my love. Have some tea."

"Mum."

"Yes?"

"Your colors have changed. You look–different."

Her mum goes quiet for a moment. When she speaks, it is with a note of finality. "Violet. A person's colors can't change. They are who they are." She stands up, smooths out her dress. She looks away from Violet for a long moment. When she turns back, she has a smile painted on her face. "Maybe it's you who has changed."

It is the first time Violet can remember being afraid of her mum.

CHAPTER FIVE

MARCY

1940

The spring air smells like lavender. Marcy breathes in the scent as she pedals down the lane. Sheep and cows graze in pastures along hedge-lined country roads, grazing contentedly in the sun. She is late for Gran's as it is, but instead of turning left onto her lane, where her Tudor-style row home sits facing the sea, she pedals straight on and parks at Greve de Lecq by the ice cream stand.

The start of school that year had come with the start of the war. It gave it that crisp, freshly ironed, new-clothes-feeling. Every mum was planting her Dig for Victory garden, every child playing Axis versus Allies. Teenagers coined the phrase, *there's a war on*, as a catch-all rationale for doing anything forbidden.

There's a war on, let's skip class, said Annette. *There's a war on, let's drive too fast in John Shiver's automobile down Five Mile Road*, said Susan. *There's a war on, let's take the boats out in high tide and try to swim back in the freezing water*, said Basil.

Marcy had done none of it: the thought of repercussions from her mother was enough to keep her far away from anything that resembled trouble.

Today, though, feels different. Eugene is leaving.

If there is one place Eugene Westover will be on a beautiful spring day like this one, Marcy knows it's the beach. And she's got to see him.

It's low tide, and the beach is scattered with tidal pools and clumps of seaweed, large rocks where teenagers bathe in the sun. Since the war began, tourism had slowed on the island, and on a day when this beach should have been packed, only a few locals—the ones who didn't need to farm or work—had ventured out.

Marcy scans the beach and sees him almost immediately. Tall, lanky, yellow, with a bouncing gait and a gorgeous mop of black curly hair, Eugene is impossible to miss. He sits on a rock with Penelope Campbell, looking very interested in what she has to say as she stretches out, tilting her face toward the sun. Several other boys pause their game of catch to watch her.

Rolling her eyes, secretly wishing she could stretch and look as glamorous as Penelope, Marcy gets in line for the ice cream truck. She'll buy Gran a ninety-nine with a chocolate flake in it, and all will be forgiven.

She stands in line when she feels him approaching. That's the thing with Eugene. She always knows when he's close. Suddenly self-conscious, she fiddles with her purse, pulling out money for the ninety-nines.

Marcy has been watching Eugene at the beach for years. Four years older than her, he has always been perfect, and perfectly out of reach. When she was younger, Eugene seemed to notice her, including her in games at church picnics, seemingly oblivious to the fact that Marcy was hopelessly in love. Then he started dating Penelope Campbell and became all gruff and choppy around the edges. Marcy would watch Eugene from the hedges of the schoolyard, the pew behind at church, wishing she could make herself less invisible.

"Your mums used to be best friends, you know," Annette told her once as they sat on the rock wall of Greve de Lecq, watching Eugene surf with his friends.

"What?" Marcy asked skeptically. She had never noticed Mrs. Westover as anything more than polite and distantly cordial with her mum.

Annette nodded. "My mum told me. Absolutely inseparable. Your mum was even Eugene's godmother."

"What happened?"

Annette shrugged. "No idea. My mum either didn't know or wouldn't tell me."

Marcy never brought up the subject with her mum. She wasn't sure how. But it gave her some quiet confidence in her thoughts about Eugene, knowing there was this thread between them.

"Marcy Foster," he says now as he nears. She'd never noticed how much she liked her full name until he said it. His voice is like creamy coffee, warm and smooth. "You've grown up."

Marcy feels a blush creep over her whole face, trying to swallow her disbelief that Eugene is actually talking to her. At fifteen, her chest finally grew in and her hair got thicker. Over the winter, she grew three inches taller. Her stomach is still far more round than her mother would like, but she has to admit that she *feels* more like a woman, looking at herself in her bedroom mirror. For Eugene to notice, though, brings a new thrill entirely.

"Hiya," she says, smiling widely in return. She knows her face betrays the fact that she's thrilled to see him, and again, she wishes she could be smooth, emerald green.

"Alright?" he asks as he steps into line beside her. She feels aware of the lining of his shirt, so close to hers, of the way that if he moved an inch, their hands would brush.

I know you, Eugene, she wants to say as she looks at his eyes, the color of deep sea. *I've watched you my whole life. I know you better than Penelope Campbell ever will.*

"Fine, thanks," she says instead. She smiles a half smile the way she's seen Penelope do it, hoping she looks beautiful and mysterious.

"You okay?" Eugene asks, frowning at her.

"Yes, yes, of course," Marcy says, dropping the smile. The line for ice cream moves forward and she steps along with it, trying to ignore the flame in her cheeks.

"I heard Arthur enlisted," he says, running a hand through his curly mop of hair.

Behind Eugene, she sees Penelope Campbell turning her emerald green head in their direction.

29

"What?" she asks.

"Your cousin."

"Oh," she says, forcing herself to stop watching his hand working its way through his hair, wishing she was that hand. "He came round to tell us this morning. He's been writing to a friend in England while waiting here for further orders. The friend says the food's not half bad."

"Well, that's a consolation. At least I'll have something to look forward to."

"He told us you were enlisting as well."

To her surprise, she cannot conceal the emotion in her voice.

"I leave next week," Eugene says. He says the words like he is trying them on, standing up straight and puffing out his chest slightly. The persona of a hero.

"That's very brave," Marcy says. "I hope you stay safe."

He holds her gaze, sending a shiver down her spine. She hardly dares to believe this is happening to her: Eugene's green eyes meeting hers, Penelope yards away. Had she known the morning would go like this, she would have at least done her hair.

"You know what I've been thinking about lately?" he asks.

"What's that?"

"Choir with Mrs. Cremps. Do you remember that? At the St. Peter Parish Church?"

Marcy laughs. "How could I forget? Mrs. Cremps always arrived twenty minutes late, smelling of cigarettes and musty perfume." Marcy was nine then, Eugene thirteen, the oldest boy in the choir. Marcy was only there because her parents made her attend, but Eugene always seemed to really love it. When he sang, he closed his eyes and lifted his chin up, looking like he floated away somewhere for the length of the song. That was before he became popular, before he decided that singing wasn't good for his reputation and quit the choir.

"Why are you thinking about that?" Marcy asks.

Eugene shrugs. "Silly reasons," he says.

Somehow, this small show of embarrassment gives Marcy courage.

"Have a go," she says. She glances briefly toward Penelope and is thrilled to see her frowning in their direction.

"I've just been thinking about why I love music."

"And why's that?"

"Because you can't even begin to assess a song until it's over. Each note is just a word on the page, a link in the story. You don't know what you've done until it's over. And everyone's talking about this war like it's the end all and be all, and maybe it is. But maybe it's also just a link in my story. A note."

The two look at each other for a moment. He radiates yellow. Marcy tries to summon the courage to touch his hand.

"That's not silly at all."

Penelope Campbell stands up and begins sauntering towards them, breaking the spell. She sways as she walks, like she is dancing, sprinkling emerald green around her. Marcy knows she is staring, but she can't look away. Penelope Campbell has somehow been given every favorable asset a woman can have: wide hips, thin waist, full lips, big hair. Marcy tries to swallow her envy.

"Eugene," Penelope calls. She tilts her head as she waves.

"Er, coming," Eugene says, waving back. "I'd better go."

"Yes," Marcy says.

"Nice talking to you, Marcy," Eugene says as he walks away.

Marcy holds out a few coins to the vendor, though she doesn't even want the ice cream anymore. "One ninety-nine," she says. "With a flake."

"Hey, Marcy," she hears. Turning around, Eugene stands there, hands in his pockets. Is she imagining it, or does he look sheepish?

"Hi," she says, ice cream in hand.

"I'll be at the Weighbridge Saturday next to ship off. If you're planning to see Arthur off, maybe I'll see you there."

Marcy squeezes her ice cream cone and feels it crack. If she were emerald green, she'd be mysterious about it. But beiges can't afford mystery.

"I'll be there."

31

He nods and turns. Marcy's ice cream falls to the ground, splattering on her wellie. She grins as she tries to wipe it off.

***

It's nearly dinnertime when Marcy arrives home that evening. Gran had pretended to be cross with Marcy for being late, and then was actually cross when Tess, her cat, bolted out of the front door and into the street. By the time Marcy found her hissing in the alleyway and came back to prune the roses, the sun was already hot in the sky. She was so distracted, replaying her conversation with Eugene, trying unsuccessfully to suppress the hope that *finally*, he had noticed her, that she pricked herself several times.

Her mum is in the kitchen, boxing up a date cake topped with Marcy's toffee sauce. Violet is the most talented baker Marcy knows, and friends are always ordering scones or tea cakes from her little business, *Bakes by Vi*.

"Gosh, I don't know *how* you manage to bake so well and keep the house so clean," friends say as they come to pick up their perfectly wrapped packages.

"Oh, it's not clean, not really," Violet insists, absentmindedly wiping a single smudge from the spotless counter.

It's the one thing her mum seems to do despite it bothering her dad. He doesn't see why Violet would need to make anything more than what he provides for her.

"It's just a hobby, David," Violet says whenever he brings it up. "Besides, it's not good for us to be eating all these cakes, is it? I won't fit into my dresses!"

Her mum is always making comments like that, about weight and size. Marcy doesn't understand why, because her mum is more feather than human: a tiny, delicate wisp. Marcy thinks the comments are reserved for her, Marcy, who has always been what her mum calls "bigger boned," whose dresses are always snug and who has to sit on her hands to keep from having a second helping at dinner.

As Marcy walks in, she takes a deep, apprehensive breath, wondering what kind of mood her mum will be in after this morning.

"Hiya, Mum," she says as she pulls off her wellies. The left one is still sticky from the ice cream this morning. A shiver of delight runs down her spine.

"Gosh, you were a long time," her mum says, tying a blue ribbon around the box. "Dinner's nearly ready. Can you put some plates out?"

Marcy heads toward the table, which is now clear of laundry aside from one pair of yellow woolen socks.

"Did you find your missing sock, then?" Marcy asks as she pulls plates down from the shelf to set the table.

Her mother tenses over the cake. "No," she says. "I made another pair."

"Oh? Gosh, that was quick," says Marcy. "Who are they for?" By the color, she thinks she already knows.

Another pause. Marcy thinks she didn't hear her and takes the plates over to the table.

Then her mother says quietly, "Louisa's boy. Eugene."

CHAPTER SIX

LOUISA
1940

Louisa sits in the conservatory of her centuries-old farmhouse in the early evening light, staring through the glass doors out to the chicken yard and then out over to the cliff that drops into the sea. The newspaper is spread out across her lap, offering details about the weather, the wartime rations, and Miss Marjorie's cow fence, which suffered sufficient damage after a hit by John Blanchard's tractor.

Louisa is thinking, against her will, about Violet. She mulls over her run-in with Violet this morning and swallows a wave of embarrassment. She doesn't want Violet to know that she is still swimming. It makes her feel more exposed than being found in the lane in a housecoat and wellies.

Back when they were friends, they used to walk past Miss Marjorie's house on a weekly basis. Marjorie loves knick-knacks; random gnomes and collectibles adorn her front yard. One gnome, who the ladies nicknamed Soppy, was in a different location every time they walked by. "Shall we go see where Soppy is today?" was the phrase Louisa would say to Violet to suggest they go for a walk. As she always does when she thinks about Violet, Louisa feels a twinge of sadness and anger, but most of all, guilt.

"Mum," Eugene says as he walks into the room with his own cup of tea. Louisa looks up, forgetting about Violet and the gnomes. He smells like the beach and looks like sunshine, and Louisa knows he's spent the day avoiding chores with his father and lounging at the beach.

She thinks he's coming to apologize. Yesterday, she caught him smoking a cigarette with Penelope Campbell behind her uncle's bank in town. She'd been so surprised to see him there, holding out a long cigarette for her, standing close, laughing about something. In the last few years, her sensitive, intuitive Eugene had become bruisy and rebellious. He had coughed when he'd tried to inhale his, and it gave Louisa some relief to know it was probably his first, that her many speeches and rants about how disgusting she found cigarettes hadn't fallen on totally deaf ears.

She's a little embarrassed as she remembers the way she marched toward him and plucked the cigarette from his mouth, asked him what in the bloody hell he thought he was doing, then ground it into the cobblestone. Penelope vanished like the smoke she was puffing, slipping away before Louisa could give her a piece of her mind.

"There's a war on, Mum," Eugene had said, half sheepish, half defiant. "And besides, Dad smokes his pipe every night."

"That's different," Louisa had wanted to say, though she knew it wasn't really different, and that Jon had never agreed with nor supported her views on smoking. So she had felt angry with him too, by the time she got home and declared that they could all fend for themselves for dinner as she was going to bed.

Now, she looks out the window and says, "Yes?"

"I've enlisted in the army."

Lifting her eyes to his chin and his nose, she wonders when his face lost its chubbiness, when those cheekbones became defined. The real question: when did he become old enough to sit across from her and give her news that would devastate her over a cup of tea? "Is this about the cigarette?" she asks. Now, she wishes she had not snuffed it out. Had she known what was coming, she'd have put it to her own lips and had a long drag.

Eugene smiles, crease lines appearing around his eyes. He sits down next to her and she catches a glimpse of the tender boy she remembers.

She wraps her hands around her cup of tea and asks with all the steadiness she can, "When do you leave?"

She tries to ignore the brittleness in her voice. She hopes he will, too.

"Saturday next," he says.

She grips her cup more tightly so that hot tea splashes over the edge and scalds her finger. "Damn," she says before she catches herself.

He pulls out a handkerchief and offers it.

"Where are you going?" she asks as she takes it, wiping off her hand.

"England, first, then who knows?" he says with that crooked smile she loves so much. "Probably France."

Louisa wants to shake him. She wants to say, "Why would you leave me, this home, this life the three of us have built together?"

She knows she should have told him more about the Great War. She had omitted stories, interrupted Jon every time he came close to telling them. Her desire had been for her son to know nothing of the cruelty people were capable of unleashing on each other. Eugene didn't know about the night terrors that continued to haunt his dad, about the number of times Louisa had woken up to yelling and thrashing, the way she had to rock Jon back to sleep as he cried in her arms.

She'd refused to talk to Eugene about this war, not wanting him to know how dire the situation was, even when he asked questions. When they saw signs in town about enlisting, Louisa would hurry Eugene past them, hoping he wouldn't see.

She swallows and takes a deep breath. She reaches for his hand and squeezes it three times. *I love you.*

Then she says briskly, "Well, the French aren't good for much, but they do make a decent croissant. If you don't bring me one back in time for my birthday next year, I shall be very cross."

Eugene smirks, and she hopes he is remembering the annual trips they took growing up on her birthday to St. Malo, twelve miles away, because she insisted it was impossible to find a good croissant in Jersey. They would sit on the stone wall, watching the waves roll in far below them, sharing pieces of the flaky, buttery crust while fighting off the seagulls.

"Of course, Mum," Eugene says. "But I can't guarantee that I won't have a bite of it first."

He stands up and says he's got to meet some friends for a football match. Louisa stares out the window until she is sure he is gone. Then she takes the teacup in her hand and throws it against the wall. To her fury, it doesn't even break.

Cursing a long string of every forbidden word she knows, she pulls her wellies on and goes outside. She walks along the edge of the garden until she reaches the hog shed, where her husband Jon is mending the roof.

As she approaches, he stops hammering. His face, though weathering, is still as handsome and rugged as the day she first met him, on a London street corner in the thick of the Great War, on her way to work at the WAAF.

"Eugene told you then," he says to her as he pulls off his work gloves and gets down from the roof. He smells like earth, like dirt and spring rain.

She pushes him. "You should have *told* him!" she says, on the brink of yelling. "You should have told him how terrible it was. He should know."

"Do you really think that would have made a difference?" Jon asks.

He wraps his arms around her and she sobs into his shoulder. The wind from the sea blows against her back.

"He's like a butterfly, Jon," she says. "He's too delicate for a place like war."

Jon raises his eyebrows. "Eugene? A butterfly?"

"You don't know him like I know him," Louisa snaps.

Jon puts his hands on Louisa's shoulders. He looks into her eyes, which are level with his. "Butterflies are strong, Lou," he says. "They can carry twice their weight."

"Bend the wing the wrong way and it will break," she says.

37

He brushes her hair out of her face.

"Let it go and it will soar."

She turns then and looks out toward the sea—at the waves rolling in, the clouds in the distance, out to where she knows war is wreaking havoc on other mothers, but she cannot bring herself to feel empathy for any of them.

"I won't lose another child," she says to Jon.

"You won't," he assures her, rubbing her back. "He's not a little boy anymore."

"I won't," she whispers. It is a prayer.

She walks back toward the house, hands stuffed in her pockets. On the doorstep is a small parcel, wrapped in brown paper and tied with twine. The soft, crinkly package bends against her hand when she picks it up.

"For Eugene," the label says, scrawled in the perfect handwriting she knows like her own.

Louisa swallows a lump as she rips the package open to reveal a pair of perfectly knit yellow socks that will serve her son well as he disappears to the trenches. She takes the socks upstairs and puts them away in her drawer.

CHAPTER SEVEN

VIOLET

1911

Violet's mother never mentions the incident at Plemont Bay again, and Violet knows better than to bring it up. She and her mum move around one another on eggshells, talking only about tangible things like the roses in the garden and the number of plates to be set at dinner. Violet wonders whether she is about to be arrested. Every time she hears sirens, she jumps, thinking someone is after her.

I killed someone, she says to herself when she is alone, the ugliness of the sentence wrapping around her insides like a weed, strong and unrelenting like the wisteria vine outside her window. Sometimes, she looks at herself in the mirror and tries to say it out loud. She never can.

Violet watches her own color change. It becomes something colder than the sky, more breakable. Sometimes, when she walks around, she feels herself draining, leaving the deeper pigments behind. *Maybe it's you that's changed,* her mother's words ring in her head.

"Rosa, dear, is there any more jam?" her father asks one morning while he sips his coffee.

"No, I'm afraid not," her mum says, mouth in a straight, firm line. Her soft, lotioned hands tremble slightly as she spreads the marmalade on the bread.

The family doesn't return to Plemont Bay for family picnics, moving instead to Five Mile Beach at St. Ouen. Violet doesn't like the flat, vast, sandy beach. She misses exploring the coves with her father, but still, she says nothing.

On her own, she tries to sort out what happened. She sneaks the newspapers up to her room at night and reads every line at the painstaking pace of an eleven-year-old, searching for any hints of a man who has fallen to his death from the cliffs. She finds nothing.

Violet wishes she could talk to Louisa about this, but Louisa hasn't been back at school since the incident. The teacher says she's moved. Violet misses her friend's kind smile, her curiosity. Sometimes she thinks that maybe if she could see Louisa, if she could just sit in her eggplant purple for a bit, she could believe in the colors again.

She could have imagined it, she allows herself to think hopefully. Maybe she isn't a murderer and isn't responsible for the death of a stranger with thick shoulders and sandy blonde hair who wore a smart suit jacket on the day of his demise. Maybe she never saw the man who looked familiar but was also unplaceable, with the long nose and the shiny black shoes pointing up on the beach.

It would be nearly possible to convince herself of this if it weren't for the dreams. A month after the incident, Violet begins to have nightmares. For three nights in a row, her head is filled with shrill screaming, the man falling, her footsteps echoing as she runs toward him, always waking up before she reaches him.

"Mummy!" She yells, asleep, into the darkness of her room. "Help me!"

Her mum runs in every night, holds her, and tells her it will be okay. Then, with a force equal to her softness, she insists, every night, that Violet was dreaming. "You've made this up, my love," she says as she strokes Violet's hair. "It's alright, it's alright, just go back to sleep."

On the fourth night, as Violet dreams about the man, she runs toward him, like she always does. Except for this time, she reminds herself, in her sleep, not to scream. Otherwise, she will wake her mum. In her dream, she gets closer to the man in the suit, closer than she's ever been before. As she approaches, she realizes he is bigger than she pictured him: a portly gentleman with straight blonde hair and a mustache. She's seen him before, maybe at church or a parish fete. He lies on the beach as though asleep.

40

Dropping to her knees, she sits next to him, a scream lodged in her throat that she doesn't allow to escape. She puts a hand on his chest, willing his heart to beat. He is silent, still.

In his coat pocket, she feels something lumpy. Reaching in, she pulls out a mass: a string of rose gold pearls.

The scream in Violet's throat can no longer be contained. She wails, in her sleep, into the night.

When her mum can finally wake her, Violet is drenched in sweat, shaking. "He had your pearls."

Violet's mum stares at her for a long moment. Then, she leans forward and whispers harshly, "Pearls? What pearls?"

"You were wearing pearls that day."

"I most certainly was not. This is enough. Do you understand me? I have had *enough*. You *imagined*—*it*—*Violet*. That is all. You imagined the whole thing. You must never speak to me about it again."

Violet nods, silent tears rolling down her cheeks.

"Rosa?" a sleepy voice calls from the hallway. Her father pokes his head around the doorway, wearing a thick robe and slippers. "Is everything alright?"

Her mum stands, collecting herself. "Yes," she says a little breathlessly, "Yes, darling, we're just fine. Violet's getting settled down now."

Leaning forward, her mum kisses her forehead. "Remember," her mum whispers. "Never mention this again."

After that night, Violet continues to dream about the man, about that day at Plemont Bay, but even in her dreams, she doesn't scream.

She never brings the incident up again. And though, over time, her mum returns to her bright, cheery self, a hard line is drawn between the two of them, one that neither seems to be able to cross. Violet's mum is no longer turquoise. She is murky and unreadable, as if she doesn't want to be found. *It must be me*, Violet thinks. *I can't be trusted.*

One evening, as her dad drinks his scotch and smokes his pipe in the living room, Violet overhears him from where she is reading a book at the top of the stairs.

"Darling, I'm worried there's something wrong with Violet."

"Oh?"

Violet hears the knitting needles click back and forth.

"She's become quite withdrawn, hasn't she? Wanting to keep to herself all the time."

"Don't worry, love, that's just growing up, isn't it?" her mother says brightly. "Don't you remember becoming moody when you reached adolescence?"

"I suppose you're right," says her dad.

Upstairs, Violet grips her book so hard that the page rips.

***

Violet steers clear of the beach. On free afternoons, when her mum sends her outside after school, Violet walks. She explores the island on foot, trudging the many footpaths and roads. Jersey, she realizes, is filled with even more diversity than she knew: a variety of plants and insects wait for her every time she ventures outdoors. Taking a basket with her, Violet collects the rocks and different flora she discovers on the island, thinking she will find a book in her dad's collection to identify them.

It is on one of these walks that Violet first sees the house at Sorel Point. Like a fortress, it stands alone at the end of a winding lane lined with blackberries. A stone house, somewhat freshly vacated, it carries the aura of having once been well-loved. Set right up against the meadow that looks out toward the sea, with an arched doorway and an overgrown front garden, the house looks like it has jumped out from the page of a storybook.

A few bunnies hop lazily across the front garden. They give her a glance, and then hop closer to the house, as though beckoning.

Turning to make sure no one is about, Violet walks up to the front door and knocks. There is no answer.

Minutes pass. Violet stands on the slate stone step engulfed in utter silence, apart from the honey bee frolicking its way through the overgrown garden.

She knocks again. Chest fluttering, she reaches out and turns the knob.

It is, amazingly, unlocked. The heavy wood door swings open in front of Violet's outstretched palm.

"Hello?" Violet calls out into the dusty foyer. Her voice echoes.

There is no reply. Violet walks across the wide-planked floors, runs her hand along the cobwebbed banister. She is already imagining the house as it was, or as it could be: with garland hanging from the large rafters, the table set in glittering dishware for Christmas, children's footsteps thundering down the stairs while the piano plays and turkey roasts in the oven.

The house claims her in an instant. Its character, its coziness, its deep windows and high ceilings. She steps inside and takes off her shoes. With the unreserved candor of a child she'd nearly forgotten, she begins to play: stoking the imaginary fire, wiping the countertop in the kitchen, dancing in the long, narrow hallway.

Outside, she eats her packed lunch on a blanket beneath the mulberry tree while the tall grass tickles her elbows. She imagines a cow pasture, a pig pen, chickens. A happy place, where no bad memories can touch her.

After that day, Violet comes back to the house again and again, leaving as soon as she finishes chores in the morning, staying until it is time to trek home for tea. She begins sneaking out her mum's cleaning supplies and spends whole days washing the windows of the house, scrubbing the floors, and sweeping around each crevice and crack. She weeds the outside gardens carefully and fills the window sills with wildflowers she picks. Bringing her dolls from home, she sets them around the old wooden table, where she pours them imaginary cups of tea and chats like a grown-up about the weather and the tides.

"Violet, dear," her mum says one afternoon as she prepares dinner, "Where are you running off to every day?"

Violet pauses, the fork she sets hovering over its place at the table. For a moment, her mum looks at her with such bright, kind eyes, that Violet remembers what their relationship was like before Plemont Bay. If she'd found the house before, she'd have come home immediately to tell her mum about it.

Her mum leans over with her oven mitts to pull out a Shepherd's Pie. Violet's mouth waters as she looks at the lamb and vegetable casserole, topped with mashed potatoes and grated cheese.

"I'll show you tomorrow, if you like," Violet says impulsively.

Her mum's smile is wide and beautiful. "I'd love that, Vi. Really," she says. For a moment, the storm clouds lift and her mum looks turquoise again. Violet looks away and tries not to see it.

***

In the morning, Violet wakes up very early to get to the house. She puts fresh flowers out everywhere and lays a blanket for the picnic her mum will pack.

She cycles home quickly, hair falling out of her plait as she rides. She pulls into her cul-de-sac.

A tall, thin man stands outside her door. Violet wonders why he doesn't knock. He wears a black hat and coat even in the warm summer sun and is sorting through his briefcase.

"Can I help you?" Violet asks as she parks her bicycle. She doesn't like the man's coat or the black suit underneath.

The man looks up, surprised. "I'm looking for a Rosa Blanche," he says.

"That's my mum."

He smiles, revealing a mouthful of stained teeth. Violet doesn't like it. "She's a lucky woman to have a daughter like you."

Violet squirms uncomfortably. "Is there something you need?"

The man shakes his head. "Nothing needed, everything's been sorted. I just wanted to give your mum these."

He pulls out of his pocket a string of rose gold pearls.

Violet recognizes them immediately. They are the pearls her dad had given her mum for her birthday. "A pearl for my pearl," he'd said, beaming proudly over his mustache. Her mum had smiled at him and clasped them around her neck.

She remembers the pearls swaying in front of her mum as she served Violet toast with strawberry jam the morning of Plemont Bay. Dots appear in Violet's vision. She feels very hot suddenly.

The door opens and her mum steps out. Violet wants to tell her to go back inside, but her mouth is like cotton and she can't speak.

"Miss Blanche," the man says. "I've been looking for you."

She sees the pearls dangling from the stranger's hand.

"Why are you here?" she asks. "I thought everything was sorted."

"It is sorted," the man replied. "But these belong to you."

Her mum shakes her head and takes a step back. "No," she says. "I don't want them."

"You better take them, if you've got any sense," the man says, shaking them in front of her face. "I'm not going to hold onto them."

"If I take them, will you leave me alone?" she asks, a note of desperation in her voice.

The man grins. "For now."

Her mum takes the pearls and puts them in a pocket. "Please," she says. "I didn't want any of this. Just leave me."

The man points a finger at Violet. "Don't forget, Miss. I can talk any time I want. It's in your best interest to stay polite."

He walks away.

Her mum reaches for Violet. "Are you alright, my love?"

Violet feels cold. "Those pearls."

Her mum leans in close and puts two hands on Violet's shoulders. Her face is angry now, and her voice a terrifying whisper.

"You must promise me—*promise me, Violet*—that you will never speak again about that man. You must never mention it. Not to your dad, to your friends, to anyone. *Do you understand me?*"

Violet can only nod.

Her mum's eyes are puffy, her hair frizzy. With a deep weariness, she says, "I need to lie down, Violet. I'm afraid I can't go on your adventure today."

Violet's mum never asks to go to her special place again, and Violet never offers.

CHAPTER EIGHT

MARCY

1940

For a week, Marcy agonizes over what to wear to the Weighbridge to send off Eugene. She visits her Auntie Ethel (salmon pink), who bakes pies in the kitchen while her other son, Basil (warm olive), mopes, his wiry frame hunched over the counter.

"What do you think I should wear, Auntie Ethel? My polka dot dress? Or navy blue?" Marcy asks as she samples a bit of pastry.

"That would be nice, dear," her auntie says absentmindedly as she rolls.

"It feels rather like a grand thing, to see a fellow off at war," Marcy says dreamily. "A sea of handkerchiefs and admirers: the epitome of bravery. Say, Basil, are you giving anything to Arthur to take to war with him?"

"Only a hammer to knock out his eyes so they're as rubbish as mine," says Basil sulkily, pushing his thick-rimmed glasses back up the bridge of his nose.

"Cheer up, Basil," Marcy says. "I'm glad you're here, even if you aren't. And I'm sure you'll find plenty to do for the war effort from home."

"Fat chance," says Basil. "Arthur's going to have all the action, miles away, while I'm stuck here baking pies. It's not fair. I've always been quicker and stronger than him. It's just these bloody eyes."

Auntie Enid hands him a rolling pin. "Roll out some pastry, then, if you're so strong," she says, but she gives his arm a gentle squeeze.

In the end, Marcy settles on a green dress and a ribbon in her hair.

She spends ages trying to tame her frizz in the mirror before she goes downstairs. On her way out the door, she grabs a pair of her dad's woolen mittens from the winter bin, thinking Eugene will need them more than he will. Everyone said the war wouldn't last long, that it would be over in a couple of months, but that was last September. It couldn't hurt to be prepared.

When she arrives at the Weighbridge, it is packed with girls and mothers saying goodbye to their beaus and sons. An army band plays a peppy song, and a massive ship docks in the St. Helier harbor, ready to depart.

Eugene stands in the middle of the crowd with his hat off. He's nervous; she can tell by the way he clenches his jaw and bobs up and down on the balls of his feet. He wears a rucksack over his uniform and runs his hand through his hair as he looks around. Penelope Campbell is nowhere in sight.

"Eugene," she calls as she walks over to him. She pulls her dress away from her stomach.

His face breaks into a big smile when he sees her. "Golly, thanks, Marcy. It was good of you to come." He takes the mittens she thrusts into his hand. "Did you make these?"

"Well, now, that's top-tier secrecy," she says. She doesn't want to admit that she swiped them from her dad. For a moment, she forgets all about the war. She can only think that a moment she's dreamed about is actually coming true: she and Eugene together, alone in a crowd. Her stomach flutters and she knows her hands are sweaty.

"I'll think of you when I wear them."

She bites her lip to keep from laughing out loud.

She asks, "Where is your mum?"

A shadow crosses over his face. He looks away and shrugs. "Couldn't make it."

And Penelope? She can't bring herself to ask.

"Loose thread," she says, reaching out to adjust a mitten. She thinks he squeezes her hand and her heart soars and breaks at the same time.

"Take care of yourself, Eugene," she says, looking up into his eyes. "Come home."

He looks at her intensely. She wonders if it is because he wants to come home to her, or because he just needs to hear it from someone.

You're the picture of the hero, Eugene, Marcy wants to say. A starched, crisp uniform, the smell of gunpowder, the hero blazing new trails for the free world.

The whistle on the ship blows. The sound is deafening. A man in uniform shouts from the deck, "Alright, boys! Time to load up."

All around Marcy and Eugene, couples are kissing and crying. Marcy realizes this could be her last chance to do what she has imagined doing for years, and in a flash of bravery equivalent to that of a soldier, she throws her arms around his neck.

He surprises her by kissing her right above her ear. His lips are soft and warm. He whispers, "Take care of yourself," and his breath tickles her skin, shooting tingles across her whole body.

Marcy wants to look into his eyes as he pulls away, to discern what he meant by that, but another fellow claps him on the shoulder. "Ready then, mate?" he asks.

Before she can look again, he has blended into the throng of all the other boys in uniform, onto the ship that will take him away from her.

He stops as he boards the boat and looks back at her: a flash of yellow burning through the sky. Knowing this is her goodbye to a childhood crush, wishing it were the goodbye of lovers, she waves her handkerchief back.

Marcy waits a long time to go back home, until long after the ship has rolled out of sight and the crowds have thinned out. Without Eugene, her world seems to have a bit less air in it. In the span of a few moments, Eugene finally noticed her and then let her go. Ambling home, the island feels crowded with women.

At home, her mum is in the garden, attacking weeds with a vengeance. Marcy drops her bag and begins to dig beside her.

"He's left, then?" Violet says as she yanks out a handful of thistles peaking up next to the tomato plants.

Without warning, the emotions of the Weighbridge overwhelm Marcy. She begins to cry, heaping, gulping sobs.

Violet's lips purse and her shoulders tense. She pauses over her vegetable patch, as though her hands are unsure whether to continue weeding or comfort her daughter. In the end, she puts one hand on Marcy's shoulder while pulling out ragwort with the other.

"Was Mrs. Westover there?" her mum asks quietly.

Marcy shakes her head, sniffling.

Violet nods, and then presses both hands deep inside the dirt. For a moment, her crisp, pale blue seems to swirl and deepen, but when Marcy looks again, it is gone.

Chapter Nine

VIOLET

1922

When she is sixteen, Violet volunteers for the war effort by knitting socks and writing letters to lonely soldiers. At eighteen, she becomes engaged to be married to a soldier who wrote back, a fellow Jerseyman named David Foster. If she still believed in the colors, he would be the color of the Jersey potato he grew up farming: a stable, reliable brown. She doesn't love him, but he is well-mannered and, more importantly, offers her an escape from her house.

She and her mum never talk about Plemont Bay. In fact, they never talk much about anything. Their conversations are stilted, Violet circling close and her mum backing away. More often than not, they end in a fight, the pent-up emotion exploding. The man in the black coat never shows up again, and Violet eventually gives up scouring paper clippings, trying to suss out what happened. *Just forget about it,* she tells herself. *It doesn't matter.*

But Violet doesn't stop visiting the house. She goes less often, as preparing a wedding chest means most of her days are spent knitting and sewing with her mum and a few other women from the church. But at least once a month, Violet gets to the house, which is, miraculously, still vacant. She wipes down the windows, prunes the roses the way her dad taught her and imagines, just for a little while, what it would be like to have a life there.

One day, Violet gathers her courage and brings David past this house while out on a walk in the early evening. They had begun awkwardly talking about their future, shyly referring to themselves as a "we," liking the way that felt on their tongues but still unsure of what that meant.

It is nearly dusk when they reach the lane. Glow worms dance around her, lighting up the path of grasses that lead up to the big stone house. It looks magnificent in the early dusk.

"There's this house I like," she says, forcing herself to remain casual, not to betray the depth of attachment she has toward this house.

She lifts the latch on the gate.

"Violet," David says nervously. "I don't think we should do this."

"Don't worry," she insists. "It's vacant." She tries to keep the excitement out of her voice.

They walk around the overgrown bramble bushes, up the lane. Suddenly, Violet feels ridiculous, vulnerable, presenting the abandoned house like this.

"There could be room for farming," Violet says. She can't say that she's imagined a thousand lovely things happening here, like child ren stacking wooden blocks on the floor in the kitchen, fresh laundry blowing the scent of lavender through the open window, building a bench on the far side of the garden to watch the colorful fishing boats come into the harbor in the evening. She doesn't tell him that this is the place where she came to have a good cry, to throw rocks in the ocean. This is the place where she collected dozens of wildflowers and held birthday parties for her dolls, where she came to daydream about her first crush in secondary school.

She doesn't say that this is the one place where she feels safe from the nightmares that haunt her, the one place where the colors don't seem so impossible. The house itself feels like a sage green, a comforting balm, ready to wash away everything bad and make room for new.

"We could," David says, and Violet knows right away, from the hesitancy in his voice, that the house will never be hers. "It's rather exposed, don't you think?"

Violet doesn't say that it was the very exposure that made her love the house. It looks like an old robust woman, standing against the backdrop of the open sea, taking the brunt of the wind and the weather but remaining resilient.

"Yes, a bit," she says instead, biting the inside of her lip.

"We couldn't afford the repair it would need," he says. "Nor does it make sense, when my dad's already left me a house and the portion of the farm. You liked Clapham house, didn't you?"

Clapham House is fine. It is a perfectly normal farmhouse. The kitchen faces south and is sunny. But it isn't magic. Violet doesn't know how to say that. She thinks her relationship with David doesn't feel safe enough yet. She doesn't know that it will never feel safe enough to say the things that reside in the space closest to her heart.

Instead, she nods and says briskly, "Of course, you're right. Silly of me to waste your time with this one."

"Never a waste of time," David says with a smile, though in his eyes, she can tell he is already thinking about something else. Violet learns then how easy it is to keep a man outside of your center, to hold him at arm's length without him ever knowing it.

On the morning of her wedding, Violet wears a lace dress, white like the caps of the sea that dance outside the church as she says her vows. Her mum dabs her eyes with her handkerchief and declares Violet a vision.

Her father comes down the stairs that morning in his suit, a package in hand. "Violet, my girl," he says with all the tenderness a father can have for the only daughter he is about to give away, "I haven't spoken with your mum about this so I hope it's alright, but I want you to have something I gave her a long time ago."

Her mum smiles at him encouragingly as he presses the parcel into his daughter's hands.

Tentatively, Violet opens the wrapping. A string of rose gold pearls falls out of the thin, brown paper into her outstretched hand.

Violet feels the cold of the round balls against her palm. She sees her mother's face, her wide eyes.

For a moment, the two look at each other, afraid.

"Well now," her dad says, oblivious to the language passing between them, "Shall I put these on you?"

Violet ducks her neck to allow her dad to fasten them. In her head, she sees only her mum's peach dress flowing in the wind, hears her screams echoing, *I'm sorry*.

Her mum reaches for her. Violet pulls away.

Still avoiding her mum's eye, she asks, "Shall we?"

She swallows the nausea rising in her stomach and they make their way toward the church.

Later, Violet tries hiding the pearls in several places in her new home after the wedding: in a drawer, next to the bed, downstairs with the utensils in the kitchen. In each location, the pearls haunt her. Eventually, she stores them on the bottom shelf of the linen closet, in a box with some hand-me-down handkerchiefs, and does her best to forget about them.

***

Even after her wedding, Violet continues to walk by the house. As she bakes and builds a kitchen of her own, she can't resist visiting this kitchen, opening the Dutch door, imagining a future child she's decided she won't have running around while she works at the stove. She hopes, though she knows it is reckless and suspects it will crush her.

David never says anything about why she hasn't gotten pregnant. She notices the way he looks longingly at other children in church and she pushes aside the guilt.

A few weeks before the wedding, Violet visited the library in town, determined to find out how to keep a pregnancy from occurring. She didn't—and doesn't—want a child, she knows this. She doesn't trust herself enough to bring up another soul and doesn't want a relationship with her daughter like the one she has with her mother.

She paced back and forth outside the library, wringing her handkerchief, summoning the courage to go in and ask.

Finally, the librarian came outside. Gray-haired and matronly, she said, "I've noticed you walking out here for over a quarter of an hour. Is there something I can help you with?"

Violet stopped pacing and looked at her, the hands wringing her handkerchief suddenly very still. "I'm getting married," she said, rather breathlessly.

"Well," the librarian said, a smile on her face. "Wonderful!"

"And I've just got questions about—about marital relations." Violet's face burned as she spoke, and she was unable to meet the librarian's eyes.

The librarian chuckled. "I'm sure you'll sort it all out, my girl. And in time, you'll have a little bundle of your own to raise."

"Well, that's just the thing," Violet said in a rush. "I was hoping to delay the little one process. Just for a few years. While we get on our feet."

Something shifted between the women. The librarian narrowed her eyes. "Children are a gift," she said. "Not a toy thing you can have at your convenience."

She turned around and walked back inside, leaving Violet in a pool of shame.

The thing is, though, Violet doesn't get pregnant. She can only chalk it up to her own volition, some kind of magic that keeps her womb hostile to new life. Her belly stays flat, her clothes fitted, and the nursery David built in their first month of marriage stays vacant. Enough time passes that people stop making hints about a baby and instead look at her with a glazed-over kind of sympathy.

Sometimes, Violet thinks she will dissolve with the shame of it all, of her confession to the librarian, her secret longing for a child, and her inability to be honest with her husband. Sometimes, she dreams about a baby and wakes up with arms that physically ache with desire. She wants to vomit then, to remind herself that a person like her can't and shouldn't bring forth a baby.

***

One morning, five years into her marriage, Violet walks up the lane that leads to Sorel Point to visit the house.

She is about to round the bramble berry bushes, anticipating the satisfying crunch her feet will make on the gravel drive as she walks up it, when she hears laughter.

Peaking through the green bushes, she sees a young couple in the front garden on a picnic blanket. The woman is smiling and rests a hand on her own large belly, perfectly rounded and pronounced.

The young man pops a bottle of champagne. "To our new home," he says, raising it while the others cheer.

The couple looks at each other with love and ease Violet hasn't felt with David even after all these years. They kiss, completely oblivious to Violet, on the other side of the bushes.

Quickly, Violet marches home.

The house never belonged to you, she tells herself, wiping hot tears from her eyes as she walks. *It wasn't yours to lose.*

She throws open the cupboard in her kitchen and she begins to bake. Scones, with ginger and currants. She pulls a jar of her best marmalade from the cupboard. She arranges them on a tray, willing herself not to feel anything, trying to stomp on the despair rising in her chest.

She carries the tray back to the couple on the blanket, basking in the glow of what is now the golden hour of the day. Twisting around the bramble bushes, she tries to forget that she knows exactly where to step. As she marches up to them, she plasters a forced smile on her face.

"Hello," she says to the couple. "I'm Violet Foster, and I live just down the road. About time someone bought this place. Congratulations on your new home."

She does not expect the woman to stand up and come barreling towards her, arms outstretched. "Violet? Violet Blanche! Come here, you old girl. How long has it been?"

CHAPTER TEN

LOUISA

1940

Louisa lays in her bed, unable to get up. She hears Eugene padding around his room, the drawers opening and closing, the second stair creaking as he descends them. He rummages around in the kitchen, opening and closing cupboards, until the kettle whistles. The smell of toast wafts up the stairs. He will slather a generous helping of orange marmalade on top of it the way he does every morning, scattering the counter with crumbs.

She knows she should get up, wrap her robe around herself, wash her face, and make her way down the narrow staircase. But she cannot. It is as though someone has filled her legs and arms with lead, chained them to the posts of the bed.

"Mum?" Eugene calls from the bottom of the stairs. He sounds vulnerable, timid. This breaks her heart.

Go to your son, she yells at herself as her eyes fixate on the dark ceiling of the room. But she cannot bear to greet him, to walk into the kitchen and wipe the crumbs off the counter, knowing they won't be there tomorrow morning. She can't bear to touch his mop of curly hair, freshly cut according to army regulation, knowing she won't be able to breathe it in the next time she wakes up.

The clock ticks beside her, each second more deafening than the next. She wills it to stop, to not take her into a future bereft of cups of tea and games of checkers with him after dinner.

He ascends the staircase, wearing his boots in the house, something she's taught him never to do. He stops at the landing, and she feels his tall, lanky frame standing on the threshold of her room.

You are a better mother than this, she urges herself.

The last time she was stuck like this was eight years ago, when she lost her baby girl. Eugene was just a boy, barely ten. For days she lay in her bed, unable to move, the quilt pulled up over her head and the curtains shut. She heard Eugene outside in the yard, laughing downstairs, but she could not get up or go to him.

After about a week, the door of her bedroom creaked open. She knew it was evening by the way the shadows came in through the closed blind, by the smells of the burnt dinner attempts coming from downstairs.

"Mum?" Eugene had whispered as he approached her bed.

With all the strength she could muster, she had managed to open her eyes and look at him. It embarrassed her, Eugene seeing her like that. She was exposed. This was not who she wanted to be as a mother.

"Mum, I'm going exploring, and Dad said I could take this," Eugene said, holding up an old Mason jar from the kitchen cupboard. "What do you fancy?"

Louisa had stared at him, unable to put words to the depths of what she wanted, to what she had hoped for that would never be. Finally, she whispered, "I fancy a piece of the sky."

Eugene had nodded, like it was a normal request, backed away carefully from the bed then raced down the stairs. After he left, Louisa regretted what she'd asked for. She should have asked for something easy, like a worm or a leaf. Why would she ask for something he couldn't find?

She dozed off, and when she woke again, there was no light coming through the curtains anymore. Eugene stood over her again. "Mum," he whispered loudly. "Mum. I have something for you."

With effort, she opened her eyes. In his hands, he held a jar of glow worms, little lights buzzing against the boundaries of the glass, defying the darkness.

"A piece of the sky," Eugene said.

Louisa had bitten her lip to keep the tears from escaping. "Thank you," she whispered, allowing the touch of his hand to bring her briefly into the land of the living.

This memory comes back to her now as her son stands over her, preparing to leave. She waits for a miracle. It doesn't come.

After a moment, Eugene leans down and kisses her forehead. "I love you, Mum," he says.

And then he is gone, and Louisa's sky crashes down.

***

For days, Louisa cannot get out of bed. She lies there after Jon comes home from the Weighbridge and gently rubs her feet. Her body remains motionless while he brings her cups of tea that grow cold while the light of the room ebbs and flows. At night, she stares up at the ceiling, listening to Jon's steady, shallow breaths, inhaling the smell of the whiskey he drinks so that sleep will come.

Her body no longer belongs to her. It is as though she hovers above it, watching herself disappear. With tremendous effort, she walks outside to the loo, then back to the bed, drawing the curtains shut behind her.

She wishes Eugene would come back to say goodbye again. It's not his leaving that will kill her, she thinks. It's the emptiness in its wake. If it meant that each morning he would come to stand in her doorway another last time, she could survive that goodbye with him again and again. Having nothing tactile to touch or smell, only memory: this is what threatens to undo her.

An indeterminate number of days after Eugene leaves, Louisa feels the bed shift as Jon gets out. He sighs heavily as his feet hit the floor. She lies in silence, listening to him watch her chest move up and down, the only proof she is still alive. She wants to reach her hand out to squeeze his waiting one, but she cannot move.

He goes downstairs and makes a cup of tea. There is a knock on the back door.

"Hello, Jon," she hears as the door swings open. "I just thought I'd pop by."

Louisa winces as she listens to Violet's crisp, efficient voice and pulls the covers over her head.

"I'm afraid Louisa isn't well, Violet," Jon says. "Thank you for coming, but she's not up for visitors at the moment."

"Yes, I know," Violet continues. "But I just need a minute with her. Thank you, Jon, and I'll take that tea up for you." Her heels click across the floor and up the stairs.

Louisa considers her options. She could roll off of the bed or try to make it to the closet to hide. But while she is still thinking all of this, the door creaks open, and Violet marches in.

"Morning, Louisa," she says too brightly. She sets a tray of tea and what smells like freshly baked scones down on the nightstand and pulls open the thick curtains so that light floods into the room.

Violet had always been so efficient, so good in a crisis. Any time Louisa had fallen apart, Violet was there, with a baked good and a cup of tea, fluffing up pillows and dusting the furniture. The thought fills Louisa with both resentment and the ability to finally cry.

Sitting down at the end of the bed, Violet pours Louisa a cup of tea. "Now then," she says. "I know this won't solve a damn thing, but it will at least get something warm in you, so there's a start."

Despite herself, Louisa smiles. She meets Violet's eyes and feels a rush of gratitude for the only person brave enough to show up in her room like this.

Pushing herself up on the pillows, she takes the scalding cup and says, "Thank you."

"And you'll need a scone. They're ginger currant."

Louisa's favorite. She is touched that Violet remembers.

Louisa bites into the scone. It tastes familiar. A memory comes back to her: she and Violet downstairs in the sitting room, hanging garland across the beams at Christmas time, a plate of ginger currant scones on the coffee table which they ate, later, with piping hot cups of tea. Eugene, barely three, spent the morning running all over the house yelling, "It's Christmas! It's Christmas!" before colliding with the stairwell and bursting into the hot, angry tears of toddlerhood.

Violet takes a sip of her own tea and says, "Bloody Hitler."

"Bloody uniforms," Louisa says back with her mouth full.

Violet raises an eyebrow.

"He wouldn't have gone if the uniforms weren't so smart," Louisa says, knowing it isn't true but needing something to blame.

Leaning forward, Violet puts a hand on Louisa's knee. "But the question is, Louisa, what are you going to do about it? About him being gone?"

"I'm going to hide here until the war is over and he appears in the doorway again."

"And realizes he was the thread that held you together?" Violet asks. "Surely the Louisa I know has more to her than that."

The scone catches in Louisa's throat, the ginger making her eyes sting. "It hurts too much to think about living again."

"Of course it hurts," Violet says as she reaches for her own scone in such a matter-of-fact voice that they could have been exchanging recipes. Only the way she keeps crossing and uncrossing her legs clues Louisa in that she's nervous. "It's the hardest thing in the world, to look darkness right in the eye and choose life anyway. But that's how we gain our weight. That's how we learn to matter."

Louisa regards Violet warily, wondering if she should speak. Normally, Louisa is never short on words or feeling, sharing her intimate thoughts even with perfect strangers, which has made her, she's been told, quite Un-British on several occasions.

But that was before.

"How?" she begins.

Violet finishes for her. "How do you learn to matter? One single moment at a time. The first thing you can do is take a bath. You stink to high heaven."

Louisa laughs. "Jon didn't say anything."

"Well, he spends all day in a hog shed, doesn't he? Let's get you out of bed."

Violet pulls Louisa out, and they walk arm in arm, Louisa still taller than Violet even with her heels on, down the creaky steps and to the kitchen, where the tub has already been filled. Louisa notices the way she and Violet still know their way around one another, taking up the space beside each other, like intricate steps of a dance they've both memorized.

Violet begins laying out the towels, checking the temperature of the bath. "I've brought you a lovely rose soap," she says. "Marcy's friend Annette dropped it off last week."

At the mention of Marcy, Louisa's warm feelings fizzle. A child who, because of her sex, is safe at home instead of off at the war. It's not Marcy Louisa resents: it's that Violet has and she doesn't. It's *everything* Violet has and Louisa doesn't.

"I'll just go upstairs and freshen up your room," says Violet. "Do you still keep the spare sheets under the bed?

She's offering a towel, white, with Louisa and Jon's initials embroidered on the front. It was a wedding present.

"No," Louisa says, her voice hard.

"Sorry?"

"Thank you, Violet, but that won't be necessary," Louisa says. She snatches the towel.

"Have I said something wrong?" asks Violet, looking alarmed. Her shoulders begin to droop ever so slightly, like the air going out of a balloon.

"Not at all," says Louisa, jutting her chin out, hands at her side to keep them from quivering. "Just that I still know how to change the sheets and take a bath." She adds a chuckle. It sounds hollow.

For a brief moment, Violet looks at her like a trapped animal: eyes round, vulnerable, caught. Then she clears her throat and snaps back to her competent, efficient self. "Of course you can. Right, well. I'll just put the soap here." Violet sets the bar on the counter. She takes one last look around the room.

"I'll be off then," she says. "Do ring if you need anything."

"Of course," says Louisa, knowing she won't.

Violet's heels continue to click across the wooden floor, like she's stamping herself all over the house. When the door closes, Louisa lets out a shaky breath.

Only after she's in the bath does she realize Violet left via the front door: the one reserved only for formal company and strangers.

CHAPTER ELEVEN

VIOLET

1922

Before Violet sees Louisa's face she sees purple. Bold, beautiful eggplant, the most vibrant color she has seen in almost two decades. It wraps around her in a glorious, pillowy fog, and Violet is filled with a stab of longing for the person she used to be, for the friend she used to have.

Louisa's broad arms engulf Violet in a giant hug. Violet, who has not been touched with such unreserved enthusiasm in years, tries to keep her shoulders from clenching up. Louisa takes a step back and surveys Violet, smiling wide. Louisa is tall and broad-shouldered, with a head of thick, flyaway curls that give her a mythical air. Her belly is round and she automatically rests a hand on it, lovingly. Her smile is still like a slice of the moon, and her whole face seems to glow.

"Gosh, look at you! How many years has it been? Still as lovely and put together as ever, aren't you Vi?"

Violet cannot speak. She nods and thrusts forward the tray of scones that was likely just crushed by Louisa's enthusiastic greeting.

"Jon. *Jon!*" Louisa says to the man who is already at her side. "You must come here. This is a dear friend of mine from when we were school girls. Violet Blanche—unless you've gone and gotten married as well?"

"Violet Foster now," she says, leaning forward to shake Jon's outstretched hand.

"Ha!" Louisa says. "Look at the two of us, old married women. Did you marry a grockle like I did? He's from Southampton. But we'll make a Jersey man of you yet, won't we love?"

Louisa beams at Jon, and he leans over to kiss her forehead.

"We met during the war, and next thing I know she's dragging me off to this faraway island," Jon says. He is handsome, in a rugged kind of way, strong in the sense that Violet somehow feels safer for having him there.

"We didn't *meet* during the war, it was a planned attack," Louisa laughs. "He bumped into me on the street and sent my purse flying. I had to talk to him just to get my money back."

"All's fair in love and war," Jon says, grinning.

Violet watches their easy candor. It is not this way between her and David. They don't joke, or giggle, or poke fun at each other. Their relationship is cordial, formal, and separate.

"Well, I'll just be off, then," she says, leaving the lovers to stare into each other's eyes.

"Don't be a stranger, Violet," says Louisa. "It's so good to see you after all these years."

Tears blur her vision the whole way home.

***

To her surprise, Louisa returns the tray a few days later. She shows up early on Monday morning: wash day. Violet is in the garden, hanging out her sheets.

Most women wear a housecoat to do their chores. Violet, like her mother, considers this sloppy and never does. Today, she is grateful she is in a proper dress and her hair is pinned back when Louisa comes round the bend.

"Morning!" Louisa calls cheerfully, carrying Violet's tray, filled to the top with cookies. Violet thinks fleetingly about how those cookies were baked in the kitchen she had longed for and swallows a pang of envy.

"I'm a dismal cook, so these are likely to taste like mud," Louisa says jovially, "but you can't return a tray empty, can you?"

Violet forces herself to smile. "I'm sure they're lovely," she says. And then, because Louisa makes no effort to move, and she also doesn't want her to move, she adds, "Won't you stay for a cup of tea?"

They sit outside on the black iron chairs in the garden. The cookies are terrible, rock hard and completely flavorless, but Violet says they hit the spot.

Louisa is so complimentary of Violet's flowers and her green thumb. "Honestly, how do you manage this?" Louisa says between bites, gesturing to the perfectly trimmed climbing roses, the wisteria, the bleeding hearts. "You *must* teach me how to garden. I've got all this lovely space in the back now and not a clue what to do with it. Whoever was there before me was a skilled gardener, and I don't know how to do her justice."

Violet swallows her cookie, thinking about the hours she put into pruning that garden, coaxing it back to life.

Louisa's color unnerves Violet. She is so purely, deeply *purple*. Violet keeps blinking, trying to push Louisa's color away the way she has learned to with everyone else, but it will not be subdued. Louisa is vibrant, rich eggplant, even more pronounced than when they were kids. Violet knows she can't trust the colors, can't trust herself.

"I shouldn't be eating all these biscuits," says Louisa. "Bad for the baby and all. But I can't stop. I've got an insatiable sweet tooth."

Violet smiles. "Is this your first?" she asks.

Louisa nods. "Took us long enough," she says. "We've been married for three years now. I was beginning to think it wouldn't happen for me."

Violet nods, trying to ignore the envy she feels as she thinks about a baby in that house.

"I'm sorry to be blunt, Violet, but– have you and David any children?"

Violet shakes her head.

Louisa pats her knee encouragingly. "Never mind, my girl. All in good time. You're plenty young yet."

"Mm," is all Violet can say as she tries to nibble at her biscuit.

"You know, Vi, I thought I would never see you again after we moved," Louisa says, crossing her legs as she leans back on the chair. "I have to admit, when we bought the house, I hoped it would bring me back to you."

Violet thinks about the loneliness after Plemont Bay, about how often she wished to talk with Louisa. "Where did you go?" Violet asks.

"We moved to LaRoque, in with my mum's mum," Louisa says. "I would say it was a difficult time, and it was for me, but I think my mum loved living with her mum. She just seemed happier once we'd moved. But yes, it was difficult."

Louisa pauses then, which seems, even in the short time they have been reacquainted, uncharacteristic.

To fill the silence, Violet asks, "Difficult how?" She's sure it can't be nearly as difficult as it was for her, though she knows she won't say anything about it.

"My dad passed away right before we moved. Cliff accident. My mum needed to get away, I think, so we left quickly. I wanted to come see you, but there was no time." She wipes an eye. "Ah! Look at me, getting so emotional and it was so long ago. But that's family, isn't it? I can't complain. It was a good childhood, in LaRoque."

Louisa doesn't notice that Violet has stopped eating. Her hands are trembling as she puts the teacup back on the table. *No*, she thinks, *it couldn't have been him*, but even as she thinks it, she finally places the portly man with the same nose Louisa has now, at a table with Louisa at the end-of-year school picnic. She sees him having a cheese and marmite sandwich, Louisa wiping a spot of marmite from his mustache.

Louisa stands up. "I'd better get on," she says. "I've got to sort out something for tea. This was lovely, Violet, truly. I'm so glad to have you back in my life."

Violet nods, trying to meet Louisa's eyes. She can't quite do it.

"You should know," Louisa says, "I've no intention of letting you go again."

Chapter Twelve

LOUISA

1940

Though Louisa doesn't want to admit it, Violet's visit becomes the impetus for forward movement again in her life. After her bath, she takes a walk outside, tightening her robe around her to protect against the chill of the morning. The rooster struts back and forth in the back garden, pausing now and then to puff out his chest and crow. Eugene used to joke about roosters, how it must be hard to be responsible for bringing out the sun every morning. As she remembers that now, a fresh jolt of pain slices through her.

She walks along the lower garden path, down by the stone wall that looks over a sheep pasture. Beyond is a steep cliff that drops into the ocean. She follows the path until it reaches the wood, full and thick, layered with trees Eugene knows by name. Eventually, the path reaches a small clearing, a circle no more than ten feet in the forest, filled with wildflowers. This clearing, which Violet planted for Louisa years ago, when she still had hopes of becoming a real gardener, is her place of refuge, where she comes to let her mind and herself unravel.

Today though, this circular garden does not offer her solace. It threatens to swallow her in her grief.

She screams into the vacant air. "I grew him. I *grew him!* He came out of me. You have to bring him back." She kicks, she pulls the grass and the flowers up and collapses to the ground.

Finally, she cries. Huge, gulping breaths escape her as she sobs.

That night she sits on the garden wall with Jon, watching the ocean change color with the evening light, watching the world move forward. If he is surprised to see her up, facing the world again, he doesn't show it. Louisa reaches for Jon's hand and he squeezes hers. They sit, shoulder to shoulder, so similar in height and breadth that they can wear the same clothes.

"I've been talking to him since he left," Jon says, adjusting his cap as he looks out into the horizon. Louisa loves his side profile—there isn't a part of his body that isn't strong, solid, sturdy. Eugene is like him in looks, but smaller, thin and delicate where Jon is not. "In my head. All the time."

"What do you say?" Louisa asks.

"I talk about the sunrises, the tide. I ask him what his regiment is like in France. I tell him what I'm making for dinner, how I miss watching him stir the eggs on the mornings he makes breakfast. I tell him the eggs never taste quite the same without him, so he'd better get back."

Louisa shifts on the wall, the breeze from the ocean tickling her skin. "When do you think we'll hear from him?"

Jon shrugs and looks out over the ocean. "He's probably in training now," he said. "No time to write."

Or he's writing to that Penelope Campbell, Louisa thinks.

"But he's safe, Lou. I feel that here." He points to his chest. "Our boy's out there."

Slowly, Louisa emerges from the cocoon. One day, she feeds the chickens, the next, makes a quiche. Whenever she feels restlessness or sadness settle over her like a blanket, she walks. She walks the cliffs, the paths by the pasture, the hills and valleys, for several hours each day.

She finally gets a letter from Eugene, short and somewhat distant. *Mum and Dad, headed to France and thank goodness, English food is rubbish. I'll be looking for a good croissant. Love E.*

Louisa saves the letter, keeps it under her pillow. She brings it to her nose, willing it to smell like him.

When her dad passed away, before they moved, Louisa took one of his dress shirts from his wardrobe. She slept with it for months, crying into it, trying to preserve the way her dad smelled. Her mum found it and was so distraught that she took it. Louisa watched her throw it into the stove one evening after she was supposed to be in bed.

She becomes manic about leaving notes for Eugene every time she goes out, just in case he appears back at home while she's away.

E, she would write. *Gone for a walk. Fresh loaf in the bread bin. Love Mum. xx*

One morning in late May, Jon calls for Louisa as it's time to leave for church. "Louisa! We're going to be late, come on already!"

"Just a minute, love," Louisa calls from the kitchen, where she scribbles a note on a bit of paper. *E, gone to church. Back by lunch. Love Mum. xx*

"For heaven's sake, he *knows* we'll be at church, it's Sunday morning," Jon says, exasperated as he comes to pull her out the door.

The first hymn has already been sung and the congregation is tucked into the hard wooden pews by the time Jon and Louisa pull open the heavy wooden door, sunlight pouring briefly over the stone floor.

They try to walk, discreetly, to the third pew from the front, where they sit every week. Violet, in a pink hat with feathers, smiles timidly at Louisa as they pass her row, and bitter envy rises up in Louisa as she watches Marcy hold Peter's hand next to her.

"I know we're all worried about the Maginot Line," the Reverend says as Louisa and Jon take their seats. He is referring to France's defense, which is said to be so strong it can never fall to the Germans. "All we can do is trust. Trust God and trust our boys."

They end the service with a hymn, *A Mighty Fortress is our God, a Bulwark Never Failing*. Louisa presses her lips together and wishes it to be true.

But a few evenings later, Louisa and Jon listen to the BBC radio as it reports scenes from the Battle of Dunkirk. Jersey men get in their boats and sail to England to help with the rescue mission.

"Winston's getting his troops out," Jon assures her. "They'll get Eugene out."

In the end, 338,000 troops are evacuated from Dunkirk.

"That's so many," Louisa says to him. "Surely Eugene was one of them."

She checks the post two, three times a day, waiting to hear from him, safely tucked away at an army base outside of London. She imagines him writing a jovial letter to her, saying she was right, that London really wasn't all it was cracked up to be.

One rainy, miserable morning, Louisa sits in the conservatory, reading as the water pellets the ceiling. Jon has taken his meat to the butcher and won't be back until teatime.

Louisa likes waking up to the rainy days, because she feels that they protect her a bit; the weather is the bad thing, so no bad news can come. It would be too ironic, she thinks, to get any bad news about Eugene today.

Then she hears the door knocker. It's the milkman, she tells herself as she stands up, though in the last two years he's knocked only once to tell her one of the pigs had escaped the pen. Or it's Ouen, the neighbor, asking for eggs, though Ouen is frail on his feet and never leaves the house in bad weather.

The telegram boy stands in the doorway, sopping wet, a puddle appearing at his feet as he stands just out of the downpour. "From the war office, Ma'am," he says as he holds out the paper, stamped with an official seal. "Shall I read it for you?"

Louisa forces herself to reach out and take the flimsy telegram. "No," she says, her fingers closing around the thin, almost transparent paper. She meets his eyes. "No, thank you, I'll read it myself."

The boy removes his hat and wrings it between his hands. "Sorry," he mumbles. He steps back into the torrential rain towards his bicycle.

Louisa closes the door and leans against it, shaking, staring at that thin paper. Why couldn't they have at least used quality paper?

She sets the telegram on the side table, then under a book. Sighing, she wanders into the kitchen and puts the kettle on for a cup of tea. She never drinks it. All afternoon, she feels the weight of the letter hover around her, heavy with significance like the moment she met Jon on a street corner in London or the moment she found her house. She thinks about how she will respond if the letter contains the worst news. Unwillingly, she thinks about Violet at home with her daughter, who will never be sent to war, and she knows that even if this is the worst news, she will not fall into the pit she was in before. She will not give Violet the satisfaction of pulling her out.

By the time Jon comes home from town at half past four, she has pulled a chair right up to the side table at the door and holds the telegram in her hands.

"Hiya Lou. Oh," Jon says as he opens the door to find her on a chair in the hallway, wrapped in a white blanket. She holds out the telegram.

Jon's eyes widen and he kneels to the ground before her, the door still flung wide.

"No," he says.

"I haven't opened it, Jon. I can't," says Louisa. "You've got to do it."

Picking up his hand, she holds it in hers for a moment before opening it, placing the envelope inside and pressing his fingers shut.

She looks at him, suddenly the strong one. "You can do this," she says, reaching out a finger to touch his jawline.

The years stretch between them, swirling around them: Eugene toddling up and down the hall in a diaper, making boats out of the furniture, drawing on the walls with pencil and hiding under the sink when he was found out. The memories hang like portraits until Jon opens the translucent paper against the light from the open door.

As Louisa watches him, her last thought before her husband breaks down in tears is that he is unwrapping light.

72

Chapter Thirteen

Violet

1922

No no no no, Violet thinks, pacing back and forth in her garden after Louisa leaves. Her pulse is racing, her hands are trembling, and she cannot get a full breath. It is as though someone has placed a heavy brick in the middle of her lungs.

It can't be the same thing. It can't. I imagined it, Violet thinks, as she remembers the portly man lying so still on the beach.

Her best friend. She ruined her best friend's life. Was she only capable of causing destruction?

Violet needs to do something. She begins to clear the dishes. She takes them inside, puts them in the sink, but scrubbing them does not drown out the yelling in her head.

Screaming. I'm sorry. My fault.

Violet stops washing. She puts her fingers to her forehead. That's it. She cannot continue in a friendship with Louisa. She'll only cause more pain.

The grief of it makes Violet want to sob. The one true friend she's ever had, back in her life and Violet can't have her. If Louisa knew what Violet had done, she'd never forgive her.

The next morning, Violet is scrubbing the floor when the door swings open.

"Good morning," comes a big, cheery voice. Violet sees purple even before she turns.

"Louisa, hi," says Violet, butterflies in her stomach as she stands up. She tries to meet Louisa's eyes but can't.

"I was out for a walk and craving a cup of tea," says Louisa. "I thought I'd pop in to say hi. We've got so much lost time to make up for."

Violet stares past Louisa, out to the open field where David is working. "I'm not so sure, Lou," she says vaguely.

"Sure of what? That you have tea? Well, no matter, I'll just have a sit down—"

"No." Violet knows her voice sounds shaky and defensive. "No, it's just— well, a lot has happened since we last saw each other."

"Don't I know it, my girl," Louisa says cheerily, taking off her shoes.

"No," Violet says sharply.

Louisa pauses and looks up, one foot suspended.

"It's just, there are some things that have happened. If you knew me, Louisa, really *knew me*, you wouldn't want to be my friend."

As she says it, Violet thinks the sorrow of it will drown her. She waits for Louisa to recoil, to put on her shoes and leave.

Instead, Louisa laughs. A full, rich, eggplant laugh that fills the room with a palpable sense of joy.

Violet finally meets her eyes. "It's not funny," she says, her nerve to tell the truth faltering.

"Violet Foster," Louisa says, her voice full of a love that threatens to crack Violet wide open, "You couldn't tell me a single thing that would make me not want to be your friend. We've all got skeletons, my girl. I've no intention of making you revisit yours."

Violet swallows a lump in her throat and it lodges somewhere in her chest. She knows that Louisa doesn't know what she's promising. Still, Louisa's words give Violet a burst of hope that she cannot quite suppress. She can't bring herself to say what she's done. The thought of being liked, after all these years, is too much to resist.

"Now," says Louisa, plopping down heavily on the chair next to the table, "How about that cup of tea?"

***

1923

"He's a happy little thing, isn't he?" Violet's mother coos.

Baby Eugene gurgles back at her grandmother, kicking his chubby legs in the air.

Violet leans back on the sofa, closing her eyes. She is tired, so tired. Louisa and Jon are in Southampton, visiting Jon's mum, who has been ill with the flu. Eugene was too young to be around sickness, so Louisa asked her to keep him while she was away.

"Of course," Violet said in a rush, eager to do anything for her friend; eager, as always, to lessen the debt that is an invisible chasm between them.

Louisa had smiled sympathetically at Violet, misreading her enthusiasm. "I'm sure a baby will happen for you one day, Vi."

They've had Eugene in the house for a week now, and Violet hates to admit how lovely it's been, though she can't remember ever being so tired. Eugene wakes up at night, missing his mummy, needing to be consoled, and Violet isn't able to fall back asleep afterwards.

David has loved having Eugene. When Violet is making dinner or doing the laundry (how does a tiny person create *so much* laundry?) she catches him, cooing at Eugene, tickling his tummy. He comes in early to pick Eugene up, taking him outside to see the Jersey cows.

Violet tries to swallow the guilt and the shame. *Stop it*, she tells herself. *You haven't done a thing to keep it from happening.*

But she knows she has.

Rosa stretches out in front of the fireplace, Eugene on her lap. She kisses his six-month-old chubby cheek.

"Were you this tired when I was a baby?" Violet asks, stifling a yawn.

"Tired? I couldn't see straight," her mum says with a laugh. "You were the devil incarnate as a baby. I used to stop bothering to even change into my pajamas at night because I knew I would be up with you."

Violet doesn't know whether she should laugh or be offended by this.

She's been having nightmares again, in those rare hours when sleep does come. She wakes up at windows, yanking them open, yelling "No!" until David awkwardly shakes her awake. By then, Eugene is almost always awake, and the cycle begins once more.

She knows she needs to ask her mum about Louisa's dad. She's been avoiding the conversation ever since that first tea with Louisa, where she found out he passed in the cliff accident.

She's tried to stuff it down, keep Plemont Bay deep in the recesses of her heart while she works on being the perfect friend to Louisa. All the while, she lives in terror that her secret will be found out, that she will lose the one real friend she's ever had.

David retires upstairs, and Violet sees her chance. "Mum," she begins, "Did you love Dad?"

"Love him?" her mum asks briskly. "What a silly question. Of course I did."

"Did you ever--was there ever anyone else?"

"What do you mean?" Rosa stops jiggling Eugen on his knee and looks at her.

Violet knows she is approaching dangerous, forbidden territory. Things between Violet and her mum have been cordial, even friendly, as long as Violet keeps the conversation light. Today, the sleep deprivation seems to keep her from stopping.

"Were you ever with another man, other than Dad?"

"That's ridiculous," her mum says, but Violet notices that her hands tighten around Eugene as she talks. "I can't believe you would even ask me that. How would you feel if I asked you about your marriage?"

"Ask away," Violet says. "It would only unsettle me if I had something to hide."

Her own voice is shaking now, and she can't believe she's prodding the way she is. She is close to something, she can tell: by the way her mum's lips have pursed into a thin line, by the way a frost has descended like a wall between the two of them.

Just tell me, Violet wants to say. *I won't judge you for anything, I just need to know. It's the only way I continue in my friendship. It's the only way I can ever have a child of my own.*

Eugene begins to cry. Her mum hands him back to Violet. Violet takes him and bounces him on her knee, trying to ignore her own sweaty palms.

"Violet," Rosa says, so sharply that Violet herself is eleven again, sitting next to her mother on the bed, worried she will slap her.

Violet forces herself to maintain eye contact, willing her mum to give her something.

For a moment, her mum opens her mouth, like she is going to speak. Then she closes it, looks away, and reaches for her purse. "I thought we outgrew these kinds of conversations," she said.

Knowing she will regret it, she pushes a bit further. "Louisa is a friend from my childhood," she says. "She moved away when I was eleven. Her dad died in a cliff accident."

Is she imagining it, or do her mum's shoulders tense? "How tragic for her," her mum says, back still turned.

"What happened to her dad? Mum, do you know?" Violet's heart races.

Her mum turns. She looks weary and small. "I haven't the faintest idea, Violet," she says, her voice quiet and fragile. "I'll see you next week."

Violet sinks onto the sofa after her mum leaves. She holds Eugene close, bouncing him up and down. "What have I done?" she asks him.

She sighs, noticing her own lips purse automatically, in the exact shape of her mother's.

Chapter Fourteen

MARCY

1940

After the goodbye at the Weighbridge, Marcy thinks about Eugene constantly. She obsesses over him. She flushes every time he appears in her mind, sure that everyone knows how hopelessly in love she is.

She starts adding routines into her day, convincing herself that if she parts her hair on the side and wears the faded green ribbon—the way she had done her hair the last time she saw him—or if she says *Eugene* in her head ten times before getting out of bed, he will be okay and unharmed.

Her days are drawn out in the torturous place between worrying about and wondering about Eugene and remembering the way he looked at her before he left, wondering what it could mean. It doesn't keep her from thinking things like, "I'll lose the last ten pounds," or "I'll learn how to be a fun conversationalist." Fixated on becoming the type of person she thinks Eugene would like, she tries to laugh more freely, to tuck her hair the right way. She begins to draw lines on the back of her legs like the other girls do when there are no pantyhose to be found.

One afternoon in late May, she pulls weeds from Mum's vegetable garden between the sprouting courgette plants, plopping them into a silver bucket. Beads of sweat gather around her temple, and she stands to dab her handkerchief against her forehead.

Annette's mum, Mrs. LeBrock (silver), comes through the picket fence. Marcy's brother Peter once said Mrs. LeBrock looks like a peacock, always wearing bright colors and strutting around with her head in everyone's business. Marcy's mum had pinched her lips and hushed him, but later, Marcy caught her laughing later as she washed dishes in the sink.

Mrs. LeBrock stops now at the vegetable garden, clearly comparing Violet's execution of the Dig for Victory campaign with her own. Marcy knows there is no comparison. Her mum's garden looks like it straight out of Women's Day Magazine: all perfect lines and neat hedges.

"Hello, Mrs. LeBrock," Marcy says, standing up.

"Ah, Marcy," says Mrs. LeBrock. "Didn't see you. You okay?"

"Fine, thanks—just dealing with some stubborn weeds."

"Well, we've all got to do our part, haven't we?" Mrs. LeBrock smiles brightly. "I'm just here to pick up a cake order from your mum. It's Mr. LeBrock's birthday."

"Of course, right inside."

"Margot! Lovely to see you," Marcy hears her mum say through the open window. "I've got your cake right in here. Won't you stay for a cup of tea?"

"A quick cup," Mrs. LeBrock says as the door swings shut. "I really do have to get back. We've been wondering about you. You've heard about the Maginot Line?"

Intrigued, Marcy crawls closer to the window, a handful of weeds between her gloved hands. They had talked of nothing for weeks but the Maginot Line, the line between Germany and France. Everyone said it would never fall, but then it did—crumpled like paper in a clenched fist. She's been listening all week for information about Eugene, scouring the paper for his name, standing too close to other ladies talking at the grocer. Marcy wonders if Mrs. LeBrock might have some information.

"Mm," says Violet amidst the clattering of teacups. "Terrible, isn't it? Especially as it involves some of our boys."

"Not Arthur?" says Mrs. LeBrock in a hushed voice.

"No, thankfully, Arthur is just fine. Ethel heard from him last week."

Margot breathes a dramatic sigh of relief. "I wish we could say the same about Louisa's boy. Eugene, isn't it?"

Marcy gasps, then puts a hand to her mouth to muffle any sound.

"What's happened to Eugene?" Violet asks sharply.

"M. I. A.," Mrs. LeBrock says importantly, as though using the acronym made her more official. "Louisa got the telegram yesterday, poor thing. She's beside herself. Peggy's husband found out from Jon this morning when he delivered the milk. Jon was sitting on the front stoop, eyes bloodshot, drink on his breath, twisting his handkerchief together. Peggy's husband thought he'd been out there all night."

No, Marcy thinks. *No, no, no.* She'd worn the green ribbon. She'd said his name ten times. He couldn't be missing.

"That's terrible," Violet says, and Marcy is surprised to hear the amount of emotion in her voice.

"Isn't it just," says Mrs. LeBrock, as lightly as if she were discussing the weather. She sets her teacup down. "Makes us grateful for girls, doesn't it? I'd better run, Violet. Thank you for the tea and here's payment for the cake."

Marcy leans against the side of the house and closes her eyes as Mrs. LeBrock walks past her.

She feels dizzy. Missing in Action. Where is he?

When she finally stands up, she opens the Dutch door to the kitchen. Her mum is scrubbing the counter furiously. "Mum?" She begins to shake. Her teeth rattle and she can't breathe. "What's happened to Eugene?"

"Marcy," her mum says, pausing to look at her with such rare empathy that Marcy wants to be a child again, curl up into her mum's arms and rest in her lap. "I know you've always been fond of him."

I love him, Mum, Marcy wants to say. But Violet is scrubbing again, her face etched in a faraway expression.

Marcy stands for a few moments, blinking back tears. When she can move again, she goes to the cupboard and pulls out the tins of flour and sugar.

"What are you doing?"

"I'm baking a cake for Mrs. Westover," she answers, trembling.

"Oh. How thoughtful. I'll help you."

"No thanks, Mum," says Marcy. "I've got to do this on my own."

Baking, for as long as Marcy can remember, has been something she does *with* her mum, for her mum, or in her mum's presence. The kitchen is her mum's turf. This is the first time that Marcy has claimed it as hers. She stands taller and pushes out her chin, knowing that she needs to do this alone but not quite understanding why.

"I see," says Violet, pursing her lips. Her tone changes, shedding sympathy and patience like a snakeskin and putting on something more abrupt. She wrings out the rag over the sink. "Well then. Please clean up the kitchen when you've finished. I don't want to find flour on the floor when I'm trying to cook dinner." Gathering a pile of washed and folded shirts from the kitchen table, she turns sharply to leave.

Marcy bakes a tea cake with fresh strawberries from the garden. Carefully and methodically, she mixes flour, eggs, and sugar and pours the batter into a round tin. The mechanical process she's done hundreds of times soothes her with its predictability and consistency. Put these ingredients together at this ratio, and you're bound to get a cake. Not so with war. Take a bunch of boys, the same age, unleash them on one another with lethal weapons. Some will make it out whole, some tattered, some not at all.

She paces the kitchen while the cake bakes, thinking about the way Eugene smells like cedar, the way he runs his hand through his hair. Someone so *alive* doesn't just become dead, Marcy tells herself.

When the timer goes off, Marcy pulls the cake out of the oven, fanning it with a towel to make it cool down faster. If she could just *see* Eugene's mum, maybe it would help— maybe it would make Eugene's disappearance just a little less terrible. She's not sure why, but she thinks maybe, if she saw Mrs. Westover, she'd be able to carry on. Her grief threatens to consume her if she stops making this damn cake.

Marcy's mum comes back into the kitchen. She looks at the cake, purses her lips as she watches Marcy begin to frost it. "You're doing that too early. The icing will melt."

"I know," Marcy says through gritted teeth. Her mum is right: the icing is dripping down the sides, making a goopy mess.

"Here," her mum says, as Marcy prepares to put the cake in a tin. She pulls a few yellow petals from the rose bush outside the front door. Leaning over Marcy, she arranges them on either side of the cake. "This will help."

Marcy nods, not meeting her mum's eyes. Carefully, she puts the lid on the tin, then carries it out to the basket of her bike.

Mrs. Westover's long gravel lane twists in a half-moon as it winds up to the house. It is lined with hydrangea bushes that bloom in deep blues and purples, and chickens roam the front garden of the stone farmhouse, pecking between the daisies and daffodils. As a little girl, whenever she cycled past it, she thought it the most pleasant place on earth. Though she'd only entered a few times for church functions, she used to imagine it on her bed at night, walking through each room in her head as she fell asleep.

Yellow, Marcy thinks, missing Eugene with a tangible ache as she dismounts her bike, gathers her cake, and stands in front of the wisteria-lined doorway.

Just before she knocks, she thinks she sees a curtain flicker in the front room, a hand move away from the front room. Is it Mrs. Westover? Marcy remembers something Gran said once, soon after Peter was born, about how grieving people are caught in a pendulum, swinging between suffocating loneliness and wanting to be alone. Marcy wonders, as she knocks, if she will open the door.

After an impossibly long minute, the lock of the door clicks, and Mrs. Westover opens it. Marcy wonders which one of them looks more terrified.

Mrs. Westover's shining physical characteristic is her hair.

Streaked with gray and white, it is curly and wiry. Today, it looks like she tried to temper it by pulling it back, but coils pop out and curl around her face. The effect is stunning.

Mrs. Westover is an eggplant purple. Marcy's sure she's never seen such a vibrant color. Regal, dignified, with wide cheekbones and broad shoulders. Her color swirls around her shawl and takes up the span of the doorway.

"Hello, Mrs. Westover?" Marcy asks it like a question. She's suddenly not sure if Mrs. Westover even knows who she is. All those Sundays Marcy has studied her at church, memorized her interactions with Eugene, she could be completely invisible to this magnanimous woman. "I'm Violet's daughter, Marcy."

Is it just her imagination, or does Mrs. Westover flinch at her mum's name? She quickly covers it with a warm smile.

"Yes, I know who you are," she says. "Please, love, call me Louisa now. You're practically grown."

Thrusting the cake in her direction, she says, "I—I mean, my mum—she made this for you. Thought you might want some cheering up."

"Well. How thoughtful of your mum." Her voice sounds thick, she might have been crying, but there is something else, at the mention of her mum, that Marcy can't place.

Louisa takes the box and lifts the lid. She looks at the cake inside and raises her eyebrows. Marcy's ears begin to burn. Why had she said it was her mum's cake? Everyone knew Violet by her cakes; her perfectly fluffed buttercream, decorative fondant and ornate marzipan. Even the beautifully arranged flower petals wouldn't convince Louisa that this was a Violet cake.

But Louisa only looks at Marcy after a moment. Her smile is warmer and more free than it was a moment ago. She says, "That's lovely. Please thank your mum for me."

There is a pause, and Marcy wonders if she should turn around and leave. Just as she is about to step off the porch, Louisa says, "Jon and I couldn't possibly eat all this ourselves. Won't you come in for a slice?"

Marcy hesitates, not sure how she should respond.

"I've already got the tea in the pot," Louisa says, a hint of desperation in her voice reminding Marcy of the swinging pendulum. "Really, Marcy. You've come at a perfect time."

"Er, okay then," Marcy says. She follows Louisa into the house, feeling like her legs and arms are too long for her body.

The two walk down the long hallway, past the living room and the kitchen into the conservatory. Marcy breathes in the scent of the house like it is an old friend. The last time she was in this house, she must have only been ten or eleven, for a children's church gathering. It still smells like cedar and lavender, and the hallway is made of such lovely pine that she resists the urge to slide down it in her stockings. Some of the other kids, whose mums were better friends with the Westovers, would tell Marcy about the legendary Sunday Roasts. Yorkshire puds, roast beef, plenty of wine, and rice puddings. In the summertime, Louisa would declare it was too nice of a day to be stuck inside, and the guests would carry the bulky wooden table out to the lawn.

Two fat, wicker chairs sit in the middle of the conservatory, facing the cliffs and the sea.

"It's quite hot back here," Mrs. Westover says. "Too hot for a cup of tea, really, but Eugene loved it back here, so I find myself..." Her voice trails off.

Marcy can already feel the back of her neck and the underneath of her arms growing damp, but she quickly says, "Oh yes, it's lovely."

Louisa says, "Make yourself comfortable; I'll just pour the tea," and disappears into the kitchen.

Marcy looks around the room. Through the glass windows, Marcy can see the sea. It feels like she could step straight out of the window and into it, though she knows it is actually fifty meters away and then down a steep cliff. Under the bench cushion, Marcy sees a bin of toy trains. Louisa must have kept them from when Eugene was small. A lump catches in her throat. She swallows, sits, tries not to think about Eugene at the other end of the sea. She tries not to wonder if he is thinking about her.

Louisa returns, carrying a tray with two steaming cups of tea and slices of cake.

"There we are," she says. "Now, Marcy, how is your family?"

"Fine, thanks," says Marcy. Then, automatically, she says, "How's yours?"

She puts a hand to her mouth, mortified. "I'm sorry. I didn't mean—"

Surprisingly, Louisa throws her head back and laughs. When she looks at Marcy again, she has tears in her eyes. "You must think me mad," she says. "Only, it's good to stop tiptoeing around the elephant and get it out, isn't it? Eugene is missing, and I won't forget about it by not talking about it." She wipes her eyes and takes a sip of her tea. "You're a good friend, to Eugene, to come out and see me like this."

Marcy swallows. She wonders how to tell Eugene's mum she loves him. She thinks about her own grief and suddenly feels ashamed for it—for thinking her grief is anything like Louisa's, anywhere close to the magnitude. How silly to think a cake could do something to salve the wound of Eugene's absence.

"He's not my friend," she blurts out. "I mean, I'd like him to be, but we don't talk much. I've been waiting for him to notice me for years."

Her ears burn as she realizes what she just said out loud.

She expects to be told to leave so Louisa can stand up and begin clearing the plates. Instead, Louisa leans forward and says, "Your lives are threaded together. You'd have found one another again eventually."

Marcy stares hard at the plate balanced on her knees, wondering what Louisa means.

They eat their cake in silence for a few moments, sweating in the sunny conservatory.

"He's alive, you know," Louisa says abruptly, defensively. "Everyone talks to me like I'm a bereaved mother. But my son is alive."

Marcy looks up at her, at the purple swirling around her hair like a hazy crown. She says, "I'm sure of it."

Louisa takes Marcy's in hers. Hers is soft, tan, smells like lotion, dotted with sunspots. "Thank you, my girl," she says.

"I think my mum misses you, Mrs. Westover—Louisa," Marcy says before she can stop herself. It comes out evenly and bluntly.

Louisa withdraws her hand and picks up her tea again, but Marcy can see the moisture pooling around her eyes. "Well," she says briskly. "I can't do anything about your mum. But you'll simply have to come back."

***

Marcy's legs ache as she pulls into her drive and mounts off her bike. She pushes open the kitchen door, breathing heavily, both from the last hill and adrenaline from her visit.

Her mum is at the kitchen table, with her arms crossed and her feet tapping the floor. Her dad, surprisingly, also sits at the table.

"Hiya, Mum. Dad?" Marcy says, as she stands in the kitchen door. Marcy's dad, David, is never in the house at this time of day. Normally, he stays in the fields until dinner.

He looks at her from the table, where his dirty hands wrap around a cup of tea. In brown work overalls, which hang on his thin frame, a tan, freckled face, and a balding head he tries to cover with a cap, Marcy's dad looks every bit the hardworking Jersey farmer. Marcy is full of love for him and walks over to kiss his forehead.

"Hello, Marcy girl," her dad says. He brushes her cheek with his finger. "Where have you been off to?"

"Marcy, the *door*," her mum snaps. She, too, has a cup of tea in front of her, but looks ragged, pinched. "You're letting all the flies in."

"Sorry," Marcy says. She closes the door and pulls off her shoes. Her parents look uncomfortable with each other, sitting at the table. In all the years she has known them, Marcy has never seen them at ease with one another. Nor has she ever seen them sit like this. At night, he usually dozes off reading the paper while Mum bakes or embroiders.

"Have a cup of tea," her mum says, pulling the cozy off of the teapot that sits in the middle of the table. Her voice is taut. "Then go find your brother."

"She should hear this, Violet," her dad says. His big brown eyes remind Marcy of a Jersey cow, sad and full of words he'll never say. She pulls out a chair next to him and sits down at the table, feeling braver in his presence than she would with just her mum.

"Hear what?" she asks as she picks up a teacup.

"Churchill's demilitarizing the island," her dad says at the very same time that Violet says, "Nothing."

Marcy is so surprised that her hands drop the floral teacup. It shatters on the floor.

"Oh, *Marcy*," her mother groans. She stands up to fetch the broom and begins to sweep aggressively.

"Sorry," Marcy says, jumping out of the way. She locks eyes with her dad, the two of them on the outside of Violet's tornado. As always, her dad looks helpless to her mum's moods, like she is a weather pattern he cannot understand. He sits at the table while she grazes his feet with the broom, picking his teacup up and putting it down for something to do.

"Churchill can't do that, Dad," Marcy says. "We're English citizens."

"He's already done it. He's leaving us completely defenseless to the Germans, and with the Maginot Line down, it's a matter of days, likely, before they arrive."

"You don't honestly think the Germans would want anything to do with us, do you? We're just islands."

Violet sweeps around Marcy's feet. Marcy steps aside. "Mum, I'm sorry."

"Never mind," Violet says, "Out of the way."

Her father asks timidly, "Do you think you've just about finished, Violet?"

"Nearly." The floor is spotless now, but Violet keeps sweeping.

"Dad," Marcy prods.

David continues. "We're a piece of British soil. They'd love to get their hands on us. Bailiff Alexander Coutanche good as said that today in his speech. Anyone who wants to evacuate has three days to do so." He takes his handkerchief and wipes his brow, looking weary.

Violet shakes the dustpan full of glass into the rubbish bin. Wiping her hands on her apron, she says, "Well, I can pack up our clothes. We can stay at my Auntie Katherine's in London for a bit, while this all blows over."

Her dad turns to her mum, thick eyebrows raised in genuine surprise. "You can't be thinking of leaving."

Marcy agrees with her dad, silently. Jersey, with its steep cliffs, high tides, and side-of-the-road fruit stands, is her home. They couldn't possibly leave.

"What other option do we have?" Violet asks. "You've just said the Germans are coming. We'll have to leave."

"Unless we stay."

"And do what?"

"Farm. Do what we've always done. We'll live off the land. What's a chap like me going to do in London?"

Her mum pauses.

"But, they could be," Violet pauses and glances sideways at Marcy. "What?"

"Well, *rapists!*" Violet blurts out, her face turning bright red.

Her dad chuckles softly and puts his handkerchief in his pocket. "They aren't rapists, Violet."

"Nancy Moss says they are," Violet says.

"Well, Nancy's leaving, so she can say whatever she bloody wants."

"Nancy and Ray? They're leaving LeCairn?"

Marcy is surprised, too. She knows Nancy loves her home, Le Cairn, just up the road.

"Aren't you worried the Germans will just take our home? Their brutish, uncivilized ways?"

"I've fought them before, in case you'd forgotten," says her father, his voice rising in pitch slightly.

"Of course I haven't forgotten," Violet snaps. "Who do you think was here waiting, listening to Bertha Bland go on about the letters you'd been writing to her?"

"Well, you won *that* war, didn't you?"

"I haven't decided."

Marcy's father turns to her with his big brown eyes. "What do you think we should do, Marcy?"

Marcy swallows. She looks at her mum, who is now focused on polishing a smudge on the handle of the sink with a tea towel. Jersey, with its steep cliffs, high tides, and side-of-the-road fruit stands, is her home. They couldn't possibly leave.

"I think we should stay," she says quietly. "This is our home."

David smiles. "That's my girl."

Violet's expression is unreadable. Finally, she says, "Well. I suppose that settles it."

She throws the tea towel on the table and stomps upstairs, leaving Marcy and her father to stare silently at one another in her wake.

CHAPTER FIFTEEN

VIOLET

1925

What Violet didn't know, as she walked up to the pregnant woman and her husband on the golden lawn of her hidden house, was that Louisa already knew Violet wanted the house.

Louisa tells her two years later, as they diced potatoes for a Sunday roast, that she and Jon stumbled out of that house like a dream. "It was too perfect. The stonework. The view," Louisa says as she wipes her hands on her apron, and Violet swallows a pit of jealousy. "I didn't think it could ever actually work out. We were just back from England, where I met Jon during the war, and I was so hopeful we could find a place on Jersey that was all our own. We found out the house belonged to Mrs. Sullivan, who had long since moved to a pink row home in Rozel."

Violet nods, keeping her eyes on her potatoes. Of course, she knows this about Mrs. Sullivan. When Violet was twelve years old, she'd looked up the deeds and traced the lady down. She'd offered Mrs. Sullivan her allowance and any pocket money she'd collect until she could get a real job and afford it herself.

Mrs. Sullivan had laughed kindly over her tea. "Now, my girl," she'd said as she rocked. "Don't go spending your life away. You might meet a young man who will feel differently about it."

Louisa puts her knife down and looks at Violet, a question in her eyes. "Mrs. Sullivan was willing to sell, of course, but after she did, she told us that you had wanted the house for years. I couldn't believe it. My best friend from childhood was still in town. And then, just a day or so later, you showed up in my garden. Together again, Violet, after all these years!"

Hearing her most vulnerable hope said out loud, Violet blinks back tears. She looks down at her potatoes and chops furiously. "Oh, that," she manages," her voice catching. "That was just a silly childhood wish."

Louisa lays a hand on Violet's arm. When she looks up, Louisa's face is full of kindness.

"It's okay if it wasn't just a childhood wish."

For a moment, Violet almost gives in to the grief of everything she lost.

Then she remembers the look on her mother's face when she shared about the man at the cliff. And so, instead, Violet stiffens.

"It was nothing, Lou," she says, scraping the potatoes into a large bowl of water. "Just a daydream. I'm happiest here, at Clapham."

As though to prove it, Violet begins furiously scrubbing her counters clean.

***

Violet tells herself that Louisa getting the house is recompense for Violet's crime. *It makes us even*, she thinks. *We both lost what we loved.* She knows it isn't the same, but it's a thread that allows her to maintain a friendship with Louisa.

She avoids conversation about her parents or about Louisa's. Anytime Louisa mentions casually in conversation (and she does so often), Violet changes the subject.

"Lemon meringue! You know, Violet, that was my dad's favorite cake."

"Oh, that's nice," Violet says, trying to keep her hands from shaking. "Goodness, it's raining again. What a lot of bad weather we've been having."

One day, Louisa plops herself down in front of the fire in the living room and says, "Vi, I've never told you much about my dad, have I?"

Violet is mending a pair of David's socks. She jumps at the mention of Louisa's dad and stabs herself in the thumb.

"Oh blast," she says, as a trickle of blood pours out. "Excuse me, Lou, I'll just fetch a plaster."

In the kitchen, Violet presses both hands against the counter, trying to breathe. Her ears burn and a drop of sweat trickles down her forehead.

I'm sorry, I'm sorry, she screams in her head to the man as he falls to the bottom of the cliff.

"Are you quite alright, Vi?" Louisa calls from the other room.

"Yes, yes, I'm coming," Violet calls back, trying to keep her voice steady.

With shaking hands, she loads up a plate with shortbread biscuits, and takes a deep breath before rushing back into the living room and diving straight into the latest piece of gossip.

"Did you hear about Helena Grange's hat getting caught in the Vicar's robe last Sunday?"

Louisa, always hungry for a good piece of scoop about Helena, leans forward with a smile. "I didn't – but do tell!"

CHAPTER SIXTEEN

LOUISA

1940

"What in the devil's name does Churchill think he's doing?" asks Louisa as she tosses aside the newspaper. "Demilitarize the island, my foot. He can't do that to us."

Next to her, Jon smokes his pipe and picks up the discarded papers. "Never liked that man. Smokes and drinks too much for his own good."

Louisa rolls her eyes. Jon has been a relentless advocate of Churchill for years, ever since he fought in the Boer Wars.

"And that Alexander Coutanche fellow, stepping in here with the Lieutenant Governor gone," Louisa continues. "What is our island coming to?" She slams her hands on the table.

With the island being demilitarized, the Lieutenant Governor would be recalled to England with the rest of the troops, leaving the Bailiff, Coutanche, in charge. Louisa doesn't actually have anything specific against Alexander, whom she has met only once and quite by accident, when she stumbled across a private party for his wife in a tearoom in St. Helier. She is annoyed by the situation, by the idea of Occupation, and mainly, what that will mean for mail coming on and off the island. How would she hear any news of Eugene if the island were to be Occupied?

"Well, it looks like if we are going to leave, we had better do so today or tomorrow," says Jon, putting the paper on the table and rubbing his eyes with his free hand. "It says here that anyone who chooses to evacuate should be at the Weighbridge for the next three days at half-four with their belongings, to be put on a boat immediately. Women and children first."

"At least they're being chivalrous about it," says Louisa sarcastically. "Run away, but let the children and women go first." Louisa knows she is being crude and unfair, but at this moment, she doesn't care.

"We're not—you don't want to leave, do you, love?" Jon asks, turning his eyes to her.

"Jon, do not be ridiculous!" Louisa says. "Of course I'm not leaving. How would Eugene ever find us?"

Jon nods, staring at the cupboard door across from him. She stops pacing and looks at her husband.

"Jon, you don't—you can't *possibly* want to leave?"

Jon says simply, "I can't lose you too."

"Where am I going, eh?" Louisa asks with a laugh. "Jerries will have to pull me cold from this house, and even then I guarantee I won't make it easy for them."

Jon smiles wearily and holds out a hand to Louisa. She reaches out to take it, but is interrupted by a knock on their door.

Louisa walks down the hallway, swallowing the thrill of anticipation she gets every time someone calls, though she knows that it couldn't possibly be Eugene, and if it were, he wouldn't knock: he'd come bounding in through the side door and immediately raid the cupboard.

It's not Eugene. It's Nancy LeCairn, Violet's neighbor, wearing layers of wool sweaters and a trench coat, perspiring on the hot summer day. Nancy and Louisa became friends through Violet and somehow managed to hold their friendship together even after hers with Violet disintegrated.

"Nancy, lovely to see you," Louisa says warmly. She stands aside to let her friend in.

Nancy shakes her head. "Thank you, but I can't stay. I've got to get to the Weighbridge. I just wanted to say goodbye."

Louisa looks past Nancy to her husband, Ray, who sits in the car with the engine running. He wears a cap, a scarf, and a tweed jacket in the hot sun. He nods to Louisa. She waves back.

"I truly wish you all the best," Louisa says. "Is your house all locked up?"

Nancy shakes her head. "No," she replies. "I left it open—I've heard that's the best way to keep the windows from being broken into. Violet's going to ask her daughter to go round and check on it for me from time to time." Nancy presses her lips together, and Louisa can tell she is trying not to cry.

"What about your valuables—your china?" Louisa asks. Every time she goes to Nancy's house, she is served tea on her grandmother's prized china.

"Oh, yes, Violet is going to look after that for me too." A little sob escapes Nancy's mouth, and Louisa puts a hand on her arm.

"What's the matter?" Louisa asks gently. She fishes for her hand-kerchief in her pocket and hands it to Nancy, who accepts it gratefully.

"I'm sure it's nothing, really," Nancy says as she blows into Louisa's handkerchief, "Only a comment Violet made when I left my china with her. I was already upset because I had just found out we couldn't retrieve Ray's money from the bank, and then to give up my china—"

"What did she say to you?"

"I shouldn't say really," says Nancy, though Louisa can tell she wants to dish.

"Go on," Louisa encourages.

"She said I shouldn't blame myself for going, that 'not everyone can be brave or strong enough to stay.'" Nancy sobs a bit. "Ray's health isn't good, you know, and we feel London is the better place for him, in the event of Occupation. But even so, it's not easy."

"I see," Louisa says stonily. Violet has never been good at saying what she means and often comes across as blunt or rude, but this feels like a new low. How could Violet say this to her friend?

"Wait here," Louisa says. She hurries upstairs to her room and opens her brown wooden jewelry box. She pulls out a long-forgotten string of rose gold pearls and walks back downstairs with them in hand.

"These will help get you started in England, until you can sort out the rest of your money," Louis says, pressing the white balls into Nancy's palm. She tries not to think about where she got them, or who they once belonged to.

"Dear me, I couldn't possibly," Nancy says, looking at the pearls. "Really, Louisa. These are precious. You might want them back one day."

Louisa sticks her chin out resolutely. "I will never want them back," she says confidently. "They mean nothing to me. Take them."

Reluctantly, Nancy puts them in her pocket. She kisses Louisa on the cheek, "Take care, love," she says.

"You too, my girl," Louisa says, trying to smile brightly. "Even if it does come to Occupation, it won't be long. You'll be home by Christmas, I'm sure of it."

"If I am, you'll come round for my pudding. I know how much Jon likes it," Nancy says as she walks toward the car.

"More than anything I make," Louisa says.

She watches Nancy drive away, not even noticing that she turns right out of the drive, back toward her house, and not left toward the Weighbridge.

***

All afternoon, Louisa fumes about Violet's comment. Quietly, she agrees with Violet. In her opinion, it takes a good deal more courage to stay in the face of Occupation. But she never would have said that out loud.

At half-four, she decides to cycle down to the Weighbridge to see what's happening.

She reaches the harbor, where Nancy and Ray sit in a half-mile queue with all the other cars of people trying to flee the island. In the end, they pull their clothes out of the trunk and carry them in their arms up to the Weighbridge, where they board a mailboat. They abandon their car and leave it in a line of other vehicles. Louisa thinks it looks like the Car Graveyard of Val d'Pleasant.

Across the weighbridge, on the other side of the harbor, Louisa sees another figure on a bicycle, looking down over the chaos. She's a beautiful woman, Louisa can tell even from this distance, with perfectly curled dark hair, high-waisted slacks, and a white blouse. It is Violet.

Louisa wonders what the coming weeks will be like for both of them, stuck on the island, for better or worse. She wonders if the island will prove big enough for them both.

Chapter Seventeen

VIOLET

1926

Violet stands at the kitchen counter, hands deep in the dough she kneads for bread. A few feet away from her, Eugene, who is suddenly three, stacks blocks, one on top of the other.

"Whee!" Eugene squeals, clapping as the blocks fall over in a heap on the brick tile floor. "Did you see how high I made that one, Miss Vi?"

Violet smiles as she kneads, enjoying the peacefulness of this moment. Mornings like this, watching Eugene while Louisa runs errands, have become the highlights of Violet's week. Secretly, she pretends that this is her child. She imagines that this is what life could be like as a mother: working in the morning sun while her toddler plays near her feet.

The side door flings open and Louisa bursts through. Violet snaps guiltily out of her daydream.

"Good morning, Vi," Louisa says cheerily as she walks over. She picks Eugene up from the floor and swings him around. "How's my darling boy?"

Eugene wraps his arms around Louisa's shoulders, burning his face in her hair. With a pang, Violet remembers what she already knew. Eugene is not hers, will never be hers.

"Hello, Lou—I wasn't expecting you back so quickly," Violet says.

"Well, I was out running my errands when I was struck with a wonderful idea," Louisa says, plopping herself down at the kitchen table. "The weather is absolutely perfect—too perfect to waste the day doing chores. So, let's go on a picnic."

"A picnic?" Eugene asks excitedly. "Can I come?"

"Of course you can, my boy," says Louisa. "And so can Vi. That's why we're here." She looks up at Violet. "Say you'll come?" she asks.

Violet hesitates. "I don't know. I've got so many chores to do."

"Oh, pish posh," Louisa says, waving a hand away. "The chores will always be there. Today will not. And I've already packed lunch."

"Well—" Violet begins.

"Excellent," Louisa says, jumping up. "I'll run upstairs and get your towels. If you wouldn't mind putting a bit of your raisin bread in my bag—I forgot to make sandwiches."

Violet smiles and rolls her eyes as Louisa disappears upstairs. She wonders what else Louisa forgot in her lunch and decides to add apples and a block of cheese.

Eugene is speaking quickly now, about the beach, making sand castles, and searching for shells. Violet decides it's a good thing Louisa has come. She puts the dough in a bowl to rise and covers it with a tea towel.

A few moments later, Louisa comes down the stairs, laden with towels. "Oh, bullocks," she hears as Louisa misses the last half-step, the way she always does.

She comes into the kitchen with a pile of towels. "Violet," she says as she sets them all on the table, "I found these in the linen closet. They look rather valuable."

In her hands, she holds a string of rose gold pearls.

Immediately, a flood of memories comes back to Violet–the lack of oxygen in her lungs, the black suit, the thick blonde mustache, the smell of sea salt, the sinking pit inside her that she had done something very, very bad.

"Oh, those," she tries to say casually, the room beginning to swim around her. "Those aren't important. You can have them, if you want."

"No, I wasn't asking for them. They just look precious, is all, like you might want them in a safe place."

"I don't want them," Violet says emphatically. "No, Lou, please, take them. I don't want them in this house."

Violet tries to take a full breath. She feels dizzy, clammy, like she is locked in a dark room and cannot find the door.

Louisa steps forward to rub Violet's shoulder. Violet recoils at the touch.

"Are you sure you're quite alright, Vi?" she asks quietly.

Violet nods, putting her head in her hands. She thinks about her mum's face, the way she slapped her, the constant nightmares. "I've suddenly got a headache coming on," she manages to say, her own voice sounding foreign to her.

"Oh dear," says Louisa, looking concerned. "Tell you what, we'll go to the beach and come back to check on you afterwards. How does that sound?"

Violet nods, not looking up. She needs quiet, to hide, to bury herself upstairs in her covers.

"Why don't I make you a nice cup of tea before I go?" Louisa suggests.

"No," Violet snaps. She tries again, more gently. "No, I just need to have a lie-down, that's all,"

"Right," Louisa nods, looking alarmed. Violet has never acted like this in front of her friend.

Violet stands up, and prepares to go upstairs. "Louisa, please. Keep the pearls," she says as she leaves.

The memory of that day plays in her mind again and again. *You imagined it*, she tells herself. *There was no man. It couldn't have been her dad.* She tries to pack up the memory and seal it. She tries to put herself to work.

Eugene and Louisa return at half two, sun-kissed, smiling and covered in sand. By then, Violet has had a bath, put the bread in the oven, dusted the furniture, and managed to pull herself together slightly, though her hands still tremble every time she leaves them idle.

"Hello," she says brightly as they make their way in, ignoring the grains of sand that sprinkle all over her newly washed floor. "Did you have a lovely time?"

Eugene looks like he's had a wonderful day, carrying an armful of shells, grinning from ear to ear.

"How are you feeling now, my love?" Louisa asks as she walks in. "You look better."

"Yes, much," Violet lies. "Where did you go?"

"I don't know if you've ever been there. It's a lovely beach up north. Lots of steps down, but Eugene did every single one, didn't you both?"

Violet knows exactly which it is but tries to keep her face pulled tight into a smile.

"You really must get there sometime, Vi. You'd love it. I think it was called Plemont Bay."

Chapter Eighteen

Marcy

1940

Right after the last of the evacuations, Marcy rides her bike to the LeCairn house, checking, as her mum had asked her to, that Nancy's house is clean and in order, all the valuables tucked away.

As she rides, her dress nearly catches on a bush of wild roses growing unkempt on the side of the road. Marcy presses on the brakes, the peach color evoking a memory.

She tries to suppress it, to keep it from forming around her, but she cannot. It grows up and around her like a tree with vines, so that even as she rides her bike on a lane in wartime she is twelve again, burning with shame as she holds a fabric the color of salmon, of early sunrise, in Boots while her distracted mother looks at fabric swaths on the counter, holding a squirming, one-year-old Peter on her hip.

Boots smells of warm leather and grain, warm and earthy. Marcy loves the way the sun comes through the window and makes a bright path on the floor. Boots has a long counter for goods and a whole shelf of candy, including black licorice, which Marcy hopes for when they're all done.

"Right, Marcy, have you picked out a color to wear for the christening?" her mum had asked her a moment before. A sliver of pride had rushed through her as she thought about standing in front of the church, holding her baby brother. She knows Eugene is going to be the altar boy. Eugene, four years older than her, tall, lanky and lately more interesting. She finds herself flustered and speechless around him in a way she doesn't understand.

"How about this one?" She says, hoping her voice sounds casual as she holds a lovely peach fabric in her hands.

Her mum raises her eyebrows, then turns back to the fabric and continues to sift through it. "Not that color, Marcy. I don't think it's quite right for someone of your frame."

Marcy recoils at the sting of the words. She forces herself to close her mouth, to look away. At twelve, she has never thought to question her frame. She shifts her weight from one leg to another, suddenly thinking about that morning when she heard her father insist she was a growing girl after a second bowl of oatmeal.

"What do you mean, my frame, Mum?" she asks.

Her mum looks around uncomfortably like this is a conversation inappropriate for Boots. "Never mind, Marcy," she whispers tersely. "Fine, we'll get it."

Before Marcy can answer, she puts the fabric on the counter. Marcy looks at Peter, or at the ladies' toiletry items, anywhere that is not Mr. LeBray. She wonders if he heard them. Did he, too, think her frame was big?

On the way home, Marcy's mum talks about the weather and the potato crop. She asks Marcy to please feed the chickens when they get home because she has to make lunch and isn't there just so much to do in a day?

Marcy tries to find the words to ask what happened at the store. Instead, she holds the bag with the fabric between her fingers like it is a stolen object.

Her mum doesn't mention the dress again as she sews and stitches it together. "Lovely," she says tersely, when Marcy tries on the finished product. She never quite meets Marcy's eyes.

"You're a vision, Marcy girl," says her dad with his big sad eyes from behind his newspaper, and Marcy feels a surge of hope.

She stands in front of the church on the morning of the christening in the peach dress next to Eugene, the altar boy. She holds Peter, and when he smacks her on the nose, the whole church laughs a little and Marcy meets Eugene's eyes.

Louisa Westover comes through the receiving line after the service with Eugene. Marcy is talking to the Granges, but she hears Louisa say to her mum, "Marcy looks lovely in that dress today."

"Oh, that," says Violet, her tone hard, determinedly casual. "I told her girls with her frame aren't suited to wear a color like that, but she insisted."

In the receiving line, Marcy's arms go tingly. She feels a blush grow up her chest and burn in her cheeks. "Excuse me," she says to the Granges.

Turning away before her mother can see her, she marches up the hill until she gets to the bit at the top where the grass grows a little taller. She takes a deep breath and lays back, trying to keep the shame that threatens to wash over her at bay.

"You're bound to get hit once the football starts," she hears. She sits up, rubbing her eyes. Eugene stands in over her, silhouetted by the sun, his mop of curly black hair dancing in the wind.

Marcy tries to laugh and looks away. She wonders what Eugene heard.

"You did a good job during the service," he continues as he flops down on the grass next to her. "It's not easy being up there, your first time."

Marcy meets his eyes, and is suddenly caught off guard by the shade of them. They are the most stunning mix of green and brown, changing even as she looks, so that she can't get a firm grasp on the color.

Her tummy turns over inside of her. Again, she feels uncomfortable, looking at Eugene in this new light.

"I should probably be getting back," she says.

"To what? Small talk and grown-up stories? No. Let's play a game instead. Guess who."

"How do you play that?" she asks.

"Easy," he says, tossing his hair. "I'm thinking of a person. You have to ask me yes or no questions until you suss out who I'm thinking of. Are you ready? Go."

"Boy or girl?" she asks, unable to keep the smile off her face.

"Girl."

"Old or young?"

"Old to us."

"Any distinguishing characteristics?"

"Oi!" he says. "Yes or no questions."

Marcy laughs. "Practice round, come on."

"Okay. Yes. An exceptionally shrill and slow voice." He stands up. "Children, child—REN!"

"Mrs. Cremps!" she says, laughing.

"And Marcy," he says, leaning over to take my hand, still talking in the voice of Mrs. Cremps, "You really *must* project this time, shoulders back, chin up."

"She did that to me last week, only she kept calling me Anna." Marcy raises her voice to do her own impersonation. "Anna, stand up straight. Anna, make a *line* from the *nape* of your neck to your *navel.*"

"Did you ever correct her?" he asks her.

"Mrs. Cremps?" she says. "Heavens, no! I let her think I was Anna the rest of the class. She might still think that's my name."

He lets go of her hand and laughs, laying back in the grass. It's so good, so victorious, to make him laugh.

Miss Lou comes up over the hill. "Eugene?" she calls.

Eugene sits up. Does Marcy imagine it, or does his face flush? He stands up, not meeting her eyes. "Well, I better run," he says.

"Okay."

He walks a few paces down the hill, then stops and turns around. "Marcy?" he says, still not quite meeting her eyes. "You look—nice—today."

Pleasure and shame pulse through her.

***

Marcy pulsates with that same blend of shame and pleasure now as she continues to pedal up the lane. Le Cairn comes into view, the now vacant home of Nancy and Ray Moss. It looks sad and very vulnerable, a grand old manor home now left to fight the war on its own.

"Marcy, dear," her mum had said before she left, "If you stop by LeCairn on the way home could you just check in the cupboards to make sure there's no more of that china? I'm just reading in the paper about looters raiding Mildred Brock's house near LeRoque." Her mum had shaken her head disapprovingly as she bit into her toast.

Marcy parks her bike on the gravel drive and walks up to the imposing wooden front door. She turns the handle and it swings right open. The Mosses, in their desire to protect the house's structure against looters, hadn't even locked the door.

The grand foyer of the house feels ominous, daunting. She peaks around, noting that all the furnishings still seem intact. The house is still warm in an eerie way, like the body of an animal right after life leaves it. Marcy shivers and wraps her arms close around her in the June heat. Plates are stacked high in the sink, slippers and work boots caked in mud lay on their side by the door.

She imagines Nancy rushing through the house for the fifteenth time, agonizing over what to take and what to leave. Marcy turns the water on and lets the sink fill with soapy water. One at a time, she washes the dirty plates and puts them on the rack to dry.

Looking around, she decides she'll take a walk upstairs. She's never been to the second floor of this house, and curiosity overpowers her. The top of the steps opens up to a landing with a bay window, through which she can see past her farm with its soft brown Jersey cows and lavender fields, down the winding lane to the parish church, to the beach at low tide and the sea. The cushioned window seat invites Marcy to sit down, so she flings the window open and plops onto the seat, letting the breeze tickle her face. If Ray could afford a house like this, she wonders, why would he ever leave? She would rather ride out an Occupation in a lush house than a war in the middle of London.

With her back against the wall, Marcy sits on the floral cushion until the sun begins to sink lower in the sky, casting a golden light on the fields. Her dad will be heading home, and dinner will be started soon, and her mum will ring the bell to come in. She heads for the stairs, stopping as she passes Nancy's bedroom. Nancy is always so stylish and put together. What had she left behind? Before Marcy quite knows what she is doing, she opens the wardrobe and peers inside.

She runs her fingers along the beautiful skirts she knows wouldn't fit her, the leather high heels, the fine jewelry. She's about to leave when she sees, on a china plate atop the dresser, a string of pearls.

Marcy walks over to them. The rose gold pearls catch the light and glisten. Unable to resist, she reaches out her fingers to touch them.

She wonders why something so obviously valuable has just been thrown on the dresser. Had Nancy forgotten them?

Overcome with an urge to put the necklace on, she clasps the string around her neck, noting with pleasure the coolness of the pearls against the back of her neck.

She catches herself in the mirror and stops. The necklace has transferred to her a sort of sophistication and grace that was missing a moment earlier. Turning back and forth, she studies her image. She looks prettier, more glamorous than she's used to. She continues to stare.

In the mirror, Marcy no longer looks like a beige. There is a sparkle to her that she hasn't seen before. She wonders if it is really that easy to change who you are. A few accessories and she can be a new person.

She unclasps the necklace, in the dim, dusty light of the room. Though she knows she is alone, she looks around and says out loud, "I'll just take this necklace home to mum." She shoves it in her dress pocket, runs down the stairs and cycles home to dinner.

"Hiya Mum, Peter," she says as she bursts through the door.

"Marcy, it's dad's favorite, Bean croc!" says Peter, looking up from his train set on the faded green rug in the living room.

"Lovely," says Marcy. She walks to the cutlery drawer to pull out knives and forks. "Good day, Mum?" she asks as she counts forks and napkins.

Her mum pulls a fresh loaf of bread from the oven, dabbing her forehead with a tea towel. "It was. Far too hot for a bean croc, but your dad asked for it."

Marcy nods. She knows Dad has felt out of sorts, like the rest of the island. Half the people disappearing almost overnight is unsettling, and the half who remain scan the sky constantly, waiting for invasion. All of them long for something familiar, and the thought of thick, warm bean crock with some crusty bread makes her mouth water.

"Did you have a chance to pop by Nancy's and everything was alright?" Her mum continues.

Marcy walks toward the table, the weight of the pearls heavy in her pocket. *Just tell her*, she thinks. But they made her glamorous. Beautiful. If she wore the pearls when Eugene came back, surely he would love her.

"Yes. All fine, Mum," she says.

"Good," her mum says, dishing out bean croc and stewed tomatoes to the waiting bowls. "Marcy, tomorrow, I hoped you would—"

She is cut off by Peter, who races into the kitchen with his train. "Marcy, Mum said you'll take me to the beach tomorrow!"

"Oh?" Marcy says, raising her eyebrows.

"I've got Knotty Knitters tomorrow, and I was really hoping you would take him," says her mum. Her monthly knitting club meets in the front parlor.

"We're going to collect big seashells, Marcy. The ones where you can hear the sea inside just like I read about in my book."

"Peter, I don't think Greve de Lecq has those kinds of shells," Marcy begins, but Peter has already left, zooming his plane around to another room.

Marcy finds it an odd request. Lately, at night, they've been able to hear the fighting in France, and it sounds like it's getting closer. Either Violet truly thinks the war won't reach them, or she has to live in a reality where it isn't an option.

That evening, she lies in bed holding the string of pearls. *They aren't yours*, she tells herself, but already she is justifying it, telling herself they were just going to sit on the dresser or be stolen by someone else.

She thinks about what Eugene would say. She wonders if he would notice that the pearls make her a different color.

Chapter Nineteen

Violet

1926

The evening is cold and blustery. David and Violet sit in front of bowls of steaming rice pudding at her mum's house near Greve de Lecq, warmed by the cast iron stove in the kitchen. David digs in heartily and Violet longs to; rice pudding is her favorite. She sits on her hands to keep herself from having more than a few bites.

"So," Violet's mum says as she scrapes the remainder of pudding in her bowl. "Are you planning to have one?"

"One what?" Violet asks, though she already knows what her mother means.

David looks up eagerly, a spot of creamy, sticky pudding on his chin. "One more bowl?" he asks. "I'd love one."

Violet's mum laughs.

"You know what I mean," her mum pushes. "A child."

David puts down his spoon. Violet can feel him looking at her and she purposely ignores his gaze.

Lately, Violet has been wanting to ask a similar question to her mother: "Did you plan to have me, or did I just happen?" She forms the words in her mouth but her voice turns to chalk every time she is about to ask. If things had been different, if their lives had not included the morning at Plemont Bay, maybe she would have been able to ask.

But Plemont Bay has happened– or maybe happened– and the trouble is that it keeps happening to Violet. In her dreams she sees the man falling, her mum (or was it her mum?) on the cliff in a peach dress. The unanswered questions circle around Violet in her sleep, making her second guess everything else while she is awake, making her irritable and short and generally a mum that no child would deserve.

Violet takes a sip of tea and looks at her mother, the unspoken words and unanswered questions swirling between both of them.

"I don't know, Mum," Violet says. "We'll just have to see."

After they are back home, Violet brings David a cup of tea.

He looks up from his newspaper at her. "Thank you, Violet," he says. For a moment, he lifts up his hand, as though to hold hers, then changes his mind and puts it down. "Are you quite alright?"

Violet knows he is thinking about her conversation with her mum, thinking that she is upset because she wants a baby. She cannot bear to meet his eyes.

"I'm fine," she says.

***

Later, Violet tells Louisa that she can't have kids.

"It's not wise," are the exact words she uses, leaving Louisa to infer that they are the doctor's words. Eugene works on a puzzle at their feet.

Louisa pats Violet's leg sympathetically. "What a shame, Violet," she says. "You must be heartbroken about it all."

Violet is heartbroken, but she doesn't say this out loud. She doesn't say that sometimes she does want a child, even desperately, so that she lies awake with a physical ache in her arms, longing for the warmth of a baby bundled in blankets. Occasionally, in the middle of the night, she'll wander into the room David left empty to eventually become a nursery. She'll sit in the old rocking chair that belonged to David's mum, hugging a pillow, hoping in vain that it will fill the ache.

Louisa wants another baby, and has been trying since she had Eugene. Violet knows she wants to fill her whole house with children, and it makes sense, because that house is meant to be full of little feet.

111

Louisa will be a wonderful mother to a whole tribe of children. Violet knows this, because she has the house and not the secrets.

"Mum, can I please have a snack?" Eugene asks.

"Of course, love," Louisa says.

Following Louisa into the kitchen, Violet says, "It's okay we don't have children. David and I are happy without them. Truly."

Chapter Twenty

Marcy

1940

Marcy and Peter pack a cooler full of berries, bread and jam. Peter sits on Marcy's handlebars as they cycle to Greve de Lecq. The pearls press against her leg through the pocket of her dress.

Later, she will wonder why she didn't hear the planes before they were right on top of her. Gran will insist that it was because of the sea roar. So loud today, she heard it inside her house with the windows up. Marcy will think it's karma because she took the pearls: that she was somehow unable to hear because of the stolen object inside her pocket, because of the lie she told that put it there.

Marcy is enjoying the pleasant sensation of being up to her elbows inside the tidal pools, hunting for crabs, watching the tuft of her brother's heavy brown hair, his little face furrowed in a brow of concern.

"Let's stop by Gran's on the way home," Peter says as they squat in the sand. "She's just restocked her black licorice and I know if Mum's not there she'll give me two pieces."

Marcy smiles. She begins to feel hot and sunburnt, their lunch long digested.

"I hope Gran's got ginger snaps too," says Peter longingly. "I fancy a ginger—oi, Marcy, look! Planes!"

Marcy looks up and sees three dots in the sky, behind the Tower on the far end of the beach.

"Are they allied planes?" Peter asks.

"Can't be," Marcy says. "We've been demilitarized. Unless—" suddenly Marcy is struck with the terrible truth of the situation.

"Peter!" She screams, grabbing his hand and running, leaving the bag of empty picnic food containers behind her. "Run!"

The planes come quickly, the noise of their engines deafening. Marcy throws Peter under one of the boats, then throws herself on top of him. The engines roar over them.

For a year, Marcy had waited for the war to come to her doorstep: at school, staring out the window, picturing every escape scenario. When it finally does, Marcy is on her knees in the wet sand at low tide, exploring the tidal pools for treasure with her five-year-old brother.

Marcy thinks they are going to die. She holds Peter's arm, which is soft and warm from the sun. She feels him breathing under her and she realizes she's never noticed how precious a breath is, how fragile and vulnerable it is for the body to expand and contract like that, over and over. In her pocket the pearls are wedged between her leg and Peter's body, little spheres that don't breathe or contract.

If she lives, Marcy thinks, she'll give the pearls back, tell her mum the truth.

As suddenly as they came in, the planes are gone, the beach silent again but for the roar of the waves, which, amazingly, kept moving in and out.

"Can you get off me now?" comes Peter's voice from underneath her.

Marcy rolls off. "Are you alright?" She asks as she sits on the sand next to him, her teeth chattering.

"Think so," Peter says. "I've still got my legs, so that's lucky."

He stretches out, looking impossibly small to have survived a bombing on a beach.

Marcy peers her head out from the side of the boat and looks out onto the deserted beach.

"We've got to get to Gran's," she says. "Just two blocks. Are you ready?"

They run across the sand, Marcy's limbs like rubber as she tries, with tremendous effort, to keep lifting, moving her body that is as heavy as stone.

Around her, others start to come out of their hiding places, dazed. She sees one man bleeding on the ground, a woman next to him screaming, "Help me! My son! Help me!"

She continues to run, gripping tightly to Peter's hand.

Gran's home is a Tudor-style row home with an opaque glass front door. Gripping Peter's arm tightly with one hand, she pounds on the door with the other.

Gran opens it, flustered, wearing a housecoat, the phone in one hand, its cord stretching to its base in the foyer.

"What in the devil are you knocking for?" she yells at Marcy, hysterical tears in her eyes as she pulls them into a hug before yelling into the phone, "They're alright, Vi! They're here!"

Gran puts the kettle on and Peter runs after her, in search of licorice. He receives three pieces.

Marcy remains on the burgundy carpet of the foyer, unable to stand up. She listens to Peter tell Gran about what happened. ("Huge planes, Gran! Loads of them! And I thought Marcy would bury me alive in the sand, I really did.")

Her mother arrives within twenty minutes. She walks in, lips pressed together in a thin, quivering line. Without a word, she crouches next to Marcy in the foyer and grasps her elbow tightly for a long moment. Finally, she pats her cheek and says, "Let's have a cup of tea, shall we?"

Gran puts her own pink shawl around Marcy, guides her to the table for a cup of tea. Pressing her toes into the burgundy carpet, Marcy suddenly says, "Gran, we've not washed our feet. We'll get the house muddy."

To her surprise, Gran laughs. "Can't stand these carpets, my girl," she says. "Your grandad wanted this color, not me. Replacing them might be the one good thing to come out of today."

They stay at Gran's all night, afraid to leave in case the Germans

115

return. Marcy lays fully dressed on the guest bed next to Peter. Long after the house is quiet, she runs her fingers over the smooth line of the pearls in her pocket.

They seem connected somehow: her theft of the pearls and the Germans. She had taken something from someone else. The Germans had tried to take something from her. Nancy had wanted something, so she took it. The Germans wanted something, so they took it.

Marcy thinks, *I'm like them.*

That's ridiculous, she replies to herself.

In the morning, a layer of white leaflets covers the ground like a dusting of snow. They contain orders from Germany demanding Jersey's unconditional surrender. They demand that all houses hang a white sheet out to signify their acquiescence.

"Absolutely preposterous," says Gran as she paces the floor, opening the blinds a fraction of an inch and then snapping them shut again. "This island isn't theirs to take."

There's a war on, thinks Marcy.

Marcy sits in the rocker, which she knows used to be her grandad's favorite chair. Pulling a blanket over her, she sits and stares at the walls of books she knows her grandad used to enjoy. She listens to her mum come down the stairs. She immediately begins to wash dishes in the kitchen.

Marcy thinks of getting up to join her when she hears the garden door open, and Gran walks in.

"Violet," says Gran, "You're up early."

"Mmm," Violet responds.

"I've just picked these up from outside. Bloody Jerries," her gran swears.

"*Mum,*" Violet whispers loudly.

Marcy peers around the corner. She notices the way her mum's shoulders tense, the way a wall goes up immediately when her own mother is involved. It has always been this way. Marcy remembers another incident, when Marcy had come home with a bad grade on her report card.

Her mum had been cross, until Gran started telling Marcy she needed to study more. Mum stood up then, took Marcy home, and never said another word about school.

"Well, they are, dropping these ridiculous leaflets like snow. The ground is covered with these papers, demanding absolute surrender. Giving us a list of impossible rules."

Violet says nothing.

"Violet," Gran says, "You mustn't blame yourself. It's not your fault they were at the beach."

Violet scrubs the dishes so hard that the water splashes up and soaks her dress. "Blast," she says, reaching for a tea towel.

"Violet?"

"Mum. *Stop it.* I didn't ask you anything."

Her mum stomps upstairs. Sighing, Gran begins to dry the dishes and put them away.

A moment later she comes down the stairs with a very groggy Peter. "Marcy! Come on. We're going."

VIOLET

1933

"There's a brave boy. Look at you cycling all on your own," Louisa coos encouragingly to Eugene, running after him for a few steps as he cycles away. "Straight on at the fork!"

She slows to a walk, falling into step with Violet behind Eugene. It's a gorgeous afternoon, and they are headed to Greve De Lecq for a swim and an ice cream.

Louisa says, "Right then. Shall we?"

Violet nods, and they begin down the drive, onto La Rue, with its winding paths and pastures filled with brown Jersey cows, grazing contentedly. The air has the faintest crisp in it, the beginnings of fall making whispers across the island.

"What did you do this week then?" asks Violet.

"Well, I went to the doctor. I've been feeling quite poorly lately," says Louisa. She looks nervous.

"Oh?" asks Violet, concerned for her friend. "I hope it's nothing serious." She remembers that a few weeks ago, Louisa had left hers early, claiming an upset stomach. She hadn't touched the blueberry lemon cake Violet had made. Louisa normally devoured baked goods with passion.

"It is quite serious," Louisa says, a smile she can't contain playing at the corners of her lips. "I'm two months along!"

"Oh," says Violet again. Then, plastering a look of excitement across her face, she says, "Oh! Well! Well, that's wonderful!"

Louisa stops walking and takes Violet's hands. "I didn't want to tell you," she said, looking straight into Violet's eyes. "I was worried it would affect things between us. I wish that you could have children too."

Louisa has been trying for another for years. For the first year, when Eugene was still a baby, Violet walked through the emotional turbulence of the month-to-month waiting. Then, slowly, Violet noticed Louisa begin to withdraw. She stopped sharing her disappointment.

When other ladies in their church became pregnant, Louisa would exclaim, "How lovely!" while squeezing Eugene's hand tightly. Once, he squirmed away, seeming to sense everything Louisa wanted from him and finding it too much.

"At least we have each other, Vi," Louisa used to say, linking Violet's arm as they left the meeting. And it made Violet feel so good to be part of something like that.

Facing Louisa now, Violet forces herself to laugh. "Change things?" she asks. "How could it? Louisa, love, I am so *very happy* for you."

Louisa's shoulders relax, visibly relieved. "Thank you, Vi," she says.

***

Over the next few months, Louisa's body begins to bulge again, and Louisa comes to life in the way only a pregnant woman can. Her body is literally blooming, carrying the heartbeat of another, and she begins to radiate joy and happiness from someplace deep within her.

"What's the worst thing you've ever done, Violet?" Louisa asks one Sunday after church as she sets her dining room table for their weekly roast. Jon and David make small talk in the sitting room about the crops and the pigs. Eugene plays checkers next to the fire.

Violet splatters the gravy she is whisking. "Oh, blast," she says as she gets a wipe. Her heart pounds.

Sand. Screaming. Falling.

"The worst thing you've ever done," Louisa says again lightly. She chuckles as she folds a napkin. "I'll tell you mine. When Jon and I were living in London in the fall of, when was it, 1921? We were in a grimy basement flat waiting for Jon to be discharged so we could come back to Jersey. One of those awful places that never got fully clean, no matter how hard you scrubbed the walls and floor."

Violet has a feeling that this will be nothing like the worst thing she's ever done. She tries to smile, to nod politely along.

"I was a terrible cook then. Not that I'm much better now, mind you. But that day, after Jon left in the morning, I decided I was going to have a nice dinner ready for him. I only made it to the market at half-eleven. The walls in that basement depressed me and I could never get out of bed on time. Well, the butcher had one indistinguishable packet of meat left. I bought it without asking for its name."

Violet pulls the chuck roast out of the oven and pierces the meat with a fork. It is tender enough that it falls apart at the fork's touch. She sets her timer for the Yorkshire puddings.

"I popped it into the oven that afternoon, with some broth and vegetables, and was so pleased with myself when Jon got home. I told him to set the table, and when I brought the pot out to the table, he said in amazement, 'Gosh, Lou, you've really done it.'"

Violet dishes the meat out onto the waiting plates, with the potatoes and steamed carrots. "I'm not really following here, Lou," says Violet. "None of this seems bad."

"Well, keep listening. "So Jon lifts up the lid, and he looks inside, and I watch disappointment just *crawl* over his face. 'What's wrong?' I asked. I looked inside. The meat was floating in the broth, still completely raw. I had never turned the oven on."

The story sounds so much like something Louisa would do today that Violet smiles, thinking of the incident.

"I was so mad at myself that I picked up a plate and threw it at the wall. It shattered into pieces, one of my good floral plates. A shard of it bounced off and hit Jon's arm."

"I've still got the scar to prove it!" yells Jon from the living room.

"Yes, he does actually," says Louisa, grimacing. "So I ran to get a towel for him to wipe up his arm and I said, 'I'm pregnant.'"

Jon walks into the room, pipe still in his mouth, and wraps an arm about Louisa. "I said, 'Are you that upset about it that you're trying to kill me off?'"

"I cried and cried," Louisa laughs. "And then Jon made me a piece of cheese on toast and told me to put my feet up."

Violet tries to laugh as the timer rings, to ignore the queasy feeling in her stomach. She pops the puds out onto plates and carries two to the table.

"So that's my dirt," says Louisa as they all sit down. "What's yours, Vi?"

Violet's throat catches.

"Violet's perfect," says David, pouring gravy over his meat. "She's never done a thing wrong in her life."

Slicing her potatoes, Violet manages a strained smile. She avoids eye contact, and wills what he's saying to be true.

***

Louisa's stomach swells over the course of the winter. Violet knits baby blankets and bonnets and tucks them into a chest for her friend. She listens as Louisa discusses where she will put the nursery, as she talks about Jon fixing up the pram, which has been broken since Louisa took Eugene on a hunt for starfish when the tide was coming in and busted the wheel on a rock.

One day, Louisa stops talking, and places her hands on her belly. "A kick," she says, the joy on her face evident. She looks at Violet. "Would you like to touch?"

Violet hesitates. She doesn't. She doesn't want to feel the life inside of Louisa: Louisa who is full of light and love, who does not know or understand the feeling of being trapped inside a bottle. But, because it is Louisa, who has been her friend all these years, she puts a hand out. The baby kicks against her open palm.

"I know it's silly, Violet, but it's moments like these that I wish my dad were here."

Violet stiffens. She tries to change the subject but can't think of anything to say.

"He loved babies. Would always point them out when we were out and about– their little toes peeking out from under the blanket in their pram. I think I got my love of children from him."

Violet closes her eyes. She sees the man fall, she feels the sand beneath her feet as she races toward him, not fast enough.

"Are you ever afraid of being happy?" Louisa asks. "Doesn't it feel risky to you, the idea of surrendering yourself to hope?"

Violet is constantly afraid. She holds her husband, her friendships, her deepest desires all at arms' length, afraid that she will lose them, that she will cause them harm, or maybe worst of all: that they will not love her in the way she loves them once they know her secret. Louisa would never truly love her if she knew what had happened at the beach.

She cannot not say this. Her friendship with Louisa is the most open, vulnerable one she's had, but still, she can't let her in this far. Instead, she says what she cannot not implement: "I think happiness is a state to be embraced eagerly, not regarded warily."

Louisa stares through the conservatory windows at the wintry sea for a long while, her hands absently rubbing her blooming belly. "You're right, Violet," she said. "There is always room to hope."

Violet begins to wonder if the sentiment could also be true of herself.

CHAPTER TWENTY-ONE

LOUISA

1940

The Occupation covers Jersey in a blanket of terrified silence, punctured only by German music and the echo of jackboots. Louisa had seen the planes come in, and had been far enough away from the beach that the bombings had sounded more like a distant *pop pop pop*.

When word gets around that the Foster children had been at the beach when the bombs hit, Louisa's chest drops and her hands go clammy, even after she hears that they managed to escape.

"They were some of the lucky ones," says Ouen, her neighbor, when he stops by for a cup of tea. "Death count is up to nine."

Louisa swallows a lump in her throat. She looks out the window at the lane that leads to Violet's. Twice, she nearly goes to see her, but never makes it to the end of her own drive.

Jon comes into the kitchen one evening with spreadsheets and lists.

"What's all that?" Louisa asks. She is trying to motivate herself to wipe down the counters and sweep the kitchen floor, but she hasn't moved from her seat at the big farmhouse table—the one Jon built early in their marriage when they thought there would be enough children to fill it.

Jon lays the sheets on the table and spreads them out. "Here's the way I see it, Lou," he says. "The Germans are going to need food."

"You're not suggesting we feed them." Louisa picks up a sheet of paper. It's an inventory of every animal they have.

"Either we feed them or they take it," Jon says. "We're one of the largest livestock farms on this side of the island. If we can show them we're useful, and cooperative, we'll be able to keep the house."

Louisa stands up. "These Germans are the reason my boy isn't home," she says, her voice shaking with anger. "You can't possibly think I'm going to *cooperate* with them."

Jon bangs his fist on the table. "Lou, are you hearing me?" he says, exasperated. "If we don't figure out how to get on their good side, there will *be* no house for him to come home to."

Jon moves around to Louisa's side of the table. "Don't you see?" he says, taking her hands. "I don't want them here, any more than you do. I hate that Eugene's gone. But the war has come to us now, and we've got to be smart about it."

They spend the next few days counting the livestock, cleaning the pens, organizing the chicken coup and marking down egg production. Just like Jon predicted, the first German truck pulls into their lane within a week.

"I'm very impressed," the officer says as he marches around the farm with a clipboard and tall boots. He looks over the notes Jon has handed him. "Did someone tell you that we would be requiring a list of livestock inventory?" His accent is thick. Louisa is desperate to spray some mud onto those spotless boots.

"We thought we would make it easy on you," Jon says with a carefree smile. Only the way he keeps wringing his hands together betrays his nerves.

The officer doesn't even go into the barn to double-check Jon's work. Instead, he just writes down Jon's numbers in a notebook and says he'll be back in November for butchering.

"Why did you give him all our information?" Louisa asks. "Now we'll hardly have any food for ourselves, every animal requisitioned to The Reich."

"Did you double check the list, Lou?"

"No. You're far more meticulous than I am."

Jon winks at her. "*Eighteen* chickens requisitioned to The Reich.

We've got twenty. And we had better butcher the extra two before November."

Every morning it seems like a new rule falls from the sky. Curfew is 11 p.m. All clocks are set to European time. No one can enter the St. Peter Airport. No criticizing the Germans. All cars confiscated for German use. All Jews must enter their names at a special registrar. In-home wireless sets are prohibited and must be turned in at once. No cycling two abreast.

That fall there is a bit of rattling news, about two British soldiers who manage to sneak back on the island. One of them is turned in to the German authorities by his own mother. Louisa cannot believe it. She takes her rage out on the kitchen floor, scrubbing it until it sparkles, for once in her life feeling as clean as Violet.

One morning, Louisa wakes up to silence and bright sunlight. She heads down to the kitchen, where a pot of tea sits under the cozy, still warm. Louisa pours some and takes it out to the garden, where she begins to snip rosemary and thyme from her window box to make a quiche.

She hears the crunching of the pea gravel and turns around. Marcy pedals up her drive. Next to her, on another bike, looks at first glance like Eugene: a boy with a ball cap, laughing as he talks to Marcy.

"Mrs. Westover!" the boy calls, and Louisa is disappointed. It is Basil Larose, Eugene's friend, Marcy's cousin. She waves back in greeting.

"What a lovely surprise," Louisa says, genuinely. She's not had visitors in weeks. "Come in for a cup of tea, please."

Marcy dismounts her bike.

Louisa squeezes her hand. She has not seen Marcy since the bombings. "I'm so glad you're alright, my girl," she says. She doesn't have an explanation for why she hasn't come to visit, why she hasn't been to see Marcy's mum.

For a moment, Marcy looks as though she might cry. Then, she shrugs and says, "I look better than poor Basil here."

She's right. As Basil leans his bike against the wall of the house,

Louisa notices a large bruise beneath his left eye, deep scrapes up and down his front leg. He carries a large, bulky potato sack.

"Basil," Louisa says. "What happened to you?"

"Nice to see you too," Basil smiles. He reveals a missing tooth and bleeding gums.

"Yes, go on Basil, you'd better tell us," says Marcy, "You told me you fought off three Jerries, but for your lack of detail I'm starting to think that might actually be the case."

Basil raises his eyebrows.

"They *did* have something to do with it!" Marcy exclaims. "Basil, what happened? They didn't think you were one of those soldiers who was hiding, did they?"

Basil sits up straight and shrugs. "No, no. Just a fortunate accident is all. Was riding my sister's bike too fast on the lane and Jerry was coming the other direction, up the hill. I knew I wouldn't be able to stop, so I just went ahead full speed. He couldn't do anything to move out of the way."

"You rode head-on into a German on Jean's bike?" Marcy asks.

"Yes."

"Bas, have you gone completely mad? You could get sent to Germany for something like that!"

"The only one going back to Germany will be that bloke, I guarantee that. He's no longer fit for fighting duty."

Louisa stares from Marcy's scowl to Basil's quiet beaming, deciding on an appropriate response.

"Is he okay?" Louisa asks.

"Breathing, if that's what you want to know. But knocked flat unconscious, and will wake up with quite the goose egg. I didn't need any questions about where I was headed or what I was doing."

"What did you do with his bike?" Marcy asks.

"Well, that's what I rode here, didn't I?" Basil says. "He ruined Jean's, so I had to chuck that into the St. Peter's reservoir. He'll have a sorry walk home, the bastard."

"Well," says Louisa. "Well."

She starts to laugh. Slowly at first, and then, as she surrenders, it becomes long and jubilant. Basil grins next to her. Marcy presses her lips together and continues to shake her head.

Finally, Basil clears his throat and says, "There's actually something I wanted to talk with you about, Mrs. Westover. The real reason I've come."

With an air of forced soberness, Louisa says, "Well, come inside first. I'm making a quiche. You can both stay for lunch."

In the kitchen, Louisa hands Marcy a knife. She skillfully chops herbs while Basil stretches out at the kitchen table.

"Go on then, Basil," Louisa prompts.

"Well, actually, it isn't news for both of you," Basil admits, looking pointedly at Marcy.

Marcy looks up in surprise. "Are you talking about me? Honestly, Basil, I am the most trustworthy person you know."

"I know," says Basil. "But this is serious business. It's War, you know, not me sending Arthur in to take my French exam."

Marcy rolls her eyes. "Like that was a smart move. Arthur can't do more than order a croissant. You should have sent me."

"Because we look so much alike, right," says Basil, but Louisa can see him softening. "Alright then, as you wish. It's only my head on the line. Have a look at this."

Louisa cracks eggs into a bowl and watches as he reaches into his potato sack. He pulls out a small contraption made of wood and wire, about the size of his palm.

"What is that?" Marcy asks, but Louisa knows.

"A crystal wireless," she says. "Brilliant."

All wireless sets were requisitioned by the army. They'd had to stand in long queues weeks ago, turning them in under the promise that they would be returned after the war. Louisa had run into Violet in line, each of them carrying a set and brimming with awkwardness as they waited in the queue.

"I remember that set," Louisa said, looking at Violet's brown one, then regretting starting a conversation.

Violet nodded eagerly. "It used to be in my kitchen, remember? We used to listen while we made our Christmas cakes every year."

Ahead of them, group of Germans stood at a table, inspecting wireless sets and writing down names.

"I ran into Nancy LeCairn," Louisa said abruptly.

Violet turns a deep scarlet. "Oh?" she asked. "I thought she'd left?"

"She has," Louisa said. "Stopped at ours on my way out. Violet—" Louisa lowered her voice, "How could you have been so mean?"

"I— I didn't mean," Violet stammered.

"I thought you were better than that," Louisa said.

Violet's eyes narrowed, and she momentarily looked angry. Louisa had never seen her look like that, and she felt a little frightened.

"You don't know me Louisa," Violet said. "You shut me out completely. You don't know me at all."

She thrust her wireless into Louisa's hand. "Please, turn this in for me. I've got to go."

Louisa was left, standing alone in the line, with a bulky wireless in each hand.

Now, Basil nods. "Let me show you how it works," he says. He fiddles with the wire.

"Where did you get this?" Marcy asks.

"Made it myself. A whole lot of them. I was so angry. Standing like sheep turning in our only key to the outside world. My parents insisted on turning in our wireless. I had to get the BBC somehow."

He fiddles with the set, trying to get the signal right.

"Bloody genius," says Louisa. "Have you got headphones?"

"There we are," he says.

Marcy and Louisa lean forward and hear the static music of the BBC radio.

"That's lovely," she says after a moment.

"Of course it is," says Basil. "But I'm not here to sell you one. I need a bit of a favor."

"What's that, Bas?"

"I need you to let me keep them here."

A thrill rushes down Louisa's spine. "Yes," she says quickly.

Basil doesn't seem to have heard her. "It's just that Dad is pretty uneasy about the whole thing, doing anything wrong by the Germans. If he knew I had these, he'd go mad."

"Basil."

"What?"

"Yes."

Basil stands up, his beat-up face lighting up in an enormous smile. "Really?"

Louisa is sure her smile is as big as Basil's. "I've been waiting–*absolutely pining*–for some way to get involved with this war. If this is going to hurt the Germans and bring my boy closer to home, then I don't need to think twice."

"Well, that's just brilliant," says Basil. "Do you need to check with Jon?"

"Jon has probably already dug a hole to hide them in," Louisa says in a rush. Truthfully, she thinks Jon might be a little more hesitant, but she'll talk him into it later. "What made you think of us, Basil? There are plenty of farmers you could have asked."

"Actually, it was Marcy's mum who gave me the idea."

"What?" Marcy and Louisa ask at the same time.

"Oh, inadvertently, mind you," Basil says. "She doesn't know she did it. I went over a few days ago and was sitting in her garden with a cup of tea and some cake."

"I bet you were," says Marcy. Basil and Arthur always seemed to know when there was free food to be had at Violet's.

"And I said to her, 'Auntie Vi, who's the most trustworthy person you know? If you had to pick anyone to keep a secret you'd carry to your grave, who'd it be?'"

"And she said it was me?" Louisa asks.

"Not at first. She looks at me a long time, she does, and at last she says, 'Well Bas, I expect it would be me, but I'm afraid I haven't got room for any more secret deposits at the moment.'" Basil chuckles.

Louisa's stomach churns uncomfortably.

"So I say, 'Who's runner up then?' and she finally says, 'That would be Louisa Westover.' She's probably the next best secret keeper on the island. So, I've come on good recommendation."

"I see," says Louisa slowly.

"I'll help, too," Marcy says, looking at both of them. Louisa turns to her, remembering she's still here.

"No," she says. *Violet would kill me*, she thinks.

"Sorry?" says Basil.

"You need help getting the crystal sets to town. I can help you with that," she says.

"Marcy," Basil begins, "You're not exactly a risk person."

"I can be risky," says Marcy. "Remember the time I went in after your mum's puppy into the ocean? And I couldn't even swim then. Or when I climbed up the tree to rescue Peter's kite?"

"This would have consequences, Marcy," says Basil.

"Lots of consequences," Louisa echoes. "Marcy, you're too young. The whole thing— it's too risky."

Puffing out her shoulders, she argues, "No more risk than it is for either of you, making or storing them. Besides, what German would suspect me to be carrying a crystal?"

"Marcy, if your mum knew about this, she would have a fit," says Louisa. She fiddles with the piece of sea glass that hangs around her neck.

Marcy steps forward, looks up into Louisa's eyes. "She isn't *going* to know about this."

"My darling, if you could just see the position you're putting me in," Louisa says.

"I'm not putting you in any position, Miss Lou. I'm of age. Eugene could do his part for the war. Basil can. You can. Why can't I?"

With her chin out and her jaw set, Marcy resembles Violet so much that Louisa has to look away. Violet always had a current of grim determination, and Louisa has a feeling Marcy isn't going to back down anytime soon. She decides to step in and side with Marcy.

"You're right," she sighs. "I can't stop you. And, no one would suspect a thing."

Marcy looks grateful for her defense.

Basil sighs. "Alright," he says reluctantly. He pushes the wireless across the table. "Deliver this to 1137 Rue de la Vallette next week. Two short knocks and three long ones. When they answer, ask for Mr. Grey, say you have some Jersey Royals for him. They'll know what you mean. And make sure they pay you."

"How much?" asks Marcy.

"Six eggs, or a slab of beef, whatever they've got. No English money—it's worthless now, with the Reichsmarks."

Marcy feels a surge of nervousness. "What will I carry it in?" she asks.

Basil looks like he's regretting his decision to let her in.

"Never mind," she says quickly. "I'll sort it out." Standing up before he can change his mind, she picks up a tea towel from the counter and wraps the wireless in it.

Louisa watches Marcy as she gets ready to leave, a lump forming in her throat.

"How likely is it that she gets caught?" Louisa asks as Marcy cycles back up the lane.

"Low," Basil says. "Jerry isn't as smart as he scares us into believing he is."

"But there's still a chance."

"There's always a chance, Miss Lou."

Louisa should have been the one to do it. She shouldn't have let Marcy take this risk.

"What will happen, Bas? If she does get caught?"

"Don't think about that. You can't let your mind go there."

After Basil and Marcy leave, Louisa goes upstairs. She opens her closet and pulls out Violet's large brown wireless set, turns it on and tunes it until she can hear the BBC.

Guiltily, she thinks about that phrase: *The next-best secret keeper on the island.* She wonders what Violet means.

CHAPTER TWENTY-TWO

MARCY

1940

Marcy waits at home for an opportunity to go to town. She gets one the next week, when her mum grows restless of cooking and baking only for her family.

"It's time for a party," Violet says one morning as she walks into the kitchen, like they had been in the middle of a conversation. "We need something to celebrate."

"Oh?" says Marcy. And then, because she cannot help herself, "It's Louisa's birthday Thursday next. Perhaps we could have tea for her?"

After saying it, she wishes she could take the words back, tuck them away unsaid. The topic of Louisa is rarely brought up in Violet's presence, even less since Marcy began visiting her regularly.

Her mum's eyes narrow. "How did you know it was her birthday?" She looks at her calendar, where Marcy notices a small red dot next to the date.

"Louisa's not one for big hoorahs," says Violet, recovering quickly. "So let's have a fall party instead."

Marcy doesn't know why she wants her mum and Louisa to be friends again. Maybe she believes it will justify her presence at Louisa's; maybe she believes it will bring Eugene back. Either way, she surprises herself with her boldness as she asks, "Will we invite her?"

Her mum begins tidying compulsively, signaling to Marcy that she's pushed far enough. "Leave the guest list to me. But you may invite Annette and Susan."

Marcy doesn't dare bring the topic of Louisa up again, but when the pale, crisp invitations are sent out, she notices none have Louisa's name on them.

The next-best secret keeper on the island, she thinks, and wonders again what happened between them.

The party is set for a Saturday afternoon in October. Peter and Marcy play with his train set on the floor of the living room that Wednesday before. Marcy's mum scrubs the grout between tiles on the kitchen floor.

As she scrubs, she says casually, "I think I'm going to wear my white dress with the pink polka dots tomorrow."

Marcy says nothing as she tugs one of Peter's trains along the track.

Her mum pushes a stray hair out of her face with her gloved hand as she continues, "It would look so lovely next to your pink dress—the one with the ruffle around the hem."

Marcy looks up, heart dropping to her stomach. "What about my green one?" she asks. "I think the ruffles on it are lovely."

"No, not that one. It's not nearly as flattering as the pink"

Bracing herself, Marcy says quietly, "I can't wear the pink."

"Why not?" asks her mum, waging war on one crevice in the tile with her toothbrush.

"It's ripped."

"It's what?" Her mum stops scrubbing. A moment later, she appears in the living room, toothbrush in hand.

"Ripped," Marcy says again, bracing for what is coming next.

"But that's your best dress! How could you possibly have ripped it?"

Riding along the lane lined with blueberry bushes, breathing in the scent of fall, daydreaming about Eugene's soft hair, imagining a life with him, Marcy wants to say. She hadn't seen the milkman coming around the corner and nearly went headfirst into the bushes.

"Honestly, Marcy. You're so careless."

The words sting Marcy. She stares at her mother, who bubbles with a socially acceptable, pale blue anger.

"I could hem it up," Marcy starts to say, but her mum has already stomped out of the room and up the steps. Peter looks at Marcy, eyes big. She pats his hand and says, "Let's keep playing, shall we?"

The door to the wardrobe opens upstairs, and then it slams shut and her footsteps march back down. She appears in the living room, holding the dress in hand.

"It's not a rip, Marcy," her mum says. "It's a massive tear. And I've only got yellow and blue thread at the moment, so I can't fix it." She taps her foot on the ground, the way she does when she's close to panicking.

Marcy knows this is her chance. She takes a deep breath. "Well, I could go to Boots in town tomorrow, and get a spool of pink thread," she says. She tries to say it causally, like she hadn't realized none of them had been anywhere near town since the Occupation began.

Her mum hesitates, pressing her lips together. "Go to town?" she says.

"Yes."

For a moment, there is only silence, and the tapping of her mum's foot into the ground as she weighs her desperation for the pink thread with her reluctance to send Marcy into town unaccompanied.

"Basil will be in town tomorrow," Marcy blurts out. "He's working at the bakery. He'll be there if I need him."

It does the trick. "There and back," her mum says. "And don't talk to anyone you don't know."

That evening Marcy packs the wireless set into a basket. She covers it with dish towels and sneaks into the kitchen to put some potatoes on top.

All night she sleeps fitfully, dreaming about the Germans tying the strand of pearls around her neck like a noose. She wakes up feeling irrational and anxious, but determined.

The early morning drags on forever. The shops don't open until ten and Marcy knows she can't leave much before that or she'll look suspicious. Her mum, too, looks at a loose end, wiping down the same counter five times and reiterating things like, "Straight into Boots and back," and "You won't look them in the eye, will you? And don't speak to them unless they speak to you."

At quarter to ten, Marcy races upstairs and rifles through her drawer. She grabs the pearls and tucks them into her pocket, to remind her, she can take things just like the Germans. They can't harm her, because she is like them.

She kisses her mum on the cheek and walks out of the house. She fetches the basket she's hidden beneath the bushes at the side of the house, and puts it on her handlebars. Turning back, she sees her mum at the window, watching her like a worried hawk.

Trying to snuff out the nerves and excitement, she pedals, as fast as she can into town.

She looks around as she bikes in on Cheapside. St. Helier has turned back in time fifty years. The streets are vacant of vehicles, and a few horses and carriages dot the street. Nazi flag hangs ominously over Le Pomme d'Or Hotel.

Marcy parks her bike in the middle of the road, watching as a parade of Germans march by, the click of their boots against the cobblestone echoing like a drum inside her, the echo made louder by the absence of cars. She is disoriented, smelling gunpowder in the air when she should be smelling fish. She looks behind her—where the sea still rolls in and out, steadily. Closing her eyes, she tries to listen to the lapping of the ocean, not the clicking of the boots.

"Oi! Watch it," she hears. Opening her eyes, a man with a brown cap pushes a milk cart toward her.

She jumps out of the way. *Don't think about the bombings*, she tells herself, even as in her head, she sees sand flying and Peter running across a bombed beach. She walks up the street, basket in hand. She'll go to Boots, then to the address. Easy as pie, quick as a wink.

Marcy can't help but look at the soldiers as she walks by. She is surprised to register they look nothing like she expected them to. They don't have the distorted faces of the propaganda posters. They are younger, taller, thinner and more attractive. Her stomach jolts guiltily as she thinks this.

As she crosses the street, she feels the eyes of two Germans on her. Worried they know what is in her basket, she walks quickly, keeping her head down. She hears laughter coming from the line and she flushes, convinced they are laughing at her. She walks so fast she worries she will pop a dress stitch.

She ducks into an alleyway to calm down, taking a few deep breaths. They couldn't know what was in the basket, she reminds herself. It just looks like a basket of potatoes.

"Marcy?"

Marcy jumps. She turns around and comes face to face, not with a German soldier, but with Penelope Campbell. Beautiful, effortless, emerald green Penelope, walking with her purse in one hand and gloves in the other, her blond hair perfectly curled and pinned back.

No wonder Eugene likes her, she thinks, involuntarily, as she approaches. *Even I like her.*

Penelope fills up the alley as she walks toward her. She clutches Marcy's hands with her perfectly soft, manicured fingers like they are best friends. A head taller than Marcy, she leans down to kiss her cheek. She smells like gardenias.

"Marcy," she says with a warmth Marcy has never heard from her before, "I've not seen you since all of this began. Have you been alright?" Marcy feels giddy with relief that she doesn't know about the crystal set. She leans in clumsily and kisses Penelope on the cheek. "We're alright, we really are," Marcy says. "And you?"

"We can't complain. Mum and I have moved in with my gran in town."

"I see," Marcy says. Briefly, she wonders what Eugene would think about that. She wonders if he worries about Penelope's safety as he falls asleep at night. Of course he does.

She thinks she should say something then, something like, *I'm sorry about Eugene,* or *I've been thinking about you.* But she doesn't, because she's not sorry for Penelope at all.

Penelope leans in and says, "Darling, let me fix your hair." She takes out a bobby pin, twisting her hair back again. "Look at all these soldiers, Marcy," she says in a casual, low voice as she presses the pin into her scalp.

Marcy flinches against her touch.

"So far from home," Penelope continues. "So desperate for women, and here we are: young, fresh, incredibly available. Why, even *you* could have your pick of the litter."

Marcy flushes. "What do you mean?"

Penelope shrugs. "There's a war on, Marcy," she says.

"We could never," Marcy says.

"I think, were the circumstances right, you'd find that you very well could," says Penelope. She winks. "Take care of yourself," she says as she flounces off.

Marcy feels dirty. Looking left and right to make sure there is no one in the alley, she clutches her basket closely to her and walks again.

And yet, even as she does, she feels the pearl necklace in her pocket, thinking again about taking things that didn't belong to her. As she leaves the alleyway, she is more aware of herself: the way her skirt brushes against her legs, the tight, stretched feeling around her fore-head where Penelope had pulled back her hair.

Focus, she tells herself. *Thread and then the radio. Do this for Basil. Do this for Eugene.*

And then her shoe catches on the uneven cobblestone. She trips.

Flying forward, she lands on her hands and knees, her basket at their side, potatoes rolling in every direction. Frantically, she gathers them into her basket, shoving them on top of the crystal set.

"Damn," she whispers as she piles them on.

Then, she hears those jackboots behind her on the cobblestone. "Excuse me, Miss," a softly accented voice asks.

Marcy's heart drops somewhere in the pit of her stomach.

Without looking up, she says, "It's alright! I'm okay, thanks!"

But the footsteps stay put. The soldier drops to his knees next to Marcy and lowers his face so it is at eye level.

"That was quite a tumble," he says, and he smiles, revealing a dim-ple in his right cheek that causes Marcy's heart to jump.

Looking at the soldier, she feels blindly around her basket. Her fingers touch the crystal set. Discreetly, she checks that it is covered by the tea towel.

"Let me help you up," the German offers. He looks about her age, maybe a bit older. His face is soft and unshaven, with a dimple on his left cheek. He looks like he couldn't grow a beard even if he tried.

Despite herself, despite the compromising and dangerous situation, Marcy cannot stop looking at the handsome face in front of her.

"You speak English?" she says, as she jams what potatoes she can find into the top of the basket.

He smiles, and the lines around his eyes and lips crease, making him look both older and younger at the same time. "Guilty as charged," he says.

Marcy jumps.

"Learned it in secondary school, and studied it in university before I was called up for service," he continues.

She stands up, glancing down at the basket to make sure the contents are covered. Then she holds it at her side, so as not to draw attention to it.

They stand there, a foot apart, staring at each other for a moment, Marcy trying not to breathe or sweat, trying not to give anything away.

The soldier shakes his head like he is coming out of a reverie. "You dropped something."

Marcy gasps. She imagined this happening, over and over in her head, with faceless Germans. "I–I don't know–"

The soldier holds up a string of pearls. "May I?"

Marcy is so relieved she could laugh. "Certainly."

He steps forward, clasps them around Marcy's neck. She tingles as his hands touch her neck.

"There you are," he says proudly. "May I ask your name?"

Marcy swallows. She doesn't want to tell him. Her mum said, talk to no one. And yet, a part of her, entirely separate from her grief and longing for Eugene, wants to give him a name.

"Marcy," she says.

"Mary?"

Mary—what a relief. Yes, she could be Mary. Let her be someone else to him, just an innocent, clumsy girl wandering through the streets. A girl who isn't guilty of conspiring or feeling flattered that a soldier wants her name.

"Yes," she says, smiling up at him.

"Mary, I'm Franc. It's a pleasure to meet you."

The dimple threatens to swallow her whole.

"And you," she says. She looks left and right, planning her exit.

"May I take you to tea? It's parsnip, I'm afraid, but this cafe says it's the best in town."

Marcy knows the one he is talking about— a cafe run by a lovely elderly couple named Albert and Betsy. She feels a jolt of strangeness, thinking about the cafe being filled with Germans.

"It is. The best in town, I mean," she says.

"Please say you'll come."

Even in the oddity, the tension of this situation, Marcy blushes. This is the first time she's ever been asked to tea by a man, even if it is the enemy.

"I'm sorry, Franc, you caught me at a bad time. I've got to run some errands for my mum."

"Well, then, shall I accompany you? I cannot allow a lady so beautiful as yourself to run errands alone."

She is both flattered and disturbed by the compliment. She looks at his dimple, thinking that she can already see his color. She pushes the thought away.

"I'm sorry," she says again. "But I really must go."

"I'll be looking for you, Mary," he says with that dimply smile that unnerves her. He tips his hat and marches off in the other direction.

She walks an extra hour, snaking up and down the streets, checking behind her every minute to make sure she isn't trailed by him.

Finally, she approaches 1137 Rue de la Vallette. Marcy stares up at the black arched doorway, the imposing knocker. She looks left and right, but she does not see Franc. Putting her hand up to the knocker, Marcy grips the cold iron, trying to keep her hands from trembling. She knocks.

Marcy arrives home flushed and breathless. She's done it. She delivered the radio to a balding old man who tried three times to invite her to stay for tea. Two offers for tea, after a lifelong drought. Marcy can't believe it. Does being part of the Resistance make her more attractive?

Marcy wants to think more about the thrill of delivering the crystal set, defying the Germans underneath their noses.

Instead, she can only think about the soldier with the dimple and how he made her heart flutter in a way that had nothing to do with her radio.

She sets her bike against the house. Her mum sweeps the front steps. Marcy walks around the corner, thread in hand, thinking her mum will be pleased with her.

But her mum doesn't smile when she looks up. Instead, she freezes, there on the porch.

"Marcy," her mum whispers.

Marcy thinks her mum is relieved to see her, that she can't believe her daughter made it home in one piece.

Trembling, Violet asks, "Where did you get those pearls?"

CHAPTER TWENTY-THREE

VIOLET

1934

Violet reads in the morning paper that low tide will be at 11 a.m. She picks up her tea and takes a sip of it, immediately spitting it out.

"Something wrong?" David asks, looking up with alarm from his sausage.

"This tea—the milk in it has gone off. Did it taste funny to you?" Violet looks at his half-empty cup.

"Tastes like it does every morning," David says, taking another sip.

They are interrupted by the side door opening.

"Hello!" Louisa calls, slightly out of breath, hand resting atop her large belly. "Is that a fresh pot of tea?"

She comes inside and plops down on a vacant seat. David nods at her and stands up, taking his plate over to the sink.

Violet pours her a cup. "Yes, but the milk has gone off, I think," she says as she passes it to Louisa.

"Well lucky for you I'm absolutely desperate for a cuppa, off or not," Louisa says. She takes a sip. "It's not off, Vi. It's perfect."

Violet, baffled, begins to wash the dishes. Eugene, ever intuitive, picks up the plates he didn't eat from and carries them over to the sink.

Violet loves Eugene. She can't help it. She loves his quiet, easy manner, his shyness. If she had a child like him, she thinks, she would be a good mother.

"Right, well I haven't actually come for a cup of tea. We're here to take you to the sea. Absolutely no excuses today. We've worked hard all week and today we'll have some fun." Louisa leans back in the chair, looking like a sultan as she rubs her belly. "David, you must make her come with us."

David looks up from the bench where he is pulling on his boots. "It is a lovely day," he says timidly, looking between them.

"Where are you going?" asks Violet.

"Plemont Bay. It's high time you actually saw it. I am going to have this baby in two months and then I won't be able to do anything fun all summer."

Violet's heart sinks. She shakes her head. "I don't want to go to Plemont Bay, Lou."

"Pish posh. You *must* come, and I'm so pregnant that I won't hear a word against it."

Recently, Violet has noticed that Plemont Bay doesn't occupy her thoughts in the same capacity that it once did. Whole days can go by where what happened, where what she did, don't even enter her mind. But it is always after a spell of those days, that her dreams are the worst.

"There are too many steps there for you," Violet says now, sweeping away a few crumbs of toast from the table.

"The steps will be fine—hang on," says Louisa, leaning in suspiciously. "I thought you hadn't been before?"

Violet pauses, panic rising in her.

"I've heard about them," she says.

"Well, today you shall see them. Come on Violet, when have I ever asked you for a favor?"

Loads of times, Violet thinks, but she says nothing. Before she can think about what is happening, Louisa has carted Eugene and Violet both off toward the beach.

Louisa's right. It is a gorgeous day, the kind that unfolds like they are already a memory. The sun seems to make the hedges greener and the pastures more lush, and when the sea comes into sight as they round the hill, Violet thinks it positively sparkles.

Louisa takes the steps slowly when they arrive, the wind ruffling the hem of her floral maternity dress as she descends.

Violet pauses at the top, an old feeling of excitement rising within her as she takes in the wet sand, which appears to stretch on for a thousand miles, peppered with patches of black rock and seaweed. This was the beach of her childhood, she thinks as she descends the stairs. It has not changed in thirty years.

The sand at the bottom is squishy between her toes. Eugene takes off running, buckets in hand, in search of shells and crustaceans, exactly the way that Violet used to. Violet remembers the magic of Plemont Bay, the new treasures that seemed to await her every time she came. For a moment she closes her eyes and allows it to wash over her.

When she opens them again, she tracks down Louisa. She is in the distance, by some of the caves on the far side of the bay, crouched down in the sand.

"Mum!" Eugene yells as he runs toward her. "Look, Mum!"

Eugene's legs carry him across the sand so that he is flying. His black, curly hair bounces on his head. Violet can see, as she gets closer that in his hands he holds a shell.

His mum smiles, reaches out to take the shell, but does not stand up. A flash of worry courses through Violet, and she begins to run toward Louisa as Eugene runs away.

Louisa's head is ducked between her knees. She puts a hand under her dress. When she pulls it out, Violet can see it is tinged with red.

No, she thinks as she runs, her past flooding back to her. *No. This cannot be the story again.*

Violet reaches Louisa, pulls her up. "We've got to get you to a hospital," she says.

"No, Vi, I'm fine. It's just—ouch!" Louisa moans and doubles back over.

Violet pushes Louisa's hair off her face, which is suddenly glistening with sweat. "Come on, Lou. Let me help you."

"It's too soon," Louisa pants, hunched over her belly. "Too soon. Can't be–ah!"

Another moan. Louisa's face is etched in pain. Violet begins to half lead, half drag her across the sand.

"Everything will be fine," Violet says, trying to keep the panic out of her voice. "Let's just get you checked out. It will be okay."

As Louisa begins to walk, she leaves a dotted trail of blood in her wake. Violet blinks back tears, keeps Louisa facing forward, arm trembling beneath the weight of her friend's body and her hope.

She waves to Eugene across the sand. He waves back and starts to come over.

"Please," Louisa says. "Keep my son away. Don't let him see me like this."

For a moment, it is as though Violet is looking at herself, years before, and more than anything else in that moment, Violet wants to keep Eugene away.

She leaves Louisa and runs toward Eugene. *Please,* she thinks as she runs. *Don't let this be his memory of Plemont Bay.*

Trying to block Louisa from Eugene's view as she reaches him, Violet passes him money for an ice cream. "Come on Eugene,'" she says in the cheeriest voice she can muster. "Let's have a race to the top, shall we? I bet you can't beat me up all those stairs."

Eugene grins. "Bet I can!" he yells, and bypassing Louisa, he races up the stone steps.

He doesn't know, Violet thinks as she returns to Louisa, who is gripping the stair handle so tightly that her knuckles turn white. "He doesn't know," she says triumphantly to Louisa. If he doesn't know, everything will be okay.

The women begin the long walk up the stairs, an impossible feat. Louisa, breathing heavily, stops to hunch over time and time again.

"Come on, Lou. That's a good girl," Violet says, rubbing her back. Marcy reaches her, out of breath.

What she holds on to, as she pulls Louisa up the rest of the stairs,

145

is that Eugene is at the top, waving triumphantly. He wasn't screaming, wasn't yelling. *Maybe he won't remember.*

"We'll sort this out, Lou," Violet says with a confidence she doesn't
feel, getting Louisa into her car. "It will all be fine. Let's just get you
to the hospital."

They drop Eugene at Violet's house. Violet sets him up with some
books and frantically waves down David in the field.

They get into David's car and Violet feels a rush of gratitude that
David insisted she learned to drive. Violet races through the streets
to the hospital while Louisa moans in pain. "I'm sorry," Violet says as
she drives, tears streaming down her cheeks. "I'm sorry."

Chapter Twenty-Four

MARCY

1940

Marcy stands in the kitchen, heart beating furiously as she raises her hand to touch the pearls.

"I– Mum," she stammers, trying to decide how to explain to her mum that she stole them from Nancy LeCairn.

Her mum drops the broom and runs upstairs. Marcy follows her to find the door to her room locked.

"Mum!" Marcy says as she knocks. "Mum, can I come in?"

There is no answer. Marcy thinks she hears her mum stifle a sob.

Marcy heads downstairs, outside to the garden. Her mum must think the very worst of her, must not want to be associated with a thief. She must know they don't belong to her. Suddenly, Marcy's entire trip out feels like one game of pretend.

Hours later, her mum comes out of her room, her eyes puffy and her mouth set in a thin, firm line. She heats the oven, pulls out the flour, ties on her apron like she is headed to war.

"Mum," Marcy begins, once she works up the courage to approach her mother.

"Forget it, Marcy. I don't want to know." Her mum beats her whisk with such intensity that Marcy backs away.

Still, Marcy can't return them. Every time she tries, she's drawn to the possibility of being someone new with them on. So she puts them in her drawer.

She and her mum move around one another, walls growing higher as Marcy senses the disapproval radiating from the person she most wants to please.

Marcy throws herself into Basil's wireless project, delivering them on her bicycle all over the island. Her mother urges her to get a job, and she says she's looking, but really, she heads to Louisa's for parsnip coffee on the porch any chance she gets.

Basil, hell-bent on making his weak eyes pay for keeping him out of the army, wages his own war wherever he can on the Germans. He whistles BBC radio tunes in town, just out of sight from the soldiers on their marches. He goes to the cinema and boos at the German propaganda before the film. The following spring, the paper reports that roads in the Rouge Bouillon district were vandalized with bright blue paint that read "Victory is British." Later, she sees dried paint up Basil's arm.

Marcy doesn't see Franc again. She avoids St. Helier, not because she is afraid of him but because she worries about what her attraction makes her. At night, occasionally, she still thinks about the dimple on his cheek, about the tingle down her spine when his hands brushed her neck. He had been so *human*. She wonders about Eugene.

As the Occupation carries on, Marcy begins to feel like a withering plant. The war that was supposed to last a few months has lasted three years, and everyone starts to worry that this occupation will never end.

At night, Marcy still dreams of yellow, of Eugene and his color coming back into her world which has been devoid of the sun. But occasionally, since her trip into town, she falls asleep thinking about burnt orange.

PART TWO

CHAPTER TWENTY-FIVE

LOUISA

1943

The first weeks after the bombings and Occupation were surreal. There was panic buying, of course: not a jar of preserves to be had in any of the stores on the island, but underneath that Louisa noticed a kind of solidarity between her and the other islanders. She ran into Penny March in the lane, Reverend Brown in the church pew, her mother's cousin along the promenade, and would say to them knowingly, "You alright? Everyone holding up okay?" as though she spoke in code.

It was as though all the islanders felt, at the very beginning, that they were above whatever mayhem brought on by the Germans—keep their chins up and they'd all get through it. Most of them, Louisa included, still believed England would rescue them any day and praise them for how calm they kept, for how much they took the Occupation in stride.

But as a bitter, hungry winter melted into spring, and then again to fall, the attitude began to shift as more and more liberties were taken away.

Then came the removal of organized groups. Scrabble club, a group Louisa had been a part of since the game's invention in 1938, was suddenly disassembled. The rules grew ever more ridiculous: no meetings of unapproved organized groups, only Germans can drive a car. As the islanders began to feel the prick a little more, they became more indignant at their common privileges being taken away.

Then some islanders realized the rules weren't the same across the board. The Germans obviously had more rations, more meat, more cheese, more freedom than the rest of the island. Some islanders realized that if they could get on the good side of the Germans, they could get access to some of those little privileges. So they began doing awful things, like calling in about who had lights on after curfew, or who had a radio.

Louisa began to doubt who she and Jon could trust. People at church, longtime neighbors, called one another in. Some of the islanders called themselves opportunists, but their opportunity came at the cost of breaking the trust of the entire island.

Now, in the spring of 1943, even the farms have begun to feel the sting of the Occupation: the lack of resources, the shortage of rations. It is no longer possible for Jon to hide livestock from the Germans; he's made himself known as a decent farmer and they visit regularly for eggs and meat. Louisa's dresses begin to hang thin, but she knows that in town, civilians are faring much worse than she is.

"We could sneak food into town for people," Louisa suggests to Jon as she half-heartedly sweeps the kitchen floor. The setting sun comes through the window, casting an orange glow on the room. "Leave it outside their doors, so that they have enough to eat."

"We'd be eaten alive," says Jon. "Attacked for how much we have."

Louisa thinks of Eugene. She wonders, the way she does daily, where he is, if he is hungry, or if some kind lady somewhere is feeding him.

"We could be quiet about it," she pushes.

Jon looks like he has more to say, like he is about to argue with her but can't quite find the heart to, when the door opens.

Louisa's stomach drops like it always does. She looks around to make sure any evidence of the crystal sets is hidden. She runs her foot over the edge of the rug, where the false floorboard sits underneath.

"Hello, Louisa, it's only Marcy and Basil!" comes a voice from the hall.

For the past few years, Louisa has been seeing Marcy and Basil on a near-daily basis. She's grown used to hearing their pedals coming up the drive while she pours her morning cup of tea. Basil bursts in with some update on the number of wireless sets distributed. Often they'll gather round their own wireless to listen to the BBC.

She's gotten used to the way Marcy leaves her shoes at the door, the way she's learned Louisa's kitchen like it was her own. Marcy is a talented cook, and seems completely at ease in Louisa's kitchen, using the ever-limited resources to make scones or Tottenham cake, dying the icing pink by adding some wild raspberry juice. Louisa feels a little guilty about the easy way between her and Marcy. She wonders what Violet would think, if she knew how chummy they had become. Pushing the thought out of her mind, she walks toward the door.

Basil and Marcy are in the entryway. Behind them, on the drive, is a large green van. They both look extremely pleased with themselves.

"Hiya," says Basil with a crooked grin. "We wondered if you could give us a hand."

"Where did you get the van, Bas?" asks Jon, a hint of worry in his voice.

Basil sticks his chest out and says, "I've been given a new job at the bakery. See, I'm their best baker, but they don't seem to appreciate my countenance with the customers, particularly the foreign ones. So now I'm the supply delivery boy."

"And they've just given you this van?" Louisa asks incredulously.

"Well, not exactly. I was meant to return it yesterday after work, but something came up."

He walks round to the back of the van. Lifting the hatch, he pulls out a large coffin. "Mr. and Mrs. Westover," he says, removing his cap, "I'm very sorry for your loss."

Something rips inside of Louisa. She grabs the railing to steady herself. Jon stiffens next to her, looking at the coffin.

"Basil!" Marcy says, looking horrified. "No, no, it's—a terrible joke, it's not what you think—oh Basil, just bring in the coffin."

Basil looks sheepish and embarrassed. "No, it's nothing like that," he looks around and lowers his voice. "Come on, just help me get this into the barn."

"I'll get you a cup of tea, Louisa," Marcy says. She takes Louisa by the arm and leads her inside.

Louisa sits down at the kitchen table and notices her hands are trembling. She rubs the sea glass necklace.

"That was an awful joke Basil made; I'm sorry Louisa," Marcy says as she puts the kettle on.

For a few minutes they sit in silence and watch the kettle. Then Marcy says abruptly, "Eugene's alright. I can feel that he's alright."

Though she knows, logically, Marcy would have no idea about Eugene being alright, she feels comforted by the statement. "Thank you, my girl," she says. "When you have a feeling that seems far-fetched at best, it's nice to know someone else does too."

Marcy pours the hot water into a mug, stirs the parsnip tea. She purses her lips the exact way Violet does, and Louisa feels a pain in her chest. For a moment, she misses that friendship with a violent surge that almost seems to equal the loss of her son.

Then she pictures Violet at her dinner table surrounded by both her children; Violet shopping with her daughter while Louisa pines for her son, Violet's son sheltered from the horrors of war on account of his age, and the anger returns, filling the gap of grief.

Basil and Jon come to the back door. Basil turns red as he says again to Louisa, "Sorry about the fright, Miss Lou."

"Never mind that, Basil," Louisa says, waving a hand. "But enough with the mystery. Whatever's in there had better be worth it."

"Oh, it is. Come out to the barn."

When the sliding doors to the barn are shut, Basil leans over the coffin and pries it open. Louisa peers over the edge of it. The whole space is packed full with not a person, but a freshly dead pig.

"Gosh and golly me," says Jon.

"That's right," says Basil, winking at Marcy, "A whole pig. Killed this morning."

Louisa whistles quietly, impressed. "How did you manage that?"

"Yesterday, one of the pigs on the Harold farm died," Basil explained. "If you remember Marietta Harold was delighted to receive a wireless as now she gets all the news from England and knows her family in the north hasn't been bombed yet. So, she calls me up and says the coroner had already confirmed the death of the pig, and would I like it?"

"Brilliant," says Louisa.

"So I said to her, 'Yes, Mrs. Harold, I'd love that,' and I took my truck after work to pick it up. Now you can call the coroner, have him register one of your pigs as dead while we pick out a nice, healthy one of yours to have for ourselves, without the Jerries getting their fat fingers in it."

Louisa stares at him for a moment, and then realizes what he's implying. "We could kill one of our pigs scot-free?" she says. "Basil, it's perfect."

"Bas, don't you want to share this with your dad? Your own family could keep the meat," says Jon. Louisa's mouth is watering and resists the urge to kick him in the shin.

Basil chuckles and shakes his head. "Wish I could," he says. "But my dad is too squeamish to get involved with anything like that. He and Mum have got their heads down, just trying to get through the war unscathed."

"I'll call the coroner," Louisa says before Jon can say anything else. "Get that pig out of the coffin."

"You're the second pig this week to die of natural causes," the coroner says while he inspects the dead animal, scribbling in his notebook.

"There is a war on, Coroner," Louisa says, hands twisting behind her back, trying to stand up as still and straight as possible.

"Yes," he says slowly, still looking suspicious.

"I'm sure you and your wife would enjoy having breakfast sausage," says Marcy in a rush.

The coroner peers over the rim of his glasses. Then he winks. "We very much would," he says. "I'll get this report in straight away."

When she is sure he's gone, Louisa clasps Marcy's hands. "You were *marvelous*."

Marcy leans in to hug her, smiling.

"I'd have loved to have a daughter like you," Louisa says without thinking. Does she imagine it, or does Marcy rest her head deeper into her shoulder? She adds quickly, "Your mum must be so proud."

Marcy looks up at her. "Honestly," she says, "You feel more like a mum to me than she does sometimes."

Louisa tries to keep the flush of pleasure out of her cheeks.

"And now look," says Marcy, grinning back. "A whole pig."

For the first time in months, Louisa giggles. She is light and airy, like a French croissant.

Chapter Twenty-Six

VIOLET

1925

By the time Louisa and Violet get to the hospital that hot summer day, Louisa's whole body is convulsing with contractions. Violet coaches her through them as best as she can, wiping the sweat off Louisa's brow, telling the nurse that they need to be admitted immediately.

Having never had a baby, Violet has no idea of the gravity of Louisa's situation. Babies are born early all the time, she tells herself. The pain Louisa is experiencing is normal. It's hard work to have a baby.

The midwife's face when she looks at Louisa tells Violet that things are most certainly not okay. She yells for a nurse and they rush to get Louisa on a bed. The midwife peppers Violet with questions, like when was Louisa due, had she been pregnant before, when did the contractions start. Violet answers them as best as she can, trying to ignore the panic rising within her.

Between contractions, the midwife tries to find a heartbeat. "Can I have a quick word?" She asks Violet. Louisa screams in pain.

"It's not looking good, I'm afraid," the midwife says in a low voice when they round the corner. "I can't find a heartbeat. But she'll have to push anyway."

"You're sure there's absolutely nothing you can do?" Violet asks, trying to keep her voice even.

The midwife looks grave. "If your friend is going to survive this, she needs to keep pushing."

Violet nods, trying to quiet the screaming inside her own head.

She returns to her chair, next to Louisa's bed, squeezing her friend's clammy hand. Their eyes meet as the room fills with more nurses.

"What did she say, Vi?" Louisa asks.

"She said you need to push, Lou," Violet says as neutrally as she can. "Come on, I'll help you. I'll be right here."

"No," Louisa had said, "About the baby. What did she say about the baby?"

Violet looks into the eyes of her dearest friend, who had hoped so much for this child. *Don't make me say this, don't make me,* she silently begs.

The room smells stale, like sweat and body fluid. Louisa's gray eyes do not break contact with hers. Finally, Violet says, "We need you to push, Lou. Just push. We'll sort everything out after that."

"I'm not going to push if there's no hope for the baby, Violet. I don't want to live without this baby– Argh!"

Louisa's body is overtaken by another contraction. She squeezes Violet's hand so hard she wonders if it will break.

"You don't mean that," Violet says when it passes, wincing as she pulls her hand free to dab Louisa's forehead. "You have Eugene, Jon, your house."

"Tell me the baby's okay," Louisa groans.

Violet takes a deep breath and says what she must, hating herself as she does it. "There's hope, Lou. There's always hope. Just push."

It is what Louisa needs to hear: the silver lining that perhaps everything will be alright, that this baby, who had grown more than any of the others and not died yet, would not die.

Louisa pushes while Violet rubs her arm. Violet cheers her on, saying, "That's it! Keep going, Lou," knowing that at the end of the pushing, it is only emptiness that waits for her.

For an hour and forty-three minutes, Violet coaxes Louisa's lifeless baby out of her body. With the final push, her little girl flops into the world, still warm but silent, and when the midwife announces quietly that she is dead, Louisa lets out a howl more haunting than any scream of labor.

"It's good you brought her when you did," the midwife says to Violet. "She's losing a lot of blood. We'll need to get her into surgery immediately."

Nurses begin pouring into the room, fiddling with dials and preparing Louisa for surgery. Violet stands in the middle of it all, frozen.

"I think it would be best if you left now, dear," says the midwife. "We'll take her from here."

As Violet begins to pull her hand away from Louisa, she realizes her friend has already let go.

"Wait," Violet says, before they wheel Louisa away. "Lou—what's the baby's name?"

"Come on, we've got to get her in," says a nurse, pressing her foot on a pedal by the bed to release the brake.

"Hope," Louisa says, in a weak voice. "Hope Evangeline."

CHAPTER TWENTY-SEVEN

LOUISA
1943

The morning after the pig incident, Louisa tidies her house in preparation for Sunday's Roast. The thought of eating until she's full makes her mouth water and gives her the energy to take on the house jobs she's been avoiding. She fluffs cushions, puts away the piles of books that clutter the end tables, gets around to finally organizing the mismatched teacups that perch precariously on her cupboard shelf. The circles of dust make the house feel hazy. When Louisa looks up momentarily from her work, she watches the way they dance and swirl when they're illuminated by the sun.

"Mummy, why do we try to get rid of dust?" Eugene had asked one afternoon when he was a small child. In a blue collared shirt and shorts, on the rug of the living room floor, building a castle out of blocks, while Louisa knitted a sweater for Jon on the sofa, the cat curled up by her feet.

She'd been taken aback like she often was by Eugene: his questions made him different. At four, she worried about him, because he would rather be inside with her than out working on the farm or roaming the countryside with the other boys. He was sensitive, and because he was a boy, she knew there would come a day when he would pretend not to be.

"Well, because it's dirty," Louisa had responded, raising her eyebrows.

She expected Eugene to shrug and go back to his castle. Instead,

160

he stood on his toes, raised an arm into the patch of sun, and waved his fingers back and forth, dancing with the dust in the light.

Louisa looked at him with his head tilted up, and got the feeling, like she often did with Eugene, that he saw things she didn't. She watched his delicate fingers sway in the light, trying to close around the specks of dust he would never catch.

"What are you thinking about, Eugene?" she finally asked.

Eugene paused, then put his hand down and returned to his blocks. "How we try to do away with the prettiest things."

Now Louisa watches the specks swirl in the window's light, and the pang of longing threatens to drown her. She turns off the stove and puts on her boots.

She'd gone to Violet about Eugene. At the beach one day, while Eugene raced in and out of the tide, she turned to Violet, in a polka dot dress and sunhat, and said, "Have you noticed Eugene is different?"

Violet ran her thumb over the shells in her lap, ones that had been deposited by Eugene. "Different how?" she asked.

"He's sensitive. Quiet. He doesn't play soldiers or pranks like the other boys. The other day he asked me about dust, about why we do away with beautiful things. I just worry he will get run over in life."

Violet shook her head and reached over for Louisa's hand. "I don't know much about other people's children. But he's a good egg, that Eugene," she said. "There's nothing wrong with being a sensitive boy. Someday Eugene will learn that too."

She had dropped in Louisa's hand a broken shell, a teal color. Louisa had made it into a necklace later, and wore it around her neck ever since. She touched it for reassurance every time Eugene said or did something that made him painfully, obviously different in the years that followed: choosing to paint or draw in the mornings rather than play rugby with his friends; how he'd listen to classical music by the fire in the evenings with his eyes closed, mouth pulled back in a small smile, like he was accessing a world far away from their Jersey farmhouse.

"He's pathetic at the chores," Jon would say when Eugene was older, exasperated at night as they got ready for bed. "He follows me along, head in the clouds, like he'd rather be absolutely anywhere else. He mixes up the feeds, forgets where the tools go."

Louisa put her hand to the necklace. "He's different, Jon. He's not like the other boys."

Jon rolled his eyes. "Different or not, he's got to find a way to earn his keep."

Now, Louisa thinks about Eugene, her fingers running over the smooth shell hanging from her neck. She feels the grief, which looms like a deep, cavernous hole, reaching out to consume her, and she grips the shell as she tries to push it back. Since puberty hit, Eugene had learned to put on a front of roughness. He started playing football, staying out late, seeing girls. And then, just when she thought he was growing out of it, when flashes of her sensitive son began to appear again, he enlisted.

Though she hasn't spoken to Violet in months, suddenly yearns to see the woman who understood her son seemingly more than she did with such desperation that she puts on her boots and marches up the gravel path, to the winding road that will provide, if not answers, remembrance.

As she rounds the final hill and approaches the cottage, Louisa's resolve begins to waver. She looks at Violet's perfectly maintained home: the way the bushes and branches have all been meticulously trimmed, the garden neatly put to bed. Nothing at all like her own garden, which sprawls about in every direction, embarrassingly grown over.

She takes a deep breath and tells herself she's come all this way, reaches up a hand to knock on the door, but before she can, it's opened.

"Louisa, hello," says Violet, looking immaculate in a purple dress, apron tied around her. Louisa can smell something baking. If Violet is uncomfortable, she doesn't show it. "Come in, please. I've got a luncheon cake that will be done in a minute. Made with potato flour, but we've got to work with what we've got, haven't we?" She steps aside, and Louisa comes in, pulling off her shoes. "Lovely morning."

"Yes, isn't it just," says Violet. "I'm grateful for it too. I haven't got enough wood to heat the house anymore when it's cold. Don't know what we'll do if the wood shortage carries on to next winter."

"Of course," says Louisa, thinking of her own drafty home. The Germans had rationed electricity, and with shipments not coming in or out, wood was in limited quantity as well. "Summer will be very welcome this year."

"Cup of tea? Parsnip, I'm afraid," said Violet. She seems causal and breezy as she fills up the kettle and places it on the stove.

"Violet," says Louisa, putting her hands in front of her, trying to look nonplussed. She wants to say, *tell me about my son. Tell me who he was and is. Tell me all your memories with him, so that I can soak them up. Give me something— I'm a starving woman.*

Instead, she says, "I've been given a pig."

"What?" says Violet.

"A pig. A dead pig, ready to eat."

"How did you manage that?"

Louisa decides not to go into details. She says, "Marcy and Basil are coming for a roast this Sunday. Won't you and David join us?"

Violet pauses. Louisa wonders if it's the mention of Marcy's name, or the fact that it has been nearly a decade since Louisa invited her in.

"I couldn't impose," Violet says, brushing past Louisa to pour the tea, her mouth set in a firm line.

"You're not imposing if you're invited," Louisa says, suddenly generous as she reaches out to take the cup of tea.

Violet pauses, and looks out the window. "We used to do Sunday roasts all the time."

Louisa swallows. The reason for the roasts ceasing hangs between them, and she feels exposed.

"I've noticed Marcy's been spending a good deal of time around you lately," Violet says, her back to Louisa. "What are you two up to?"

163

Louisa swallows a splash of guilt, coughing up her tea. She can't tell Violet what she is doing, but she knows if the roles were reversed, she would be desperate to know what Eugene was up to.

"Just visiting, really," says Louisa as lightly as she can. "I think she misses Eugene."

"Yes, perhaps," says Violet icily. Then she turns. "I found her wearing the pearls. The ones I gave you."

"She what?" Louisa asks, confused. She thinks back to giving them to Nancy. How had Marcy gotten hold of them? "I... I thought you didn't care about those."

"I didn't."

"Well, you don't have to come." Louisa wonders why she came here. It is too complicated, too messy, to try and fix her friendship with Violet.

"Alright, then," Violet says. She says it quickly, like she can read Louisa's mind, and wants to accept before she changes it. "I'll bring a rice pudding for dessert."

"Lovely," says Louisa, though already she can feel herself closing back up. She needs to get out of Violet's house.

She sets the teacup down. "Come round after church." And then, because she can't resist, "I'll make the roast potatoes just the way Marcy likes them."

"Right," Violet says, lips pressed in a firm line again.

Louisa puts on her coat and is back out the door, a sinking feeling in her stomach as she walks. *Why*, she wonders, can she no longer interact with Violet the way she used to? Why must her words always be cutting, guarded, designed to keep her at arms' length? She walks along the stony ground, both wondering and knowing at the same time.

CHAPTER TWENTY-EIGHT

MARCY

1943

By May of 1943, food rations have been reduced to 11 oz. of meat per week, 2 oz. of butter, 3 oz. of sugar.

"Impossible!" her mum huffs each week when she returns with an armful of food from the shop down the road. "How am I meant to feed my family, let alone carry on a business, with these measly portions?"

Ever resourceful, her mum finds ways. She evaporates sea water to make salt, brews tea from shredded carrots, parsley, nettles, pea pods and bramble leaves. Coffee is produced from dried acorns or roasted parsnips and sugar beet. She makes cakes without eggs, breads without flour.

"Almost tastes real," her dad says with a grin, sipping his evening coffee. Her mum doesn't look at him, but presses her lips together as she looks into her knitting like she is trying not to smile.

Her mum replaces Victoria Sponge with Luncheon Cake, thickened with potato flour and milk, replacing the egg with baking powder.

"Rubbish, isn't it?" She says to Marcy one morning, as she pulls the slightly flattened, lopsided cake out of the oven. "See if I haven't any jam left in the cupboard. We've got to make it edible somehow."

Even with her mother's improvisations, Marcy begins to go hungry. For the first time in her life, she wakes up in the morning feeling the bumpy ridges of her ribs against her skin, the hollow feeling inside her. Her dresses begin to hang more loosely, and remembers again what it is to have room for a full breath of air.

"It's good, I bought those a little small," her mum says, nodding with approval at Marcy's slacks as she eats a boiled potato for breakfast. "Now they're perfect."

***

On the warm Friday morning just after the pig incident Marcy rides her bike to her friend Annette's house, where she and Susan lounge on the rug in the attic bedroom, flipping through old magazines.

"Summer is going to feel so different this year," says Susan (navy blue), yawning as she rolls onto her back. "No picnics on the beach, no lounging in the sun."

"Girls, *girls!*" Annette says from her wardrobe, where she holds clothes in front of her body and looks at herself in the mirror. "This is depressing. And I am tired of being depressed. We need to do something fun."

"Oh, not again, Annette," says Susan, covering her eyes with her hands. "I told you, that's dangerous. You need to drop it!"

Marcy looks from Annette to Susan, not understanding. "What are you on about?" she asks.

Susan rolls her eyes. "Annette hasn't told you about the soiree this weekend?"

Marcy sits up, brushing against the scratchy rug. "Soiree? But where?"

Annette throws her head back and laughs, making Marcy feel like she's missed something important. "It's at the St. Brelade Hotel."

Marcy knows that the Germans have taken over St. Brelade's Hotel. It's prime real estate, with such a lovely view of the water.

"I see," she says.

Annette continues to stare at her, eyebrows raised, until Marcy understands what she means. "You can't be serious."

Annette tosses the clothes in her hand aside. She climbs up onto the bed, tucks her feet under her knees like a cat. Smoothing out her skirt, she says casually, "What's the harm? It's been so *boring* since the Occupation began. We've hardly had a lick of fun. It's tomorrow night. What do you think, Marcy? Say you'll go."

A wisp of burnt orange flashes across Marcy's subconscious, and though she hasn't breathed a word about Franc to anyone, least of all Annette and Susan, she imagines for a moment them at the ball together. In that forbidden moment she goes back and forth between the shame and the thrill of the desire to see him, wanting nothing more to do with him and longing to know what could happen.

"There'll be Germans there, Annette," Marcy says.

"Of course there will be Germans there," Annette says, leaning forward on the bed. "Handsome, lonely Jerries who want a girl to dance with."

"I don't know if it's a good idea."

Marcy thinks about the radios, about the pig and Sunday's upcoming hog roast. To even be around a German would be a danger for her now. She thinks about Eugene, about how proud he might be to know she'd been part of the Resistance. And still, the embers of burnt orange stoke within her.

"Pish posh, Marcy. It will be grand and you know it. Besides, it's not like your mum's going to find out about it. She never even has to know the soiree happened."

"Well, I most definitely am *not* going," Susan says firmly, twirling her hair with her index finger. "It's betrayal, isn't it? I can't imagine what my mum would say if she found out, let alone David." She'd been seeing David Greene since about twelve hours before he left for the war, and loved to go on at any given moment about how serious they were.

"For heaven's sake Susan! It's not like we're going to *marry* the Germans," Annette says as she stands up. "It's one carefree night. Consider it part of the war effort, if you want to. We'll dress up, have a night out, and drive those Jerries to such distraction that they'll forget to report for duty the next day, so really, our boys will thank us in the end."

For a moment, Marcy forgets about the war. She forgets about Allied and Axis powers, about country loyalties, about the resistance. She doesn't even think about Eugene. For one, blissful breath, she is only a teenager, weighing the possibility of going to a dance.

"I've nothing to wear," Marcy says.

Annette walks to her closet and pulls out a dress. It is more like a black swan in dress form: feathery, lacy, with sleeves that travel to the elbow and a skirt full and lush.

"Wear this," she says.

Marcy wants that dress, and badly. She has never before worn anything so expensive or well-made. It pays to have a father who is a banker, she thinks.

"It won't fit me," she says, trying to keep her voice even.

"Try it," Annette says. She holds it out like she is daring Marcy. "You've lost weight, you know, since the Occupation began."

Marcy tries it. She pulls it on, and it is tight, very tight around the waist, but Annette is able to button it.

"Gosh, Marcy," Annette says, raising her dark eyebrows. "You look—"

"I love it," Marcy says, quickly, before Annette can say anything about how she looks in it. She looks at herself from different angles in the mirror—there is not an ounce of beige to be found. She could be a neon pink, or a royal blue. She thinks again about the pearls now tucked away in her top drawer, about how they would look paired with this dress.

"Well?" says Annette, tapping her foot.

Marcy wants to say yes. But as she turns to Annette, the sun reflects on the vase by Annette's bedside table—bright, glaring yellow.

"I shouldn't," she says as she pulls the dress off. "It's not right."

Susan sticks her chin out. "We couldn't possibly." She smiles at Annette like a little child who has gotten her way.

"You going to a dance won't do one iota to bring Eugene back," Annette says quietly.

"I—what?" Marcy asks, flustered. "Who says I'm thinking about Eugene?"

Annette laughs and waves a hand. "Come on Marcy, we both know you've been mad about him for years. But," she adds gently, "You can't waste away, pining after him. Would he really begrudge you one dance?"

"No," says Marcy quietly, folding up the dress. She thinks, for one more forbidden moment, about what it would feel like to spin with burnt orange on the dance floor.

"Say you'll come. Just one night of fun."

Marcy sighs, her resolve wavering. "Alright," she says. "Just to keep you out of trouble."

Annette squeals and Susan frowns. "Marcy, it's going to be wonderful!" she says.

Marcy tries to suppress the guilty thrill that rises within her. She tries to suppress the words Penelope Campbell whispered in her ear: *even you could have your pick.*

She tries not to think about how good it would feel, for one night, to have what she wants.

CHAPTER TWENTY-NINE

VIOLET

1925

In the weeks after Louisa loses the baby at Plemont Bay, she becomes like a child. Violet rushes through her own chores every morning and packs a lunch of rye bread and marmite to take to Louisa's. She answers with the bare minimum, stares off into the distance when Violet is around. Violet eventually leaves her in bed and spends the day with Eugene. They go for walks, pick wildflowers to leave in vases around the kitchen.

Violet tells herself that Louisa is grieving, that she can't bear to face Violet because she can't face her own grief. It can't be because Violet had told Louisa to hope. It can't be because, once again, Violet was there to witness the unthinkable at Plemont Bay.

Still, the guilt Violet feels is like a millstone around her neck. The nightmares have gotten worse, only they are populated now by not only the man on the cliff, but Louisa's baby. Violet's legs are glued to the sand and she cannot move to save either of them.

Violet begins to think her friendship with Louisa is dangerous. How much damage could she continue to do to this woman and still call her friend? Violet wonders if there is anything, absolutely anything she can do that will make up for it. She throws herself into caring for Eugene as though he were her own.

One day in the fall, Louisa is outside when Violet arrives. She sits in a wicker chair in the garden. Violet hurries inside to make some tea, and when she comes back out, Eugene has his arms wrapped around his mum's shoulders, his head leaning on her slightly as he crouches next to her. Violet stops, uncomfortable at the display of affection. She sets the tea down and hurries back in to fetch Louisa a blanket.

Louisa looks up and smiles at Violet: the first smile Violet has seen since before she lost the baby. Violet smiles back timidly, and pours a cup of tea.

"I've got one beautiful child here, haven't I?" Louisa says as she drinks her tea, watching Eugene play. "Maybe I'll have to let that be enough."

Violet nods. She has heard enough from the doctors and nurses to know that Louisa won't be able to get pregnant again, that she can't safely bring any more children into the world.

And then, for her own news.

Violet looks at her hands, which rest on the stomach that finally, after all these years of emptiness, bears a secret. She knows it is too soon, that she shouldn't tell Louisa when she is this raw in her grief.

Louisa notices Violet doesn't have a tea cup. "Are you not having any?" she asks.

"No," Violet says. "Tea just tastes funny to me lately."

Louisa's eyes narrow, a knowing look on her face. "Why does tea taste funny?" she asks.

Violet tries to lie. "I've just had a bit of an upset stomach."

"Tea tasted off for me when I was first pregnant with Hope," Louisa says, her voice full and gurgled, like the tears would burst through at any moment. She smiles sadly at Violet. "I'd give anything for it to taste funny again."

Violet nods. She jiggles her knee.

"Violet!" Louisa says suddenly. She leans forward, toward Louisa. "You're not—"

"I'm expecting," Violet blurts out. As soon as she says the words, she regrets them, wishing she would have found a more tactful way to say it. She keeps talking, trying to hide how uncomfortable she is. "Due in the early spring, April I think."

The teacup in Louisa's hand begins to tremble. Louisa has a smile plastered on her face, and Violet sees the tears welling up behind her eyes. "Well, that's, gosh."

She looks away from Violet, straight ahead, biting her lip. Wrapped in a blanket, Louisa looks so small and uncharacteristically meek.

"I was worried about telling you," Violet continues, unable to stop talking. "Worried it might be too soon."

"No, no, it's your news, my girl," Louisa says, though Violet can tell it pains her to say it, to put on any facade of happiness.

Violet squirms inside. Will she ever stop causing this woman pain?

"I thought--forgive me, but I thought you couldn't have more children?" Louisa asks after a long silence. Violet hears a trace of bitterness in her voice. She can tell Louisa is trying not to break.

Violet had never confessed *why* she couldn't have more children. How it had finally happened, Violet didn't know. Her only explanation was that it happened right about the time she stopped obsessing so much over Plemont Bay. It was before Louisa lost her baby, in those fleeting few weeks where she was beginning to think she could be free of it. She had let her guard down; that was her only explanation. It wasn't scientific or rational, but Violet knew that was the only reason. She'd allowed herself to hope, allowed her body to make room for something other than grief, and suddenly it was bursting with a life she'd never be able to maintain.

"I don't want it," Violet says. Her confession hangs in the air. "I don't want to be a mother?"

"What do you mean, you don't want it?" For the first time, Louisa sounds cold.

"I don't," Violet says, heart beating fast. This is the closest she has come to being truthful. "I can't. I'm not fit to be a mum. I don't know how it happened. All I know is that I don't want it."

"Violet Foster, you surely can't mean that," Louisa says sternly.

Louisa is right. Of course Violet wants it. She doesn't want to be herself. She wishes she could be a good mum. And the thought of bringing a baby into the world, right after Louisa's loss— it is too unfair.

Louisa looks at her. She leans forward, and for the first time since the incident, Violet sees something like hope in her puffy, bloodshot eyes.

"You really, really don't want it?" she asks.

Violet takes a deep breath. She could be honest with her friend. She could tell her why. But looking at Louisa, so fragile and raw, Violet knows she can't.

"No. I really, really don't."

Louisa looks out again over the sea. When she speaks again, it's so quietly that Violet's not sure she heard her.

"Give me the baby, Vi," Louisa says it like it's a question.

"I—pardon?"

"You don't want the baby. I can't have more babies. Give me your baby."

"Lou, that's impossible. What would people say?" Even as she says it, Violet feels a glimmer of possibility. Louisa, who is a good, calm mother. Louisa, who has no complications with her own mother or children, who knows how to let people in, who doesn't harbor secrets: what she could save her child from if Louisa became her mother.

"Who cares what people think, Vi?" Louisa says, a desperate kind of smile on her face.

Even as Violet follows the possibility through to its implications, she already knows what she knows: though she doesn't think she can mother it, she won't give it up. The thought of watching her own baby in Louisa's arms, grow with Louisa, call her mummy, Violet can't. She will never be the kind of mother Louisa is. If she were, maybe she'd be better at giving her child what was best for them.

But looking at the hope on Louisa's face, Violet can't say anything. She can't crush the sprout of joy. So she takes Louisa's hand, and does the cruelest thing she's ever done. Worse than killing someone on the beach, worse than telling her friend to push.

"I'll think about it, Lou. Let me have a think. Now, let's get you some more tea."

Louisa, like a trusting child, hands her empty cup to her friend and waits for it to be filled.

CHAPTER THIRTY

LOUISA

1943

Friday evening before the roast Louisa hears from her neighbor Owen about a black market connection in town where she can buy flour. *Real* flour, for Yorkshire puds, which would be perfect with their dinner.

She paces the living room, bemoaning the cost of goods and the black market. "People you thought had more decency than that, Jon, buying and trading on the black market. Helena Grange, do you remember her? *Jon.*"

Jon, who had dozed off while reading his paper, startles awake. "Helena? Yes, yes—I remember her."

"Owen says she's selling her eggs for five Reichsmarks a dozen. Can you believe the nerve of her? Going to get rich off the war, happy to let her neighbors starve if they can't pay. Honestly, it makes me sick."

Jon grunts, and rests his head back on his chair, leaving Louisa to her own swirling thoughts.

That night, Louisa dreams about Eugene. She'd begun to dream about him in the most peculiar way: heavy like she's underwater, and always at Plemont Bay.

In this dream, she is walking, very early in the morning in her nightgown, her hair flowing gracefully in a way it never does when she's awake. She is looking for shells, which surprises her because that was Eugene's thing.

She looks down into the water of a tidal pool, salty and clear, and there is Eugene, tucked up into a pure white shell.

"Eugene," she says, splashing her hand frantically into the water. "Are you there?" She pulls him out of the shell, and he unfolds and expands, until he is sitting next to her on the sand. In the dream, she touches his ears, breathes in the scent of his washed hair, runs her hand across the hint of stubble on the cheeks which were once velvety soft. "Eugene," she says, over and over, her voice muted and thick.

"It's okay, Mum," he says with that crooked smile that makes her ache. His voice, unlike hers, is perfectly clear, like he is used to being underwater and it no longer phases him. He stretches out on the sand with his impossibly long legs, leaning back onto the rucksack he still wears on his back. "I've got your croissant in here somewhere." He pats his pocket, looking for it.

Louisa wants to tell him about the bombings, the white sheets she hung outside her window, the sound of the jackboots against the pavement, the balding officer who came to take count of all her animals. She wants to tell him about the radios, about Basil and Marcy, about how every time she watches a radio set leave her home, she feels as though it is one more blow against the Germans who have taken her most precious thing away.

She cannot say any of this. Instead, she says, "You remember that cliff path, the one on the North coast, between Plemont Bay and Sorel Point?"

Eugene looks at her, his lips playing in a small smile. "The one you did on your hands and knees, insisting it wasn't funny when Dad and I laughed?"

She swats his hand playfully. "Well, it wasn't. Anyway, I've been walking that path, two or three times a week."

"Mum, you swore you'd never walk it again."

"I know, Eu," she says. "But it makes me feel alive."

Eugene leans forward, touches her leg. His touch is electric in her dream state, reminding her of the days when he was a newborn and she couldn't wrap her mind around the miracle of a tiny being with limbs, grown within her, moving outside of her.

"What are you doing this summer Mum?" he asks. "Are you and

dad going to have your outdoor roasts and your day long picnics by the sea?"

Louisa sighs. "That will be tricky this year. They've blocked off the beaches and are starving us on their rations. Although your friend Basil did secure me a whole pig. We're having a shoulder roast Sunday."

Eugene laughs. "That sounds like Basil. Make sure you have it with a Yorkshire pud."

Louisa doesn't want to tell him about the flour and the black market.

"Eugene, why did you change? You weren't ready for a place like war. You used to be so sensitive."

"I still am. But you have to let people shift. That was the thing between us, Mum. There wasn't room for me to change."

Louisa is confused. Eugene stands up and walks away.

She watches him walk away, noticing as he walks that the footprints he leaves in the sand are stained red. Looking up after him, she sees his boots are dripping with blood.

"Eugene!" she calls. "Eugene, you're bleeding!"

He continues walking, straight to the sea, until he has disappeared beneath it, leaving only the deep red footprints in his wake.

She tries to run after him, but her legs are made of lead. After a few steps, she falls to the ground, unable to move. Turning, she sees another trail of red—crimson spots leading up to a woman with a bulging belly, crouched in the sand, crying out in pain, wearing a blue dress, her hair blowing in the wind, while her son hands her a piece of sea glass and runs away.

"Keep moving," she calls out to the woman, to herself, hunched over in pain. "If you keep moving you won't lose her."

But the younger Louisa cannot hear. The older Louisa crawls forward, frantically trying to cover up the red splotches in the sand, but they don't rub out, no matter how she tries.

She wakes up thrashing in the sheets, calling for the children she grew but could not save.

***

In the morning, after her cup of parsnip tea and toast (no butter), Louisa writes her address on a slip of paper and puts it in her purse. She leaves a note on the counter.

"E, gone to town, back in the afternoon, fresh berries in the colander in the sink. Love Mum x."

She pulls her bike out of the shed.

"Jon," she calls into the hog shed, raising her voice into the summer wind. "I'm going into town."

Jon appears, pushing a wheelbarrow. "What for?"

"Real flour."

"And just how are you going to get your hands on that?" he says, but with a small smirk, like he already knows Louisa's plan.

"It's the only way," Louis says, puffing out her shoulders and trying to look dignified.

Jon puts a hand on each shoulder. "Lou," he says with concern, "Those people—they are selfish and dangerous. They aren't like Basil. If they're caught, they'll pull us under with them. Are you sure we should get involved?"

"I need real flour for the Yorkshire Puds. They're Eugene's favorite."

Jon traces her cheek with one finger and says sadly, "Yorkshire Puds won't bring him back."

Louisa's lips tremble. Then she snaps, "I know it won't."

She turns away and begins to push her bike down the drive furiously. Hot tears well up in her eyes.

"Lou," Jon calls out to her when she is nearly at the end of the drive. She turns around. He is walking toward her with a small basket.

"What's this?" she asks. She peers inside to see a dozen eggs. "Jon, I can't take these. What will you say to the collector?" Every Thursday, a German collector comes around to collect eggs from their farm.

Jon shrugs. "I'll say the hens are tired. You try laying an egg in this wind. Give Helena a run for her money."

177

Louisa throws her arms around him. "Thank you," she says into his shoulder.

"He'll come back. I know it."

"Jon," she says as he pulls back.

"Yes?"

She wants to ask if she stifled Eugene, if she didn't give him room to change. But she cannot ask. She's afraid to be responsible for the answer.

"Nothing. I'll see you this afternoon."

***

By the time Louisa arrives in town, her legs are like jelly. With fewer rations, she becomes easily winded. She pulls up outside of Helena's townhome and knocks on her bright pink door.

After a moment, Helena answers, her hair still in rollers. "Gave me a right fright, knocking this early in the morning," Helena says as she moves aside to let Louisa in. "To what do I owe the pleasure?"

"Nice to see you Helena," Louisa says briskly, trying to keep from sweating too profusely as she cools down in the foyer. "I wondered if you could point me in the right direction for flour."

Helena stops with her back turned to her. Slowly she turns round. "Changed your tune a bit, have you," she says. "All high and mighty to us last week, when we were just making the most of the lot given to us, and now you want to take part in it?'

Louisa sticks her chin out. "I want to make Yorkshire Puds," she says. "And I can substitute ingredients for most things but for these I need real flour. They were Eugene's favorite."

At the mention of her missing son, Helena softens. "Well, you'll have to go to Harry LeDrue, over by the Weighbridge. He'll be able to help you."

"Thank you Helena," Louisa says, both bolstered and sickened at the same time.

"And, don't take the Esplanade," Helena warns as Louisa turns to leave. "You may run into some trouble."

"Oh?"

"With all the new workers the Germans have brought over, with the Organization Todt," Helena explains. "They like to parade them up and down the Esplanade at this hour."

"What new workers?" Louisa asks, confused. "From France?"

"You've really got your head in the sand, haven't you, Louisa?" Helena asks. "Don't you read the news?"

Louisa hadn't been reading the news, not in some time, after finding out it was mostly German propaganda.

"They're prisoners of war, from Russia, Eastern Europe, Spain," Helena says dismissively. "Here to work on fortifications."

The phrase *prisoners of war* made something tick inside of Louisa. That could be her son. Her Eugene could be a prisoner of war, back on this island. Knowing it's irrational and entirely unreasonable, Louisa still lets the thought grow inside of her: a glowing ball of hope.

Barely saying goodbye to Helena, Louisa pushes the door open, hops on her bike and races round the bend to the Esplanade.

Helena was right. A group of Germans in uniform march a herd of raggedy, impossibly thin men up the Esplanade, laughing and jeering at them as they stagger. Forty or fifty men, some looking younger than her son, wearing scraps of clothing, women's dresses, barefoot on the rough cobblestone street.

Louisa wonders if she is dreaming again as she inches closer. The men have hollow eyes, sagging skin, ribs she can see through their thin clothing. As they march past her, she scans for her son, both willing him to be there and hoping he hasn't known suffering like this.

She reaches into her basket and feels the cool, soft round of the egg. As discreetly as she can, she holds out an egg as the workers walk by. Immediately, it is grabbed out of her hand. One by one, trying to avoid the eyes of the Germans who march and jeer at the back, she hands out the dozen eggs.

The last egg in her outstretched hand is picked up by a boy with eyes the same color as her son's: startling, blazing green. Louisa is taken aback, and the egg falls to the ground, cracking on the cobblestone. Without missing a beat, the boy drops to his knees and begins licking raw egg off of the pavement.

"Oi! Move!" Yells a German from the rear.

The boy scrambles to his feet. He is already being shoved along by the throng of the crowd.

Louisa can't lose him. Reaching into her purse, she pulls out a slip of paper with her address on it, the one she brought with her this morning in case she needed it for deliveries, and tucks it into his hand. Their eyes meet, and then he is pushed forward by the crowd.

"Ma'am," the German soldier asks as he reaches her. "Was someone bothering you?"

Louisa looks at him, amazed at her own naivety. She had convinced herself, in this war, that the Germans were a decent kind of enemy, who tipped their hat in the street and at least were polite as they ripped freedoms from the Occupied. But now, watching these boys, these living skeletons march in the cold, Louisa quietly rages. Still, she says politely, "No, just dropped my basket," and walks away.

Now, without any eggs to bargain on the black market, Louisa turns and heads back home, praying that, wherever Eugene is, he is safer than that.

Jon comes out of the shed the moment Louisa pulls into the drive. She dismounts and walks past him, not saying anything.

"What's happened?" he asks, following through the door into the kitchen. "Did you run into trouble?"

Louisa sinks down on the chair in the kitchen, empty handed. She presses her fingers to her temple.

"Lou. You're scaring me," Jon says.

Finally, she looks up. "Prisoners, being marched on the Esplanade. I don't know where they're from. Russia? Spain? Some of them were wearing dresses."

To her surprise, Jon nods. "The Organization Todt," he says.

Louisa smacks her hand against her leg. "Bloody hell, Jon. And you didn't think to tell me about this?"

Jon's shoulder sag. "I was worried you would…"

"Worried about what, that I go looking for them, thinking Eugene was there?"

"Yes."

"Well, I did." Louisa puts her hands to her face. She thinks about the boy with Eugene's eyes. She looks at Jon again and speaks more softly. "What are they doing here?"

"They're here to build fortifications, against a possible allied invasion."

"Well they don't look like they could build much. I could break them in half with my two fingers." Louisa shudders.

"I don't think they're being paid, or given much food. Living conditions are pretty terrible. Lou—I'm sorry I didn't tell you."

Louisa leans back in her chair, thinking about Eugene's words in her dream: *there was never room to change.* "It's fine, Jon," she says, feeling weary.

They sit in the thick silence of their safe, warm farmhouse while spring blooms around them.

CHAPTER THIRTY-ONE

VIOLET

1925

Weeks go by, and Violet begins to show. Louisa says nothing about their previous conversation. Violet convinces herself that Louisa is embarrassed she said something, or maybe that she's forgotten completely.

But Louisa is not the type of woman to be embarrassed by anything, and Violet knows, by the way Louisa asks after her health, by the way she touches her own empty stomach, that she hasn't forgotten.

She thinks sometimes about the way Louisa would love her if she gave her this baby. She thinks about how much easier it would be to be a doting auntie than a mum again, about how *good* it would be to see Louisa with her arms full again. But then she feels the baby kick. She thinks about its heartbeat, drumming inside of her, and she cannot think of letting it go. She is bound, for better or worse, to her child.

David has noticed Violet is showing, Violet can tell by the way his gaze lingers over her stomach when she stands up from the table. He is either too polite or too self-conscious to say anything.

Finally, Violet cannot stand it any longer. One Saturday morning, they sit around the breakfast table. David mops up the egg yolk with his toast. Violet, still nauseous, moves the egg around with her fork.

"Where is the old crib?" she says abruptly into the silence.

David stares at her. Even the way he blinks reminds her of a Jersey cow: slow and sad. "The crib?"

"Yes, David, the baby crib," Violet snaps. "The one your parents gave us after we were married."

"It's in the barn," he says. His eyes travel to her stomach. Instinctively, Violet pulls at her blouse.

"Right," she says as she stands up to clear the plates.

"Will we be needing it, then?" David asks.

Violet pauses, her back to David. She turns around, and for possibly the first time in her marriage, she lets him look at her. With a plate in each hand, she lets her blouse tighten around her stomach, and for an instant, lets herself be the wife who gives her husband what he's always wanted. "Yes," she says. She feels full of power and mystery.

His eyes travel up her body. He stands up, walks toward her, reaches out a hesitant hand and puts it on her stomach. His face breaks into a smile, and she feels one tug at her own lips.

"You'll be a perfect mum," he whispers.

For one beautiful moment, she believes him. She imagines their life with a little set of feet pattering around them, someone to help her in the garden, making pies.

Then, she turns toward the sink and sees the flowers on the counter that Louisa picked for her last week. Immediately she feels sick to her stomach.

Thrusting the plate with the uneaten egg into David's hands, Violet heaves over the sink.

"Are you alright, Violet?" he asks. Hesitantly, he touches her hair. She bristles at his touch.

"Fine," she answers sharply. "I just need a minute."

He pulls his boots on and opens the door. Violet grips the side of the sink until her knuckles turn white.

When his footsteps are finally outside, Violet sinks to the ground. Putting her head in her hands, she tries not to cry: for the pain she cannot stop causing, for everything just out of reach.

***

183

Violet sits outside in the fading autumn light, waiting for David to come in from the potato field. She listens to the tide roll in, wraps her shawl around her against the cool breeze.

He finally shows up, in his overalls, muddy boots and hat. "Violet," he says as he approaches the house. He looks surprised to see her just sitting outside, not tending to or cleaning something. "Alright?"

Violet slides over to make room for him on the bench. "Fancy a sit-down?" She tries to sound casual. In all their years of marriage, they've never had a sit down like this on the bench.

David sits down heavily on the bench. He stretches his feet out in front of him and pulls off his boots.

"Nice night," he says. "Are you sure you're quite well, Violet?"

Violet stares straight ahead, wondering how to say what she's been mulling over for weeks.

"Do you ever feel afraid to want something?"

"I'm not sure what you mean," David says.

"I mean, do you ever feel like you don't deserve to be happy?"

He looks at the hand resting instinctively on her stomach. "Is this about the baby?" he asks.

She turns toward him, torn between what she is going to say and what she wants to say. Finally, she says, "I don't– I don't think I want the baby, David."

"What?"

"I don't want it. I can't raise it."

"I don't understand."

"I think we should give the baby to someone else."

"The baby?" David leans forward. "You mean *our* baby?"

Violet turns toward him, surprised to see the flash of anger in his eyes.

"Of course I mean our baby," Violet says, cheeks flushing.

"Just checking, because you're talking about all this like it's a recipe." His voice is hard, brittle.

"I know it's not a recipe. It's just, there are things you don't know about me David."

"Clearly," David says, standing up. He turns toward the house.

"I won't be a good mother," Violet calls after him.

David pauses at the door. "I don't know why this life isn't enough for you Violet. I thought you wanted children. I thought we both did. But that baby is not just yours. And if I have to raise it myself, I will."

Violet wonders again why there is always a gap between what she means and what she says.

***

In early December, Violet and Louisa make mince pies in Louisa's kitchen. It's an unusually warm day for early December and they take a break outside.

They sit in silence, listening to the distant waves. Taking a deep breath, Violet says as casually as she can, "Louisa."

"Yes, my dear?"

Violet wants to say that she can't give her the baby, that she tried to tell David and it didn't go well. But before she can say anything, Louisa says, "Oh, I nearly forgot. Come look at these, Violet."

Louisa points to a row of freshly dug-up dirt. "Can you see this?"

Violet smiles at the messy garden work. "It looks like you've put some bulbs in."

"I have. My first time. I planted irises in honor of Hope."

Violet nods quietly. The baby inside her kicks.

"And I planted daffodils. To celebrate new life."

She smiles at Violet's expanding stomach. She looks with such longing and hopefulness that Violet wants to cry.

Violet tells herself, *it is okay to keep your own baby,* even as she feels she has no right to it. She looks at the woman who has lost so much, on account of Violet, and knows she cannot deny her this.

As though she can read her mind, Louisa says, "Has your mind changed, Violet? About the baby?"

Even as she says it, she brims with a fragile hope that makes Violet want to weep.

Violet cannot bring herself to talk about her conversation with David, about the way he looks at her now like she is unsafe.

She pats Louisa's hands. "Those pies will be ready, I expect," she says.

Walking into the kitchen, Violet dabs at her eye with a tea towel. She doesn't know how to fix the mess she's gotten into without hurting everyone around her. She knows, no matter what she does, she'll be the one to hurt the most.

Chapter Thirty-Two

Violet

1926

On a bright, crisp, Monday morning in early spring Violet is hanging out her wash when she feels a sharp, stabbing pain come over her body. *It can't be time,* she thinks. She rushes inside, to make a soup for dinner. She folds a basket of sheets, bending over to breathe through each contraction. When David comes in for lunch, she is trying to sweep the floor, doubling over and clutching her stomach.

"Violet," he says sharply, rushing to her side. She drops the broom as a contraction overtakes her. She leans forward and bites her lip so she won't scream. "I'll get Louisa," he says, opening the door.

"*No,*" Violet says sharply. The plan was always to have Louisa at the birth, but today, Violet doesn't want her there. She knows she cannot accept Louisa's help when she is about to hurt either Louisa or David. She wants a few moments with this child that are only hers.

"There's no time, David," she says. "You'll have to help me."

She expects David to squirm, to turn white or to say he can't do it. Instead, he seems to step into himself in a way she hasn't seen before. He nods with the quiet capability of a man who has delivered calves, pigs, and sheep. "I'll get the water," he says. He smiles at Violet. "We're going to do this Violet. We're going to have a baby."

Violet grins back, her teeth chattering. Then she is overwhelmed by another contraction. She silently focuses on the handle of a cabinet.

The birth is surprisingly quick for a first baby. Violet is amazed at how calm she feels, just her and David. David could be talking about the potato harvest, the way he coaches Violet on when to push.

Violet gives birth to a girl, Marcy Iris Foster. "She's gorgeous," David says as he picks her up. His sleeves are rolled up and his shirt is unbuttoned, but as Violet looks at him, sinking back into her pillows, she thinks for the first time that she never noticed how handsome he is.

"Look what you've done," David says, bringing Marcy over to her. He places her daughter in her arms. Violet expects to be overwhelmed by love, by the bond between mother and child that Louisa always spoke about. Instead, Marcy begins to cry and Violet is unsure of what to do.

"Do you need help?" David asks, a look of concern on his face.

Violet knows he has helped plenty of young calves but this is different. With an onset of new vulnerability and exposure, she pulls the sheet up over her. "No," she says, a little too sharply. "No, I can sort this out."

David backs up, hands at his sides. "Right," he says. "I'll er, I'll make a cup of tea."

He leaves the room, and Violet looks down at the bundle in her arms, and wonders why the only emotion she can conjure is grief.

***

Two days later, Violet sits in the nursery, rocking Marcy next to her in the bassinet. Violet is dressed and she has done her hair, despite having no sleep the night before. Her secret to looking so put together? Violet let Marcy cry while she got dressed. This pains her to remember.

Violet's life overnight has become a long string of failures: because her dress doesn't fit, because the laundry is overflowing with dirty diapers and because really, all she wanted was for someone else to get up with Marcy in the night. She could not find the delight that the other mothers talked about, the delight that was so obvious on David's face.

Marcy is a fussy baby. She cries and then she screams. Violet tries to pick her up to calm her but the screams seem to crawl into Violet's head, reverberating there until she wants to scream too, and she finds herself sobbing, holding her baby, saying, "I'm sorry, sorry, sorry."

Violet's thoughts are interrupted by footsteps coming up the stairs. Louisa, in characteristic bluntness, bursts through the nursery door.

"I've just heard the news, my girl," she says, "Although you should have told me, when you were in labor. I would have helped."

She fills the room with her large presence and stands over Marcy. "Well isn't she just," she coos. "May I?"

Violet nods, unable to bring herself to meet Louisa's eyes.

Louisa leans down and picks up Marcy with a sense of reverence that only amplifies Violet's shame. Tears well up in Louisa's eyes as she holds Marcy to her chest, leans down to kiss her cheek. "Hello, my gorgeous girl," she says.

"Her name is Marcy," Violet says. She is surprised by the sharpness in her own voice.

Louisa raises her eyebrows at her. "Of course it is," she says. "Now, Vi, we've got to discuss how this arrangement will work. I expect you'll want to keep her here until you sort the milk out, but Jon's got the room all ready for whenever you're ready. I wasn't even going to tell him our plan until I was sure of what you'd decided; didn't want to get his hopes up, but when I heard she'd been born I just couldn't keep it to myself. The four of us should get together of course, have a chat about how all of this will work."

Violet sighs. In a voice that breaks, she says, "Louisa."

"Yes?"

"I can't give you the baby." She notices that she doesn't say Marcy's name.

Louisa smiles at her, a strained, thin smile that seems to take tremendous effort. "Oh, Violet, don't worry. Of course you can't."

"David would never have it. And I know—I know I said I didn't want it, but I can't give it up, Lou. You understand, don't you?"

Louisa stares straight ahead. She nods without making eye contact. Her arms continue to hold Marcy.

"I know it's not fair, Lou. You're such a good mum. You should never have lost Hope. And I want more than anything for you to have a baby but. But I can't give you mine."

"No, it was silly of me to have asked," Louisa says. Her voice sounds like it is going to break.

The words hang between them. Violet tells herself, *it is okay to keep your own baby*, even as she feels that she has no right to it.

Louisa speaks. "I imagine you're exhausted. I should let you get on and have a lie-down."

With trembling hands, she puts Marcy back in her bassinet.

"Louisa—" Violet says.

Louisa stops. She meets Violet's eyes. Violet cannot say anything to convey what she feels.

Louisa nods. She turns and leaves.

Marcy begins to scream and Violet leans back in the rocker, covering her face with her hands.

***

In the weeks and months that follow, Violet stays away from Louisa's house, out of shame or anger, she isn't sure. At Christmas, Violet leaves flowers at the end of the lane, but doesn't dare go up it.

Instead of having play dates every few weeks in Louisa's garden or at the beach, she begins to have playdates with other ladies from church, ladies who never seem to have a problem getting pregnant, who add more children like they are adding decorations, easily and seemingly without thought. Violet pretends she is like them, waltzing through motherhood unencumbered by ghosts. She drags Marcy along. As the days turn into months and then to years, Violet tries not to notice that none of the other mothers reach out to Marcy or try to include her; that none of the mothers have become friends with Violet the way Louisa did.

She waits and waits for Louisa to walk back into her life, to pick up where they left off. But Louisa never does. Things become strained between them, awkward and halting where they once were smooth and easy. Violet takes it as punishment, tries to accept that this is just the price of the culmination of what she's done.

One morning, when Marcy is six months old, Louisa shows up on the front drive. Eager to see her friend, Violet rushes outside.

"Lou," she says breathlessly. "Gosh, it's good to see you."

"Hello, Violet," says Louisa. Violet stops short at the formal use of her name.

Thrusting a wrapped paper package into her hand, Louisa says, "This is for you. And for—the baby."

"Thank you, Lou," Violet says quietly, holding the package in her arms.

"Yes, well I don't need them anymore, do I?" Louisa says with a forced brightness. "And, I'm happy for you Violet. Really."

Violet looks into her friend's face and sees the cloud of grief move across it. Violet doesn't know how to enter that. She wants to say, *I would so rather this be you*, but that feels too trite and too sad, because it could have been, if Violet were a real friend. Her grief and Louisa's joy, that is easier for Violet. She can put her own feelings to the side, and live in celebration of her friend. But when it is Violet who has what Louisa most wants, Violet cannot live with Louisa's pain.

So, although she has not had a lovely tea, or a lovely few months since Louisa walked out of her life, she says, "We've just had the most wonderful tea with some ladies from church."

"Oh?" Louisa asks, surprised.

"Yes," Violet continues in a rush. "And I've got some extra biscuits. Would you care to have one?"

Louisa looks at her for a long moment, like she is trying to figure out just what Violet means.

"No thank you," she finally says. "I've got to get back."

Violet nods, and watches as her friend walks away.

Inside the house, she opens the package. It contains all the booties, sweaters, and hats Violet had knitted for Louisa, in whites and grays and pale yellows.

CHAPTER THIRTY-THREE

MARCY

1943

The night of the soiree at St. Brelarde's Hotel, Marcy stands pressed against the wall, stomach tucked into the back of her ribs, trying to make herself invisible.

She wonders again, looking at the decked-out dance hall, bunting and ribbon strung across the ceiling, why she agreed to it. Maybe she thought she could be like Penelope Campbell. Maybe she thought she could just be a teenager, having a bit of fun.

She realizes, standing against the wall, that she is nothing like Penelope Campbell. She is incapable of frivolous fun. The only feeling she can muster is guilt.

Marcy looks across the dance floor. Annette is the one who is *actually* having fun. She had practically danced her way through the front door of the hotel, leaving Marcy's side as soon as they were through it for a handsome blonde soldier. Marcy glimpses her now, across the dim, smoky dance floor. She is twirling and laughing with a different man.

Marcy dodges a waiter coming out of the kitchen, carrying a beautifully arranged tray of foods she hasn't seen in months: camembert, fig, jam, and steak. On the stage, Billie Rodgers, a girl from her class, sings in a blue glittery dress. It seems brazen and risky to Marcy, to stand up there, where everyone can see her. She wonders what Billie's mum would think about her being here.

What would her own mum think? Marcy swallows a pit of dread. Involuntarily, she pictures the shocked crumpling of her mum's face, finding out Marcy wasn't actually at Susan's studying. Her mum, who cares so much about what others think, hearing news of her being at a party with a load of Germans.

Standing in the dim light, watching the other girls flip and toss their hair, touch the wrist of a German coyly, looking up at them from the corners of their eyes, Marcy swallows. *I'm not like them*, she thinks. *I'm part of the Resistance.* Even as she says it to herself, she cannot make herself believe it.

She touches the pearl necklace against her chest. She almost hadn't worn it today, but Annette had insisted she needed something to go with the black dress.

"Have you got anything, Marcy? Anything grown up and flattering?" Annette asked earlier that week as she rummaged through Marcy's drawers.

"I don't think so," Marcy had mumbled.

Annette pulled the necklace out of the top drawer. "Gosh, where did you get these pearls? They're lovely."

Marcy looked at the pearls. "Those don't look quite right for the dress," she tried to protest.

"They're perfect. You *must* wear these, Marcy." Without asking, she clasped them around Marcy's neck.

They both looked at Marcy's reflection in the mirror.

"Wow," Annette whispered. "You don't even look like yourself."

Marcy swallowed and thought of her mother.

Now, she runs her hands along the pearl string.

It's just one night, Marcy insists to herself. *I'm not like them.* But still, she cannot fully shake the thought.

Beginning to feel claustrophobic and panicked, Marcy looks for the exit. She'll explain to Annette later, she thinks as she begins to walk.

"Mary? Is that you?"

Franc's voice is so soft, Marcy is surprised she hears it. She turns around, coming face to face with vibrant burnt orange.

"Hello there," she says, a little breathless, hand still on the string of pearls.

He's a handsome boy. A straight nose, sweet smile. In ordinary times, she can't believe he'd ever be interested in her—but in Jersey in 1940 there's a surplus of men, a shortage of girls. He's so tall that his presence feels intimidating. Marcy steps back to look up at him.

"You look taller than the last time I saw you," she blurts out.

He laughs. "Perhaps, the boots. But it is very good to see you. I have thought of you."

"I've thought about you too." Marcy feels herself blush a deep crimson as she says it.

He reaches out his pinky finger, grazes it against her own. She looks at his dimple. When she'd come in, she was trying to sort out everyone else's color. Now, the whole room is deep orange.

He says, "Would you care to dance?"

Marcy's heart races as she clutches her purse.

Furtive Fritz is listening, be careful what you say. The saying is everywhere amongst the islanders—Peter even said it this morning. Marcy hears it now in her head, vibrating around inside, making her dizzy.

But Franc is a magnet, a current of color, and she cannot resist stepping into it. She holds his pinky finger, wondering how such a small touch can light up her whole body. He puts his hand on the small of her back and steps closer.

"Let me just put my purse down," Marcy says breathlessly.

Franc wraps his arm around her waist, and Marcy cannot breathe. She has never danced with a man before, never felt arms like that on the small of her back. He smells like citrus.

Suddenly, Eugene pops into her mind, Eugene who always smelled of cedar and lavender, and she feels confused.

"You are very beautiful, Mary," says Franc, leaning in toward her.

"Do you have a girl back home?" she asks.

"No," he says tenderly. "Never had a girl but you."

"I find that hard to believe," she says. She has to tip her chin all the way back to see him.

He lifts her hand and spins her around. The whole dance floor is orange.

But only for a moment. He pulls her close, traces her face with his finger, stops at her chin, and she stares at his frosty blue eyes thinking she might drown in them. And then the music stops, everyone claps, and Marcy has the feeling of one who has just fallen asleep unintentionally.

"I'm so sorry," she says, feeling flustered. "What's the time?"

Franc checks his watch as the band begins to play another tune. "Twenty-five past eight," he says. "Are you alright?"

Marcy is conflicted, ridden with both guilt and desire. "I need to sit down," she says.

"Of course," says Franc, offering his arm. She takes it and they walk to the table where her purse is. Plopping into her chair for show, she stretches her legs out and sighs.

"Can I offer you a drink?" He asks politely.

"That would be lovely," Marcy says.

As he walks away, Marcy looks at the other girls around the dance hall. They are leaning into soldiers, laughing, throwing back champagne. Marcy judges them, until she remembers she looks like one of them. If any of them go back home and tell their mothers that she was at the St. Brelade hotel tonight, she'll be marked just like them: put in a box checked *betraying one's country*.

A tall, voluptuous woman stands up. She's gorgeous, maybe the most beautiful woman Marcy has ever seen. Her deep auburn hair is pinned back, and she wears a red dress that hugs every curve in her hip. She smokes a long cigarette. Someone hands her a glass of champagne. As she picks it up, someone bumps her arm—or she tips it intentionally— and it splatters on her dress.

"Well now I've done it," she says loudly, laughing as she sways a little, looking tipsy. "I must be sauced. On a new dress, too."

Three Germans stand up immediately and offer her handkerchiefs, which she brushes off with a wave. "Thank you boys, but that won't do it," she laughs. "Point me to the ladies' room."

The lady saunters off, her dress shimmying back and forth as she moves.

Marcy watches her saunter off, her dress shimmying back and forth as she moves. She stands up, turning every head as she moves across the dance hall.

The lady walks right by Marcy's table. To Marcy's surprise, she leans over and whispers in her ear, "Meet me in the loo."

Marcy blushes. Had this gorgeous woman actually spoken to her? And why ask her to meet in the loo?

Marcy looks around, sure that everyone is watching her. She waits until the woman disappears around the corner, then stands up and follows her, willing herself to blend in.

Inside, the ladies' room, the woman towers over the sink in her sparkly heels, dabbing her dress with a towel. She glances up at Marcy, raising her perfectly trimmed eyebrows. Her color is scarlet, deeper than the dress. Marcy feels spellbound by her.

"Lock the door," says the woman. "Hurry, before anyone else tries to come in."

Marcy turns the lock, her fingers fumbling. "I'm sorry," she begins the conversation. "I think you might have me confused with someone else."

Bernadette stops dabbing her dress. "You sell crystal sets, right?"

"I—pardon?"

"Crystal sets. The wireless. I've seen you all over St. Helier."

Marcy feels dizzy. Was what she was doing so obvious?

"I—I'm not sure what you mean," she says quickly. She's not about to announce to a woman at a Jerry dance that she works for the Resistance.

The woman waves her hand breezily. "I'm Bernadette Braun. The worst Jerrybag in town." She laughs, but it is hollow and pained. "According to any patriotic Jerseyman you ask."

Marcy swallows, unsure of what to say.

"Never mind that I've got a sick son to feed. Never mind that half of Jersey is willing to sell quietly on the black market but if I do it publicly I'm worse than the lot." Bernadette leans forward. "I need radios," she says. "My friends need radios."

"Why?" Marcy asks.

"Why does anyone? Hope? Assurance that the Allies are, in fact, coming for us?"

She goes back to dabbing her dress. "I can pay you in money, but I think I've got something more valuable for you than that."

"What?"

"Information. Things we overhear."

"What would we do with that?" Marcy asks. Her heart is pounding inside her chest.

"Whatever you want that could cause a fuss. Steal, pillage, make life difficult. I read about the V signs in the Bullion District."

Marcy squirms. She had told Basil not to paint the V for Victory sign all over the road and houses, but he hadn't listened. She worried that the blue paint that lingered on his arm for days would give him away, but Basil seemed untouchable.

Bernadette snaps her purse shut. She looks at Marcy, pressing her red lips together.

Shimmery maroon, Marcy thinks.

"What you're doing is dangerous work, you know. The Germans aren't daft."

"I know," Marcy says, thinking about Franc's dimple.

"You're brave," Bernadette says with a small, approving smile. "Young too—always good to have youth on your side in the war."

She begins walking toward the door. "You get me radios. I'll give you names," she says over her shoulder.

Marcy doesn't know what to say. "Er—okay," she finally stammers.

"But, just remember how this is going to look for you, being here tonight. Associating with me. People talk, you know."

She turns and walks out the door.

Marcy composes herself in the mirror, trying to stop her hands shaking.

"I'm sorry," she says to Franc when she finally returns to the table. He stands up, and she feels him, close to her. She wants to reach out and touch the fabric of the shirt on his chest, wants to know if he feels as warm and soft as she imagines he will. Instead, she says, "I'm not feeling well. I'll be going now."

"Oh?" he says with concern, tucking a strand of hair behind her ear. "May I walk you home then?"

She wants to say yes. She wants to lean into him, to soak up this attention, to revel in what it feels like to be wanted.

"No, thank you, Franc. I'm quite alright."

She turns and walks quickly into the night, thinking that it isn't too far to Susan's—that she could get there on her bike in twenty minutes, so long as no one stops her.

She thinks about how she'll have to tell Basil about the dance. She'll focus on Bernadette, the types of cheeses served, maybe even Billie Rodgers dancing on stage. Certainly though, she won't tell him about the soldier, the color of raging autumn, who smells like citrus and dances like he is part–bird. That soldier, as far as Marcy is concerned, is history.

"Mary?" Marcy hears the soft voice slice through the quiet of the night.

Against her better judgment, she turns.

CHAPTER THIRTY-FOUR

VIOLET

1940

As talk of war comes closer to home, Violet notices a change in her daughter. Lately, Marcy has begun to talk about colors. She lays them out in front of her and uses them as a roadmap, labeling people in their shades, categorizing the world around her by pigment. It is as though the war has given her a new filter and voice.

Marcy asks her mum things like, "Did Grandad ever tell you his color?" while she gazes absentmindedly out the window. "Was he a gold, Mum? I wish I could be a gold, not boring old beige."

Violet pretends to ignore Marcy. She keeps her head down, focuses on the daily chores necessary to running a household: weeding the flower beds, frying the eggs, sweeping the porch, washing and ironing the sheets. Thinking about colors is for people who have the luxury of both innocence and imagination, both things Violet has put away for quite some time.

But she does know colors. This is what she keeps hidden from her daughter, her husband, herself. Colors are her first language, the way she is most adept at seeing the world. Before Plemont Bay, Violet knew her mother to be turquoise, herself to be like sea glass. She used to absorb information eagerly, to possess a love of learning. She used to connect with her mother over their curiosity about the world around them.

After Plemont Bay, though, her mother changed. She became stormier, and turquoise didn't fit her anymore. Colors didn't work, she realized. They were a whimsical, nonsensical way of looking at the world. People are people. She put the frivolity of colors and people behind her.

Except in her dreams. Violet's dreams are full of color, the people around her filled to the brim with different shades. Louisa is eggplant purple. Peter is a forest green. Eugene scatters the color of daffodil everywhere he goes. And her daughter is gold. Gold like a wheat field at sunset in late summer; gold like a starfish in the sand at the beach.

Violet's dreams are more real to her than waking. In them she becomes the color of sea glass again, takes on a freer, more transparent self. Her daughter shines with her true color, not obscuring it the way she does when she's awake. Louisa's baby Hope, a pale pink, stretches to her full size, which is wider than the sky.

Except always, just as Violet begins to settle into these dreams, she is returned to Plemont Bay, running from a world full of color to one devoid of it.

Before he leaves for the war, Eugene stops by. He comes just before eleven, Violet's quietest hour of the day, when Peter is out exploring and Marcy is at Gran's, trimming roses.

"Eugene," Violet answers the door breathlessly. Behind her, a pile of laundry is scattered on the kitchen table. Her nephew Arthur has already been around that morning and shared news about enlisting.

Violet looks at Eugene and her heart breaks. For eighteen years, she has watched the curly mop of hair on his head grow, his legs become long and gangly. She has known this infectious smile and gentle manner her entire life. Eugene is an old soul. He cannot be sent to a place like war. He's not made for it.

"Sorry to pop by unannounced like this, Miss Vi," he says easily. Even when Louisa dropped her nickname, Eugene never did. He's had an easy and familiar way with her his whole life, and Violet loves him for it.

Violet thinks about how sad Marcy will be that she's missed him. She knows how Marcy feels about Eugene: anyone with eyes can see she's hopelessly in love.

"Please, Eugene, come in," she says. "I'll put a cuppa on."

Eugene sits at the kitchen table, all legs and knees. "I ran into Marcy this morning, at Greve de Lecq," he says, and the hint of a blush creeps up his neck.

Violet thinks first about how late that must have made Marcy for pruning roses, and how she was sure to hear about it next time she spoke with her mum— something Violet undertook these days only when absolutely necessary.

"Yes, well," she says, not knowing how else to respond. "I heard you're headed off to war."

"Word travels fast."

"Small island."

Eugene sighs, stretches out his legs. "The thing is, Miss Vi, when I enlisted, I thought it would make me a hero. I thought it would finally make my mum."

"Eugene, she *does* see you."

"As a grown man, not a little boy."

Violet is quiet.

"But when–if–I come back," he continues in a rush, "I'd like permission to see Marcy."

"My Marcy?" Violet asks. She is surprised. Not that he would see what she sees in Marcy, but that he would be thinking about this now.

Eugene nods. His face turns crimson. "I can't say anything to her now. If I don't come home I want her to be able to move on. But when I think about my life, she's the only person I want in it. I'm going to marry her one day, if she'll let me."

Violet is surprised at his honesty, candor, and at his ability to believe that perhaps life could work out for him the way he hopes it will. For a moment, she pictures her daughter with Eugene, happy and whole in marriage in a way Violet has never known.

Louisa would be Marcy's mother-in-law. She thinks about Marcy, going round to Louisa's for tea, leaving Violet at home. In her mind, they grow and weave together, forming a bond that is entirely separate from her. Marcy gains another mother: a better mother. Maybe the mother she should have had.

201

She thinks about the ashes of their friendship. Would a future shared grandchild alleviate some of the past hurts and pain?

Violet doesn't know. She doesn't know if the happiness of those she loves most would only bring her pain.

Eugene mistakes her silence for disapproval. He stands up, straightens his shirt. "Of course, I don't need an answer yet," he says. "Let's wait and see if I make it back first, shall I?"

Violet looks at him, is overcome with love and protection for this boy who has felt more like a son. "Have you told your mum you've enlisted?"

"Not yet." Eugene shifts, looking uncomfortable. "Off to do that now."

"Eugene."

"Yes?"

"You don't have to be so bruised, around your mum. What I mean is, you don't have to act so tough."

"I don't think I'm exactly acting tough," Eugene says, looking offended.

"Why else would you be spending time with a girl like Penelope Campbell?"

Eugene raises his eyebrows. "It's—that's not serious. I hope you know that. What I just said about Marcy—"

Violet waves a hand away. "Do you want to go to war?"

Eugene's face looks pained. Violet knows that he doesn't want to go, of course he doesn't, but he doesn't feel he has a choice.

Violet watches him walk away, feeling that once again she is responsible for hurting the people she most loves.

***

Eugene's visit reminds Violet of a time a few years back, at Peter's christening. Another surprise pregnancy, another wave of guilt made worse only by David's complete joy. By this time, she and Louisa barely spoke to each other. Marcy was twelve and well in love with Eugene, obvious to everyone except herself.

Violet had insisted the whole family wear new clothes, and spent days making cakes and scones to have in the churchyard afterwards. While she baked, she wondered if Louisa would be there. She told herself it wouldn't matter to her either way.

The morning of the christening, looking out into the pews, she was both shocked and thrilled that Louisa came. It had been so long, she thinks. Maybe Louisa was ready to turn over a new leaf. Maybe they could finally put the past behind them and begin the friendship anew. After all, the christening had been announced for weeks, Louisa simply wouldn't have come to church if she didn't want to be there.

Violet was antsy as she greeted people in the receiving line after church, switching Peter from one arm to the other.

Finally, Louisa was next in line.

"So lovely to have you here," Violet said, uncontainable joy spilling out over her as she greeted Louisa. "Really. Thank you so much for coming."

"Well, Eugene was the altar boy, so I had to come," said Louisa.

"Oh," Violet said, taking a step back. The disappointment hit like a pit inside her stomach. Louisa hadn't been there for her after all.

"But, what a lovely boy," Louisa continued, looking at Peter. And then, after a moment's hesitation, she asked, "Can I hold him?"

Violet handed him over. Louisa held him in her arms the way she held Marcy that first time: eyes closed, breathing in deeply, pressing her lips to her head. "Hello, little Peter," she said warmly, waving a finger at him. He grabbed it, giggling.

Deflated, Violet noticed how at peace Peter, who didn't like strangers, seemed with Louisa. Unable to suppress the urge, she reached out to grab him back.

"Oh," Louisa said, eyebrows raised. She handed Peter back.

Violet pulled him to her chest, possessively. Then, looking at Louisa's empty arms, she once again felt a deep pity and grief she didn't know how to express.

Louisa said, "Marcy looks lovely today."

And Violet, who was self-conscious about what she had, and somehow thought that openly enjoying it would make Louisa's pain worse, tried to downplay the daughter and the dress she was proud of. "Oh, that," she said casually. "I tried to tell her that color wasn't suited to her frame, but she insisted."

She didn't know what she hoped for: maybe that Louisa would laugh, or that it would thaw the frost between them. Instead, Louisa frowned at her like she was seeing her for the first time.

"Take care, Violet," she said, and moved along.

And Violet, who had her arms and home so full, wondered why she felt so empty.

Later, as Louisa and Eugene were leaving, Violet watched Louisa put a hand on Marcy's arm, and say something that made her daughter smile.

What had she said? Violet wondered the rest of the day, the thought consuming her so that she couldn't even think about what a success the christening had been.

She tried to ask Marcy casually that night as they cleaned up after dinner. "Looked like you had a nice time with Eugene today," she said.

Marcy smiled sheepishly. "Yes," she answered simply. Violet waited for her to say more, but she only blushed into the teacup she was drying.

"What did Louisa say to you?" As Violet asked, she thought her voice sounded harsh, unnatural.

Marcy paused, like she wasn't sure whether or not she should answer.

"You can tell me," Violet encouraged her. "Go on. What did she say?"

Marcy paused. She turned away as she stacked the teacup back into the cupboard. "She said I looked beautiful in peach."

***

When the house is empty again, Eugene gone and Marcy not home yet, Violet abandons her laundry and begins frantically knitting a thick pair of socks. She hopes the stitches will say all she can't: *I love you, I love you, I'm sorry.*

CHAPTER THIRTY-FIVE

MARCY

1943

In the cool, wintry air outside of the St. Brelade hotel, Marcy and Franc walk toward the ocean, even though Marcy knows the beach will be off-limits. For five minutes, they walk in an awkward silence.

"I miss being on the water," Marcy says. All access to boats has been restricted since the Germans took over. Even fishermen are only allowed out certain hours of the day, which almost never align with the proper tides, and they had to paint their boats so that they could be seen from shore.

Marcy can't look at Franc, because even in the darkness, all she can see is burnt orange. He's beautiful, and also the enemy. She worries about what will happen if she lets herself look at him again. This is not a predicament Marcy is used to, and the irony—that he is a person she cannot have—is not lost on her.

But Franc takes a step closer to her. His hand brushes her fingers, and his touch is warm, electric.

"Mary," he says quietly, his words a breath that circles around her. "I've not stopped thinking about you since I saw you the first time, the day you dropped your pearls."

"Well, you should stop thinking about me," Marcy says, her voice cracking slightly. She looks down.

"Ending the war is more possible than that," he says, and his fingers reach up to her face, tracing the outline of her ear.

Marcy hears other soldiers around her, the drunk yells and laughter in the dark of the night. "I shouldn't be out here; it's after curfew. I do need to get home."

"I'm an officer in the Organization Todt. No one is going to touch you, so long as you're with me."

The way he says the name, *Organization Todt*, sends a shiver down Marcy's spine. It sounds so official; so like war.

"What's the Organization Todt?" asks Marcy. "I've not heard of it." Franc smirks. "Above my pay grade, I'm afraid. I can only say it's very important to the war effort as a whole. And, being an officer makes me untouchable. You're safe, with me."

Marcy hears the rush of the sea just a few feet away, the heavy pounding of her own heart. She takes a step backward. "It's dangerous, Franc. You and me, we're enemies."

He steps forward toward her, closing the gap between them. She clenches her fists together to keep herself from throwing her arms around his neck.

"Mary, we might be a lot of things. But one thing I can assure you: I am not your enemy."

He puts his arms on her waist, and she cannot resist him anymore. She steps forward, touches his neck, puts her face into his chest. She is young and curious, he is handsome and new.

He looks at her and she knows he is going to kiss her. Even as she thinks it, her stomach drops, and she wishes he were Eugene.

Their lips meet once, and then twice, until Marcy, normally level-headed and sensible, has forgotten both the war and the radios, and only knows a hunger for the man who does not even know her name.

***

The clock in Susan's front hall reads ten past three in the morning by the time Marcy makes it there. She tiptoes in, willing her feet not to cause the staircase to creak.

"How was it?" Susan murmurs as Marcy climbs into the li-lo on the floor. She has the voice of a person who has not yet slept, waiting for Marcy and Annette to come home.

Marcy thinks about the night in flashes: Bernadette's red dress, spilled champagne, *Tea for Two*, the cold night air, Franc's hands on the nape of her neck, his thumb caressing the space behind her ear, the radios. She thinks about her body, about Franc's, resistance and collaboration like two ends of a breath. A whispered promise to meet him by the rocks at St. Brelade's Bay on Monday, the thrill of anticipating his hands on her waist again.

"Oh, it was fine," she says casually. "You didn't miss much. Not something I'll go to again."

Susan sighs, and lays back down. "I told you," she says smugly. "At least you've not been caught."

Yes, Marcy thinks in the darkness.

An hour later, Annette stumbles in, giggling as she bumps into the dresser, smelling like smoke. Susan is asleep now, snoring softly.

"Marcy," she whispers loudly. "Are you awake?" Marcy sits up.

"Oh good," she says, in a normal voice. Marcy worries about Susan's mum coming in. "I had the most lovely time, didn't you? All those men, all those songs."

"Mmm," Marcy says, keeping her tone noncommittal.

"And the *dancing*! It was glorious to dance. That's the worst part about these wars, the way they take all the fun away."

Marcy thinks, with pleasure and guilt, that she'd not had so much fun in years.

"Mmm," she says again, trying to speak quietly, hoping Annette would follow suit.

"Shame nothing will come of any of it," she says. "We've had our fun. We're done now, until the war's end, aren't we?"

In the morning, Annette wakes up with a strong headache and swears she's done with dances for the remainder of the war.

"I'm serious," she says in response to Marcy's raised eyebrows, while Susan rummages through the cupboards downstairs in search of real coffee. "I've had my fun. Now it's time for me to grow up and be mature about this whole thing. I'll be a patriotic citizen when the boys come home."

Marcy stretches out in the li-lo. She thinks about Bernadette, about meeting her again to pass off radios. Touching the pearls inside her pocket, she hopes, even as she hates herself for it, that it will also mean seeing Franc again.

"What's the time, Susan?" Marcy asks as she finally gets up. "I've got to meet Mum at church."

CHAPTER THIRTY-SIX

VIOLET

1943

The back of Violet's legs press into the hard pew, hands clasped around her hymnal, which is sticky in the humid church. She sings, "Onward Christian Soldiers," sharing her hymnbook with David, next to Marcy and Peter, who share their own. Violet loves to hear their voices, all singing together. David harmonizes, Marcy sings the melody, Peter belts the words out wholeheartedly and off tune. It makes Violet emotional, to think about their voices mingling and matching, creating something beautiful.

She remembers a time when Marcy was little, when she stared up at Violet with a faint smile the whole time they sang. After they'd sat down again to listen to the sermon, leaned over and said, "You've got a voice like an angel, Mummy."

How easy it should have been, to squeeze Marcy's hand; to smile at her, kiss the top of her hair. Instead, Violet, embarrassed that someone would hear and think she was vain, told Marcy to be quiet in church.

She thinks about that now, as the final hymn ends and people file out of the pews, as she watches Marcy make her way through the crowd of churchgoers to Louisa. She watches Louisa, curly hair flying in every direction, smile warmly back, and then loop her arm through Marcy's as they walk out of the church.

Violet gathers her purse, looks to Peter, who squirms next to her, eager to get outside, and says to David, "Right then," but he is already off, shaking hands with the minister.

She waits in line to greet the minister, all the while stealing glances at her daughter and Louisa, who are now chatting beyond the church's door. Why shouldn't she join them? They're hers, after all. She steps out of line and walks toward them.

"Hi Mum," Marcy says. She smiles and steps toward her tentatively. Violet wishes not everything about her daughter was so reluctant, like she was constantly afraid of offending. "Erm—Louisa says we can go straight to her house for lunch."

"Right," says Violet. "Lovely." She smiles at Louisa and suddenly she is the tentative one, trying again to receive approval from this friend who lets her in and then shuts her out. Trying to connect with her daughter, she says, "I bet you're tired, up all night chatting at Susan's."

"Yes," Marcy says, looking away. "Looks like Dad's nearly ready, then."

David is shaking the Reverend's hand. Violet hears them talking about rations and curfew. "Can't complain, it's not been so bad," says David.

"Right," Violet says, again, looking at Louisa. "Shall we go then?"

"I don't see why not," Louisa says. Smiling in the sunshine, putting a finger to her forehead to brush away a stray ringlet, she looks for a moment like she did so many years ago: happy, unencumbered, free. Violet can't help but smile back.

They walk up the lane, up the hill, the backdrop of the sea behind them, to the house Violet has long wanted but Louisa has had. Louisa and Violet walk next to each other, and Violet remembers the way their strides match one another perfectly. Countless times, they had made this walk after church on Sunday, along the hedged lanes and to Louisa's house. Today they talk because silence is no longer comfortable: Violet chats about her knitting circle; Louisa asks questions about yarn quality and pearl rows.

"Goodness me," Violet says, slightly out of breath, as they pass the neighbor with gnomes all over her front garden. "She's still got them."

Louisa laughs, and clasps Violet's elbow. "You never could stand those gnomes," she says warmly.

"You were the one who always wanted to shuffle them around," Violet replies. "You would always ask me if we should check on Soppy, and I knew you were up to no good."

"I don't remember you objecting."

The two laugh, and then Louisa seems to realize she is touching Violet's elbow and immediately lets go. Violet stares straight ahead, legs heavy as she walks.

Violet hears Peter scurrying behind them, the intermittent voices of Jon and David as they discuss crops and farm animals. On a breezy Sunday in June, one could almost forget that their island was Occupied.

As Louisa's house comes into view, Violet actively pushes away the pang of jealousy that rises up in her. *It's not yours, it was never yours.*

And yet, inside, greeted by the smell of a roast, fresh flowers on the table, Violet feels as though she is stepping into a place she dreamed up as a child.

"I'll set the table," Marcy says. She opens the drawer and pulls out the knives and forks, polishing them quickly with a napkin.

Violet, used to having jobs, to being needed, to setting the pace, is suddenly at a loss for what to do. Wringing her hands together, she walks into the back conservatory, looking out across the meadow and to the sea.

"Alright there, Auntie Violet?" she hears, and turns around to see her nephew, Basil.

"What are you doing here, Basil?" she asks, kissing him on each cheek.

"Well, you haven't heard then," he says with a smug grin. "I'm the provider of the feast."

"You're *what?*" Violet asks.

"Long story," he says. "But you mustn't tell Mum and Dad. They'd be furious if they knew."

Violet knows he's right. His mum Ethel is in no way fond of the Germans, but she isn't about to stick her neck out to fight them. Her philosophy is to keep her head down and carry on. It's been Violet's philosophy as well.

"Right, we're ready," Louisa calls from the kitchen.

The wooden table is laid with a floral tablecloth, set with Louisa's finest china. Plates of sliced pork, potatoes, and carrots sit in the center.

"Gosh, Louisa," says Violet. "This looks *wonderful*."

"Oh, thank you," says Louisa with a smile. "I wanted to make Yorkshire Puds, but you know it's just not possible without real flour."

The seven of them sit down around the table: Jon, Louisa, Basil, Marcy, Peter, Violet and David. As they tuck in, for a moment there is an awkward silence, all the women silently fishing for conversation, all the men lost in the rare pleasure of bountiful meat.

Violet says, "Do you remember the Sunday we had a roast on the boat?"

"Oh, yes," answers Jon with a laugh. "We thought it would be such a good idea, until the wind picked up."

"And Eugene got so sick, didn't he," continues Violet excitedly. "He was so green, he couldn't even look at us having our rice pudding."

"He never ate rice pudding again since, as far as I know," says Louisa with a smile.

There is silence again, as all of them seemed to realize again that Eugene wasn't there, and might never be there again.

"This *is* lovely," says Violet, in a tone she hopes will convey her earnestness. "Thank you for having our family."

"Well, of course we *had* to have Basil and Marcy here, didn't we, and we are glad you both could come," Louisa says. It stings Violet, the casualness, the odd closeness Louisa's developed with Marcy.

"Why did you *have* to invite Basil and Marcy?" Violet asks, sharply.

"Well, with all the time they've been spending here, of course, helping," replies Louisa.

Violet looks at Marcy. Her face has turned bright red and her hand trembles as it grips around her fork.

David clears his throat, and Jon asks who would like more water.

Violet, knowing this will not end well, that she is likely making a fool of herself, continues.

"Helping with what?" she asks.

Basil looks down at his plate. Louisa looks at Marcy, and it maddens Violet to see Louisa and her daughter in on something, she is so obviously on the outside.

"Mum, Dad, we've been doing our part for the war." Marcy winces as she talks, like she is waiting for an explosion.

"And what part is that?" Violet asks. Her heart is racing.

"We've—well, we've been taking the German marching songs and putting English words to them," Marcy says in a rush.

Violet knows it's a lie by the way Louisa's eyebrows raise, by Basil's sudden shoulder drop, by Jon's smirk. They are up to something—the four of them, and it doesn't include Violet.

Abruptly, she stands up. She can't bear to be laughed out, to be shut out by her daughter and her old best friend.

"Excuse me," she says as humiliation courses through her. "I just need the loo." Ducking her head, she walks quickly toward the back door.

She stands in the garden of the house she loved first. She wants to wreak havoc on the overgrown garden, to pull out the hydrangea bush and throw it across the yard.

After a moment, she hears the back door open. She is about to tell David to go away when a very different hand reaches out. She looks up to Jon, offering her a cigarette. Wordlessly, she takes it and has a long drag, watching as the smoke disappears into the wind.

"She's hurt, you know," Jon says.

"It's not my fault, what happened to Hope," Violet snaps back. *It's not my fault, I kept my own baby,* she says in her head, though she cannot shake the feeling that it very much is.

"Sometimes unjustified hurt makes it that much worse."

CHAPTER THIRTY-SEVEN

LOUISA

1943

Louisa pushes the pork around her plate, suddenly not hungry, wishing she had never invited Violet in the first place.

It was worse that, after Violet ran away like a wounded animal, Jon shot Louisa a look and followed her outside.

Louisa looks at Marcy, whose face burns red while she shuffles the potatoes around on her plate. She wonders why she hasn't said anything, why she kept this hidden from her mother.

David breaks the silence first. "You should have told us," he says quietly, looking at his plate.

"Dad," Marcy begins.

"We're your parents."

"And what would you have said, if I told you? You've both tried so hard to pretend this war isn't happening, like the Germans aren't taking your milk and your eggs."

David's mouth sets in a firm line, his big brown eyes filled with something like anger. "I never forgot about them. Not in twenty-five years."

Louisa knows he is thinking about the first war. She's never heard him speak of his time in the service.

"I'm sorry, Dad."

The table returns to its terrible silence. Louisa fishes for conversation. She lands on the topic that's been heavy on her mind all weekend: the forced laborers.

"They've turned some of the schools into camps," she says to the table as she finishes her story about the eggs. "They're packed in, living in awful conditions. Forced to sleep at night piled on top of each other, left to fend for themselves to find food, marched through town utterly humiliated every morning. They're completely starved by the Organization Todt."

"Organization Todt?" Marcy asks sharply. Her eyebrows are raised in surprise. "What do you know about them?"

"They're the devil incarnate. The ones spearheading this whole thing," says Basil. "Put here specially to make the lives of these prisoners a living hell."

"What prisoners?" asks Marcy.

"Good gracious Marcy, have you *been* to town?" Louisa asks, forgetting momentarily that she only just found out about the prisoners herself. "Building fortifications, bunkers, who knows. But they are working them into the ground."

"Not just for the laborers, either," says David. "Ouen Lecoat, who lives down the way from us, came by last week to tell us that they're starting to raid nearby farms at night for food. One farmer in St. Peter's spent last week in hospital, after a Russian stabbed him trying to get after the food."

"Well of course they are, they're starving," says Louisa.

"We're not too far away from that ourselves," counters David. "Ouen suggested we get our hands on some bats, keep them with us at night in case our farm is next."

Louisa raises her eyebrows. "I'm sure he did. Well, no matter. I've got a system."

"System?" asks Basil. "For what?"

"For feeding them, of course. I've been asking around, and have found out that a load of the prisoners are housed at Grouville Marsh, which means, they actually march up a road a quarter mile from here on their way to work."

"And we're to ambush them on their marches?" asks Basil, winking conspiratorially at Peter.

"No—we'll feed them, of course. Leave food for them in the bushes."

The rest of the table is silent. David looks out the window; Marcy pushes her fork around on her plate.

"Are you quite alright, Marcy?" asks Louisa. "You've gone very quiet." She wonders if Marcy is worried about Violet.

"It's nothing," says Marcy, shaking her head.

"How are you going to feed them?" asks David, leaning forward. "We've all hardly got enough to feed ourselves with our current rations."

Exasperated, Louisa bangs her fist on the table.

"They could be my son!" she yells, surprising herself with the volume of her voice. Marcy flinches at the sudden movement. "When I saw them at the Weighbridge, I saw a boy with eyes the same color as Eugene's—"

"Sea-green," says Marcy quietly, glancing up at Louisa.

"Yes," Louisa says. "Any of these boys could be my son. Our Eugene might be captured, and forced to march up and down somewhere, and I *pray* that some other mother would find it in her to feed him."

The room is silent but for the ticking clock.

At that moment, Violet and Jon walk back in, cheeks pink from the cold air.

"Ah, you're back," says Louisa, too brightly. Then, because she's not ready just yet to sit around the table with Violet, she says, "I'll put the coffee on."

***

In the kitchen, she arranges the floral cups onto a tray. Her fingers shake with anger as she thinks about Eugene. How dare David question her, she thinks. Reaching up to the corner, she looks for bowls on which to serve Violet's pudding.

She hears Basil and Jon laugh in the other room, presumably at a joke Basil made to hastily change the subject. She opens the kitchen door and steps outside to compose herself. Walking around to the back of the potting shed, she presses herself against the siding. Breathing deeply, she closes her eyes. How she misses Eugene, the sea glass of his eyes, the soft touch of his hand. She feels like an animal in the magnitude of her longing.

She hears a rustle, and then the distinctive sound of a man clearing his throat. Louisa opens her eyes, and covers her mouth to keep from screaming.

Eugene's eyes are staring back at her.

CHAPTER THIRTY-EIGHT

VIOLET

1943

Violet fumes silently as they walk home from Louisa's, David and Peter trailing a half step behind her. Marcy walks on her own, off to the side, arms folded across her chest.

Clutching her purse as she walks, she thinks about how Louisa didn't even have the decency—or nerve—to come out and say goodbye in person.

"I'm sorry but you all must go," she'd called from beyond the kitchen door. "Immediately."

Jon had gone into the kitchen, then came out quickly and said he was terribly sorry but everyone really must go. Marcy looked from Violet to the kitchen door, like she couldn't decide.

"You heard Jon," Violet had said as she drew herself up to her full height, trying to maintain her dignity.

Her daughter had stood up and followed, but there was an inward resistance, a rebellion, that unnerved Violet.

"I'll be right out," David said, surprising her most. "I just need a quick word with Louisa."

"I hardly think this is the time," said Violet, standing in the doorway.

"I'll catch up," said David, and though his voice was gentle, he was firm.

The rest of the day is tense at home.

"What did you talk to Louisa about?" Violet asks David as he

219

sits in the parlor flipping through the paper. She dusts around him, picking up a vase on the side table.

David shakes his head. "Nothing worth repeating," he says. He turns the page of a paper.

Violet slams the vase on the table and walks away.

Even Peter seems to pick up on his mother's mood and stays upstairs in his room. For dinner, they have day-old bread without butter and weak parsnip tea.

At half past nine, David puts his book down on the table, takes off his reading glasses, and rubs his eyes with a heaviness she is not used to seeing in him. He stares at her for a long moment across the room, where she sits with her knitting. She puts down her knitting and stares back at him, to the eyes that have revealed so little about his soul. Holding up her finger slightly, she almost reaches toward him.

At that moment, he stands up. "Goodnight, dear," he says as he passes by, as the pantleg of his trouser barely grazes her shoulder. "Don't stay up too late."

"I won't," says Violet as she resumes her knitting, knowing she will, that sleep won't come anywhere near her tonight.

Now, as Violet sits in candlelight, she thinks again that Louisa is the better mother. She had watched the way Marcy confidently set the table and Louisa's exclamation, "Well *done*, my girl," when Marcy showed her the fancy way she had folded the cloth napkins. Marcy was grown, a woman by all accounts. She was old enough to marry, to have her own babies. Surely, a girl of that age shouldn't be so pleased with something as trivial as napkin folding. Except, it wasn't the napkin folding. It was the way the two moved together, the way she used to with Louisa. She had been replaced by both of them.

Louisa's obvious delight in Marcy unnerved Violet. The way she had acted today– like she had some kind of ownership over what was Violet's flesh and blood.

She thinks again, like she does too often, about the months after Violet's decision to keep Marcy.

Louisa never apologized, Violet realizes. She sits up straighter. *Lou-*

isa tried to take my baby and I've been feeling guilty all this time for it. Guilty about what she's taken from Louisa, guilty about what Marcy would think of her if she ever found out.

Louisa thought she had some kind of claim to Violet's baby, and Violet had been led to believe the same thing. And now, it seems like Louisa is exercising that claim.

I won't let her, Violet thinks suddenly. I won't let her take Marcy, just because she lost Hope, just because she's lost Eugene, just because I got pregnant again. That doesn't mean she can have my child.

The clock reads nearly one in the morning. Violet walks to the cupboard and throws it open, pulling out anything that can be used for baking; potato flour, ground acorns, shredded carrots. She bakes the most beautiful wartime scones, symmetrical, fluffy and airy. Next, Violet bakes a cake, and then a loaf of bread, smacking the dough on the counter so the flour came up in puffs of dust that landed on her apron like flecks of snow. Her rations will be gone by sunrise, Violet knows this, and still she cannot stop tearing through them like they will save her. For once, she doesn't clean as she bakes, allowing the pans to pile up in the sink, the flour and sugar to scatter the floor like snow. Her hair falls out of her pins while she manically stirs.

By the time David comes downstairs at quarter past five in the morning, Violet is frying the bacon Jon sent her home with on the stove, not bothering to wipe up the little splotches of grease as they fall on the counter.

"Good morning," David says hesitantly, almost like it is a question.

"Hello," says Violet brightly, brushing a stray strand of dark hair out of her eyes. "Thought you'd like a full breakfast this morning, to start the week off well."

David cautiously takes a piece of bread, and sits down at the table. He eats and drinks in silence. He hunches over the table, his broad shoulders rising up and down as he breathes, and Violet is reminded again of how little she knows the man in front of her: how they have built their lives around each other, dividing and conquering but never meeting. The grief of it catches in her throat. What if she had told him her secret? Could their marriage have been different? She turns away from the stranger in her kitchen, begins hastily gathering items onto a tray: parsnip tea, a scone, some bread and bacon.

She gathers her tray and marches up the wooden staircase, the air getting chillier as she climbs. Outside of Marcy's room, she pauses, unsure of how to approach the woman sleeping on the other side of the door.

Just as she is about to lose her courage, to turn around and head back downstairs, Marcy opens the door, fully dressed.

"Mum?" Marcy asks in surprise. "Are you alright?"

Violet is again struck by the care of her daughter, the innate kindness and concern. And she hears the harshness of her own voice in her response. "What are you doing, up and dressed so early?"

Marcy raises her eyebrows. "I didn't sleep very well," she says. "And I've got work."

Violet sticks her chin out, sure she looks silly carrying a tray laden with food, still in yesterday's clothes, her hair and eyes wild. But she steps in, sits on the bed, trying to look comfortable and casual. Stiffly, she says, "I thought we could have tea."

Marcy raises her eyebrows. "Now?" she asks.

"Yes, now," Violet says. She sets the tray on the bedside table and begins pouring tea into the cups.

She expects Marcy, who is normally so eager for any attention, so much so that Violet has come to resent her for it because it reminds her of the ways she has failed her daughter, to rush forward and take a cup. Instead, Marcy hesitates, standing where she is in her room, the comb still held midway through her hair. "Why?" She asks.

Violet laughs uncomfortably. How can she say, *because I don't want to lose you, because I don't want you to wish Louisa was your mum, because I love you and for some reason, that has been the hardest thing in the world to convey to you.* She says, "Oh come on, Marcy, I just thought it would be nice. We've done this before, haven't we?" Though, even as she says it, Violet knows that she has never sought just her daughter out for tea like this.

222

Marcy sets the comb down on the dresser and walks toward the bed. She sits down opposite her mother and warily takes a cup of tea from her outstretched hand, and Violet surges with unexpected relief.

"Right, then," she says, leaning back onto Marcy's thin pillow. She should have a reason for being here, some sort of conversation starter. She says, "Basil says you seem to be enjoying your work as a book-keeper at the bakery."

Marcy nods.

"But you can't do that forever—what are you planning to do afterward?" Violet continues. She could be talking to a perfect stranger.

Marcy takes a sip of tea. "I don't know yet," she says slowly.

"Yes, well, soon enough, you'll fall in love and marry, I expect," Violet says. "I was only a few years older than you when I married your dad."

"There's not much available now, is there?" she says, looking out the window.

Violet thinks of Eugene, and wonders if Marcy knows how he feels. She wonders if she should tell her. Then she thinks about Louisa and changes her mind.

She looks around. "So, what do you and Louisa talk about?" she asks, knowing even as she says it her voice is brittle and tense.

"What do you mean?" Marcy asks.

"When you two are together. What do you talk about?"

Marcy looks out the window and shrugs. "All kinds of things," she says. Looking at her mum, she says, "What did the two of you used to talk about, when you were friends?"

"We still are friends," Violet snaps.

"We don't talk about you, if that's what you're worried about," Marcy says.

Violet wants to touch her daughter's leg. She wants to say, *I don't care what you talk about. I just want to be part of it.*

"What I'm worried about," Violet says, standing up, "Is you winding up in some prison somewhere because you have your head full of a bunch of hot air."

Now Marcy stands up. "We're helping the war effort, Mum."

"What are the lot of you going to do for the war?" Violet says, her heart racing. "What are you going to do to fix this? You can't make them go away!"

"We can try!" says Marcy. "They nearly killed me, Mum, don't you remember? That day on the beach. They nearly killed me. Or do you only remember Peter?" "Of course I remember," Violet says, her face now very close to Marcy's. "I think about it every day. And that's why I want you to stay away from Louisa. Stay out of trouble. Keep your head down, survive the war."

"I can't, Mum. I'm helping. I'm helping with the war effort."

"Not under my roof," Violet says. This conversation has taken a track she hasn't meant to go, but she cannot make herself back off. "I forbid you to see that woman."

She expects Marcy to cave, because she's always caved. But instead, Marcy stands tall, squares her shoulders, and says, "Okay then. I'll leave."

"You'll *what?*" Violet moves toward the door. "Don't be ridiculous."

"I'm a grown woman, Mum. You can't make me feel small anymore."

With that, Marcy gathers her school bag, a pillow, the pink and white quilt Violet made for her when she was little, and marches past her mother and down the stairs. Violet hears the screen door slam and the bicycle wheels on the gravel driveway, carrying her love away from her.

CHAPTER THIRTY-NINE

LOUISA

1943

They are Eugene's eyes, but it is not Eugene.

The unkempt boy standing before her has thick black hair matted against his gaunt face. His cheekbones stick out like sharp lines, making the sockets sunken and dark. But his eyes carry all the light and intelligence of her son's.

"Eugene?" She whispers, her throat dry. Her heart pounds in her chest, and with her hands, she touches the rough wood of the potting shed wall to steady herself.

The man extends his arm, opens his palm flat to show a crumpled, worn piece of paper in it. She takes a breath, looks closer to see her own address, in her own handwriting.

"I was just talking about you," she says, breathless, both disappointed and relieved this shell of a man is not her son. "I saw you at the Weighbridge."

He says nothing in response, only stares at her, and she realizes he does not understand. She takes him by the hand and guides him toward the house, her own legs shaky.

Opening the kitchen door, she sits him down at the small table near the counter. She walks to the door that separates the kitchen from the formal dining room. "Everyone," she calls. "I'm sorry, but you really must go. Immediately."

There's a pregnant pause in the other room. Then Jon says, "You okay, Lou?"

"Yes, but everyone must leave. Really."

"Excuse me one moment," says Jon as his chair scrapes against the floor.

Louisa glances at the boy she's led into her house, who followed her so willingly, like a puppy after his owner.

"Come on, Lou," Jon says as he pushes open the door. "Can't you just—"

He enters the kitchen and stops talking abruptly. His mouth hangs open as he looks at the emaciated fellow standing in front of him.

"His eyes," Jon begins.

"I know," says Louisa.

Jon leaves the kitchen. She hears him say, "I'm terribly sorry, but you really must go, now."

He sees them to the door.

Louisa and the boy stare at each other. He is fidgety, and she worries he will bolt from his chair any moment. She tries to smile reassuringly.

"Louisa," comes a voice on the other side of the door.

Louisa cracks it open. "Not a good time, David," she says.

"It will only take a minute." David puts a hand on the frame to keep Louisa from closing the door.

Louisa uses her body to block the boy from David's view. "What?" She says, unable to hide her exasperation.

David clears his throat. "My Marcy," he says quietly. "I know there's history with you and Violet. But don't you compromise my Marcy." He blinks with his long, sad eyelashes.

"I would never," Louisa whispers. Even as she says it, a deep blush creeps up her chest. Never had she thought David even noticed. Now she wonders what else he's seen.

David nods, looking like he's about to say more. Instead, he clears his throat again. "Okay then," he says.

He turns and walks away.

***

226

"Jon," her husband says to the boy in the kitchen, pointing to his chest. The boy nods and shakes Jon's hand. It is only then that Louisa notices he is wheezing slightly, that just to stand appears to be taking considerable effort.

She guides him through to the dining room, sits him down at the large table. He wears a thin ripped t-shirt, trousers that are cut off at the shins. She glances at his hair, thinking that he probably has lice at best, scabies at worst.

Jon follows her in, with a plate from the roast and a few of Violet's parsnips. The boy begins eating aggressively, with both hands, shoveling the food in so that he can scarcely take a wheezy breath.

Louisa and Jon watch him, and she knows he is silently praying the same prayer: don't let this be the fate of my own son.

He smells of feces, body odor and sweat. She leaves him eating there with Jon and goes into the kitchen to run him a bath.

Her hands tremble as she boils the water, sets up the large tub, pulls a bar of soap out from the cupboard. She draws the blinds and locks the kitchen door, puts a towel on the counter. She goes up to Eugene's room and pulls out a blue shirt and brown slacks, his razor and brush.

With a lot of gestures, she shows the boy the bath and the soap, and then leaves to give him privacy. She and Jon stand in the dining room, foreheads pressed against each other.

"Do we send him back to the camp?" Jon asks.

"How can we?" Louisa says. "He looks like all his bones will fall apart if we push him out the door."

"We can't keep him," Jon says. "If someone finds out we'll be sent to Germany. And how can we feed him?"

"I don't know," Louisa says. Her heart is still racing. "But he's someone's son."

They are interrupted by a howl from the kitchen.

Louisa peaks her head through the door, and sees the boy, crouched over in the tub, his back covered in fresh gashes. He must have just poured a cup of water over himself.

She gasps, without thinking, and he turns toward her. Their eyes meet, he in the tub, openly bleeding, she fully dressed, outwardly whole. Lowering her eyes, she backs out of the room.

After a long while, he emerges from the kitchen, dressed and shaved. Still thin and ragged, with his hair combed and face washed, he looks human.

He looks tired. Jon says, "Why don't you lie down upstairs?"

The boy does not understand, so Jon takes him up. Louisa listens to their footsteps above her, imagining Jon standing in the room he has avoided since his son left. She closes her eyes and hears him pointing out the dresser, the drawer with the pajamas, the water next to the bed, Eugene's painting of Rozel harbor.

When Jon comes back downstairs, her eyes are still closed, her head pressed against the back of the chair. He puts a hand on her shoulder, and she looks up at him.

"We've got to keep him," she says. "We haven't a choice."

She expects an argument, a protest, a list of reasons why they cannot do what she knows they must. Instead, he flops heavily onto the seat next to her and says, "I know."

The memory of a long-ago conversation comes to her, of Violet saying something similar. "It's my baby, Lou. I can't give up what's fallen into my lap. I haven't a choice."

Louisa pushes away the thought.

CHAPTER FORTY

MARCY

1943

Marcy pedals into the cold wind with the pink and white quilt tucked bulkily under one arm. Her heart pounds like an erratic drumbeat.

When she was twelve and Eugne was fifteen, Eugene had come over one day by himself. , She'd heard her mum's surprise downstairs, when Eugene showed up at the door and asked, "Is Marcy home?"

Marcy, elated, had grabbed the quilt and come running into the kitchen. "Hi Eugene," she said, unable to keep the grin off her face. "What are you doing here?"

"Erm," Eugene said. He ran a hand through his mop of curly hair. "You weren't at choir practice this week. I brought you the music so you wouldn't fall behind."

"Thank you," Marcy said, taking the sheet music out of his hand. And then, because she was desperate to keep him there, she said, "I was just headed out to sit on the grass and look at the clouds. Would you care to join me?"

She felt her mum's eyebrows raise. *What a silly thing to ask*, Marcy immediately reprimanded herself.

Eugene surprised her with a large smile in return. "I love looking at the clouds," he said. "I'll join you for a minute."

"Don't mess up that quilt, Marcy," her mother's voice warned as she carried it out to the garden.

They spent a few minutes looking at shapes. Marcy felt awkward and in the way, but Eugene seemed perfectly comfortable, like it was the most natural thing in the world to sit with someone and look at shapes in the sky.

"There's a frog, look," Eugene said, pointing. "Can you see it?"

"I thought it was more of a seahorse," said Marcy.

Eugene chuckled. "Yes, I see it."

Marcy sat up, unable to keep herself from blurting out what was on her mind, said, "Did you know our mums used to be best friends?"

Eugene smiled at her. "Not only did I know it. I remember it. I used to call your mum Auntie Vi."

"I don't know why, but I get this feeling that Mum blames me. There's something that happened since I was born that made them not friends anymore."

He stared at her, thick curly hair falling into his face. She felt herself blush.

"Ah, Marcy," he said. "All mums are complicated. Prerequisite for the job."

"My mum's not," Marcy said, crossing her arms. "She thinks I'm too loud and misbehaving. She doesn't want to take me anywhere."

He smiled, and again, she felt her stomach flip flop. "Someday, Marcy," he said quietly. "I'm going to ask you to marry me."

Marcy's chest fluttered. Did he mean it? Would she marry him? Already, she knew the answer.

She swatted him away. "Honestly, Eugene, you don't want to marry me," she said, trying to laugh.

He rolled onto his stomach propped onto his elbows, suddenly looking much older than fifteen. "I will if you learn how to cook as well as your mum."

Months later, when he became popular and too busy to stare at the clouds with her, she would wonder if the whole conversation was only a dream.

***

Marcy pulls up to the Tudor-style home and parks her bike next to the yellow roses growing up the garden wall.

Opening up the front door, she calls into the house, "Gran? Are you home?"

Gran's head peers around the corner, hair still in rollers. "Marcy! I wasn't expecting you. Are you here to trim the roses?"

Marcy thinks for a moment about the nature of her relationship with Gran. She sees Gran every other week in the spring and summer months, when she comes to prune the roses. Other than that, she rarely sees her. Standing in the foyer now, with no apparent reason for coming, Marcy is at a loss for what to say.

Gran looks her over, taking in the quilt under her arm. "Gracious child, what's happened? You look like a wreck."

Marcy smiles weakly. "I could use a cup of tea, Gran."

Gran nods. "Better come in, then."

In the kitchen, Marcy sits at the wooden table while her Gran washes out the teapot. Gran's kitchen has barely changed in Marcy's lifetime: the same floral curtains above the window, the same black and white tile, the same bread bin on the counter. It brings her a little comfort, to see something consistent.

In the center of the table, Marcy sees a box of handwritten recipes. "What are these?"

"Oh, just cleaning out," Gran responds. "Going through my things to lighten the load a bit."

Marcy picks up the recipe cards. She reads Gran's recipe for Bean Crock, for ginger lemonade and Victoria sponge cake. Notes are scribbled in her perfect handwriting along the sides like, "Made for Violet's 5th birthday, very good," and "Had this at the beach."

Marcy comes to a card that is written in a child's large writing. It says, "Perfect Jam by Violet and Mummy."

"What's this?" Marcy asks, holding up the card.

Gran sets the full teapot on the table. "Oh," she says, picking it up. "A jam Violet and I used to make together every year when the strawberries were ripe."

231

"Mum hates strawberry jam," Marcy says. "Always has."

Gran's eyes cloud over for a moment. Clearing her throat, she says, "Are you going to tell me what you're doing here or do I have to pry it out of you?"

Marcy sighs. She puts the recipe cards back in the box and closes the lid. "Mum and I had a massive row," she says.

"About what?"

"About me being myself," Marcy says. "I'm a grown woman and she refuses to acknowledge it."

"Oh?" Gran says. She pours the tea.

Marcy continues to speak into the awkward space between them. She's not used to confiding in her grandmother. "I was wondering– if it's not too much trouble, that is. Could I stay here with you for a bit?"

"Ah, my girl," Gran says as she pours Marcy her tea. "I'd love that. Heaven knows I've seen too little of you. But you must go home, if you are so grown up. You've got to go back to your mum and make it right."

Marcy nods, defeated.

"But if you'd really like, Marcy, I can have a word with your mum," Gran continues. "Try to smooth things over. Mothers often say things they don't mean."

"Thank you Gran," Marcy says, though she wonders how Gran would manage to smooth anything over with her mum. Any time they talk their relationship only seems to get worse.

Gran looks pleased, and neither of them seems to know what to say to each other in the silence that follows.

Marcy stands up. She wants to see Louisa, to explain what happened, and to see if she is okay after yesterday.

"Oh, and Gran?"

"Yes, my dear?"

She pulls out the pearls, and sets them on the table. "When you do talk to her, would you take these to Mum? She thinks I stole them, and she's been upset with me since."

With a shaking hand, Gran picks up the pearls. "I see," she says.

Gran doesn't stand up when Marcy turns to leave.

Chapter Forty-One

VIOLET

1943

The kitchen is silent, apart from the sound of forks scraping against the china bowls as Peter and David finish off the rest of their wartime rice pudding—made with only a splash of milk and a quarter of the sugar, so that it can hardly be called a sweet. Violet swirls her fork around her own bowl, the knot in her stomach twisting ever tighter whenever she tries to take a bite.

David hasn't spoken to her all day. He blames her, she knows this, and she wears the blame like a suffocating blanket. Peter asked for six hours straight, "Where is Marcy? What time is Marcy coming home?"

Violet had brushed him off with vague answers and timelines, until she lost her patience and snapped, "*Enough*, Peter! She'll come back when she comes back."

David, who was pulling off his work boots at the time, muttered, "Going to run him off too, are you?"

Violet stirred her stew vigorously, ignoring him. She tried to swallow back the well of emotion that nauseated her, made her wonder how the vision she had for her life and her family back in the days when she used to visit the house had turned out so differently in practice.

David stands now and clears the table, setting the bowls of rice pudding in the sink. Peter sits at the table quietly, playing with his napkin. Violet remembers when she made rice pudding as a celebratory food: when someone had done well on a test, or David had an especially good harvest. They'd eat rice pudding by the fire, doing puzzles or playing games in its warm glow. On those occasions, she had felt so proud of her little family, of the safety she provided for them through food.

This evening, she feels none of that. Peter says, "Can I leave the table?"

"Would you like me to do a puzzle with you this evening?" Violet asks, desperate to connect with someone in her family, for one of her kin to need her.

Peter shrugs. "No thanks, Mum. I want to look at my books."

"Of course," says Violet quickly. Standing up, she collects the placemats and carries them into the kitchen.

David has stacked the dishes inside the sink, and is standing with his arms crossed looking out the dark window into the black night. Their black-out curtains should be drawn by now, and Violet resists the urge to reach past him to draw it.

"She's a grown woman, David," Violet says, with a calmness she does not feel. "She has a right to leave. I didn't force her."

"Didn't you?" David turns toward her with his face like a stone. She isn't used to this kind of coldness, this kind of attention, from her husband.

"She wants to be part of the Resistance," Violet whispers. "I was trying to protect her."

"From the Germans? Or Louisa?" says David.

Violet is shocked, exposed. David has never given her, in all their years of marriage, any kind of inkling that he knows about the rift in Louisa and Violet's friendship. She wonders why he brings this up now.

Suddenly there is a knock at the door, startling Violet and making her jump.

"Open up!" A male voice calls from the outside. "Now!"

"Get back," David whispers. "Into the living room, with Peter."

Violet goes as far as the doorframe when David opens the door. A German soldier stands in the doorframe, large and threatening in his uniform and hat.

"Can I help you?" says David. His voice is tense, like a rubber band stretched tight.

"What is the meaning of this?" The German asks as he storms into the room. He is big, Violet notices from the threshold of the living room, much bigger than her husband. Instinctively she looks for Peter, who has glanced up from his book with vague concern and curiosity.

Pointing to the lamp on the kitchen counter, then the open window, he says, "Are you sending a signal to England? Showing them where to bomb?"

"We're very sorry," says David, standing in between the soldier and Violet. "We completely forgot; we'll put the curtain down now—"

The German soldier pushes the oil lamp off of the counter. The glass shatters as it hits the floor. Violet gasps, then puts a hand to her mouth to stifle it. Peter runs over, wrapping his arms around Violet's waist. She puts a hand protectively on his head, pushing him slightly behind her.

"It will be worse for you, if this happens again," says the soldier. "From now on, do as you are told."

Turning, he stalks back out the door, slamming it shut behind him. Only then does Violet hear the sound of a motor, of wheels screeching as they drive away.

Violet falls to the floor as he leaves, laying her head against the wall. Peter touches her arm and says, "We showed him, didn't we, Mum?"

David begins picking up the pieces of broken glass from the shattered lamp. He pulls down the blackout shade. His fists are shaking.

"Don't you see what I was trying to protect her from?" Violet whispers, after a long silence. "If that was over a blackout curtain, imagine what she would face over something—whatever it is she's doing—contraband ."

David stands over the sink with the broken glass, looking older, more defeated, than he had a moment ago.

"I miss her," he says, and Violet is surprised at the rare display of tenderness. "I miss my girl."

CHAPTER FORTY-TWO

MARCY

1943

Leaving Greve De Lecq, Marcy rides north toward Sorel Point on her bicycle.

She pulls into Louisa's drive, propelled forward by the thought of a good cup of tea and a good cry. Louisa, at some point in her life, was hurt by Violet. Marcy has gathered this much. Surely Louisa will be sympathetic to Marcy's complaints.

She tries the handle on Louisa's door, but to her surprise, it is locked. Louisa never locks the door. "They want me that badly, they can have me," she always says, while Jon rolls his eyes. "You mean you'll just let me deal with it," he says.

Marcy knocks.

"Who is it?" Louisa's voice comes from the other side of the door, tense and tight.

"It's only me, Marcy," she says in a rush, like Louisa might not know her voice. "I'm sorry to come by so early."

The door opens, but only a tiny crack.

"What are you doing here?" Louisa asks, her voice sharp, the inch of her face Marcy can see etched into a deep frown.

"I've had a row with Mum," she blurts out. "About the roast yesterday." She feels like a schoolgirl telling tales.

Louisa stands there, appraising Marcy, and it feels very much like their visit right after Eugene went missing, when Marcy stood on the porch with a cake wondering if Louisa was going to answer the door. Marcy's ears burn as she stands there, beginning to feel foolish for coming.

She is just about to say, "Right, well I'll just be going," when Louisa pulls open the door.

"In," she says. "Quickly."

Marcy looks back over her shoulder as she is ushered through the entryway, trying to sort out who could be watching them. Louisa shuts and locks the door behind her, turning the deadbolt with a definite click.

"Are you alright?" Marcy asks.

"There's someone I'd like you to meet," says Louisa.

Marcy follows Louisa down the hallway to the kitchen. She forgets about her mum when she sees a thin young man with jet-black hair sitting at the table in Eugene's clothes.

"Oh," she says.

"He's from the camps," says Louisa in a rush. "Showed up yesterday, during lunch. I couldn't say no."

Marcy cannot look away from him. It is startling, Eugene's eyes on another man's body.

Louisa's hand finds hers and she squeezes.

"How are you going to feed him?" Marcy asks. She has noticed the way Louisa has become hollow over the last months, how airy and loose her dresses have become and how she hoists her trousers up with a belt.

"Well, for now we've got the pig. And I had food set aside that I was going to share with the prisoners that he'll get."

"But what about the other prisoners?"

"I don't have enough Marcy. I would need extra rations, and who can get that these days, unless you have money for the black market?"

Marcy looks at the boy again, who has been silent, hands folded in front of him. Even in his quietness, his thin frame and broken-down body, she can see his strength. He has a man's strength, on his arms, in his face, his shoulders and gait.

Franc flashes into her mind, burnt orange. She thinks about his dimple, his uniform, and what she's failed to notice until now: his power. She remembers what Basil said about the Organization Todt. Looking at the boy in front of her, she wonders how Franc, the boy who misses home and has a dimple in his smile, could possibly be responsible for this boy's condition.

If a man wears his strength on his arms, she wonders where a woman wears hers. She looks at the boy and wonders if there is a girl at home who wears a blue barrette for him, who says his name ten times before her feet hit the cold floor in the morning.

If Eugene, like this boy, is at the mercy of another woman some-where in Europe, she hopes the woman would stop at nothing to save him.

Just this morning Marcy had been thinking about kissing Franc's dimple. She had thought about sliding her arm through his, asking him to tell her more about the farm he grew up on. Now she feels sick. She doesn't want to have any part with the Organization who nearly killed the boy in front of her. But she thinks about the dance, the lavish food, the excess, and she knows what to do.

"I know how to find you extra rations, Miss Lou."

CHAPTER FORTY-THREE

VIOLET

1943

"Margot," Violet says, smiling at the woman in the doorway, trying to act like she's caught in her nightgown every day. "Lovely to see you."

"Have I come at a bad time?" Margot, Annett's mum asks.

"Not at all," Violet says, thinking that it should be quite obvious that it is a bad time. "Can I make you a cup of tea?"

Marcy still hasn't returned home. Violet hadn't slept, tossing and turning in the sheets. She replayed their conversation again and again, as though that can change the inevitable outcome, and will bring her girl back.

At dawn, she gave up the pretense of sleep. Wrapping a robe around her, she tiptoed into Marcy's room.

Violet thought of Marcy at Louisa's. She pictured the two of them waking up, having a cup of coffee in the sunroom, laughing about how they had managed to shake free of Violet.

The shame of it is too much for Violet. So instead she channeled her energy into cleaning. Taking Marcy's room apart, bit by bit, Violet deep-cleaned every inch. She dusted behind the bed frame, washed the windows, folded every item of clothing perfectly and tucked it into Marcy's drawers. She thought about the fact that she had bought it too small, about how she wanted to protect Marcy from a world where women are judged by their size. If Marcy was like Violet, unable to fit in anywhere, at least she should be able to feel like she could fit into her clothes.

The sun was well into the sky as Violet began mopping the floors, which is how Margot came to find her in her nightgown.

"Thank you, but no," says Margot now, pulling off her white gloves. She looks around. "I've actually come about a rather delicate matter."

"Oh?"

"Are we quite alone? Marcy isn't in, is she?"

Violet flushes.

"Not at the moment," Violet says, trying to keep her tone casual.

"Good," says Margot. Leaning in, she says, "It's about Marcy's whereabouts."

"Oh?" Violet's underarms begin to perspire. She wishes Margot had left the door open for some air.

"Yes," continues Margot. "You see, I was going through Annette's clothes, trying to sort out what I could take apart and sew into something else. Her sisters keep growing and there are no new clothes to be found."

Violet nods. She has had the same problem outfitting Peter. With no new clothes or supplies on the island, she's taken to making shirts out of her old curtains.

"Well, I found a black gown—one she only wears for fancy occasions, and I was going to take it apart when I noticed a stain on the skirt."

"That's a shame," says Violet, pulling her gown tighter around her.

"Yes," says Margot. "But when I asked Annette about it, she said she hadn't worn the dress at all recently. I had to push her a bit—you know my Annette isn't one to sell others out—but she admitted that the dress had been worn by Marcy."

"Oh?" Violet asks, still confused about where the conversation is headed. Her first thought is that Marcy is quite a different size from Annette, but with the stricter rations, it seems like by now everyone on the island is more or less the same size: too thin. Violet thinks about all the times she encouraged Marcy to eat less and wishes she could take every one of them back.

So instead of asking about the size difference, Violet asks, "What occasion would she have had to wear that dress, Margot?"

"Well that's just the thing," says Margot, too eagerly, like she has been rehearsing this conversation and waiting for this moment. "I pushed Annette and said, 'What would Marcy have needed a dress like that for?' And finally, she gave in and said Marcy was desperate to go to a dance.'"

"At the Parish Hall?" Violet asks. St. Mary's parish hosted a dance every once in a while, but with hardly any eligible men, it never seemed to attract many young girls.

Margot leans forward. "At St. Brelade's."

"But that's been taken over by the Germans."

"Exactly." Margot looks like a cat who has a mouse between its paws. "Annette says she tried to stop her, but that Marcy was bent on attending."

"That doesn't sound like Marcy," Violet says skeptically.

"War makes us all do strange things, doesn't it?" Margot asks. "I hope I don't really need to explain the implications for Marcy, being seen at a dance like that. You know girls who attend those kinds of events take on a certain name."

"What's that?"

"Jerrybag."

Violet has never heard the term *Jerrybag*, but she can deduce its meaning quickly enough. The term both makes her bristle and recoil at the thought of the word being in any way associated with her daughter.

"I'm sorry, Margot, but I think your daughter must be mistaken," says Violet coldly, standing with the kettle in one hand. "Marcy would never attend a dance hosted by Germans."

"Are you suggesting my Annette was making this up?"

"I'm saying it seems to be interesting that she knows so much about it. And it is her dress," says Violet crossly. "Now, I'm afraid I must ask you to leave."

Margot bristles. "You're making a mistake, Violet," she says. "Your daughter is headed down a slippery path. If I know it, countless others must as well, though they lack the compassion to tell you. If you loved your daughter you'd—"

"I'd thank you not to speak to me about loving my daughter," says Violet. She storms over to the kitchen door and holds it open for Margot. "Good day, Margot."

Margot grabs her purse and storms toward the door. "Pride cometh before a fall," she says to Violet. "You'll regret this."

Violet closes the door behind her, biting her lip so hard that she draws blood. *It can't be true,* she thinks to herself.

But it could be true. Violet realizes she knows nothing about what Marcy has been up to, these last months, maybe even years, of the Occupation.

Louisa would know, Violet realizes. Louisa would know exactly what Marcy has been doing. And she hasn't seemed fit to tell Violet, so Violet must find out on her own.

She remembers Louisa mentioned Helena and the Black Market at the roast on Sunday. Violet and Marcy know Helena from years back, when they were all put on food organization for the St. Mary's summer fete, which Helena helped with because her sister lived in the parish. Neither Louisa nor Violet could stand Helena's bossiness or loud mannerisms and Louisa nearly got them both into trouble by trying to imitate Helena right to her face.

If ever there was an island busy body, it is Helena. Violet decides to get dressed and head to town, to gather the crumbs of what is happening.

Chapter Forty-Four

Marcy

1943

The sun is high and hot the next day by the time Marcy parks her bike near the Weighbridge in town. Franc had said he would be at the Pomme D'Or Hotel all week, and as Marcy looks across the street, she sees a group of Germans smoking and laughing on the front steps.

Pinching her cheeks, forcing herself to stand up straight, Marcy walks toward the group of men. *He liked you the other night,* she reminded herself. *He'll like you just fine today.*

Franc lazily on the step next to the others, taking a long drag out of his cigarette. He is attractive, she cannot deny it, and her stomach flutters as she looks at him. Then, she remembers the boy in Louisa's kitchen. Marcy is confused by her attraction and her anger.

The men look up as Marcy's heels click closer. Then Franc stands up and smiles. "Mary," he says. Marcy cannot help it, she loves the way his voice sounds. She blushes as she thinks about kissing him the other night, about his hands in her hair and his breath in her ear.

The other soldiers laugh at Franc, slap him on the back as he walks away from the group toward Marcy.

"Mary," Franc says. "I was beginning to think I would never see you again." His fingers brush against hers, shooting electricity through her.

"I didn't know that I would either," Marcy says honestly. "I'm sorry for not coming earlier..."

Franc puts a finger to her lips. "Never mind that," he says. "You are here now, yes?"

He takes her hand, sending a thrill up her arm. Hand in hand, they walk towards town in broad daylight. Marcy worries about what people will think, and then chastises herself for worrying because it is the only way to get more rations.

"Are you off work today?" Marcy asks as they stroll. She wants to know what Franc does, in the Organization Todt. She wants to know if he knows there are people suffering, like the boy in Louisa's kitchen. She wants to know what he is responsible for.

"My shift begins later on," Franc says. "Why don't we get some bread for a picnic?"

"A picnic would be lovely," she says.

They walk up High Street. Marcy feels the glances of other women on her. She is thankful that she has not recognized anyone yet.

Marcy looks at Franc, gets a glimpse of that glorious dimple.

"What do you do at work, Franc?" she asks.

He squeezes her hand. "I'd tell you, but I'd rather not waste the day bored out of my mind," he says. "It's a lot of logistics."

Marcy nods. She wants to cry, to press him for details, but she knows she cannot. Franc, dimples and all, cannot catch on to any of her suspicions.

Instead, she says, "Who are all those people, working on the island? There's an awful lot of them."

Franc waves a hand away. "Don't worry about them. They are doing work for the Reich."

"It's just—they all look rather thin."

A shadow comes over Franc, turning him from burnt orange to something darker. "They're criminals, Mary. All of them. Here to pay out a sentence. You can't expect them to feast."

"What have they done wrong?" Marcy knows she's approaching dangerous ground, but she needs to know where Franc stands.

Franc shrugs. "I only listen to my orders. I am told they are criminals. Who am I to ask why?"

244

"But some are so young, I just don't see what they could have actually done."

"There's a war on Mary. We want to get through it so we do as we're told." Franc speaks with a note of finality.

"Even if that means letting someone else suffer?"

"Isn't that what war is?"

Franc tries to grab her hand. Marcy suppresses the urge to move away. All she can remember is the way that Eugene used to move crickets outside rather than step on them. The stark difference, between Eugene and Franc, seems to dissolve any attraction she had for Franc.

After a moment, she changes the subject. She begins to talk about her picnics at St. Ouen's Bay as a child, lugging all their belongings from home to the sand.

"But how did you get everything down?" asked Franc. "It's such a steep drop down to St. Ouen's."

"We'd lower it in a picnic basket over the side of the cliff," Marcy says, laughing at how it must sound to someone who has never done it. "China tea cups, a bean crock, chairs and all. It took ages. Once we set everything up, we'd have a scalding hot cup of tea in the summer sun."

She thinks about the beach now, covered with landmines to keep the islanders in and the Allied Forces out.

"And what would you do, when you were there at the beach?"

"Well, sometimes our whole church would go for picnics. And when that happened, Eugene and I would hunt together for shells."

"Eugene is your brother?" Franc asks.

"No. A friend."

Saying Eugene's name out loud gives Marcy a pang of loneliness.

Franc stops her in the street. He looks at her, traces her jawline with his finger. She shivers, thinking about the night of the dance, kissing him in the dark.

"I've never done this before," she whispers. She wants to run away.

"Dated a soldier?" he asks with a smile, and Marcy sees again the boy who stopped to pick up her belongings when she fell on the sidewalk.

"Dated the enemy," she replies.

He nods, his face inching closer to hers so that his breath tickles her skin. Marcy suppresses a wave of nausea. "I think that makes you the enemy, too," he says.

He smells like smoke and citrus. The hair on her skin prickles. She doesn't know how to get out of this.

"I'm not like you, Franc," she says.

"Well, that's a good thing, Mary."

Just as he leans in to kiss her, her stomach growls loudly. She remembers she hasn't eaten since the day before.

Franc's hand is still on her waist. He moves it around to her stomach. "Have you got a lion in there?" he asks.

Marcy knows this is her chance. "How embarrassing," she says, trying to laugh as she shakes her head. "It's just—I—my family and I—we're hungry. We don't have enough to eat."

Franc frowns at her, and for a moment, Marcy wonders if he is going to question her. He knows she lives on a farm, that she has access to potatoes and fresh milk.

Instead, though, he begins to walk again. "Why didn't you say so?" he says, pulling Marcy along. "If it's rations you want, I can get you rations."

They take a left at the top of the hill, rounding the corner to where a group of women stand outside a butcher shop, ration cards in hand.

Marcy, realizing what Franc is about to do, begins to panic.

"Actually, Franc," she says, "Don't worry about the rations."

"Nonsense," says Franc. "I can't let you go hungry, Marcy."

He walks right up to the throng of women.

"Miss Bernadette," he says.

A tall, beautiful ginger turns around. Marcy immediately recognizes Bernadette from the dance.

If Bernadette is surprised to see her, she doesn't show it. Smiling smoothly at both of them, she steps momentarily out of line.

"Officer," she says to Franc. "What a pleasant surprise."

Franc nods. "Bernadette, this is Mary."

Bernadette nods. "We met the other night at the lovely dance."

"Of course."

The other women in the line begin to look at Bernadette and Marcy. A few of them start to whisper. Marcy fights the urge to run.

"Mary here needs some extra rations," he says. "I hoped you could help her with that."

"Of course I can," says Bernadette. "We'll get you taken care of right here with this grocer."

"But—this isn't my store," Marcy says. "I'm registered at a store in St. Mary's." Islanders were since the Occupation only allowed to purchase goods at their local store.

"No matter," says Bernadette with a wave. "We know this grocer." She winks at Franc.

"Meet me after you get your rations, back at the hotel," Franc says. "I've got some work to wrap up, and then we'll have a picnic."

Marcy doesn't ask why he suddenly doesn't want to stand in a ration line, but she says nothing.

To Bernadette, Franc says, "I'll see you Wednesday evening, for dinner. Officer Fraudt invited me."

"Lovely," Bernadette says brightly. "Marcy, you'd be welcome to join us as well."

"Mary," says Franc. "Her name is Mary."

Bernadette looks confused for a moment. Marcy gives her a slight nod and she continues. "Oh yes, my apologies. Slip of the tongue. Say you'll come Wednesday, Mary."

"Alright then," says Marcy, not wanting to go but unable to say no when she stands in the ration line at Franc's mercy.

Franc kisses her forehead and marches off, leaving Marcy in line with Bernadette.

"Well, that's a confusing trick, switching your name like that," she whispers as she gets in line again. "Could get you into a lot of trouble."

"I thought it was better he didn't know my real name," Marcy whispers back.

Bernadette shakes her head. "You young people can be so foolish," she says.

They step back in line. Marcy notices the women around them step back.

"Well, you'll have to come on Wednesday evening. You can bring the crystal sets. And you can meet some of my friends."

Marcy nods, feeling uncomfortable.

"I'll need you to come as your happiest, most charming self. We get these men drinking and they share all kinds of classified information."

Marcy swallows. The stakes of the resistance have suddenly spiked: Marcy seeing a German, Louisa hiding a laborer. Basil will be so jealous when he finds out, she thinks.

"How do these rations work?" Marcy asks. She looks down at Bernadette's book, noticing that extra allotments have been made to it. Where most people only receive four oz. of meat per week, Bernadette was allowed eight.

"The grocer here is friendly with the Germans," says Bernadette. "I tell him you're with me, and he'll give you double rations here." She pauses, then lowers her voice. "I don't need to tell you how dangerous it would be for you if anyone found out what you were using these rations for."

Marcy stares at her, wondering how Bernadette seems to know what she is up to.

Just then, an older lady walks up the street. She's wearing a threadbare floral dress and rubber tires fashioned into shoes. In one hand she carries an armful of shopping bags, a cane in the other, and she struggles to keep hold of everything.

"Excuse me," Bernadette says loudly, stepping slightly out from her place in line as the woman passes. "May I help you with those?" The woman frowns at Bernadette, then spits at her feet. "Don't need no help from a Jerrybag," she says loudly, and hobbles on.

Bernadette blushes, then stares straight ahead.

The old woman seems to give the others standing in line more courage.

"Go away, Jerrybag," one woman calls from further up in the queue. "We don't want you or your sort in our line."

"Yes, get your rations your own way, and leave the honest people to get their rations in peace," says another woman.

Bernadette draws herself up to her full height and continues to stare straight ahead. "Stay calm, Marcy," she says. "Half these women buy on the Black Market. We have every right to be here."

"The young one with her is a Jerrybag too!" Calls another woman. "Sleeping with the enemy just for some extra sweets."

Marcy tries to let the comments roll off of her. The crowd begins to chant around them: *Jerry-bag. Jerry-Bag.*

Then, amidst the cries, Marcy hears another voice.

"Marcy?"

Marcy turns and sees her mother standing in the street, in pale blue heels and a matching purse, hurt and confusion written across her face.

Chapter Forty-Five

LOUISA

1943

Louisa tries to keep herself busy so she won't think about the boy in her house. Through the living room, Louisa can see the boy perched on the edge of the sofa, head buried in the English-Russian dictionary Louisa found in Eugene's room, from the time he was fourteen when went through his Dostoyevsky phase. Obsessed with *The Brothers Karamazov*, Eugene had purchased the dictionary at a rummage sale, insistent that he would learn enough Russian to read the book in the original language. He joined a football team that fall and never spoke about learning Russian, or *The Brothers K*, again.

You never allowed me to change, Louisa thinks about Eugene's words in her dream. She remembers how upset she'd been, when Eugene said he didn't want to read anymore, that he wanted to go out and be with his friends. "But, you're a reader," she had insisted to him, always proud of how much and at what level he read.

"And now I'm a football player," Eugene had said, grabbing his bag and letting the door slam behind him.

Louisa had pulled that dusty dictionary off the shelf this morning and ran her fingers over the thin pages, a wave of guilt washing over her. She gave the dictionary to the boy at breakfast.

Now, she prepares herself to enter the room, once, then twice. She bursts through the door, and finds herself standing in the middle of the sitting room, which suddenly feels much too small.

"Hello," she says as she brushes her hands on her apron. She is consciously aware that this is the first time she's been alone with him since he arrived at her house.

He looks at his dictionary for a moment, then up at her. "Good– morning," he asks slowly, stumbling over the words. "How are you?"

Louisa watches him, his brow furrowed in concentration, hands, which are still stained brown and calloused, holding the fragile paper between his fingers like it is something precious to him, like if he presses it too hard everything that has come to him will disintegrate in his hands.

She stares into his eyes, a living hope for her son.

"Fine, thank you," says Louisa. "And you?"

He looks down again, carefully running that stained finger down the lines of words. His finger stops. After studying it for a moment, he looks up.

"Good. Thank you," he replies, leaving out the *h* in *thank you,* the d in good ringing like a t. It is enough.

They both nod eagerly, neither of them sure what to say next.

Louisa finds the mustard yellow sofa she and Jon have had since they bought the house and plops down onto the thread-bare fabric. She wonders how her home looks to him. To her, until Eugene left, it has been a place of warmth, of redemption. Now, she notices the faded rug, the thin upholstery, the dreary curtains. It seems like when Eugene left, he took everything with him.

And then, either because she cannot help herself, or because there is a safety in knowing the boy cannot understand her, Louisa begins to talk.

"My boy loved to paint—watercolors. He loved to paint the sunset and the water, right outside our window." Louisa gestures toward the window in the back of the house—the row of glass doors in the con- servatory that lead to the sea. I probably have thousands of paintings he's done. I can't throw away a single one."

The boy crosses his legs and sits back. Louisa continues to talk.

"He stopped painting a few years ago. Said he was too busy with other things like football and girls. I was livid. Absolutely raging mad. Told him he was throwing away his talent. Jon went to all the football matches, and I refused to go. Sat at home looking at his watercolors, thinking my boy had left me. I had no idea."

She rubs her forehead.

"I used to think—well," she pauses. "You can't understand me, can you?"

The boy continues to stare at her blankly, granting Louisa the boldness to say what she's never said out loud.

"I used to think that he wasn't enough. I wanted more children, you see. Had another girl. She—I lost her. And for years, I was lost in that grief, even after I was finally able to get my head above it. I was treading in it, wishing I had more than what was given me, wishing Eugene had a sister. There was this idea in my head that I had let everyone down. I was less of a mother because I was only a mother to one. The only way to absolve that guilt was for my own child to be perfect. I was locking him in a golden cage and didn't know it."

She wipes her eyes, which are beginning to brim with tears.

"It wasn't until Eugene told me that he was leaving for war that I realized what I had, but something kept me from going back. It's like I took him for granted, all this time, thinking he would always be here. I could wish for more because of what I already had; because of what Eugene already was. Awful, when I say it out loud, isn't it?"

The boy sets the dictionary aside and leans forward, rubbing his hands on his knees. Louisa continues to talk with the sense that she has lost control, the words spilling out.

"I'm sure your mum is worried sick about you, just like I am about my Eugene. I should ask your name, that's what I would want another mum to do about my son. You've got his eyes, have I told you that? They're just like my son's. It makes me long for him so much that I can't even ask about you."

Louisa feels a sob push its way up her throat. She swallows to keep it from escaping her mouth. Putting her head in her hands, she presses her palms against her eyes, until the pressure makes her think they will burst open.

The boy stands up. He puts a hand, lightly, on Louisa's shoulder. She reaches up and grabs it, opens her eyes, which are seeing black dots. He pulls her to her feet.

Pointing to his chest with his large, stained hand, he says, "Fedor." Louisa wonders briefly if he understood everything she just said. But from his blank expression, she realizes he simply wants to connect with her.

She points to her own chest. "Louisa," she says.

They stand there, together, in their new knowledge of each other. Fedor puts his arms out, and Louisa falls into them.

The sob that had been caught inside her throat escapes, and she weeps, as she stands with her troubles in the arms of the boy who has troubles of his own. Both are carrying burdens far too heavy, but they walk the road together. For this moment, Louisa's house becomes full again.

For now, it is enough.

***

For a blissful afternoon, Louisa lives in a dream where her boy with green eyes is returned to her. Fedor sleeps in her son's bed, wears his clothes, sits at his place at the table. He scarfs down everything Louisa feeds him: fried eggs, bacon, weak tea.

She talks to him: she can't stop herself. Because he can't understand her, Louisa feels safe. Every memory of Eugene, it seems, has flooded to the surface. She talks about the way he ate toast, crust first, how he liked to walk on the balls of his feet, the way he bit his lip when concentrated and how sometimes he would come home after a Math test with a bleeding lip from biting it so hard.

Bringing out journals, she sits at the table with Fedor and goes through the complete history of Eugene's childhood. Fedor listens patiently, not understanding, but nodding at every opportunity.

"You'll bore him, Lou," Jon says when he comes inside.

"He's not bored, he's interested. Aren't you, Fedor?" she asks him.

Fedor smiles politely and watches.

Basil comes by late that afternoon. If he is surprised to see a runaway in the house, he does not show it. He tells them about the conditions at the camp. He had ridden his bike to Grouville, where Fedor was. "Completely crowded," he says. "Buried on top of one another. Sleeping out in the elements."

"Who are they?"

"Poles, Russians, Spaniards," says Basil. "I saw one woman whose bowl was empty. She crawled around, holding out her bowl to people like she was asking, 'Can I have a bite? Just one bite?' One man carried her bowl up to the O.T. Guards. They laughed, and then began to hit him, until eventually he fell over, unconscious."

Louisa shakes her head, trying to block the image out.

"What are they doing here, Basil?" asks Jon.

"Building, of some sort. Tunnels, fortifications. Perhaps to protect from an Allied invasion."

"Well, you're safe now, aren't you," Louisa says to Fedor, patting his leg.

***

Louisa wakes up in the middle of the night with a start. Pushing back the quilt, she sits up and wraps her arms around herself. Putting a match to the lamp, she slips out of bed, wincing as her bare feet hit the wooden floor.

Jon groans in his sleep as he rolls over. "Go back to bed, love," she whispers, touching his forehead.

She puts on her robe, takes the lamp and tiptoes downstairs, trying to shake the displacement and unease that awakened her. Fetching a glass of water, she sits down with the lamp at the kitchen table, thinking about all she would do for a cup of tea right now.

It was the dream that awakened her, she thinks as she watches the lamp cast shadows on the far wall, flickering gently, like calm, lapping waves. The dream she has almost nightly now: Eugene at the beach, walking away from her. Except, tonight, when Eugene looked at her, his face twisted into the boy's face—the boy asleep in her son's bed. His curly hair morphed into thick black, his face slender and gaunt. Reaching out to her with hands that were not his—long and slender— but the boy's, scraped and cracking, filthy with a black that will not wash out in the bath water.

And then, the boy morphs again, into Violet's boy, Peter. He is dirty and helpless, and he is being sucked into the sea's current. Louisa reaches out and tries to save him, but he won't take her help. "Mummy!" he calls. "I want my mum!"

Louisa recoils, in the dream. She slides back into the sand, falling into the shell, until she wakes up.

As she sits in the dark kitchen, Louisa thinks about Peter. She barely knows the boy, having only spoken with him on a few occasions. Embarrassment, or jealousy, or unmet longing, keeps her from ever approaching him.

She thinks about those months after Marcy's birth, after Violet told her she would be keeping the baby, how Louisa couldn't reach out to her. Louisa knew, of course, that Violet's baby wasn't hers. She knew she couldn't have it. But the desire for a baby, the jealousy mixed with the deep grief, all clouded Louisa's vision, and the only thing that gave her any clarity was blaming Violet.

Ridiculous, she thinks, taking another sip of her water. *I knew Marcy wasn't mine.* But the unease lingers.

The lock jiggles on the front door. Louisa jumps up. She grabs the rolling pin from the shelf next to her, and tiptoes toward the door. It swings open, and Louisa yells, "Get out!" as she swings her pin.

Marcy ducks just in time, narrowly missing the wooden weapon. She's carrying a paper bag, and it spills out over the floor. "Louisa!" she says, crouched on the ground. "It's just me!"

255

Louisa drops the wooden pin, embarrassed. She slams the door shut and locks it. "You should have knocked, or announced yourself," she mumbles as she stoops to help Marcy retrieve her items.

"You gave me the key before I left, remember?" Marcy whispers back. "I thought everyone would be asleep."

"What are you doing out so late, Marcy? And on such a misty night? You'll catch your death, if not by the Germans, by cold." She leans forward to pick up a dark tin. Flipping it over, she squints in the dim light as she reads the label. *English breakfast tea.*

"Where in the devil's den did you get your hands on real tea?" Louisa whispers.

Marcy sits on the floor, legs pulled into her chest, next to the pile of goods: chocolate, cheese, bread, and tea.

"I told you I'd get you rations," she says with a shrug, but for a fleeting moment, Marcy looks raw, in the way she'd seen her mum look: like a wounded deer, exposed to a life not made for a sensitive heart.

Louisa should have noticed Marcy was still out when she went to bed. Marcy had a row with her mum. She'd spent a night at Gran's but after finding out about the Russian, wanted to stay with Louisa to help.

Louisa had been so busy, taking care of the boy, hatching escape plans in case anyone should show up. Finally, at around midnight, she'd fallen into a fitful sleep on her bed, only to be awakened by her dream.

In her head, she runs through the possible ways Marcy could have gotten her hands on these rations, and every way leads to a place where she is not comfortable.

Marcy begins picking up the boxes and tins of food. "Where shall I put these, then?" she asks.

"Marcy," says Louisa softly, and as soon as she speaks, she knows what she must say. "I cannot allow this. Whatever you're doing to get these foods—we'll be okay without them."

As she says this, her stomach grumbles, loudly. Louisa presses her hands against the hollow of her stomach, where she has not eaten for giving her bread and soup to the boy, making large pots to put out in the bushes for the workers to take on their way in and out of the tunnels.

Marcy raises her eyebrows. "All I did was speak to Basil's client, Bernadette," she says. "It was really easy— she knows people and she's—she's just so *grateful* for the crystal sets we've given her and her friends."

Picking up a tin of canned salmon, Marcy stands up and walks toward the kitchen, tenderly, like the floor is full of air pockets she will slip through if she steps in the wrong place.

Could that be it? Louisa wonders, relief swirling around her like a rope, beckoning her to reach out and grab it. Could it just be that a good, grateful person in town wanted to show some support? Standing up, stretching her arms over her, she follows Marcy into the kitchen, legs heavy with the desire for sleep.

"Is that really all, my girl?" Louisa says quietly, standing at Marcy's back, longing to put a hand on her shoulder, to stroke her dark hair. "You know I view you almost as—well, your mum and I...what I'm trying to say is that I care for you a great deal, and putting yourself in harm's way— it's just not worth it for the rations. We live on a farm, for heaven's sake."

The girl's shoulders tense, and her fingers press into the counter. After a moment, she says, "Even on a farm, food doesn't go very far, not when the Germans keep taking it all and you're trying to feed all their workers."

"We can manage!" says Louisa, though she really doesn't know how they will. She clenches her fists together to keep from grabbing the box of tea.

"Really, Louisa. I'm quite alright, honestly! Just tired. But no one forced me into anything, truly. Let's go to bed, so that we can dream about a precious, real cuppa in the morning."

Louisa pauses. She's not used to not knowing, and she doesn't think Marcy is telling her the full truth. But if she's asked, and Marcy insists she's fine, well, what else can Louisa really do but trust her and keep an eye on her?

"You just be careful, my girl," she says solemnly. "No amount of rations is worth tearing yourself in half."

Marcy heads toward the stairs, carrying one of the lanterns in her hand. At their base, she pauses, and turns back to Louisa one more time. "I'd do anything for him, you know," she says quietly.

Marcy's face is cast into light by the lantern, so that she appears to be glowing. "Absolutely anything."

She turns and heads to bed.

Louisa carefully organizes the new rations into the cupboard before going to bed. She dreams that night fitfully, not of the boy with her son's eyes, but of the look on Marcy's face, who turns into Violet, who says:

"I would have done anything for you. Absolutely anything."

When she wakes, her pillow is wet with tears.

CHAPTER FORTY-SIX

VIOLET

1943

Violet hated that Margot was spreading horrid rumors about her daughter, hated her more because it was true.

There is her daughter, in a ration line that isn't hers, being called a Jerrybag in the middle of the street in broad daylight.

Marcy's face, when she turns, is etched with guilt. She steps forward and says, "Mum?"

Violet shakes her head. She backs away. *This* was what her daughter was up to? The "war effort?"

Even as she knows that this couldn't be what was happening at Louisa's house, that Louisa would never work with the enemy like this, she feels betrayed. Either Louisa didn't know what Marcy was up to, which was bad enough--if Louisa was going to play second mother, she should at least be a responsible one—or worse: Louisa had known, and had said nothing.

Violet gathers her shopping and spins on her heel.

Walking away from her daughter feels like the most un-motherly thing Violet has ever done, and yet her pride and hurt will not let her do otherwise.

She walks along the Esplanade, right up to the street Helena lives on. Not ready to knock yet, Violet sits heavily on a bench.

How foolish it seems now, for her to have taken the bus to St. Helier, to look for Helena, to try to find out what was going on with her daughter, when her daughter was broadcasting who she was to all the world.

Violet wipes a tear as she stares out into the harbor, where fishing boats are going out into the sea at a bizarre hour, to line up with German regulations.

Violet sighs, brushing a stray hair out of her face. *Foolish girl*, she thinks. Marcy has generally been so responsible. She wonders what could have gotten into her, what kind of attention a German would have had to have given her daughter to make her interested.

Dating the enemy, if that's what Marcy was doing, terrifies Violet. She worries about what will happen to Marcy, when and if the war tables turn. Her heart clenches at the thought of Marcy being on the wrong side of history, of what those women if the ration line would do to her daughter if there were no German officer to protect her.

Violet looks out at the ocean and thinks about Eugene's visit and his intentions. She wonders if she could have prevented all of this by sharing what Eugene had said. She closes her eyes and sees herself again, running across the sand, trying to save someone she's already lost.

"Is this seat taken?" Violet hears a voice behind her.

Violet jumps and turns around. Helena stands over her, bursting out of her dark purple dress: the only woman on the island who has gained weight during the Occupation.

"Helena," she says. "What a surprise. I– I was just on my way to see you."

"Thought as much," says Helena, a murky, navy blue, plopping down next to her so that the bench shakes. "Usually when people want to see me they wait on this bench for a while. Deciding if their conscience will allow them to knock." She unwraps a package in her hands: scones. Real, fluffy, scones, with candied ginger. "People hate the Black Market, until they get hungry enough."

She offers Violet a scone. Violet can smell it from where she sits and knows it has been made with real flour, butter, eggs. She sits on her hands to keep from taking it.

"Suit yourself, then," Helena says. She takes a big bite of her scone, dropping crumbles onto her skirt. "So, what is it you've come to see me for? Buying or selling?"

"I beg your pardon?" Violet asks.

"Are you looking to buy goods or sell them? I know you live on a farm and likely have enough to spare. You could make a pretty penny."

"Oh—neither. Helena, I came to ask you a question."

"Oh?"

Now that Violet sits here with Helena, she cannot bring herself to ask outright about Louisa or Marcy. Instead, she says, "There's a woman I just saw in the ration line. She's maybe about my age, red hair. All the other women in the line were calling her a Jerrybag."

"Mm-hmm," Helena nods as she chews her scone. "That would be Bernadette. She's notorious around these parts."

"For what?"

"For being such a brazen Jerrybag. Lives with a German, don't she, and has them coming in and out her house all the day long. Her poor mum and child, forced to watch it all happen and can't do a thing about it."

Violet nods. "I see," she says.

"War comes to an end and she'll be in for it, she will. People can only forgive so much for so long."

Violet swallows a fresh surge of panic at what will happen to her daughter.

"Say," Helena says, "Haven't spoken much to Louisa, have you?"

"What does Louisa have to do with anything?" Violet asks, though she knows it's the whole reason she's here— to find out what Louisa is up to.

"Well, she came here the same way you did not too long ago, wanting to buy real flour. Not seen her since and the contact I gave her said she never came through. But she's been up to some things, I'm sure of it. Had a fishy look about her when she came round."

Violet says nothing.

"How do you know about that Jerrybag, anyway?" Helena asks.

Violet sighs. She is torn between loyalty to Louisa and panic for her daughter. Panic wins out.

"This is confidential," she prefaces.

Helena pats her leg and says, "Of course it is, dear."

"Louisa and my daughter Marcy are up to something. Something they shouldn't be. And it seems to me that woman—Bernadette? —has something to do with it all."

"Oh?" Helena leans in.

Violet wonders if she's said too much.

"I'm sure it's nothing," says Violet quickly, standing up.

"I'll tell you what," says Helena, standing up as well. Crumbs from her scones fall off of her dress and onto the ground. "I can ask around a bit. Find out what that Bernadette woman is up to and if it's got anything to do with your daughter and friend."

"You won't—asking around won't get them into any trouble, will it?" Violet asks.

"Not in the least," says Helena. "I can be very secretive. But, it will cost you."

"Cost me?"

"I'll need something I can sell. Food, jewelry, perhaps your neighbor's exclusive china?" Helena speaks with a greedy shine in her eyes.

Violet's stomach sinks. She is sure she has made a mistake, getting involved with Helena. She lifts her chin and says, "You find out information, and then I'll pay you."

She expects Helena to argue. Instead, Helena smiles and says, "Fair enough. I like a woman who knows how to bargain."

All the way home, Violet wonders what she has done.

CHAPTER FORTY-SEVEN

LOUISA

1943

"I don't know what the solution is, Lou, I'm just saying, we can't keep him here for the rest of the war."

Jon and Louisa are standing in the kitchen. Louisa is washing dishes and then passing them to Jon, who dries them with a towel. Fedor is sweeping the floor around them.

"He can hear you, Jon," Louisa says.

"He can't understand a thing."

"Jon, why can't we keep him? What harm is he doing here?"

"We're in danger every minute he is in our house. If we get caught, they'll take us off the island."

Louisa bites her lip. She knows he is right. "We can't send him back," she says. "What if he were Eugene?"

This question, "What if he were Eugene," is the center around which all their conversations circle. Louisa keeps hoping that if it's Eugene, somewhere across the continent, stranded at a person's house, that someone is brave and bold enough to keep him.

"We can't send him back, of course not," says Jon. "But there's got to be a safer place than ours. Ouen's been over twice in the past two days. It won't be long before someone drops in unannounced. Or until a German comes back to collect our eggs. We need to get him to a more remote place."

Louisa nods. "You're right," she admits. "Let's ask Basil when he comes round. Maybe he'll have an idea."

Just then, there is a knock on the door. Louisa jumps, setting down the plate she is washing in the sink. She looks at Jon.

"I'll get it," she says.

Jon nods. He gestures to Fedor, who has stopped sweeping, and pulls him out of the house toward the potting shed. "Tell me when it's all clear," he whispers.

Louisa brushes her hands off on her apron and walks toward the front door. "Just a minute!" she calls loudly. She pauses, trying to calm her breath and her racing heart.

Whoever is at the door knocks again.

"Yes," Louisa snaps, "I'm coming!"

Flustered, she whips open the door and comes face to face with Violet's mother.

"Oh," she says. "Hello."

Louisa has met Violet's mother, Rosa, only a handful of times, but she would recognize her anywhere. Tall and thin, Rosa has a glamorous air about her even in her seventies. She has the face of a woman who has always been beautiful and knows it. Somehow, in 1943, in the middle of an Occupation and years of supply shortages, Rosa looks as stylish and put together as ever. She wears a checkered skirt suit and navy blue pumps, and might be the only woman on the island who still has access to lipstick.

"Louisa," Rosa says mildly, "I do hope I haven't interrupted you."

"Not at all," Louisa says, trying to act like everything is perfectly normal, like she sees her ex-best friend's mother all the time. "Please, come in."

She leads Rosa into the sitting room, then notices Eugene's shoes, which Fedor has been borrowing, next to the coffee table. "Actually," she says, turning around abruptly, "It's such a lovely day. Why don't we sit in the front garden?"

The front garden is barely a garden at all. A bistro table on a small patio, surrounded by the overgrown plants that Violet used to maintain for Louisa. This summer, the space has become overrun with weeds.

Rosa sits, and Louisa studies her for a moment as she removes her apron. Louisa knows the relationship between Violet and her mum is not, and has never been good. Once, years ago, Louisa had pressed Violet about it, wanting to get to the bottom of what happened between them so she could fix it.

"It's not one thing, Lou, it's just the way she is— the way she and I are together," Violet had said as she scrubbed her pans clean. "We just—we just *miss* each other."

Louisa had been there once, when the two of them were together. It was after Eugene's christening, at a tea in the garden at Violet's. Louisa decided to invite Violet's mum, and Violet had warned her she would regret it. The two barely spoke to each other, and when they did, Violet's shoulders tensed, and she always responded defensively.

"Are there forks, Violet?" her mum had asked, walking through the yard with cakes on little plates.

"Of course there are forks," Violet had responded, holding a handful of cloth napkins.

"Well let me have the napkins, and you can go find them," Rosa had said. "Can't keep our guests waiting, can we?"

Violet had said nothing, but had slammed the door much harder than necessary on her way inside.

Now, Rosa looks back at Louisa, resting her hands in her lap. "I suppose you are wondering why I'm here," she begins.

"It's lovely to see you, at any rate," says Louisa. She prays Jon will stay with Fedor inside the shed. "Can I get you some tea?"

Rose put a hand up to silence her. "I'll be quick," she says. "Louisa, I know things between you and my daughter have been—different— for some time now,"

Louisa bristles. "How did you know that?" she asks. Then, realizing she's been rude, she says, "Forgive me, I–"

"No matter," Rosa says, waving her hand with a dismissive air. "It's a fair question. My daughter might not confide in me, but I stopped hearing about you for long enough to know something had happened. Right around the time I stopped hearing about the baby you were going to have."

A fresh pang of grief hits Louisa. "I lost her."

Rosa sighs. She opens her purse and pulls out a string of rose-gold pearls. She sets them down on the table. They gleam in the sunlight.

"Where did you get those?" Louisa asks her. "I gave those to Nancy LeCairn before she evacuated the island."

Even as she asks the question, Louisa remembers the day she found the pearls in Violet's closet, the way Violet had turned white and insisted Louisa kept them, like the pearls were a ghost Violet needed to shake.

"Louisa," Rosa says. "You are by now far along enough in your time as a mother to have regrets, are you not?"

In her mind's eye, Violet waits in her garden for Louisa to get out of bed, Violet's belly shines round and large, Violet holds Peter out to Louisa at his christening, like she is offering him as tribute. *You never let people change.*

"Yes," she answers.

Rosa looks out toward the front garden for a moment, and presses her fingers to her temple, as though very tired. "Violet's father gave me those pearls on my birthday, many years ago," she says. "They cost him a fortune, far more than we could afford. Said he did it because he loved me, but I knew that wasn't the real reason."

"What other reason could there be?" asks Louisa.

"To keep me."

"Pardon?" Louisa leans forward, confused.

Rosa sighs. "I grew up with money, a lot more money than my husband ever had. Our family had means, connections, and I threw it all away when I married so far below my class."

Louisa does not understand why Rosa, someone she barely knows, is confiding in her like this.

"Richard did well for himself, becoming a banker, but he was always insecure about what he made and whether I could ever be truly happy with him. So he overspent. He took out loans and lines of credit to buy gifts for me, like these pearls, or new dresses, or shoes. He never believed me when I told him I was happy with him, that I loved him for who he was, not what he gave me."

"I see," says Louisa, because she has no idea what else to say.

"One day, while Richard was out, a man came to the door wearing a black suit. He said he was calling in one of Richard's loans, and if it wasn't paid, we would lose the house. At the time, Violet was around ten or eleven, and I couldn't stand the thought of her losing her home. Thinking I could use some of the conversation skills from my upbringing, I invited him inside."

Rosa twists the bracelets on her wrist now, taking a deep breath before she continues. "I made him a cup of tea while he told me about Richard's overspending. It was even worse than I had imagined. The worst part was it was all for me. He had only done it to keep me, even though he must have known he couldn't pay it back.

"The man—he took a liking to me, I suppose. He enjoyed my company. I'm ashamed to say it now, but I liked him too. And he made it clear that there were other ways I could help to pay off my husband's debt."

Louisa gasps now, before she can help herself. "Surely, not!" she says.

Rosa waves a hand, dismissing Louisa's alarm. "Happens more often than you might think, my dear. Men in power using vulnerable women: a story old as history itself. And really, he was so charming, so powerful. It wasn't just him. I liked him. In a twisted, upside-down kind of way."

"But—it sounds like you loved Richard."

"I did love him. More than anything. That's why I kept his debt from closing in on him."

"Did he know?"

Rosa looks away. "I have wondered," she says. "But someone else in our family did."

"Who?" Louisa leans forward.

"Time went on and this man and I became more and more

involved. He was sometimes wonderful, larger than life. Other days he was depressed, mean and cold. I began to feel trapped with him."

Rosa pauses her story. She looks at Louisa with one eyebrow raised.

Louisa swallows. This man sounds familiar to her, like a man from a long ago dream.

"One morning, I met the man on the cliffs at Plemont Bay. By this time he was the sole holder of Richard's debts, and I wondered if I could pay him off completely, to get him to leave me alone for good. I brought these pearls, hoping they would work against our debt.

"It was a beautiful morning, I remember. The sun was fresh and crisp, there was a light breeze, and I was hopeful, so hopeful. The man took the pearls and told me I still owed more. He—he kissed me there, on the beach, and the feeling I remember was that I was drowning."

Louisa shifts in her seat.

"Then I heard my daughter's voice. She called up to me, from the bottom of the beach. My heart—there are no words for what the sight of her on the beach did in my heart. You hope to be so much for your kids, but there inevitably comes a time when they discover you as human, in all your flaws. I just didn't expect it to be so soon."

Louisa aches for Violet.

"I yelled back to her, and I stepped away from the man. He tried to hold me tighter and I pushed him away. But as I stepped back—" she pauses, covering her eyes with her fingers for a moment.

"What happened?" Louisa asks, as gently as she can.

"When I stepped back, I caught him by surprise. And, he fell."

"Fell down?"

"Fell off the cliff. Right down to where Violet was."

Louisa sucks her breath in. For once in her life, she is speechless.

"Are you alright, Louisa?" Rosa asks. She looks at Louisa with her piercing eyes.

Louisa's hands have gone clammy. "Yes," she finally says. "Yes, I'm alright. It's just—my father also died in a cliff accident. But that was miles away from Plemont Bay."

Rosa says nothing. She continues to stare at Louisa, not even blinking.

"It couldn't be. It wasn't..."

"It was," Rosa whispers the words. She reaches out her hands toward Louisa.

Louisa pulls away. She stands up and begins to pace around the tiny garden table.

"No. No, it can't be. Mummy said the accident happened at—"

She trails off. She realized she didn't actually know where the accident happened; her mother never said. She vaguely referred to the cliff accident, and Louisa had somehow been able to convince herself the accident happened in some faraway land, like France or Italy. The thought of it happening in the same place where she had lost her own baby overstimulates her in a way she is not used to.

When it came to her father, Louisa had thought she was far enough away from the grief that it couldn't choke her anymore with its rawness. Time and space is supposed to heal everything, and with enough of it, she had convinced herself that this was true. She made her father a fairy tale figure, someone two-dimensional and benign, who loved desserts and fell asleep reading the paper. But now, listening to Rosa talk about it, she sees him in color. She sees the big, efficacious man who takes up every room he is in. She remembers his singing voice, the way it seemed to wrap around her. She remembers the rows he had with her mum, the way he would yell and the way her hands would shake afterwards while she buttered the toast. She remembers, finally, the way he would draw into himself, the way it seemed like no one could reach him. After he died, she remembers the crushing, dizzying ocean of grief, but today, she also remembers the way her mum seemed light. After he died, she started singing again.

She sits back down at the table, stares at a loose stone near her foot. She tries to focus on breathing, in and out.

Rosa, seemingly unaware of the way Louisa's world is closing in on her, continues. "When he died, for a brief moment, I realized we were free. Richard was free from his debt. We wouldn't lose the house. Violet was safe. And Richard's pride was left intact. But then I got home, and Violet—she wasn't right. She was traumatized, of course, by what happened, thinking the man falling off the cliff was her fault. I couldn't explain to her what happened. I could never tell her that was your dad. And I couldn't risk Richard finding out about everything. I made a mistake, I know that now, and I wish I could take it back."

"What did you do?"

"I lied to her. Told her I was never there, insisted she made the whole thing up."

"You *lied?*" Louisa hangs on the precipice of fear and rage. She opens and closes her hands to keep herself from slapping this woman.

"I couldn't risk Richard knowing about it. I thought, she's eleven, she's bound to forget. But then a man showed up with the pearls and she saw them, recognized them from Plemont Bay. I insisted she had imagined it. And things—well, things have never been the same between us since. Quite frankly, I think Violet's never stopped blaming herself."

Louisa leans back, letting the revelation wash over her. *Violet*, she says in her head, *that was so much to carry, all these years*. She suddenly understands Violet's reservations, her inability to let people in, the tension between her and Marcy. All these years, what Violet has been seeking is pardon.

"Did she know?" Louisa asks. "Did she know it was my dad?"

Rosa shrugs. "I don't know," she says finally.

"Why didn't you ever tell her?" Louisa asks. "Why didn't you say something, after Richard died?"

"Pride and time are a strong callus, my girl," Rosa says. "There's too much between us now. But—it's not too late for you."

Rosa pushes the pearls toward Louisa. "Don't you think our girl has worn the blame for things she didn't do long enough?"

The words hit Louisa like a punch to the gut. She wonders how Rosa could have known all of that.

"You're the best friend Violet has ever known," Rosa says. "She needs you. Don't keep locking her out."

Rosa stands and picks up her purse. "Thank you for having me," she says. Louisa feels relief at her departure and slumps back into her chair. "And, I'm sorry for your loss. For all of them."

Louisa doesn't know what to do with the conflicting emotions inside of her. She wants to dismiss Rosa as a lunatic. And yet something deep within her tells her this information is true, the way she knows fall is coming before a single leaf has turned just by the way the air changes.

"One more thing," Rosa says over her shoulder as she leaves.

"Dear God, no," Louisa mumbles.

"You need to be more discreet about that fugitive you're hiding."

Louisa sits straight up. "I beg your pardon?" she asks, heart racing.

"I could see him through the curtains in the window. I heard the potting shed open while I was waiting for you to answer the door. Do yourselves a favor and get that boy a better place to hide."

Louisa watches, stunned, as Rosa makes her way down the drive.

CHAPTER FORTY-EIGHT

VIOLET

1943

For two days, Violet combats the nausea in her stomach by weeding her garden ferociously. On Wednesday there is a strong breeze and she can smell the salt of the sea as she digs her hands into the dirt. She wonders again if she said too much to Helena. Twice she packs up to walk to Louisa's and warn her, and then twice she unpacks and stays.

After another tense dinner, and putting Peter to bed, Violet returns to the garden. She sets up the cages for her tomato plants while the June sun hangs low in the sky.

For a moment, Violet pauses in her work and looks up. The island is beautiful this time of year, with flowers blooming all over the hedges, cows grazing happily in pastures, and the lavender and potato fields coming into themselves.

"Vi! Miss Vi!" A whisper comes from the hedge at the back of her garden. The greenery shakes.

Violet's heart catches in her chest. "Who's there?" she whispers back. A memory washes over her: Peter playing hide and seek in the hedge as children, running in and out of thick green bush in bare feet, squealing as he ran.

"Miss Vi, it's me," the voice says, and it sounds to Violet like it is coming out of a dream. Her hand covers her mouth, her heart catches in her throat as she sees the color of daffodil, of sunshine, of lemon peeking out of the hedge just an arm's length away from her.

He's alive. Eugene Westover is alive, with his sea green eyes, his unruly curly hair, the dimples in his cheeks. He's thin, so thin, but aren't they all, by now? And when he smiles, Violet cannot restrain herself.

"Eugene," she says, and rushes to give him a hug, scratching herself in the thick hedge. "Eugene, you're alive."

"I'm alive, Miss Vi," Eugene says as he pats her back. He smells like cedar and lavender, and his thin arms, those arms that as a baby were so chubby and plush, circle around like he is wrapping his arms around a tree.

He is dressed in civilian clothes that she knows aren't his. They are too bulky, too scratchy, to be something Louisa would have dressed him in.

"Come out of this brush so I can look at you," Violet says, when she's sure she can speak without crying.

"Are you sure it's quite safe?" Eugene asks quietly. "No one around?"

"It's only me and my tomato plants, Eugene," she says. "So unless they start talking, I think you're quite safe."

She laughs involuntarily, and she starts to tremble. He laughs too, and they look at each other like they can't quite believe what is happening.

"Would you like a cup of tea?" she asks, when she can speak again.

Eugene runs his hand through his hair, which has become unruly and wild. "Thank you, but I can't, Miss Vi. I don't have much time."

"What do you mean, much time?" Violet asks. "You're back on Occupied Jersey. You've all the time in the world."

Eugene shakes his head. "I leave again tonight, Miss Vi."

"Leave?" Violet has the strangest sense that she is dreaming, that she will blink and Eugene will disappear before her eyes. "Now just a minute, young man. You disappear for three years, and then somehow manage to show up on Occupied Jersey, and now you're telling me you're just going to turn around and leave? I don't think so. You come into the kitchen right now and at least let me feed you before you disappear again."

Eugene begins to smirk, and then quickly hides it. "Yes, ma'am" he says with a salute, and follows her inside.

Violet walks the whole way two steps ahead of him, and when he comes in, she says, "For heaven's sake, take off those muddy shoes," and she pulls out the chair at the kitchen table for him to sit down. She busies herself by pouring a glass of milk, putting some cold potatoes and ham on a plate.

When she slides the plate in front of him, he reaches out and touches her hand. She looks at him and sees his eyes are glistening.

"Eugene, are you quite alright?" she asks.

Eugene nods, wiping his eyes quickly. "It's nothing," he says, trying to sound gruff. "I've just missed this—all of this."

Violet moves her hand away, and swallows the lump in her throat. She pulls out the chair next to him and plops down into it. "Right," she says briskly. "Tell me what's happened. Last we heard you were Missing In Action."

Eugene takes a bite of potato and chews with his eyes closed. Violet taps the table impatiently.

"I was knocked down at Dunkirk trying to board the boats," he says. "It was chaos, madness. The Germans were after us, on one end, the boats were leaving on the other. I was elbowed in the head, knocked down, stepped on. Completely passed out on the sand. Woke up in the middle of the night, surrounded by dead bodies."

Violet puts a hand to her mouth.

"I was too weak to move, but another soldier noticed I was alive and got me out of there. He carried me through the French countryside, and together we ended up at a barn near St. Malo. The owners of the farm kept us fed and let us sleep in the hayloft. Once I recovered, I was desperate to get back to my regiment, but it was too dangerous. I've been in hiding for nearly three years, posing as a Frenchman and working on a farm. My mum would be so ashamed," he jokes.

"Finally, my farmer friend secured me a boat. The French are so concerned about Allies coming from the North that, with some careful planning, we were able to slip away, and get onto Jersey. We're stopping here to resupply, and then going to England to report again for duty."

"Eugene," Violet says. "You've left so much out in that story if you weren't sitting in front of me I'd not believe a word of it. You're not a sailor. It's forty miles across to St. Malo. Even if you could sail the distance, the beaches of Jersey are heavily mined. It would be nearly impossible to make it onto these beaches in one piece, never mind unseen."

Eugene looks at her, and Violet knows that either for her sake or his nerves, he is not going to explain any further. "It nearly was," is all he says.

Violet sighs. "Well, it's going to be even harder to get back off," she says, throwing her hands in the air. "And a lot farther to England."

"Yes."

"And you're dead set on doing it, I suppose."

"I am."

"No way I'll convince you otherwise?"

"I'm afraid not, Miss Vi."

Eugene smiles, and Violet's heart cracks.

"Well," she says. "What do you need from me?"

CHAPTER FORTY-NINE

MARCY

1943

"Marcy—I mean, Mary, darling, I'm so glad you could come," says Bernadette loudly on Wednesday evening as she opens the door.

Marcy steps inside, conscious of the bit of tire rubber she stuffed into the bottom of her pump to patch up a hole in the foot. She tucks her hair, which she had spent over an hour trying to tame, behind her right ear.

"They're here, waiting in the dining room," Bernadette whispers as she leans in to kiss Marcy's cheek. "Three officers, and they've already had quite a lot to drink. And there's one more woman in the mix, someone new."

"Oh?" Marcy asks breathlessly.

"Name's Helena. I don't trust her as far as I can throw her, which isn't far at all. Only person on the island who has managed to get fat in the war."

Marcy nods, her stomach sinking. "Yes, I'm familiar."

Bernadette steps aside to let Marcy in, and leads her to the dining room. Her house smells of cigarette smoke, lamb and mint. As she walks, her sparkling blue dress that hugs every curve shimmers in the candlelight.

Just before she steps into the dining room, Marcy gets a glimpse of herself in the hallway mirror. She has lost so much weight, since the war began, that her face doesn't even look like her own anymore. It is hollow, angular, far more grown-up looking. On her legs, she had drawn a dark line to make it look like she was wearing stockings. She checks now, to ensure the pencil hadn't smudged.

"And here's our girl," Bernadette says as she pushes open the door to the dining room.

Marcy is greeted by the smell of whiskey and smoke in her eyes. Franc comes over and kisses her cheek. "Hello, my darling," he whispers in her ear. Marcy tries not to flinch.

"Mary," says Bernadette, "You'll sit over here, next to Franc. And may I introduce you to Officer Fraudt?"

A tall, gruff, balding man stands up.

Marcy holds out her hand. "A pleasure," she says.

"And this is Major Zorhorst," Bernadette says, gesturing to a plump, short man next to Officer Fraudt.

"Major Zorhorst works with me in the Organization Todt," Franc says.

"Franc told us you were ravishing, but we did not expect you to look like royalty," says Major Zorhorst. "We've heard so much about you."

Marcy laughs, and as she does, she gets the sense that she is playing a part. "Good things I hope—but if not, don't tell me, otherwise I'll have to leave." Major Zorhorst chuckles.

"And this," says Bernadette, gesturing to the portly woman on the end of the table who is still seated, "Is Miss Helena Grange."

"Pleasure to meet you again," Marcy says, turning to her. "I'm Mary."

She meets the woman's eye and remembers being with Eugene at church in the summer, building forts under the tables while all the mums set up for something—was it the summer fete? She remembers Eugene chasing her, and her running into a very solid pair of legs, the hand that took her by the ear over to her mum, and said what a misbehaving, unkempt child she was.

Her mother, to her surprise, had not been embarrassed. She held her chin high and said, "I'll thank you for letting me be the child's mother, Helena."

Now, Helena looks at her, eyes narrowed. "Mary?"

Marcy swallows. "Yes," she says, hoping her voice is confident.

"Right," Bernadette says quickly. "Shall we eat?"

Helena leans closer. "Because," she continues loudly, "I could have been sure your name was Marcy."

There is a tense, pregnant pause. Marcy feels Franc looking at her, feels the blush rising from her chest up to her cheeks. She laughs nervously. "No, it's Mary."

"Mary, Marcy, they're confusing, aren't they?" Bernadette asks cheerfully with a clap of her hands. "Close enough to get muddled up."

"No one on this island can get my name right," says Major Zohorst with a chuckle. "I've heard every variation: Zebra, Zane, Zolt. I've stopped correcting."

"Well, here we'll just call you Jolly," says Bernadette, holding up a bottle of wine. "Who cares for another?"

They all sit around the table, which is filled with candles, laden with trays of lamb and roast potatoes. "Are those real Yorkshire puds, Bernadette?" she asks as the plates are passed around.

Bernadette winks at her. "Amazing what you can do with the rations these men provide," she says. She puts a hand on Officer Fraudt's arm and smiles at him.

Wine. Yorkshire Puds. Roast potatoes. Lamb and mint sauce. This is what a person who betrays their island can have. All the richness in the world at the cost of a soul. A whole inheritance for a meal. Marcy swallows her own nausea as she takes a pud and passes the platter.

"Yes, it seems you're at the receiving end of a generous hand, aren't you?" asks Helena.

Bernadette rolls her eyes at Marcy. Marcy wonders what Helena has done to secure an invitation to this dinner, as it definitely does not appear that she and Bernadette are friends.

Marcy can tell that Franc has already had quite a bit to drink. He laughs at everything Officer Zohorst says, none of which Marcy actually finds funny. His hand finds her leg, and travels higher and higher up her skirt. She tries her best to slide away discreetly, wondering how, even knowing what she knows about where he works and what he does, she can still feel attraction to him.

Bernadette laughs, flirts, and asks seemingly trivial questions about work and rations. Marcy marvels at her ability to act.

Helena eats, and eats, and eats. She has three helpings of lamb, takes her time drizzling the mint sauce over the top, and chews each piece thoroughly. She seems to be paying no attention to the conversation.

Talk eventually shifts to the work the Organization Todt was doing on the island, the fortresses being built.

"And cheers to Franc, for all his work on the Hohlgangsanlage tunnels," says Major Zohorst.

Bernadette claps and raises her glass. "That's wonderful, Franc," she says.

"What are those?" asks Marcy.

"Hospital," says Franc, at the same time that Major Zohorst says "Shelter." The two look at each other and begin to laugh.

"He's got those sorry workers working to the edge of their life for their next meal," says Officer Fraudt.

Franc smiles. "Not all of them, just the Russians and the Poles."

Marcy looks at him. He *did* know what their conditions were. Even worse, he'd had a part in making them that way.

His hand is still on her leg. She resists the urge to squirm.

"Which reminds me," says Major Zohorst, "Why I invited this lovely lady." He gestures to Helena, who pauses mid-bite.

"Oh?" asks Franc.

"Yes," says Major Zohorst. "She said she had a piece of information we might want to hear."

Helena continues to chew, staring directly at Marcy. Marcy looks down at her plate.

"Well," Helena says, "Perhaps Marcy—oh, I'm sorry, I mean, *Mary*—can add to this, but I've noticed some suspicious activity going on at the north end of the island in Greve de Lecq, with a certain woman named Louisa Westover."

Marcy drops her fork. It clatters on the plate. "Sorry," she says, fumbling to pick it up.

"What kind of activity?" Franc asks, leaning forward.

Helena waits. She waits until Marcy looks up and meets her eyes. "She's hiding someone," Helena says.

"A German?"

"No. A worker. Isn't she, Marcy?"

Marcy's head goes cold. Her hands start to shake. "I've no idea what you're talking about," she says. "And please call me Mary."

Helena turns toward the Germans. "She lives at Honeymeade Cottage, on Rue de Cortes. She—*Mary*, are you quite alright?"

Marcy is leaning over the table, head nearly touching her plate.

"I'm sorry, I suddenly feel very faint," Marcy says. The room spins around her.

"It must be the wine," Bernadette interjects, standing up. "Come outside and get some air, Marcy. You'll feel better."

"I'll be back," Marcy whispers to Franc.

"Mary," she hears Franc say, as his chair scrapes backward and he stands up.

Marcy turns, heart pounding. "Yes?" she asks.

"Bernadette— she called you Marcy."

For a moment, Marcy stands in stunned, exposed silence, like a trapped rabbit.

Bernadette swoops to her rescue. With a loud laugh, she says, "Oh, I've always been rubbish with names. And with Helena getting confused, it just rubbed off. It is Mary. A slip of the tongue."

Marcy laughs, like it is a funny joke. Franc doesn't, but continues to stare, with a frown on his face.

"Come Mary," says Bernadette, guiding her from the room. "Let's get you some air."

Quickly, she guides Marcy through the kitchen and out to the back door.

"Bernadette," Marcy says, "I've got to get to Louisa. I've got to warn her before they go."

Bernadette nods. "Take my car," she says. "There's a pass on the dashboard giving you permission to drive. No one will stop you for long. I'll tell them you're lying down. Hurry. You must go."

Marcy nods. She runs out to Bernadette's car, black and glistening in the late evening light. The engine revs as it comes to life. Like a madwoman, she drives out of town, through the winding roads of the countryside.

She drives like she is trying to reach Eugene.

Chapter Fifty

LOUISA
1943

Louisa sits as close to the open window as she can without falling out. There's a cool breeze outside. Tonight, she misses Eugene with a fierceness she cannot quench. He feels close, closer than he's felt in years, almost as though she could reach out into the wind and touch him.

Jon is at Basil's for the evening. They are in his parents' barn, brainstorming places for Fedor to go. If Rosa could figure out he was hiding here, Louisa knows it is only a matter of time before someone else does. And yet, she hates the thought of him leaving, not filling the house anymore with his presence.

Louisa shudders again as she rethinks her conversation with Rosa. The grief and sadness around her dad seems to have come pouring out like a locked up dam. She finds herself confused and irritable, fluctuating between thinking Rosa is lying and feeling the truth wrapping around her like a weight she cannot escape.

She wants to talk to someone about it. For once in her life, she's not ready to speak with Jon. Jon never knew her father. The person she most wants to talk to right now is Violet. She wants to tell Violet her mother is a lunatic. She wants to validate every fear Violet has ever had about herself. And she wants to slap Violet for never telling her earlier.

Fedor stands in the middle of the living room, playing the violin. As he plays, Louisa is reminded of a poem she read several years before becoming a mum, about teaching your children to notice the taste of a clementine: a perfectly round sphere, already divided into individual cases that burst into sweet juice when pressed on. She loved that poem, and used to think about all the ways she and Eugene would enjoy life together; the things she would stop and notice.

What you don't learn about being a mum until you are up to your elbows in it is that you are busy, so very busy. There is washing, feeding, sweeping the floor on repeat all day, nursing and burping all night. As Eugene grew bigger, she would think of the poem occasionally, about how she should stop and ask her son about what he was noticing, what he enjoyed.

But there was always so much to do: people to cook for, a playdate to get to, washing to hang, gardens to weed.

Now, Louisa thinks about how clementines have become such a rarity in the war. She misses the sharp citrus, the lingering sweetness, the stickiness on her face and fingers.

As Fedor plays, Louisa promises herself that if Eugene comes back, she will notice him– all of him. She will take him exactly as he is: football player, painter, reader, poet. She will only ever be glad that she has him.

A sudden banging on the door snaps her from her reverie. Fedor stops playing, looking startled. "Wait there," Louisa says.

She walks down the hall to the door, her body chilled away from the stove. Wrapping her robe tighter around her, she says, "Who's there?"

"Louisa!" Marcy's voice screams from the other side. "I forgot my key. Hurry! Open up!"

Louisa unlocks and opens the door. "Good gracious, child," she says. "What's all the fuss about?"

Marcy looks winded, panicked. "They're coming," she says, her voice hoarse. She wears a shimmery dress and no shoes.

Louisa's stomach drops. "Who?" she asks, though she knows who already.

"We've got to get Fedor out, to hide any evidence. Now!"

Until that moment, the gravity of what Louisa had done, whom she had hidden, and at what risk, had not been fully understood. Now, she feels as though she will be sick with the realization of what this could cost her, and those she loves.

"But how—" she begins to ask.

"Helena Grange told them. She must have been spying on you. Fedor!" Marcy calls. "Get in my car. Hurry!"

Fedor comes around the corner, still holding the violin.

"That stupid, evil woman," Louisa says. She pictures Helena, a spider, spinning a sticky web and trapping them all.

Marcy looks at Louisa. "Get him in the back seat, on the floor. Cover him with blankets. I'm going to clear out his room."

With startling competency, Marcy races upstairs.

Louisa stands in the foyer, dumbfounded. Instead of rushing Fedor to the waiting car, she says, "Fedor, have you got a pen? I need to leave a note for Eugene."

Fedor, who cannot understand what is happening to him, nor can he control his fate, stares back at Louisa.

"A pen. Please," Louisa says loudly. "Get me a pen!"

She storms into the kitchen, opening and closing drawers, searching for the elusive pen and paper she can't find.

Finally, on the back of a napkin. "*E. Gone out for a bit. Will come back the first moment I can. Eggs in the chicken coup and if it's still springtime when you come don't forget to pick strawberries from the garden. Love Mum xx.*"

"Louisa!" Marcy screams as she races back down the stairs. "Now! We've got to go!"

Louisa stares at the kitchen, the place where she cooked and laughed with her family for so many years. She knows she might be seeing it for the last time, and is filled with despair at not knowing what to look for.

CHAPTER FIFTY-ONE

VIOLET

1943

The evening feels cool and clean as Violet steps out into it. It's a clear night, and she knows she'll be able to see the stars if she stays out for long.

She's convinced Eugene to rest for a few hours in Marcy's room.

"My boat leaves at three in the morning," he protested to her. "I'm meeting my partner at midnight. I should stay awake."

"Nonsense," she had said. "I'll stay up for you while I pack up your supplies."

Exhaustion won out, and he agreed to go upstairs.

"Are you sure you don't want to see your mum?" she asked at least three times. "She would want to see you."

Even as she said it, she thought about Marcy over at Louisa's.

It's not the same, she told herself, but it feels exactly the same.

"I can't see her, Miss Vi. I think it would crush her if she saw me and then I left again. I just can't do that to her."

"She's stronger than you think," Violet said.

Eugene shakes her head. "You didn't see her, the day I left."

Violet wants to say she did see her, soon after, and that she also watched Louisa resurrect again, like a phoenix, but she knows Eugene has made his decision.

And, after he is asleep, she also makes hers.

It's a ten-minute walk to Louisa's house. All the way, Violet wonders if she is doing the right thing.

She thinks about Louisa, about the way she lay in bed after Eugene left. She thinks about how Louisa was made to be a mother, about how good and natural she was at it.

Suddenly, it occurs to Violet that she, too, is made to be a mother. Louisa may have been the more natural one, but Violet, too, is a mother who loves her children.

And it is because she understands that love, that need, that she stands outside Louisa's door and finds the courage to knock.

She sticks her chin out, practices what she is going to say when Louisa answers. "I think you should know he's here" she rehearses. "Eugene. He's at my house."

No one answers the door. Frustrated, Violet knocks again, louder. "Louisa!" she calls. "I need to speak with you."

Are they in there, hiding from her? Laughing from the other side of the door? Violet shakes her head. *Do this because you are a mother,* she tells herself. "Louisa!" She yells. "I know you don't want to see me but it's important! Come to the door, or I'm coming in!"

Still no answer.

"Right," says Violet. Taking a deep breath, she reaches for the handle and turns. The door, to her surprise, swings open, the way it did all those years ago, when she set foot in it for the first time.

"Hello?" Violet calls as she steps in. "Anyone home?"

The house is silent. Violet switches on a light in the living room, the one with the purple shade she and Louisa had bought together years ago.

It's empty. There's no one home.

She walks around the house, calling for her friend, her daughter. "Louisa! Marcy! Where are you both?"

On the counter in the kitchen there is a note, written on a cloth napkin. Violet reads it: it's for Eugene.

Where have they gone?

She hears the engine of a car pull into the driveway. Looking at the cloth napkin, she tucks it into her dress pocket.

Next to where the note was, on the counter, is Louisa's identification card. Violet grabs that as well, tucks it into her pocket next to the note.

The sound of car doors slamming echoes outside, and jackboots crunch on the pavement. Behind them, with a proud smirk on her face, is Helena Grange.

A group of soldiers storm inside: three men, all appearing to be a little drunk. Violet sticks her chest out and faces them, trying to keep her lips from chattering.

"Are you Louisa Westover?" One of them demands in accented English. "We have orders to search your house for suspicious activity."

"Really," Violet begins. "I don't think this is necessary."

But already, the group is tearing through the house, slamming doors, opening drawers. The record player is thrown to the ground, albums strewn across the carpet.

They flip over the pink couch in the living room, the one Violet and Louisa shared thousands of cups of tea on. As they destroy the house, all Violet can think is that this, here, is where her happiest memories are, as a lonely little girl, as a woman, as a mother.

The soldiers head upstairs, leaving Violet and Helena alone together.

"What are you doing here?" Violet whispers to Helena.

"You asked me to find out what was going on," says Helena, looking like she is very much enjoying the events of the evening. "But don't forget—you still owe me."

Violet does a frantic sweep of the room with her eyes, trying to find anything incriminating.

"Ah! I've found something!" comes a voice from upstairs. She hears excited talking in German. Violet panics as she wonders what they have found.

Then, on the living room bookshelf, she sees it: a string of rose gold pearls. From across the room she feels the weight they carry: the blame, the secrets, the way they have inhibited her.

"Helena, if I pay you, will you keep quiet, no matter what happens next?" she asks.

"If it's enough," Helena says. "What do you have in mind?"

Violet walks over to the pearls. They are cold and heavy in her hands. "These are real pearls. You can get anything you want with those on the black market. Just keep quiet, okay?"

Helena smiles. "You and Louisa were always a smug pair," she says. "But payment is payment. I'll keep quiet."

A young soldier, handsome and lanky, comes downstairs with a victorious expression on his face. "A wireless," he says with a grin.

"That's enough to arrest her," the officer says. "We're going to be taking you in."

"That's not all," says the boy. He pulls a book from behind his back. "An English-Russian dictionary."

Now Violet audibly gasps. A dictionary. Russian. Of course. She puts together the newspaper reports of laborers on the island, of Ouen offering her a bat, of Marcy disappearing for ages at a time. She realizes, suddenly, what Louisa was doing, why Marcy was getting rations. Louisa, mother of every young person she meets, had simply been saving another mother's son.

The Commandant steps toward Violet. "You are Louisa Westover, yes?" he asks.

Violet nods.

"Identification card, please," he says.

Violet thrusts the card into his hand. She is thankful, at that moment, that the pictures are blurry, that Louisa's hair looks black in the photo, for the dim lighting in the kitchen which would make the photo impossible to scrutinize.

She's right. With barely a look, the Commandant tosses the card aside and steps toward her. "You defied the orders of the Third Reich by harboring a wireless."

Violet says nothing.

"And why, may I ask, do you have an English Russian Dictionary?"

Violet shrugs. "I love the language," she says.

"And why, does it say, on the front cover, Fedor Morozov, 1943?"

"Dear God," says Helena. "What an idiot."

Did it say that? What was that boy thinking? "I don't know," she says.

The Commandant steps forward and grabs Violet by the shoulders. He shakes her. "You don't know?" he yells. "What do you mean, you don't know?"

Violet tries to create the illusion of calm as she repeats, "I don't know."

"Take her in," says the young, handsome soldier. "We'll get more out of questioning her from the prison."

As they lead her across the gravel, Violet feels a desperate urge to bake a cake, to lose herself in exact measurements of flour, sugar, and egg.

Another car, a lorry, pulls into the drive at breakneck speed. *Please,* she thinks. *Don't let it be Louisa.*

Marcy throws open the door and climbs out, wearing a shimmery black dress. She runs over to them. Violet watches her eyes widen in recognition. Violet shakes her head, silently warning her daughter not to say anything.

"Franc?" Marcy asks, her voice trembling. "What's this about?"

"Mary? What are you doing here?" the young, handsome soldier asks sharply, a hint of annoyance in his voice. "I thought you were resting. Though I couldn't find you when I came upstairs."

Violet looks from the soldier to Marcy, registering the intimacy of the words *upstairs* and *resting.*

"I—I went to a friend of Bernadette's to get headache oil," she says quickly. "When I came back and saw you'd all gone, Bernadette said you'd come to this address."

Violet's heart aches for her clever girl, as she pieces together what she'd done. Marcy wasn't a Jerrybag at all. Marcy had saved Louisa, and whoever the boy was. Violet wonders how Marcy found out about Helena's betrayal—and if she knew about Violet's own part in it.

Violet thinks about Eugene, asleep in Marcy's bed at her house. He'll miss his boat if she doesn't wake him up.

Hoping Marcy will get her meaning, she says, "My house is yellow. Full of daffodils."

Marcy looks at her, and Violet cannot tell if she understands.

"Quiet," Franc says.

"Yellow?" Marcy asks.

"Dripping yellow," Violet says desperately. She can't think of another way to tell Marcy.

"What does she mean, yellow?" Franc asks. "Her house is stone."

Marcy looks at Franc. "I don't know," she says.

"You don't know or you won't tell me?" Franc says, his eyes narrowing.

"How should I know what that means? Maybe she's just painted? Franc, please listen to me. This woman hasn't done anything wrong."

"This woman," Franc says, pulling Violet's arm forcefully, "Has betrayed the Reich by hiding Russian prisoners. We are taking her in for questioning."

"What?" Marcy asks. "You can't!"

"Mary--Do you know this woman?" he asks sharply.

Marcy stares at her mother, tears welling up in the corners of her eyes. Violet knows if Marcy speaks, it will be over for them both.

"No," says Violet. "I've never seen that girl before in my life."

It is the kindest, most sacrificial thing Violet has ever done for her daughter: to disown her in front of a crowd.

Chapter Fifty-Two

MARCY

1943

Marcy follows Franc and her mother toward the car. "You can't take her Franc, she's mad. You heard her comment just now about colors. She must be driving herself crazy, living alone up here," Marcy pleads. "Please, don't do this."

Franc swats her away, like she is a pesky fly. "You should not poke your head where it doesn't belong," he says to her.

"Where will you take her?" she asks frantically as he and Officer Zohorst shove her mother into the car.

"Germany. First thing in the morning."

"No," Marcy says. "Please, don't do this. If you love me, please don't do this."

Franc turns. "Mary," he says. "If I didn't know better I would think you had some kind of connection with this woman. Now, stand back and allow me to do my job."

He gives Marcy a little push, and she stumbles to the gravel. She watches her mum stiffen as she gets into the car.

"I'm alright," she says. But she is not alright, because her mum is about to take the blame for what she never did, what she never even knew about.

"Yellow," her mum says again as Franc pushes her inside. She says it desperately, like she is begging.

"Quiet," says Franc.

The car pulls out of the drive. Marcy screams after it, "No! I'm sorry!"

Yellow. The last word her mum had said to her. She wonders if it means what she hopes it means, if her mum can really understand color.

But Eugene, back, it is impossible. Almost as impossible as her mum driving away in a German car to prison.

The door to Louisa's house opens. Helena walks out, clutching her purse in one hand, and wearing around her neck a string of rose gold pearls.

"Where did you get those?" Marcy asks slowly, standing up.

"What, these?" Helena asks casually, her fingers running over the smooth pearls on her neck. "Beautiful, aren't they? Your mum gave them to me."

"My *mum?*" Marcy asks. "Why?"

"Paying me to keep quiet. Which I will, for now. But cross me again, *Mary*," she winks at Marcy, "And I will find my voice very quickly, I assure you."

"You're terrible," Marcy says. She says it with surprise; she's not accustomed to calling grownups terrible.

Helena walks up to Marcy and leans in very close, so that Marcy can smell the lamb on her breath.

"Yes," she whispers. "But so is war, my girl. If you want to survive this, I'd recommend you get to being terrible yourself, quickly."

Helena stands up again, brushes off her dress, and walks away, into the darkening sky. Marcy wonders if she's upset that the soldiers left without her.

Marcy gets back in the lorry, reverses it out of the drive, and heads toward Basil's, thinking about what her mum said. Her legs are loose like jelly, and her heart is racing, thinking about what will happen to her mum, about the island without her mum on it.

Her mum saved her. Louisa too. She wasn't responsible for any of what they'd done; in fact, they'd done their best to keep her out of it, and still, she saved them.

Marcy begins to think that maybe she doesn't know her mum as well as she thought. Maybe she doesn't know her mum at all.

Yellow.

She has to see for herself.

Marcy slams the pedals on the brakes, remembering the word her mum used.

At the fork in the road, instead of going right towards Basil's house, she turns left, toward her own. The house is dark, and she is thankful the back door is unlocked as she sneaks inside.

The smell of home hits her first: baking and cinnamon. It is a punch to Marcy's gut, this home and these smells her mother created and has now left. Surely, she begs silently, surely they will not send her away to Germany.

She stands in the kitchen, where all the familiar dishes lay drying on the rack, where the floral tea towel hangs over the stove, where the wide plank hardwoods are swept and scrubbed spotlessly.

"Mum?" she asks, quietly into the room.

"Marcy?" a voice answers.

Marcy gasps. She grips the chair. "Who—who is that?"

A shadowy figure emerges from the darkness. "Marcy," the voice says, full of warmth and familiarity. "It's me."

And then Marcy sees it, all over her house. Yellow, dripping from the walls, yellow on the floor. Lemon and daffodil and sunshine bouncing off the darkness, bringing light to everything it touches.

Eugene comes closer, so that Marcy can make out his face in the dark kitchen.

"Oh, Eugene," Marcy says. Without thinking, she steps forward and throws her arms around him. He is skinny, so skinny, but he is soft and smooth and full of goodness. "Eugene," she says into his neck. "I knew you'd come back."

Eugene holds her close, and for that moment, Marcy's whole world feels complete. He's here, she's here, and they are not missing each other. Eugene is back, and now they can do anything. Marcy bites her lip to hold back a sob.

But too quickly, Eugene pulls away. He says, "It isn't for long, Marcy. I'm on my way out right now."

Marcy steps back, hands falling limply at her side. "What? Eugene, no. You can't leave."

"I know it's short, but,"

"No, Eu. The island is occupied. The beaches are mined. They have watch guards at every wretched tower they've built across the island. You'll die if you try to leave."

Eugene looks at her, traces her face with his finger. Marcy expects him to argue, to give him all the reasons why he must go: honor, duty, finishing what he started. He says nothing though, only continues to touch her face.

"What are you doing?" she asks quietly.

"Tracing your face."

"To remember it when you go?" she cannot keep the bitterness from her voice.

"No," he says. "I already have it memorized. Marcy, I traced your face every night in my head the last three years. I know your nose, your cheekbones, your chin. And when I come back—and I will come back—I'm going to ask you to marry me and I hope you'll say yes."

Marcy wonders if this is a dream: it must be a dream. But she can smell him and she can feel his finger on her face, and before she can convince it not to, she can feel her body begin to hope.

"What about Penelope Campbell?"

Eugene shrugs. "She was a phase," he says. "You're the real deal. It was your face I thought about at night, not Penelope's."

"Emerald green."

"What?"

Marcy shakes her head. "Never mind. Does your mum know you're here?" she asks.

"No," Eugene said. "I came to your mum. It would crush mine, if she saw me and had to let me go again. But I knew that was where your mum was headed tonight. She thought I was asleep, and she went to tell your mum I was here. I was just writing a note, explaining why I had to leave."

"But Eugene, that's just the thing, something's happened to Mum—"

Just then, the door rattles. "Eu," says a gruff voice with a French accent from the other side. "Eugene, open the door."

Eugene pulls open the kitchen door. On the other side is a small Frenchman with wild hair. "Eugene," he insists, ignoring Marcy completely, "We must go. The Germans have made an arrest, and the soldiers have left their lookout posts around our departure post. We must go, and immediately."

Eugene squeezes Marcy's hand one more time. "I will come back to you, Marcy," he says.

And then, like the end of a breath, he is gone. She hears their footsteps across the gravel yard, and wonders where they are going. The kitchen is silent and dark again, all the yellow blown away by the wind of the open door. Marcy wonders if she imagined the whole encounter, if Eugene was ever really here, if he meant any of what he said.

The arrest. Her mum. Marcy's head begins to pound as she leaves her home and runs across the lavender field to Basil's parents' barn. She is panting, dizzy, shaking with fear and adrenaline when she makes it up the ladder to the top of the hayloft.

"Hello?" she calls softly to the lumps in the hay, where Louisa and Fedor hide.

She sees shapes rustling.

"Marcy?" Basil's voice comes across the barn. "Marcy, we're all here."

Marcy collapses into the hay.

"Everything alright?" Basil asks. She can hear him shuffling as he makes his way closer. "Did you get everything from the house?"

"Mum," Marcy sobs.

"Your mum's not here—at least I hope not," says Basil.

"No," Marcy begins to cry in earnest, and tries to choke out her words between sobs. "They took Mum."

"What?" Louisa says, sitting straight up, pulling a piece of straw from her face. "What do you mean?"

"She was there when I arrived. She pretended to be you." Marcy is anxious, dizzy. She feels disconnected from her body. She wants her mum.

"Well, that's impossible. She can't have. My identity card is right—" Marcy hears Louisa pat her pocket for her card. "Oh, bloody hell."

"They've taken her to prison. To H. M. La Moye," says Marcy. She shakes all over.

"No," says Jon. "They can't. She's had nothing to do with any of this."

"Well, I've got to go in and make it right," says Louisa, standing up.

"No," says Basil. "No, you can't. That will only make it worse. They'll take both of you. Louisa, Violet chose to do this. She didn't have to."

"Why?" Marcy asks.

There is a pause. Then, Basil speaks into the darkness.

"Well, isn't it obvious? She loves you both, more than herself."

CHAPTER FIFTY-THREE

LOUISA

1943

"Basil, enough of this. Get me your torch," Louisa demands. Her heart is beating like it will jump out of her chest. She puts a hand there, to keep it intact. She is panicked, for Violet's sake. Violet, who has put herself on the line again, who wore the blame for something she hasn't done. Louisa cannot let her do it again.

"Miss Lou, I'm afraid I can't do that," begins Basil.

"Oh, blast you all!" Louisa stands up in the darkness and brushes hay off her legs. "I'll do it myself."

Fumbling in the darkness, Louisa searches for the ladder.

"Lou, you can't," Jon says. In the black of the hayloft, he finds her and pulls her back down.

"Jon, I need to," Louisa says. "I can't let her carry this. I have to go."

"What are you going to say?" Jon asks. "Who are you going to convince, in the middle of the night? All you are going to do is get you both sent to Germany."

"Don't you understand?" Louisa's voice is rising, but she cannot control it. "I cannot sit by and do nothing!"

"But you will make things *worse* by doing something just to assuage your own conscience," Jon says. He holds her down, his arm around her waist.

"He's right, you know," says Basil. "Violet wasn't forced into anything."

"No," Marcy agrees. "She chose this."

"Yes, she chose it," says Louisa, head in her hands. "She chose it because she *always* chooses it, because she has worn the blame for something she didn't do her whole life."

There is a pause. Then Marcy asks, "What do you mean?"

"I mean—never mind," Louisa says. For Violet's sake, Louisa cannot share her secret. "But, I need to get over there, to talk to someone."

"Let's go at first light," Jon says. "We'll find someone to talk to."

"Like hell you won't," says Basil. "They'll be making an example, publicly, of Louisa Westover, who defied the Nazis to protect a Russian. You go, and you put yourselves, and Fedor in danger. Violet gave herself up to protect you three, and you won't make that vain by showing up in St. Helier in broad daylight. Marcy and I will go."

The matter is settled, or settled enough. Jon suggests they rest. Fedor, who cannot understand, pats Louisa's hand.

Sleep doesn't come close to Louisa that night. She breathes in the smell of hay, listens to the occasional flap of a barn swallow's wing in its nest above them. *Violet*, she says in her head. *Violet, all I want is for you to be free.*

At the first sign of light, when Basil makes his way down from the hayloft, Louisa is waiting for him outside.

"Lou," he says, shaking his head, "You can't come."

"I snuck over to Violet's," she says, holding up a hat and scarf. "I'll blend."

Basil, in the dim pre-dawn light, opens his mouth to protest.

"Basil," she says, before he can speak. "I have been friends with Violet longer than you have been alive. She needs me to be there this morning. Trust me."

Basil hesitates, then seems to give up. "Alright, then," he says with a nod. "Let's take the lorry. Let's go."

Silently, they ride into town, just the two of them. Louisa prays as they ride, "Please, let her be okay. Please please please."

As they approach the weighbridge in the rising sun, they see a woman, being led by a guard on either side to a ship waiting in the harbor.

"That's her," Louisa says. She yells into the wind, "Violet!"

Violet does not hear. Louisa parks the truck and runs down the hill and onto the Weighbridge. "Hello! Excuse me!" she calls to the guards. "I need to talk to her."

The guards don't turn, but Violet does. Louisa, in desperation, yells the only thing she can think to say. "It's not your fault, Vi! Plemont Bay—none of it was your fault."

Violet and Louisa stare at one another on the dock, lost in a moment of time that is entirely separate. Violet's hair blows in the wind. She wears a cream cardigan, blue slacks.

"What did you say?" Violet asks.

"Not your fault," Louisa says, cupping her hands over her mouth. "Your mum says you saved her, at Plemont Bay. And—and you saved me, too. That day with Hope."

Another soldier comes up behind Louisa and grabs her arm. "I'm afraid you must leave, Miss," he says to her.

"I should never have asked you for your baby," Louisa yells. "Especially because I know what it's like to lose one. I should never have done it." The tears fall freely now down her cheeks.

The guards holding Violet have stopped, for a moment. Violet speaks to Louisa, and it is as though it is only the two of them in the world.

"You know what I was thinking about last night?" she says. "In that cold cell, with my head against the bar, I was thinking about that time that you and I walked all the way to St. Katherine's Bay because Eugene wanted to see the sea from the top of Gorey Castle. The three of us: me, you, and Eugene, walked all morning. We stood at the top, in the wind, and we laughed at the way the wind blew our hair about, the way it threatened to blow away the bag of sandwiches we had packed."

"I remember," says Louisa.

"We bought 99s all with a flake, and tried to eat them just like the tourists do, in the wind before they melted."

"Yes," says Louisa. Eugene had got a big splotch of it on his shirt, she remembers.

"When I got home that day, my cheeks hurt from laughing, my legs sore from walking, I thought, I never could have imagined being so happy. You gave that to me, Lou. You gave me that happiness."

"Violet," Louisa says. "Don't do this. Don't go."

The guards begin to pull Violet away again.

"Wait!" says Louisa, into the wind. "Wait! You've got the wrong person."

"Come on, Miss," The guard holding Louisa's arm begins to pull her back off the dock.

"No, no! You don't understand! She did nothing wrong!"

The guard has both arms now, and is yanking her backward.

"Tell Marcy I know the colors," Violet calls back, as they push her onto the boat. "Tell her she's gold. She's always been gold."

"I'll tell her."

Violet yells one more thing. "Take care of my Marcy," she yells as she is pulled away. "Be the mum I can't."

The guard shoves Louisa off the weighbridge. He spits and threatens her. She hears Basil explaining that Louisa is mad, she didn't mean any of it.

Louisa looks past the guard, to Violet's hair blowing in the wind as she steps onto the boat. In all the time she's known her, it is now, bound by chains, that she is the most free.

CHAPTER FIFTY-FOUR

MARCY

1943—1945

By the time Marcy wakes up in the hayloft, it is already early light. With a start, Marcy jumps up and runs outside, looking left and right for her Auntie Enid.

Louisa has taken the lorry. Marcy heads to town on Basil's bike, riding as best as she can in her heels. When she makes it to the weighbridge, she knows her mother is gone, by the way Louisa lays curled up over the concrete, sobbing as Basil tries to move her to a place where she won't attract so much attention.

"Get out of here for her," Marcy says, when she reaches Louisa. She puts a hand on her wild, gray hair. "Don't let her sacrifice be in vain. Come on."

It is the only thing that seems to work. They move Louisa away from the center of town, pausing to sit on a bench when they are nearly on the outskirts.

"She shouldn't have done it," Louisa says, shaking with her head in her hands. "That should be me."

"Well," says Marcy, in a much more matter-of-fact tone than she is feeling, "It isn't you. And the only way we can make that sacrifice worthwhile is by saving as many of those workers as we can."

Louisa stops crying. She looks up at Marcy. "She called you a gold, my girl," Louisa says.

"A gold?" Marcy thinks over the words. "She knew about the colors?"

"I don't know a thing about colors," Louisa said. "And even I can tell she was right. Not many people like you in the world."

Marcy looks out over the sea, thinking about her mum, who left so much unsaid, who knew so much more than Marcy realized.

"Well then," she says. "Help me, Lou. Help me be a gold."

***

Marcy moves back into her home. She finds her father sitting with Peter on the doorstep, eyes red and puffy.

"I thought she left me," he said, head in his hands. "I thought she left."

"No, Dad. She saved us."

"I never knew her, not really," he says. "It was like there was a part of her no one could ever reach."

Marcy takes his hand and silently agrees.

Louisa and Marcy work tirelessly with Basil and Bernadette, creating a network of hiding places across the island. They set up systems for securing identification cards, rations, and safe houses.

Marcy doesn't tell Louisa about Eugene. She thinks Eugene is right: that it would crush her. She hears nothing about a pair of allied soldiers captured on the Channel Island shores, so she assumes he has made it back to England. Another life, saved by Violet's sacrifice.

Two months after her mother is taken away, Marcy leaves Bernadette's in the late afternoon. On the main street, she watches Franc walk arm in arm with Penelope Campbell. She feels nothing, not even towards Penelope. There are plenty of other German men out there, with access to rations, cigarettes, and information.

She and Louisa work endlessly, until the end of the war, when it is no longer safe for her to go out on the street without being harassed. Bernadette is tarred and feathered by angry islanders convinced that she was only using the war to climb ladders, without a clue about the sacrifices Bernadette made for all of them.

Marcy stays inside during the Liberation. All the way from her home, she hears fireworks, shouts and cheers. Later, Louisa and Basil say the dancing will go on for days, that Union Jack bunting is hung all across the square, that the soldiers looked so pathetic leaving with their flags in hand, heads down.

Every day, Marcy tends to her mum's garden. Every day, she watches for the colors she loves to come walking up the lane. She hopes and she hopes and she hopes.

VIOLET

1945

Violet wasn't meant to be at Plemont Bay the day the man fell off the cliff. That's what she's always believed about herself. Except that maybe she was. Maybe she was the only person who could have been at Plemont Bay that morning, the only person who could have possibly saved her mum. When Violet begins to think this way, the shape of her life changes. She begins to realize that she is more of the sum of the places she's been, that her life is more than cursed, more than a burden on other people.

Violet survives the war. She doesn't do it out of sheer luck or by her own cleverness, she knows this. No one survives Ravensbruck by luck. It is a living hell, maybe worse than hell—crawling with lice, hopelessness, cruelty, starvation.

"I'm not meant to be here! I did nothing wrong!" This is the temptation Violet fights when she first arrives. Except, over time she begins to realize that no one there did anything wrong. Only the people holding them there are guilty of anything.

Ironically, it is in a prison camp that Violet lets go of what is not hers to carry.

Violet survives because of a memory. In it, she is at Plemont Bay once again, but as a grown-up. She is with Marcy, Eugene, her mum, Peter, Louisa and Jon on the beach, spread out across a picnic basket, where remnants of their cheese, bread and homemade buns sit in the middle. David's arm is close enough to touch, and she passes him her thermos of tea. He takes it.

The sun is setting. It has been one of those perfectly warm days that has left their skin sun-kissed and their hair windblown.

There are no ghosts, no pearls, waiting for her at Plemont Bay this time. Nothing lurking in the coves or on the cliffs. There is only color. The memory is in her future.

The End

ReadMore

▐▌Press

DISCOVERING THE NEXT BESTSELLER

Would you like a
FREE WWII historical
fiction audiobook?

This audiobook is valued at 14.99$ on Amazon and is exclusively free for Readmore Press' readers!

To get your free audiobook, and to sign up for our newsletter where we send you more exclusive bonus content every month,

Scan the QR code

Readmore Press is a publisher that focuses on high-end, quality historical fiction.
We love giving the world moving stories, emotional accounts, and tear-filled happy endings.

We hope to see you again in our next book!

Never stop reading, Readmore Press

AUTHOR'S NOTE

I have been captivated by stories of Jersey's Occupation since I first heard them as a child on my grandad's knee. His father, Clarence Cristin, owned Cristin's, a Tobacconist and Photographic shop on Mulcaster Street in St. Helier. During the bombing, the windows were shattered. My grandad would talk about how they had been there at the shop that very morning, but decided to visit an aunt's house outside of town and were not present at the time of the bombing.

On the 28th of June, 1940, the German aircraft dropped bombs on La Rocque Harbour in Jersey and at St Peter Port in Guernsey. The islands had been demilitarized by Churchill only days before. Forty-four Channel Islanders were killed that day (10 on Jersey, 33 on Guernsey, 1 at sea), and over 100 were injured.

Due to the physical restrictions of my characters, I took the artistic license to relocate the bombing from La Rocque Harbour to Greve de Lecq on the northern end. I tried to keep as many other details the same as possible, using several first-hand accounts that described the bombings as resources.

The Channel Islands surrendered two days after the bombings, becoming the only part of Great Britain to be occupied by Germany during the war. In the years that followed, many islanders demonstrated significant bravery in the face of Occupation. They resisted in the ways they could: keeping wireless sets, finding ways to shelter and aid escaped forced laborers, painting the "V" for Victory sign on German houses and property. These brave islanders paid for their actions with prison time and some with their lives.

One islander who demonstrated immense courage and compassion was Louisa Gould, a Jersey shopkeeper in St. Ouen and the mother of two sons who enlisted in the British armed forces (Ralph was killed in action in 1941). During the war, the Nazis used many captured Russian soldiers as forced laborers to build their fortifications on the Channel Island. Ms. Gould, in a display of extraordinary bravery, hid Fyodr Polycarpovitch Burriy for eighteen months in her home. When warned about the possible consequences, Ms. Gould would simply say, "I have to do something for another mother's son."

In 1944, the Germans searched Ms. Gould's house after a neighbor reported her activities. They did not find Burriy, but upon finding a Russian-English dictionary and a scrap of paper addressed to Burriy, they arrested and charged Ms. Gould for harboring both a slave worker and a radio. Ms. Gould was sent to Ravensbruck, where she died in 1945.

Louisa Westover was inspired by the fortitude and heroism of Louisa Gould. Her story and circumstances are different enough that I changed her name to Westover, but it is my hope that I captured some of that daring and compassionate spirit so evident in the life of Louisa Gould.

I'm grateful to the friends and relatives in Jersey who allowed me to interview them about their experiences during the occupation. Many of their experiences have found their way into this book. I'm indebted to their generosity, but more so, to their outstanding moral character, which prompted them to resist and act in the ways they did.

In particular, Jean Sullivan, Anne Kearsey, Jean and Kevin Le Scelleur, and Alison Genders proved to be wells of knowledge when it came to the timeline of the Occupation and sharing personal experiences that helped to shape the novel.

The research of Roy McLoughlin (Living With the Enemy), R.C.F. Maugham (Jersey Under the Jackboot), Nan Le Ruez (Jersey Occupation Diary) and Dr. John Lewis (A Doctor's Occupation) all proved immensely helpful in developing my understanding of the occupied years in Jersey. All remaining timeline discrepancies or historical inaccuracies are the fault of my own.

ACKNOWLEDGMENTS

The idea for this book grew out of a project I began about wartime recipes on Jersey while working toward my MFA at Chatham University. I'm grateful to Sherrie Flick for seeing the story behind the recipes and for encouraging me to pursue it.

Thank you to the many people on the island of Jersey who helped this book come to fruition. Jean Sullivan was nothing but generous with her time and expansive knowledge of both the island and our family history, and she became a dear friend in the process. Trudie and Howard De La Haye hosted us in Jersey so that I could do my research. My granny, Jean Le Scelleur, and her husband, Kevin, let me into their childhood during the Occupation, and introduced me to a wealth of friends who shared their stories with me. Auntie Anne and Uncle John took the Occupation from being a thing on a page and made it something I could touch.

Thank you to Dani Zrihen and all the wonderful people at ReadMore Press who believed in this book enough to bring it into the light. Thank you to Lisa Slage Robinson, who read the earliest drafts; also to Lily Lindon and Tash Barsby from The Novelry, who helped give the manuscript its shape.

Thank you to my parents and siblings, who have invested in this story with an energy that has rivaled my own, and to my in-laws, whose support has been unwavering.

Most importantly, thank you to my husband, Andrew, who was there for the rejection as well as the acceptance, who is the color yellow. And to my three children, June, Rosie, and Jack, who made the progress on this book far slower and richer than I ever imagined.

Made in United States
North Haven, CT
21 September 2024